JAMES HOGG

# *Queen Hynde*

THE STIRLING / SOUTH CAROLINA RESEARCH EDITION OF
**THE COLLECTED WORKS OF JAMES HOGG**
GENERAL EDITOR – DOUGLAS S. MACK

THE STIRLING / SOUTH CAROLINA RESEARCH EDITION OF
# THE COLLECTED WORKS OF JAMES HOGG
## GENERAL EDITOR – DOUGLAS S. MACK

Volumes are numbered in the order of their publication in
the Stirling / South Carolina Research Edition

# JAMES HOGG

# Queen Hynde

Edited by
Suzanne Gilbert and Douglas S. Mack

EDINBURGH UNIVERSITY PRESS
1998

© Edinburgh University Press, 1998

Edinburgh University Press
22 George Square
Edinburgh
EH8 9LF

Typeset at the University of Stirling
Printed by The University Press, Cambridge

ISBN 0 7486 0934 2

A CIP record for this book is available from the British Library

The Stirling / South Carolina Research Edition of

# The Collected Works of James Hogg

## Advisory Board

*Chairman* Prof. David Daiches

*General Editor* Dr Douglas S. Mack

*Secretary* Dr Gillian Hughes

*Co-ordinator, University of South Carolina* Prof. Patrick Scott

*Ex Officio (University of Stirling)*
The Principal
Head, Centre for Scottish Literature and Culture
Head, Department of English Studies
Head, School of Arts

*Members*
Prof. Ian Campbell (University of Edinburgh)
Thomas Crawford (University of Aberdeen)
Dr P. D. Garside (University of Wales, Cardiff)
Ms Jackie Jones (Edinburgh University Press)
Ms G. E. McFadzean (University of Stirling)
Dr Christopher MacLachlan (University of St Andrews)
Prof. G. Ross Roy (University of South Carolina)
Prof. Jill Rubenstein (University of Cincinnati)
Dr A. R. Turnbull (University of Edinburgh)
Prof. Roderick Watson (University of Stirling)

## The Aims of the Edition

James Hogg lived from 1770 till 1835. He was regarded by his contemporaries as one of the leading writers of the day, but the nature of his fame was influenced by the fact that, as a young man, he had been a self-educated shepherd. The third edition (1814) of his poem *The Queen's Wake* contains an 'Advertisement' which begins as follows.

The Publisher having been favoured with letters from gentlemen in various parts of the United Kingdom respecting the Author of the *Queen's Wake*, and most of them expressing doubts of his being a Scotch Shepherd, he takes this opportunity of assuring the

public, that *The Queen's Wake* is really and truly the production
of *James Hogg*, a common Shepherd, bred among the moun-
tains of Ettrick Forest, who went to service when only seven
years of age; and since that period has never received any edu-
cation whatever.

The view of Hogg taken by his contemporaries is also reflected in
the various early reviews of *The Private Memoirs and Confessions of a
Justified Sinner*, which appeared anonymously in 1824. As Gillian
Hughes has shown in the *Newsletter of the James Hogg Society* no. 1,
many of these reviews identify Hogg as the author, and see the novel
as presenting 'an incongruous mixture of the strongest powers with
the strongest absurdities'. The Scotch Shepherd was regarded as a
man of powerful and original talent, but it was felt that his lack of
education caused his work to be marred by frequent failures in dis-
cretion, in expression, and in knowledge of the world. Worst of all
was Hogg's lack of what was called 'delicacy', a failing which caused
him to deal in his writings with subjects (such as prostitution) which
were felt to be unsuitable for mention in polite literature. Hogg was
regarded as a man of undoubted genius, but his genius was felt to be
seriously flawed.

A posthumous collected edition of Hogg was published in the late
1830s. As was perhaps natural in the circumstances, the publishers
(Blackie & Son of Glasgow) took pains to smooth away what they took
to be the rough edges of Hogg's writing, and to remove his numerous
'indelicacies'. This process was taken even further in the 1860s, when
the Rev. Thomas Thomson prepared a revised edition of Hogg's *Works*
for publication by Blackie. These Blackie editions present a bland and
lifeless version of Hogg's writings. It was in this version that Hogg
was read by the Victorians. Unsurprisingly, he came to be regarded as
a minor figure, of no great importance or interest.

The second half of the twentieth century has seen a substantial re-
vival of Hogg's reputation; and he is now generally considered to be
one of Scotland's major writers. This new reputation is based on a few
works which have been republished in editions based on his original
texts. Nevertheless, a number of Hogg's major works remain out of
print. Indeed, some have been out of print for more than a century
and a half, while others, still less fortunate, have never been published
at all in their original, unbowdlerised condition.

Hogg is thus a major writer whose true stature was not recognised
in his own lifetime because his social origins led to his being smoth-
ered in genteel condescension; and whose true stature has not been
recognised since, because of a lack of adequate editions. The poet

Douglas Dunn wrote of Hogg in the *Glasgow Herald* in September 1988: 'I can't help but think that in almost any other country of Europe a complete, modern edition of a comparable author would have been available long ago'. The Stirling / South Carolina Edition of James Hogg seeks to fill the gap identified by Douglas Dunn. When completed the edition will run to thirty-one volumes; and it will cover Hogg's prose, his poetry, and his plays.

## Acknowledgements

The research for the early volumes of the Stirling / South Carolina Edition of James Hogg has been sustained by funding and other support generously made available by the University of Stirling and by the University of South Carolina. Valuable grants or donations have also been received from the Carnegie Trust for the Universities of Scotland, from the Modern Humanities Research Association, from the Association for Scottish Literary Studies, and from the James Hogg Society. The work of the Edition could not have been carried on without the support of these bodies.

Douglas S. Mack<br>General Editor

## Volume Editors' Acknowledgements

Suzanne Gilbert's work on this edition was made possible by the award of a Modern Humanities Research Association Research Fellowship at the University of Stirling during the academic year 1996–97; and a grant from the Carnegie Trust for the Universities of Scotland enabled Douglas Mack to work on the manuscript of *Queen Hynde* at the Huntington Library, San Marino, California during January 1996. Furthermore, the University of South Carolina's W. Ormiston Roy Research Fellowship for 1995 was awarded to Douglas Mack; and this made possible an extended period of work on *Queen Hynde* at the University of South Carolina's Thomas Cooper Library, which holds a superb collection of Scottish material. We are most grateful to these bodies for their support.

The present volume could not have been prepared without the help and advice of a large number of people. Peter Garside and Gillian Hughes, with their habitual but remarkable generosity, read the editors' drafts, checked documents, and made many detailed and valuable comments and suggestions. At the University of South viii

Caroilina, Patrick Scott, Jill Hufnagel, and Susan Rogers made valuable contributions to the research undertaken for this volume. The editors also wish to express particular thanks to Valentina Bold of the University of Aberdeen for information and advice; to Alistair Daniel (a Publishing Studies student at the University of Stirling during academic year 1996–97) for helpful discussions on editorial theory; to Micah Gilbert, for advice and assistance with regard to computing and many other matters; to Antony Hasler of the University of Indiana; to Ian McGowan and Alasdair Macrae of the Department of English Studies at the University of Stirling; to John MacInnes of the School of Scottish Studies, University of Edinburgh; to Robin MacLachlan of the James Hogg Society; to Wilma Mack and to Gordon Willis, both of Stirling University Library; to Brian Murdoch of the Department of German at the University of Stirling; to Fiona Stafford of Somerville Colege, Oxford; to the staff of Stirling University Library; to the staff of the National Library of Scotland; to the staff of the Thomas Cooper Library, Columbia, South Carolina; to the staff of the Huntington Library, San Marino, California; and to many other people for assistance of various kinds.

We are also most grateful to the following institutions for access to Hogg manuscripts, and for permission to publish material derived from Hogg manuscripts in their care: the Huntington Library, San Marino, California; the Trustees of the National Library of Scotland; and the Longman Archive.

The volume editors accept full responsibility for the errors and omissions in the present volume: these would have been much more numerous but for the assistance of the people and institutions we have thanked. Both volume editors made a contribution to every part of the edition. However, Suzanne Gilbert is chiefly responsible for sections 3 and 4 of the Introduction, for the Appendix on Beregonium, for the Notes, and for the Glossary; while Douglas Mack is chiefly responsible for the remainder of the Introduction, for editing the text, for the Note on the Text, and for the List of Emendations.

Suzanne Gilbert
Douglas S. Mack

# Contents

# Introduction

## 1. Contexts: A Scotch Shepherd and his Epic Poem.

*Queen Hynde* is James Hogg's epic poem about the origins and roots of the Scottish nation. However, for many of his contemporaries, Hogg must have seemed a deeply improbable candidate for the role of epic poet. Epic, after all, was regarded as the highest and the noblest of all the various poetic genres: and who could regard a self-educated farm-worker like Hogg as a person to be taken seriously as a rival to Homer and Virgil?

This unlikely epic poet was born in 1770 in Ettrick Forest, a remote sheep-farming area in the Scottish Borders.[1] Because of the bankruptcy of his father (a farmer) in 1777, Hogg had little formal education, and much of his childhood was spent in real hardship as he earned his keep by doing menial farm work (herding cows and the like) on various farms. In his late teens the barely literate future author of *Queen Hynde* graduated to employment as an Ettrick shepherd; and he worked in this capacity at Blackhouse farm throughout the 1790s, when he was in his twenties. During the 1790s Hogg had access to a good library; and in effect he educated himself at Blackhouse with the help and encouragement of his employer's son William Laidlaw, who was in later life to become the manager of Sir Walter Scott's Abbotsford estate in the Scottish Borders.

Hogg eventually left Blackhouse in 1800. In the years between 1800 and 1810 he was in his thirties, and this period saw him alternating between spells of work as a hired shepherd and various attempts to establish himself as a farmer. During these years Hogg had several articles published in the *Scots Magazine*, some of them signed 'The Ettrick Shepherd', a pen-name he continued to use from time to time throughout the remainder of his life.[2] While in his thirties Hogg also gained a modest reputation as a poet, a reputation based largely on his book *The Mountain Bard* (Edinburgh: Constable, 1807). In spite of the valuable assistance provided by his literary earnings, however, Hogg's farming schemes did not prosper. In 1809 he became bankrupt; and in 1810, having no other resource, he set out for Edinburgh to seek to carve out a future for himself as a full-time writer. He was by now forty years old.

Financially, the years immediately following 1810 were difficult for Hogg. Indeed, he would have been hard-pressed to survive them if it had not been for help provided by John Grieve, an old Ettrick friend who was now a hatter in the Scottish capital. However, Hogg's fortunes began to change for the better with the publication in the spring of 1813 of his well-received book-length poem *The Queen's Wake*.

The third edition (1814) of *The Queen's Wake* contains an 'Advertisement' by the poem's publisher, George Goldie. Goldie writes as follows:

> THE *Publisher having been favoured with letters from gentlemen in various parts of the United Kingdom respecting the Author of the* QUEEN'S WAKE, *and most of them expressing doubts of his being a Scotch Shepherd; he takes this opportunity of assuring the Public, that* THE QUEEN'S WAKE *is really and truly the production of* JAMES HOGG, *a* common shepherd, *bred among the mountains of Ettrick Forest, who went to service when only seven years of age; and since that period has never received any education whatever. Upon the consistency of this statement, with the merits of the following Work, it does not become him to make any observation; all he wishes to say is, that it is* strictly true, *which he states upon the best of all possible authority—his own knowledge.*

Although *The Queen's Wake* was really and truly the production of a common Scotch shepherd, it quickly ran through several editions, and it established Hogg's reputation as one of the leading British poets of his generation. Indeed, for the remainder of his life Hogg would be regularly described by his publishers, on title-pages and in advertisements, as 'The Author of *The Queen's Wake*'.

No doubt much encouraged by this turn of events, the author of *The Queen's Wake* began to operate in ways designed to confirm and exploit his new status as the rival of Scott and Byron among the fashionable poets of the 1810s. As a result, Hogg's poetic output was formidable in the years immediately following the first appearance of *The Queen's Wake* in 1813. The third edition of this poem contained important revisions, and was published in 1814. The revised *Queen's Wake* was followed in 1815 by *Pilgrims of the Sun*, a book-length poem which Hogg dedicated to Byron. *Mador of the Moor*, a book-length poem which echoes and interrogates Scott's *Lady of the Lake*, followed in 1816. Next came *The Poetic Mirror* (1816), a volume of Hogg's brilliant poetic parodies (of Scott, Byron, Coleridge, Wordsworth, Hogg, and others); and 1817 saw the publication of *Dramatic Tales*, a two-volume collection which reflects Hogg's long-standing interest in the theatre.[3]

In the years immediately after the publication of *The Queen's Wake*, then, Hogg was widely regarded as a significant poet. On another level, however, there was a tendency to regard him as a remarkable and amusing freak of nature: the shepherd-poet shared a talking dog's ability to attract attention. This was the context in which Hogg conceived the plan of writing an epic poem; and it is a context that *Queen Hynde* confronts with a wry, amused relish. The narrator of Hogg's epic is the well-known figure of the Ettrick Shepherd; and the Shepherd frequently breaks into the flow of the main narrative in order to address his readers, personified by the Maid, or Maids, of Dunedin (the Gaelic name for Edinburgh). Unwilling to rest content with being merely the peer of Scott and Byron, this unusual Scotch Shepherd, in his role as narrator of *Queen Hynde*, is fully aware of his audacity in embarking on the task of emulating Homer, Virgil, and Milton; and the tone of Hogg's epic—characteristically—combines insouciance, self-mocking playfulness, and real seriousness.

*The Queen's Wake* had immediately been recognised by its first readers as a major poem; and the fact that it had been written by a common Scotch shepherd added a delightful spice of novelty. Inevitably, however, Hogg's subsequent offerings came as less of a surprise; and his middle-class Edinburgh audience began to feel uncomfortable about a subversive strand discernible in the writings of this uncouth farm-worker. For this audience, a naive heaven-taught rustic would have been very welcome to produce pretty and unthreatening pastoral pieces that drew on the curious traditions of the old Scotch peasantry; but in most of his writings Hogg was after bigger game. As a result, Book First of *Queen Hynde* concludes with a declaration of independence from the limitations imposed by fashionable Edinburgh's perception of the Ettrick Shepherd's proper role. In making this declaration, the Shepherd (as narrator) offers an outrageous and funny passage full of sexual innuendo; and he then continues as follows.

> Maid of Dunedin, thou may'st see,
> Though long I strove to pleasure thee,
> That now I've changed my timid tone,
> And sing to please myself alone;
> And thou wilt read, when, well I wot,
> I care not whether you do or not. ( p.30)

In part because of Hogg's unwillingness to restrict himself wholly to the role of Edinburgh's tame shepherd-poet, the poems and plays that he produced in the aftermath of *The Queen's Wake* met with a

mixed reception. This failure to match the outstanding popular suc-
cess of *The Queen's Wake* was to cast a shadow over the projected
epic, *Queen Hynde*. The circumstances are discussed in Hogg's auto-
biography, *Memoir of the Author's Life*:

> The small degree of interest that these dramas [*Dramatic Tales*]
> excited in the world finished my dramatic and poetical career.
> I had adopted a resolution of writing a drama every year as
> long as I lived, hoping to make myself perfect by degrees, as a
> man does in his calling, by serving an apprenticeship; but the
> failure of these to excite notice fully convinced me, that either
> this was not the age to appreciate the qualities of dramatic
> composition, or that I was not possessed of the talents fitting
> me for such an undertaking: and so I gave up the ambitious
> design.
>
> Before this period, all the poems that I had published had
> been begun and written by chance and at random, without
> any previous design. I had at that time commenced an epic
> poem on a regular plan, and I finished two books of it, pluming
> myself that it was to prove my greatest work. But, seeing that
> the poetical part of these dramas excited no interest in the
> public, I felt conscious that no poetry I should ever be able to
> write would do so; or, if it did, the success would hinge upon
> some casualty, on which it did not behove me to rely. So,
> from that day to this, save now and then an idle song to be-
> guile a leisure hour, I determined to write no more poetry.
>
> Several years subsequent to this, at the earnest intreaties
> of some literary friends, I once more set to work and finished
> this poem, which I entitled "Queen Hynde," in a time shorter
> than any person would believe.[4]

Hogg asserts here that *Queen Hynde* was composed in two stages,
with a gap of some years between; and his manuscript (which sur-
vives in the Huntington Library in San Marino, California) con-
tains watermarks and other indications which strongly suggest that
the poem was indeed begun in or around 1817, and that it was in-
deed completed in the months leading up to its publication in 1824.
The evidence provided by the manuscript also suggests that the ear-
lier, 1817, section of the poem ends at Book Third line 1071.[5]

During the years between 1817 and 1824 various prose fictions
by Hogg were published. These included *The Brownie of Bodsbeck*
(1818); *Winter Evening Tales* (1820); *The Three Perils of Man* (1822);
*The Three Perils of Woman* (1823); and *The Private Memoirs and Confes-*

*sions of a Justified Sinner* (1824). It would appear, then, that Hogg planned and began to write his epic poem in the aftermath of the success of *The Queen's Wake*; and that he completed and published it around the time that he was writing *The Private Memoirs and Confessions of a Justified Sinner*. That is to say, *Queen Hynde* was written when Hogg was at the height of his powers; and, as we have seen from the *Memoir of the Author's Life*, his own expectation was that his epic poem 'was to prove my greatest work'.

It is clear that *Queen Hynde*'s Edinburgh publisher William Blackwood initially shared Hogg's high hopes for the poem. Writing to Hogg on 4 December 1824, a few days before publication, Blackwood commented as follows:

> I have read the whole of Queen Hynde, and I am quite sure it will make a sensation. There are as fine things in it as you have ever written, and there are as queer ones that will be good food for the critics.[6]

It appears that these high hopes for *Queen Hynde* were shared by Hogg's friend Sir Walter Scott. Hogg comments as follows on Scott's reaction to *Queen Hynde* in his *Anecdotes of Sir W. Scott*, a text written shortly after Scott's death in 1832:

> He once promised to review a work of mine I think Queen Hynde but he never did it although he had expressed his warmest approbation of it before several friends. I asked him a good while afterwards why he had not kept his word. "Why the truth is Hogg" said he "that I began the thing and took a number of notes marking quotations but I found that in reviewing it I would have been thought to have been reviewing myself. I found that I must have begun with THE WAKE or perhaps THE MOUNTAIN BARD and summed up; and upon the whole I felt that we were so much of the same school that if I had given as favourable a review as I intended to have done that it would have been viewed in the light of having applauded my own works."
>
> I cannot say that these were Sir Walter's very words but they were precisely to that purport. But I, like other dissapointed men not being quite satisfied replied in these very words which I can vouch for. "Dear Mr Scott ye could never think that I was in the chivalry school like you. I'm the king o' the mountain and fairy school a far higher ane nor your's."
>
> "Well but the higher the ascent the greater may be the fall Hogg so say never a word more about that."[7]

*Queen Hynde* did not in the event fulfil the confident hopes with which it was launched. It was published in London by Longman, and the records of the Longman firm show that the print run of the first edition was 1500 copies. However, by June 1825 (some six months after publication) more than a thousand copies still remained unsold; and most of the edition was eventually remaindered.[8] In his discussion of this disappointment in his *Memoir of the Author's Life*, Hogg's warm affection for his epic is very evident:

> It is said the multitude never are wrong, but, in this instance, I must take Mr. Wordsworth's plan, and maintain that they *were* wrong. I need not say how grievously I was disappointed, as what unsuccessful candidate for immortal fame is not? But it would have been well could I have refrained from exposing myself. I was invited to a public dinner given by a great number of young friends, a sort of worshippers of mine (for I have a number of those in Scotland). It was to congratulate me on my new work, and drink success to it. The president made a speech, in which, after some laudatory remarks on the new poem, he boldly and broadly asserted that it was much inferior to their beloved "Queen's Wake". I was indignantly wroth, denying his assertion both in principle and position, and maintained not only that it was infinitely superior to the "Queen's Wake," but I offered to bet the price of the edition with any or all of them that it was the best epic poem that ever had been produced in Scotland. None of them would take the bet, but as few backed me. I will however stake my credit on "Queen Hynde." It was unfortunate that the plot should have been laid in an age so early that we have no interest in it. ( p.41)

## 2. Contexts: *Waverley*, Ossian, Dr Johnson, Camelot, Gaelic Poetry, and St Columba.

'Tha tím, am fiadh, an coille Hallaig'
[ 'Time, the deer, is in the wood of Hallaig' ]
Sorley MacLean, 'Hallaig'

The main events of Hogg's epic take place on the west coast of the Highlands of Scotland, at the fabled ancient Scottish capital city of Beregon. As we have seen, Hogg began to write *Queen Hynde* around 1817, that is to say, not very long after the publication in 1814 of another account of Highland Scotland: *Waverley*, Scott's ground-break-

ing historical novel of the Jacobite rising of 1745–46. Claire Lamont
has argued persuasively that the date of *Waverley*'s publication is
significant:

> The novel had a long incubation period, but the major part of
> it was written in the first half of 1814; it was published in the
> July of that year. Consider the significance of that date: the
> end of the long Napoleonic wars was in sight. During them
> many smaller countries of Europe had been defeated by in-
> vading French armies, bringing with them modern ideas de-
> riving from the first intellectual impetus of the French Revo-
> lution itself. Reflecting on the Revolution and its aftermath, as
> any thinking person of his day must, Scott was driven to con-
> sider the conquest of an earlier small country on principles
> that considered themselves to be enlightened. His own. The
> importance of what Scott did is that he made Highland Scot-
> land into a paradigmatic culture; it is a culture described in
> terms of its destruction, in some ways its inevitable destruc-
> tion.

Lamont goes on to point out that the presentation of Highland
Scotland in *Waverley* has much in common with some of the most
interesting fictions of the late twentieth century:

> Let us consider where some of the greatest new writing in
> English is now to be found. In those literatures emerging from
> a colonial past. Literatures of the Caribbean, of Africa, of In-
> dia. If I had to name any one theme common in those litera-
> tures and beyond it is this: the imposition of colonial rule on a
> traditional culture, and the tragic destruction of that culture
> under the complex of pressures that might be summed up
> best as 'the modern world'. And who was the first novelist to
> give us this vision? Scott. And which was the first culture so
> presented? Highland Scotland.[9]

*Queen Hynde* responds to *Waverley* and its concerns in various ways.
For example, Scott's novel presents a narrative in which a fictional
character (Edward Waverley) is brought into contact, not only with
fictional characters and events, but also with historical characters
and events (for example Prince Charles Edward and the battle of
Prestonpans). *Queen Hynde*, like *Waverley*, offers a mixture of the his-
torical and the fictional. One of the central characters in Hogg's epic
is the historical St Columba (521–597). This Irish holy man founded
a monastery on the island of Iona, in the Gaelic-speaking Highlands;

and Columba has been remembered with affection for well over a thousand years as a figure of central importance in the process by which Christianity was established in Scotland. Another historical figure in the poem is Aedán (d.606), a King of Scots, who (in the historical record as well as in Hogg's epic) grew up in Ireland, and inherited his ancestral throne with the help of St Columba. Hogg's Queen Hynde herself, on the other hand, is a monarch unknown to the historical record. Likewise, Hynde's capital city of Beregon can best be described as a Scottish Camelot: a place, that is to say, which powerfully inhabits a nation's imagination and legends, but which is less securely grounded in sober and mundane history.

Scott's historical fictions often display a sense of the characteristic features of particular periods of Scottish history: *Waverley* is very much a novel about the 1740s; and *Redgauntlet* is very much a novel about Scotland a generation after the 'Forty-five. In contrast, *Queen Hynde*'s picture of the Scots in Beregon is not by any means a meticulous reconstruction of the Scotland of the sixth century. Rather, echoes from many periods of Scotland's history are to be heard in the Beregon of Hogg's epic. For example, one of the central characters of *Queen Hynde* is M‚Houston, a man of the people who wields a sword no-one else is strong enough to use, as he defends Scotland from an invading king; and in this M‚Houston provides an echo of folk-memories of William Wallace, who lived some seven centuries after the time of Saint Columba. Likewise, the Notes of the present edition show (for example) that *Queen Hynde* has various echoes of *Macbeth*; and the Notes also show that the description (pp.160–61) of the race between Eon of Elry and Feldborg is in fact based on a race that took place in Scotland some thirteen centuries after the time of Saint Columba. In short, this Scottish epic offers a portrait of Scotland, rather than a portrait of the details of Scottish life at a particular period.

It appears, then, that *Queen Hynde* is not simply an imitation of *Waverley*; but nevertheless *Waverley* is manifestly one of the ingredients in the mix that goes to make up *Queen Hynde*. Another ingredient is provided by one of the most famous literary texts of eighteenth-century Scotland: it is clear that Hynde's palace of 'Selma' in her capital city of Beregon draws its being from Fingal's 'Selma' in James Macpherson's Ossianic epic *Fingal*.

The presence of *Fingal* in *Queen Hynde* comes as no surprise: a Scottish poet of Hogg's generation who set out to compose an epic would inevitably write with a consciousness of the controversy surrounding *Fingal* and Macpherson's other *Ossian* poems; and, as we shall see, *Queen Hynde* can be read as a complex and subtle response to the heated debate that had long raged around Macpherson's *Ossian*.

James Macpherson had been born in the Highland district of Badenoch in 1736, in the territory of his uncle, the clan chief Ewan Macpherson of Cluny. James was therefore born only twenty-nine years after the Union of 1707 between England and Scotland had created the new multi-nation state of Britain; and he was a child of an impressionable age when the Jacobite rising of 1745–46 took place. Macpherson of Cluny and his followers were prominent in Prince Charles's Jacobite army; and the young James Macpherson had the traumatic experience of seeing the triumphant hopes of his relatives in 1745 dissolve into catastrophic defeat at Culloden in 1746.

Hogg shared the deep interest in the Jacobite experience of 1745–46 that can be traced both in Macpherson's *Ossian* epics and in Scott's *Waverley*. For example, Hogg's *The Three Perils of Woman* (1823) contains a particularly powerful evocation of the plight of Gaelic-speaking Highland Scotland in the aftermath of Culloden; and the years during which *Queen Hynde* was composed also saw the publication of Hogg's *Jacobite Relics* (1819 and 1821), a two-volume collection of Jacobite songs garnered from various sources, including Gaelic ones.

James Macpherson's personal experience of the aftermath of Culloden has been summed up as follows by Fiona Stafford, in her Introduction to an edition of Macpherson's *Poems of Ossian* published in 1996 by the Edinburgh University Press:

> With defeat came disgrace for Clan Macpherson, as Cluny Castle was razed and much of the local community destroyed by the violence of the victorious army. [...] Between the ages of ten and eighteen, James Macpherson thus lived through scenes of appalling violence, and saw his home and family under the constant threat of further oppression. During this period, a series of measures were implemented to crush the distinctive Highland way of life, and render the region safe for ever. After 1746, the tartan plaid was banned, and no Highlander allowed to carry arms or play the bagpipes. The estates of prominent rebel chiefs ( including Cluny ) were forfeited to the Crown, while the ancient systems of ward-holding and heritable jurisdiction were abolished. Such measures were a more Draconian development from the earlier, relatively peaceful, attempts to open communications and transport networks in the Highlands, and to encourage the use of English rather than Gaelic. But it is in the context of

· systematic cultural destruction that Macpherson's efforts to collect old heroic poetry can be seen; they were, at least in part, an attempt to repair some of the damage to the Highlands sustained in the wake of the Jacobite Risings.[10]

In 1752 the teenage James Macpherson became a student at the University of Aberdeen. At Aberdeen, he encountered the theories of the philosophers of the Scottish Enlightenment, theories that placed great value on the epic poetry of allegedly 'primitive' societies like the one into which Macpherson himself had been born. For example, Thomas Blackwell of the University of Aberdeen had produced a pioneering *Enquiry into the Life and Writings of Homer* (1735); and, naturally enough, ideas like Blackwell's encouraged the young Macpherson to see potential value in the familiar poetry and traditions of his own native Gaelic culture. That culture, having recently suffered military conquest, was now desolated and despised; and it is easy to understand why Macpherson would be fired by a desire to reassert its dignity and worth.

An important place in Macpherson's native culture was held by poems and traditions concerning the ancient warrior-bard Ossian; and Macpherson imaginatively re-created and embellished this material in texts which he presented as his own prose translations into English of third-century Gaelic epics by Ossian. Fiona Stafford gives the following account of the processes involved:

In the years following Macpherson's death in 1796, the Highland Society of Scotland set up a Committee of investigation which concluded that, although Macpherson had not produced close translations of individual poems, he had nevertheless drawn on the traditional tales collected in his tours, using certain recognisable characters, plots and episodes. He also developed his own very distinctive measured prose as the medium for presenting the Gaelic material in English, and while this was indebted to the prose tales of Gaelic Scotland, it also reflected Macpherson's academically influenced preconceptions about the nature of early poetry. For while he undoubtedly came across a large number of heroic ballads in the Highlands, he seems to have regarded his sources somewhat dismissively as the broken remains of great Celtic epics, and to have seen the task of recovery in the light of sympathetic restoration, rather than as a painstaking translation of the miscellaneous mass.[11]

Understandably, given the circumstances of their composition in the wake of devastating military defeat in 1746, Macpherson's *Ossian* epics are imbued with a deep melancholy that is redolent of desolating loss, of heroism in the face of defeat. Ossianic melancholy proved to be attractive to readers in a period in which Romanticism was developing; and Macpherson's *Ossian* poems took Europe by storm in the later eighteenth century. Indeed, Ossian came to be widely regarded throughout Europe as the peer of Homer as an epic poet.

Nevertheless, Macpherson's *Ossian* texts called forth hostility as well as enthusiasm. Famously, Dr Samuel Johnson (among others) vigorously questioned the authenticity of these allegedly ancient Gaelic epics; and *Queen Hynde* can be read as a response to Johnson's view of *Ossian*, as well as being a response to the *Ossian* epics themselves. Johnson had travelled to the Highlands in 1773, in the company of James Boswell; and Boswell published an account of this tour in his *Journal of a Tour to the Hebrides, with Samuel Johnson, LL.D.* Hogg's accounts of his own tours in the Highlands in 1802, 1803, and 1804 show him to be very conscious of following in the footsteps of Johnson and Boswell.[12]

Johnson's attack on the authenticity of Macpherson's *Ossian* was much resented in Scotland; and it is not difficult to understand the motives that lay behind the desire of many Scots to spring to Macpherson's defence. Scottish cultural self-confidence had been severely shaken by the incorporating Union with England of 1707, and by the events of 1745–46; and, for many Scots, defence of the authenticity of Macpherson's *Ossian* seemed to provide a much-needed pathway towards the recovery of self-respect. Similar forces can be seen at work in the desire of modern, post-colonial Africans to find evidence, in the impressive ruins of Great Zimbabwe, of an advanced pre-colonial African society.

Johnson took a different view. This complex and much-admired Englishman is not, perhaps, to be seen to best advantage in his various dealings with Scotland and the Scots; but, however that may be, it appears that Johnson instinctively interpreted his own country's military conquest of Highland Scotland in 1746 as an enlightened process that would bring progress to a backward and barbarous people. Boswell's *Journal of a Tour to the Hebrides* (a text with which Hogg appears to have been familiar), records Johnson's opinions:

> Dr. Johnson got into one of his fits of railing at the Scots. He owned that they had been a very learned nation for a hundred years, from about 1550 to about 1650; but that they afforded the only instance of a people among whom the arts of civil life did not advance in proportion with learning; that

they had hardly any trade, any money, or any elegance, be-
fore the Union; that it was strange that, with all the advan-
tages possessed by other nations, they had not any of those
conveniences and embellishments which are the fruit of in-
dustry, till they came in contact with a civilized people. 'We
taught you, (said he,) and we'll do the same in time to all
barbarous nations,–to the Cherokees,–and at last to the Ouran-
Outangs;[13]

Johnson's views on this matter–however robust, and however
useful as a justification for the British Empire–would be unlikely to
inspire affectionate assent among Scots or among Cherokees; or
among orang-outangs, for that matter. At any rate, Boswell (a Scot)
records his own defensive response:

> Boswell. 'We had wine before the Union.'—Johnson. 'No, sir;
> you had some weak stuff, the refuse of France, which would
> not make you drunk.'—Boswell. 'I assure you, sir, there was a
> great deal of drunkenness.'—Johnson. 'No, sir; there were peo-
> ple who died of dropsies, which they contracted in trying to
> get drunk.' (p.348)

Queen Hynde can be read as a playful assertion (in response to
Johnson) that pre-Union Scotland had even more to commend it
than Boswell's wine and drunkenness: for example, it also had
Beregon, the Scottish Camelot.

If the hostile and defensive Scottish reaction to Johnson can be
readily understood, so too can Johnson's desire to dismiss pre-
Union Scotland. How can a person of decency feel comfortable about
the military conquests of a great imperial power? If such events are
not interpreted as the benign and enlightened imposition of progress,
they can begin to appear uncomfortably like looting and armed rob-
bery. Johnson naturally wished to interpret his country's military
conquest of Highland Scotland in 1746 (only twenty-seven years
before his own Highland tour) as a benign event; and this meant
that he was pre-disposed to see the old Gaelic-speaking Highland
society as essentially backward and crudely primitive: not at all the
kind of society that could have produced a rival to Homer, but rather
a society inhabited by the equivalent of the barbarous Cherokees or
the scarcely more barbarous 'Ouran-Outangs'. This is the context
in which Johnson writes as follows, in his Journey to the Western Isles of
Scotland, about the language and culture of Highland Scotland:

> Of the Earse [Gaelic] language, as I understood nothing, I can-
> not say more than I have been told. It is the rude speech of a

barbarous people, who had few thoughts to express, and were content, as they conceived grossly, to be grossly understood. After what has lately been talked of Highland Bards, and Highland genius [Johnson's reference is to the enthusiastic response to Macpherson's *Ossian*], many will startle when they are told, that the *Earse* was never a written language; that there is not in the world an Earse manuscript a hundred years old; and that the sounds of the Highlanders were never expressed by letters, till some little books of piety were translated, and a metrical version of the Psalms was made by the Synod of *Argyle*. ( pp.101–02)

This makes it abundantly clear that Johnson, in the Highlands with Boswell in 1773, did not take much interest in the barbarous Earse sounds through which his Highland hosts sought to communicate what he assumed to be their few thoughts and their gross conceptions. Confirmation of this is provided in Boswell's *Journal*:

We here [at Corrichatachin in the island of Skye] enjoyed the comfort of a table plentifully furnished, the satisfaction of which was heightened by a numerous and cheerful company; and we for the first time had a specimen of the joyous social manners of the inhabitants of the Highlands. They talked in their own ancient language, with fluent vivacity, and sung many Earse songs with such spirit, that, though Dr. Johnson was treated with the greatest respect and attention, there were moments in which he seemed to be forgotten. For myself, though but a *Lowlander*, having picked up a few words of the language, I presumed to mingle in their mirth, and joined in the chorusses with as much glee as any of the company. Dr. Johnson being fatigued with his journey, retired early to his chamber, where he composed the following Ode, addressed to Mrs. Thrale:
ODA.
*Permeo terras, ubi nuda rupes* [...]   ( pp.271–72)

Disturbed by the fluent vivacity of barbarous Gaelic, the great man retires to his bedroom to seek solace in the more familiar comforts of Latin, the tongue of civilisation. As it happens, however, Johnson is mistaken when he writes that '*Earse* was never a written language'; and that 'there is not in the world an Earse manuscript a hundred years old'. Scottish Gaelic manuscripts of some antiquity (for example *The Book of the Dean of Lismore*) do in fact exist; and the speakers of Scottish Gaelic share an ancient and rich cultural inheritance with the speakers of Irish Gaelic. Indeed, Johnson's view of the controversy over *Ossian* is not supported by the modern scholarly consensus, as articulated by Fiona Stafford and others. This consensus accepts that Macpherson's *Ossian* texts are not direct translations of ancient Gaelic epics; but nevertheless it rejects Johnson's view that these texts deserve to be dismissed as mere fakes, mere forgeries.

Macpherson's *Ossian* texts, that is to say, are now coming to be recognised and valued as imaginative re-creations, for a modern British culture, of the traditional narrative material of the ancient culture of Gaelic Scotland. It thus appears that, in considering Macpherson's *Ossian*, we enter territory that has a good deal in common with Arthurian romance, another body of traditional narrative material which proved to be ripe for imaginative re-creation. Indeed, Hogg specifically indicates *Queen Hynde*'s connections with King Arthur and Camelot in a note about one of his poem's central characters. The character in question is M,Houston, the future King Aedán. Hogg writes:

> This hero's name is, it seems, wrong spelled throughout; a natural error of a lowlander. It ought, I am told, to have been M,Uiston; signifying the son of Eugene. He was the son of king Eugenius, the third of that name, long the accomplice, but at last the conqueror, of the far-famed Arthur. (p.218)

Here Hogg appears to be drawing upon (and altering for his own purposes) material from Raphael Holinshed, *The Scottish Chronicle*, a text that would have been readily available to him, for example in a two-volume edition of 1805 (Arbroath: J. Findlay). This text provides an account of Eugenius, the third King of Scots of that name, who acted in alliance with King Arthur, but later won a great victory over him (I, 197–202). *The Scottish Chronicle* goes on to give an account of the alliance between Saint Columba and Aedán (I, 203-11). The persons and events of *Queen Hynde* are thus firmly linked with the glamour of the chivalric romance of the Arthurian world.

A parallel between Macpherson's *Ossian* narratives and Arthurian romance has been pointed out by the nineteenth-century historian John Hill Burton:

> It has been found necessary to give this short account of the brilliant romances which record the chivalry at the courts of the two phantom monarchs, Arthur and Fingal. That they arose out of the political conditions connected with the decay of the Roman power, and the progress of those influences that

made the Scotland and the England of later days, is in itself
a fact, even if nothing but the meagreness of our historical
knowledge of the period was the cause of their existence.[14]

In his book *The Making of History* (London and Toronto: Associ-
ated University Presses, 1986), Ian Haywood has suggested that
Macpherson's *Ossian* can be seen as an early manifestation of the
kind of historical fiction that was to flourish in the nineteenth cen-
tury. Crucially, however, Haywood suggests that in Macpherson's
eighteenth-century generation retrospectively imagined historical
fictions (as later written by the author of *Waverley* and his many fol-
lowers) had still to become established as an accepted literary genre;
and, as a result, Macpherson's *Ossian* texts sought to present them-
selves to their first readers as historical relics, rather than as self-
proclaimed historical fictions.

A somewhat different line could be taken, a generation later, by
*Queen Hynde*; and Hogg's epic follows *Waverley* in proclaiming itself
to be a retrospectively imagined fiction. Hogg's poem about the roots
of the Scottish nation, that is to say, overtly weaves together histori-
cal and fictional persons and events as it playfully constructs an im-
aginative vision of what pre-Union Scotland might have been like.
It is in this spirit that the narrator of *Queen Hynde* declares that he will
proceed by 'Raising from ancient days a queen, / And maids that
were, or might have been' (p.56). It appears, then, that *Queen Hynde*
presents itself as a construction of a human, fallible, funny, heroic,
and attractive pre-Union Highland Scotland. In short, Hogg's epic
offers itself as a more sympathetic alternative to Johnson's construc-
tion of a land of grunting, barbarous Scotch orang-outangs.

Macpherson's *Ossian*, Johnson's *Journey to the Western Islands of Scot-
land*, Scott's *Waverley*, and Hogg's *Queen Hynde* all reflect the concerns
of their present as they create their versions of the Scottish past.
Thus *Ossian* constructs a vision of the past that will restore self-
respect to those defeated in 1746. *Waverley* likewise constructs a pic-
ture of the traditional Highland culture defeated at Culloden in 1746;
but Scott's novel regards that defeat as an inevitable consequence of
progress, and seeks to identify those features of the old society that
have to be left behind as Scotland consolidates its position in the
enlightened new world of Hanoverian North Britain. However,
*Waverley* also identifies those features of the old world that can be
valued and preserved by the still comparatively new British state.
Scott's novel can thus be seen as encouraging Scottish loyalty to the
British crown and the British Empire. As a text that usefully sup-
ported Scotland's place in the British political status quo of 1814,

*Waverley* helped to pave the way for Queen Victoria's tartan-draped Balmoral; and it also helped to pave the way for the various kilted Highland regiments that fought and died for the British Imperial cause during the long reign of the great Queen-Empress.

*Queen Hynde* is fully aware of *Waverley*, and of *Ossian*, and of Johnson; but, as we shall see, Hogg's poem sets out to construct its own distinctive version of the Highland past. In doing so, *Queen Hynde* (like *Waverley* and *Ossian*) is prepared to find things to value in traditional Highland culture. Hogg's poem thus has a good deal in common with various other significant Scottish contributions to European Romanticism, contributions which tend to subvert and disrupt comfortable British metropolitan assumptions like Dr Johnson's. For those who shared Johnson's world-view, the values and the glories of civilisation were to be identified with London, the centre of the British Empire; and deviations from the cultural norms of the British metropolis were, by definition, to be regarded as manifestations of the second-rate, the backward, the provincial. *Queen Hynde* is one of a number of Scottish texts that subvert such assumptions by being open to the potential value of the voice of the Scottish 'margins'; and Hogg's epic seeks to allow that 'marginal' voice to be heard.

Similar attempts to allow the Scottish 'margins' to speak can be found in the eighteenth-century revival of Scots vernacular poetry in the writings of Allan Ramsay, Robert Fergusson, and Robert Burns; in Burns's much-admired efforts in collecting and imaginatively re-creating the corpus of traditional Scottish song; in the flowering of the Scottish Gaelic tradition in poems of eighteenth-century figures like Alasdair MacMhaighstir Alasdair; in aspects of Sir Walter Scott's powerfully influential fictive re-creations of the Scottish past in the Waverley Novels; in aspects of Macpherson's *Ossian* epics; and in the many sympathetic presentations of the marginalised and the powerless to be found in the various fictions of James Hogg (that well-known Scotch shepherd, the Author of *The Queen's Wake*).

As it sets out to humanise and valorise pre-Union Highland Scotland, *Queen Hynde* (like *Ossian*) draws strength from existing Gaelic texts. At first sight this may seem surprising; but Hogg was a frequent visitor to the Highlands, and it would appear that, as a result, he acquired a basic knowledge of Gaelic. There is also evidence that he had access to Gaelic texts in translation.[15]

Book Third of *Queen Hynde* contains an extended description of a voyage by M,Houston and Columba from Ireland to Scotland, through a fearsome storm; and it is difficult to avoid seeing this passage as Hogg's homage to one of the masterpieces of eighteenth-century Gaelic poetry, 'Birlinn Chlann Raghnaill' / 'Clanranald's Galley', by Alasdair MacMhaighstir Alasdair / Alexander MacDonald (1695?–1770?). This long poem culminates in an extended description of the galley's storm-tossed voyage from Scotland to Ireland. The quotations that follow are extracts from Iain Crichton Smith's translation of 'Birlinn Chlann Raghnaill'.

> Grey-headed wave-leaders towering
>     with sour roarings,
> their followers with smoking trumpets
>     blaring, pouring.
>
> When the ship was poised on wave crest
>     in proud fashion
> it was needful to strike sail
>     with quick precision.
>
> When the valleys nearly swallowed us
>     by suction
> we fed her cloth to take her up to
>     resurrection. [...]
>
> But when the ocean could not beat us
>     make us yield
> she became a smiling meadow,
>     summer field.
>
> Though there was no bolt unbending,
>     sail intact,
> yard unwrenched or ring unweakened,
>     oar uncracked.[16]

The voyage of M,Houston and Columba in *Queen Hynde* echoes 'Birlinn Chlann Raghnaill' with an exuberant relish and energy:

> "Hold by the cords–" M,Houston yelled.
> (Gods how the monks and rowers held!)
> "To see the bottom of the main
> We but descend to rise again."
> Down went the bark, with stern upright,
> Down many fathoms from the light.
> As sea-bird, mid the breakers tossed,
> Screaming and fluttering off the coast,
> Dives from the surf of belch and foam,
> To seek a milder calmer home,

So sought the bark her downward way,
From meeting waves and mounting spray.  (pp.88–89)

Likewise, Hogg's portrait of his fictional monarch Queen Hynde seems to owe something to another eighteenth-century Gaelic poetic masterpiece, 'Moladh Beinn Dóbhrain' / 'Praise of Ben Dorian' by Donnchadh Bàn Mac an t-Saoir / Duncan Ban Macintyre (1724–1812). This long Gaelic poem echoes the complex and sophisticated structure of pibroch (the great classical music of the Highland bagpipe). A 'hind' is a female deer, and 'Moladh Beinn Dóbhrain' evokes the pleasures and the spiritual renewal to be experienced in hunting deer on Ben Dorian. The quotation which follows is a short extract from Iain Crichton Smith's translation of 'Moladh Beinn Dóbhrain'.

Hind, nimble and slender,
with her calves strung behind her
lightly ascending
the cool mountain passes
through Harper's Dell winding
on their elegant courses.

Accelerant, speedy,
when she moves her slim body
earth knows nought of this lady
but the tips of her nails.
Even light would be tardy
to the flash of her pulse.

Dynamic, erratic,
by greenery spinning,
this troupe never static,
their minds free from sinning.

Coquettes of the body,
slim-leggèd and ready,
no age makes them tardy,
no grief nor disease.[17]

It might fairly be said that 'Moladh Beinn Dóbhrain' celebrates feelings akin to those of the Sioux for 'Pte' (the buffalo) and for the ancestral heartland of 'Paha Sapa' (the Black Hills); and Hogg associates such feelings with his Queen Hynde. Interestingly, Donnchadh Bàn was entirely an oral poet: he could neither read nor write, but he could recite his own poetry as well as large quantities of other

Gaelic verse. A gamekeeper who ended his days in Edinburgh, where he joined the City Guard and sold whisky, Donnchadh Bàn was a Highland barbarian who would undoubtedly have appealed to that other literary outsider and barbarous yokel, the Ettrick Shepherd. Clearly, Donnchadh Bàn could reasonably be described as a modern Ossian; but it appears that his path and Dr Johnson's did not cross when they were both in Edinburgh in the autumn of 1773. Perhaps, alas, there would not have been a significant meeting of minds even if their paths had crossed. It is one of the rich ironies of the Scottish Enlightenment that the Edinburgh literati, speculating passionately about Ossian, seemed totally unable to make themselves fully aware of the presence in their city of a major oral Gaelic poet. If a farm-worker like Hogg was hard to take seriously as another Homer, it was equally difficult to perceive another Ossian in the person of a disreputable seller of cheap whisky. Nevertheless, Iain Crichton Smith (himself a major Gaelic poet) is on secure ground when he asserts that 'Duncan Ban's reputation remains high and surely *Ben Dorian* will remain as one of the great poems in Gaelic, musical, fertile, sunny and joyful'.[18]

'Real' Gaelic poetry, then, is powerfully present in various ways in Hogg's epic; and so is Macpherson's *Ossian*. We have seen that Hynde's palace of Selma derives from the Selma of *Fingal*, one of Macpherson's *Ossian* epics; and many other detailed comparisons can be drawn between the two poems. For example, *Fingal*, like *Queen Hynde*, is divided into six Books; in both texts there is an invasion of the British Isles by Scandinavian forces; and in both texts the resources of Scotland and Ireland combine to defeat the invaders.

This does not mean, however, that *Queen Hynde* is simply an imitation of *Fingal*. In creating its own distinctive view of the Highland past, Hogg's epic is to some extent self-consciously in dispute with *Ossian*, with *Waverley*, and with Gaelic poetry. As a result, the description of the storm in *Queen Hynde* reflects 'Birlinn Chlann Raghnaill' with an exuberant energy that is both affectionate and parodic. Hogg's epic, likewise, partly echoes and partly distances itself from the versions of the Highland past offered by Macpherson and Scott.

For example, *Queen Hynde* distances itself from *Ossian* by making use of the possibilities opened up by *Waverley*. Scott's novel had firmly established the new genre of retrospectively imagined historical fiction; and as a result Hogg's epic (unlike *Fingal*) has no need to pass itself off as an authentic historical relic. Rather, *Queen Hynde* glories in presenting itself as a modern poem, as an epic modern bardic performance in which the Author of *The Queen's Wake* exhibits his mastery of the Ossianic material. Again and again in the addresses to the Maids of Dunedin, Hogg enjoys himself with self-mocking relish by foregrounding the fact that this epic is a performance by the Ettrick Shepherd. This text even offers an exuberant parody of the Shepherd's performance to the Maids of Dunedin when, in Book Second, a vain and self-important farm worker narrates his adventures among the Vikings to the Queen ' 'mid her maids' (pp.33–39).

All this, of course, does not make for a tone of solemn Ossianic melancholy. Capable of being utterly hilarious (especially when wicked Wene is on-stage), *Queen Hynde* is *Fingal* with jokes; and the jokes involve an element of parody, as Hogg's epic gently sends up its Ossianic predecessor. The parody is affectionate and sympathetic rather than hostile, however. This can be detected, for example, in the tone of the evocation of Ossian in Book Second of Hogg's poem. Scottish sentinels, awaiting King Eric's Viking invasion of Scotland's coast, hear 'a soft lay of sorrow' which is:

> Much like the funeral song of pain
> Which minstrel pours o'er warrior slain.
> And well the strains to sorrow true
> Of Ossian's airy harp they knew,
> Which his rapt spirit from the sky
> Gave to the breeze that journeyed bye;
> And well they knew, the omen drear
> Boded of danger death and weir.    (pp.41–42)

As well as mixing affection and parody in its references to *Ossian*, Hogg's epic also mixes affection and parody in its references to Scott's writings. For example, Book First of *Queen Hynde* contains a description of a voyage in which Hynde and her court sail gloriously from Beregon round the Island of Mull to Iona. This passage interconnects with the opening Canto of Scott's *The Lord of the Isles* (1815), in which a fleet of Highland galleys appear in the Sound of Mull:

> Lord Ronald's fleet swept by,
> Streamer'd with silk, and trick'd with gold,
> Mann'd with the noble and the bold
>     Of Island chivalry. [...]

> And each proud galley, as she pass'd,
> To the wild cadence of the blast
>     Gave wilder minstrelsy.[19]

Scott's writings, like Macpherson's, show a willingness to find value in the old culture of Highland Scotland; and *Queen Hynde* shares that willingness. Hogg's poem, however, is not noticeably anxious to follow Scott in locating value with 'the noble and the bold / Of Island chivalry'. It will be remembered that Hogg, disappointed at Scott's failure to review *Queen Hynde*, had given vent to his feelings by saying 'Dear Mr Scott ye could never think that I was in the chivalry school like you. I'm the king o' the mountain and fairy school a far higher ane nor your's'. *Queen Hynde* both celebrates and sends up 'the chivalry school': and the send-up can be devastating. In Hogg's poem, Donald Gorm, the Lord of the Isle of Skye, is a leading example of 'Island chivalry'; but the glamour and value of the old chivalric code of heroic violence do not emerge unscathed from *Queen Hynde*'s account of the slaying, by an infuriated Donald Gorm, of his captive, the priest of Odin:

> Cursing and foaming in his rage,
> Sheer to the belt he clove the sage;
> To either side one half did bow,
> His head and breast were cleft in two;
> An eye was left on either cheek,
> And half a tongue, to see, and speak.
> O never was so vile a blow,
> Or such a bloody wreck of wo!   ( p.108)

This is Pythonesque in its surreal exuberance; but in spite of its enjoyment of the subversive and the grotesque, Hogg's epic has serious purposes in mind. No less than Macpherson, Hogg seeks to take on the epic poet's traditional role of patriotic mythmaker; like Macpherson, he seeks to generate a myth of national origins that will help to restore Scottish self-respect, severely dented as a result of the Union and of Culloden.

The presence in the poem of St Columba, the holy man of Iona, gives an indication of the place where Hogg's epic seeks to locate the value to be found in pre-Union Highland Scotland. Ample precedent for an epic poem with Christian themes had been provided by Milton's *Paradise Lost*; and Hogg's epic offers a Christianised version of Macpherson's heroic myth of the roots of the Scottish nation. This is not to suggest that Columba's personal heroism is the point at issue. Rather, the epic heroism at Scotland's origin is interpreted in *Queen Hynde* as a process through which Columba's Christian values of love and forgiveness replace old pagan values of violence, bloodlust, and rape. Hogg's epic is not simply a chivalric contest between Eiden and Eric, the heroic champions of the two contending nations; more significantly it is a contest between Columba and the bloodthirsty priests of Odin (whose chief delight is to find virgins to sacrifice to their gods).

In all this, Hogg seems to be offering an alternative to the view of Scottish history offered by Scott's *Waverley*. Scott's novel offers a vision of progress in which the heroic violence and the old feudal ways of Jacobitism are left behind, to be replaced by the modern, rational, Hanoverian, law-abiding world of the Scottish Enlightenment. In Hogg's epic, in contrast, the old ways are replaced by the values of Saint Columba, rather than the values of Adam Smith and David Hume.

In taking this path, Hogg's epic seems to offer its story of St Columba and King Aedán as a Christian parallel to the Old Testament story of the prophet Samuel and King David. Samuel, acting on God's instructions, selects David as the future King of Israel (I Samuel 16.1–13); and likewise Columba, acting on God's instructions, selects Aedán as the future King of Scots. Before he comes into his kingdom, David has many trials and adventures: for example, he has to defeat the Philistine champion Goliath in single combat (I Samuel 17.38–54); and he has to overcome the armies of the Philistines, which are invading the city of Keilah (I Samuel 23.1–5). Aedán, likewise, has to defeat the Viking leader Eric in single combat; and he also has to overcome the Viking armies which are invading Beregon. *Queen Hynde* sometimes gives the name 'Keila Bay' to Beregon's Ardmucknish Bay, no doubt because 'Kiel' is a local place-name; but there may also be a reference to the Biblical Keilah. Eventually Aedán, like David, wins the victory; and like David he fulfils his nation's destiny by reigning as a godly monarch.

As we shall see, all this ties in very well with a particular strand of Scotland's sense of itself in Hogg's day and generation. Like many non-aristocratic Scots of his time, Hogg tended to define his identity by finding deep significance in the anti-aristocratic struggles of the seventeenth-century Scottish Covenanters for civil and religious liberty. It is significant that, around the time Hogg was beginning to write *Queen Hynde*, the victory of the Covenanters in battle against the Royalists at Drumclog in 1679 was called to mind when, as the historian David Stevenson puts it:

> thousands of 'democrats', mainly textile workers engaged in industrial agitation, marched to the battlefield of Drumclog to commemorate the victory obtained by their ancestors over the government and their social superiors—and to celebrate the news of Napoleon's escape from Elba![20]

This march of the 'democrats' took place in 1815, as did the Battle of Waterloo; the next year, 1816, saw the composition and publication of Scott's *Old Mortality*; and the composition of *Queen Hynde* also began around this period. A hostile view of the Covenanters is offered by *Old Mortality*, which presents them as bigoted and violent revolutionary fanatics. *Old Mortality* is in effect a defence of the values of the political status quo under which Scott lived; and, in its framing narrative, it seeks to contain the revolutionary energies of the now long-dead Covenanters in the graves tended by the elderly and eccentric figure of Robert Paterson, 'Old Mortality'. In its main narrative, Scott's novel locates positive values in Henry Morton, who opposes the fanaticism of both Royalists and Covenanters, and who is in effect a personification of the ethos of the gentlemanly elite of the North Britain of Scott's own day.

When *Old Mortality* was published, Scott was a judge who was energetically consolidating his position as the owner of an expanding country estate; and he was shortly to become a baronet. Naturally, his perspective on the political status quo of the day differed from that of a common Scotch shepherd turned impecunious professional writer. Hogg's sympathies lay with the Covenanters as defenders of the rights and religious culture of 'the lower orders in Scotland' (as members of Scott's gentlemanly circle might have put it). As a result, the perspective on these matters offered by *Queen Hynde* differs significantly from the perspective offered by *Old Mortality*. David Stevenson has shown that many Covenanters saw the signing of the National Covenant in 1638 as 'the glorious marriage day of the Kingdom with God', an event through which the Scots could be seen to be 'in a sense the successors to the Jews, clearly chosen by God, awarded a unique status'.[21] This is the context in which *Queen Hynde* offers the story of Columba and Aedán as a parallel to the story of Samuel and David; and it is a context that allows Hogg's epic to imply that the radical and characteristically Scottish heroism of the plebeian Covenanters is a natural outcome of the Christian legacy of Columba, a legacy from the roots of the nation's story. With this in mind, it is worth remembering that, for a speaker of Scots, the word 'hind' can suggest a farm servant or peasant, as well as a female deer on Ben Dorian. It is also worth remembering that M‚Houston, in Hogg's epic, is a despised peasant boor before he emerges into his kingly role: indeed, this male hero of Hogg's epic is frequently described as a 'hind' in *Queen Hynde*.[22] It appears, then, that the royal Hynde and M‚Houston, with their patron Columba, have much in common with their fellow-Scots, the superstitious but devout Covenanters who suffered and died on the mountains during the Killing Time of the late seventeenth century. That, at any rate, seems to be the view of 'the king o' the mountain and fairy school' of poetry, as he asserts his difference from Scott, the king of 'the chivalry school'.

If the Christianising of the Ossianic material helps to articulate Hogg's differences from Scott, it also helps to articulate his differences from Johnson. A high point of the journey of Johnson and Boswell to the Hebrides in 1773 came when they arrived on Iona, Columba's island. This seems to have been a profoundly moving experience for both men. Johnson writes warmly about the significance of Iona, in a passage that has much in common with *Queen Hynde*'s assertion of the value and significance of Columba's championing of the Christian cause in sixth-century Scotland:

> We were now treading that illustrious Island, which was once the luminary of the *Caledonian* regions, whence savage clans and roving barbarians derived the benefits of knowledge, and the blessings of religion. [...] That man is little to be envied, whose patriotism would not gain force upon the plain of *Marathon*, or whose piety would not grow warmer among the ruins of *Iona*! (p.131)

However, Johnson's reverence for the monastic life of Iona does not extend to the society in which that monastic life operated: his 'roving barbarians' are the Viking invaders who eventually devastated Columba's island; but the 'savage clans' are the local population. Johnson asserts that the light of civilisation had once nobly shone from Iona; but (following a line of thought typical of Empire) he assumes that the noble light had to be brought to the local savages from outside. Indeed it appears that, in Johnson's view, the light had all too quickly been snuffed out in the surrounding darkness of Highland Scotland's 'savage clans':

> The chapel of the nunnery is now used by the inhabitants as a kind of general cow-house, and the bottom is consequently too miry for examination. [...] In one of the churches was a marble altar, which the superstition of the inhabitants has destroyed. Their opinion was, that a fragment of this stone was a defence against shipwrecks, fire, and miscarriages. In one corner of the church the bason for holy water is yet unbroken. (pp.132–33)

For Johnson, the benign and civilising legacy of Columba has been allowed to fall into ruin by the barbarous Scots; and the ruin is

eloquently exemplified by the fact that the superstitious Scotch peas-
ants of Iona have converted the chapel into a 'miry' cow-house. A
superstitious Scotch peasant himself (among other things), Hogg saw
matters from a different perspective. In an essay published in 1807,
he reflects on his own Highland tours, and on Dr Johnson.

> I remember reading, how Dr Johnson asked one of the minis-
> ters of Skye, "Who were the most barbarous clans in the High-
> lands?" He answered, that "they were those bordering upon
> the Lowlands." This asseveration the Doctor treated as ab-
> surd, and occasioned by prejudice. I am convinced, however,
> that Mr M'Queen was perfectly right: at least it appeared to
> me, that the inhabitants on the western coast and Hebrides,
> were the most indefatigable, and the most abstemious, people
> that I ever saw in my life; whilst those of the interior, on the
> contrary, were much given to idleness, tippling, and lying.[23]

These comments take issue with a Johnson who assumes (Hogg
implies) that the darkness of barbarism will be removed by contact
with a more civilised society. Given such assumptions, it seems self-
evident that the barbarous and savage Cherokees could have noth-
ing of value in their culture before they came in contact with the
benign civilising influence of their European conquerors. Hogg, in
contrast, seems comfortable with the assumption that the people of
the remote and 'marginal' western coast of Highland Scotland could
have had something of value in their culture even before they had
the benefits of civilisation imposed on them through conquest.

The Ettrick Shepherd, as narrator of *Queen Hynde*, is himself a
man from a remote margin; and this superstitious Scotch peasant
finds it natural to assume that Columba's legacy had been kept hon-
ourably intact, after more than a thousand years, by those other
superstitious Scotch peasants, the heroic, devout, if sometimes ab-
surd and bigoted Covenanters. Robert Burns, another plebeian voice
from the Scottish margins, expresses a view of the Covenanters that
seems to be akin to Hogg's:

> The Solemn League and Covenant
>    Now brings a smile, now brings a tear.
> But sacred Freedom, too, was theirs;
>    If thou 'rt a slave, indulge thy sneer.[24]

This short poem conveys a real and deep sense that there was some-
thing about the Covenanters that was worthy of respect: 'If thou 'rt
a slave, indulge thy sneer'. Nevertheless, an inclination to smile at
the absurdities of the Covenanters is equally manifest—as indeed

might be expected from a poem by the author of 'Holy Willie's
Prayer'. *Queen Hynde* shows a parallel willingness to find real value
in the Scotland of Hynde, Columba, and Aedán; and Hogg's poem
also shows a parallel willingness to laugh at the all-too-human ab-
surdity of its epic Scottish figures. This complex approach can be
seen in the description of the storm-tossed voyage from Ireland to
Scotland, made by Aedán / M,Houston, Columba, and the monks.
Things come to a crisis, and it appears that their boat is about to
sink:

> Again the waves rolled o'er the deck;
> But, be it told with due respect,
> At this dire moment, who should call
> From ridge of wave and tossing fall,
> But the good seer! Not seen till now;
> Washed from his hold, they knew not how,
> Blinded with cowl of many a fold,
> And wildly capering as he rolled.   (p.89)

That very rough diamond M,Houston then catches Columba, hold-
ing him 'stedfast as a rock'. Columba calls 'From ridge of wave and
tossing fall'; and M,Houston shouts 'o'er the swell / With maniac
laugh and demon yell'. Immediately afterwards the boat rounds 'the
point of low Kintyre' and enters calmer waters:

> Now were they breasting mountain steep;
> Now plunging 'mid the foamy deep;
> Anon they wheeled from out the roar,
> And swept along a weather shore,
> Beneath the bank of brake and tree,
> Upon a smooth and tranquil sea.   (p.90)

Immediately afterwards Columba proceeds to convert the pagan
M,Houston to Christianity:

> The holy sire, to tears constrained,
> The doctrine of the cross explained:
> The Fall–The covenant above;
> And wonders of redeeming love.   (p.91)

We have seen that the storm-tossed voyage of Hogg's poem ech-
oes Alasdair MacMhaighstir Alasdair's 'Birlinn Chlann-Raghnaill';
but there are also echoes here of the biblical story of Jesus stilling
the storm. This is recorded as follows in Matthew 8.23–27:

And when he was entered into a ship, his disciples followed

him. And, behold, there arose a great tempest in the sea, inso-
much that the ship was covered with the waves: but he was
asleep. And his disciples came to *him*, and awoke him, saying,
Lord, save us: we perish. And he saith unto them, Why are
ye fearful, O ye of little faith? Then he arose, and rebuked the
winds and the sea; and there was a great calm. But the men
marvelled, saying, What manner of man is this, that even the
winds and the sea obey him!

Columba and Aedán likewise experience the stilling of 'a great tem-
pest in the sea'; and this foreshadows the ending of the poem, which
ushers in the peace and calm of Aedán's 'long and holy reign' (p.216).
The stilling of the storm in Hogg's Scottish epic thus echoes a mani-
festation of Christ's power from Matthew's gospel; but nevertheless
Saint Columba is not a superhuman figure in *Queen Hynde*. Quite the
contrary, in fact. Although he is Christ's Apostle to the Scots,
Columba is a very human figure indeed in Hogg's poem: someone
capable of slipping on a banana skin, as it were, at the precise mo-
ment when his great work for Christ's cause is coming to fruition.

*Queen Hynde*, then, perceives both real value and human absurd-
ity in Highland Scotland. This desire to see human life as a combi-
nation of high achievement and the banana skin is characteristic of
Hogg's fictions; and in *The Three Perils of Woman* (1823), Hogg's nar-
rator provides a comment that seems entirely relevant to *Queen Hynde*.
The narrator's remark is directed at that very M,Houston-like fig-
ure, Richard Rickleton:

I am sorry to be obliged to wind up my tale with these letters;
but it is with domestic histories, as with all other affairs of
life.–Certain individuals wind themselves into the tissue of
every one of them, without whom the tale would be more
pure, and the web of life more smooth and equal; but neither
of them so diversified or characteristic. We must therefore be
content still to take human life as it is, with all its loveliness,
folly, and incongruity.[25]

For Johnson, the inhabitants of the old Highland Scotland 'had
few thoughts to express, and were content, as they conceived grossly,
to be grossly understood': sub-human beings, in effect. *Queen Hynde*
responds to this; but in responding, Hogg's epic resists the tempta-
tion to celebrate the deeds of superhuman heroes and heroines. The
Columba, Wene, and Saint Oran of *Queen Hynde* are manifestly im-
perfect figures; but, equally, they are not sub-human. In responding
to Johnson, Hogg's epic asserts that the Scotland of Columba, like

the Scotland of the modern Maid of Dunedin, is capable of exhibiting 'human life as it is, with all its loveliness, folly, and incongruity'.

## 3. Contexts: Scott, Byron, and Romantic Poetry.

At the time Hogg wrote the first books of *Queen Hynde*, he was still basking in the acclaim that *The Queen's Wake* had earned and confident of his poetic abilities. Though his work was compared to Scott's, the originality of his great poem had been noted and he was considered a talent in his own right. But Hogg's narrative poetry certainly invites comparisons with Scott's string of popular metrical romances. Between 1805 and 1815, Scott produced seven major narrative poems: *The Lay of the Last Minstrel* (1805), *Marmion* (1808), *The Lady of the Lake* (1810), *Don Roderick* (1811), *Rokeby* and *The Bridal of Triermain* (1813), and *The Lord of the Isles* (1815). In critical response to *Queen Hynde*, Hogg was aligned with Scott in his 'Last Minstrel' mode; but though *Queen Hynde*, like Scott's poem, foregrounds the bard's telling of an ancient tale, it goes further in establishing a strong and unique central voice that opens two worlds to his audience: the modern, 'enlightened' world of Edinburgh (Dunedin) and the mist-shrouded legendary world of ancient Beregon. For its subject matter, *Queen Hynde* perhaps owes a debt to Wordsworth's *White Doe of Rylstone* (1815), but more to another Scott poem, *The Lord of the Isles*, which appeared in January 1815 and whose fame perhaps was eclipsed both by *Waverley* and Lord Byron's appearance on the poetical scene. The setting of the first part of *The Lord of the Isles* is very near that of Queen Hynde on the western coast of Scotland, though 700 years later at the time of Robert the Bruce. As in *Queen Hynde* the action revolves around a ruin, in Scott's case the remains of the castle of Atornish perched on a promontory of Morvern across the sound from the island of Mull. Scott's autumn 1814 travels in the area (known as the 'Lighthouse Tour') inspired his poem, and in the journal he kept of the tour he mentions Beregonium, 'once, it is said, a British capital city'. Both the poem and his accounts to Hogg, whether in person or via this journal, may have sparked Hogg's imagination as well, reminding him of his own 1804 excursion to the western Highlands and islands, which had been serialised in the *Scots Magazine* in 1808 and 1809.[26]

In the first canto of *The Lord of the Isles*, Scott addresses his reader in a manner very like Hogg's in *Queen Hynde*: 'So shalt thou list, and haply not unmoved, / To a wild tale of Albyn's warrior day; / In distant lands, by the rough West reproved, / Still live some reliques

of the ancient lay'. The relics he refers to are the tombs of Scottish
heroes and kings 'amid the pathless wastes of Reay', in Harris, and
'in Iona's piles' (p.5). An excerpt from Scott's poem, written in his
characteristic rapid octosyllabic couplets, illustrates some similari-
ties to *Queen Hynde*:

> "WAKE, Maid of Lorn!" the Minstrels sung.
> Thy rugged halls, Artornish! rung,
> And the dark seas, thy towers that lave,
> Heaved on the beach a softer wave,
> As mid the tuneful choir to keep
> The diapason of the Deep.
> Lull'd were the winds on Inninmore,
> And green Loch-Alline's woodland shore,
> As if wild woods and waves had pleasure
> In listing to the lovely measure.  (p.6)

Surface resemblances aside, however, in terms of narrative style,
language, and tone, Hogg's poem departs radically from Scott's. The
voice of Hogg's poem is energetic and forthright; while Scott's is
more conventionally poetic. Hogg expands the role of the speaker-
bard; and his incorporation of humour, parody, and mock-heroic
means that *Queen Hynde* resembles more closely Byron's *Don Juan*
than Scott's metrical romance.

Byron certainly is another major poetic force to be considered.
His poetic career parallels Hogg's, with both poets benefiting from
Scott's influence and popularity, yet each taking narrative poetry in
a decidedly individual direction. By 1814 Byron was creating a sen-
sation with the first two cantos of *Childe Harold's Pilgrimage* (1812)
and with his exotic and dramatic *Oriental Tales*. Byron's *The Giaour*
and *The Bride of Abydos* appeared in 1813, and *The Corsair* and *Lara* in
1814. *Queen Hynde*, likewise, was begun around the middle of the
1810s. In some ways, however, Hogg's poem resembles more closely
a later phase of Byron, that of *Don Juan*. By the time of Byron's
death in April 1824, sixteen cantos of *Don Juan* had been published
(between 1819 and 1824). Hogg wrote the second part of *Queen
Hynde* in the year cantos XV and XVI were published and shortly after
Byron's death. *Queen Hynde* was written rapidly, like the individual
cantos of *Don Juan*, a poem, according to the *Norton Anthology* (II, 566),
best 'read rapidly, at a conversational pace'. Like *Don Juan*, *Queen Hynde*
parodies medieval chivalric romance (though Arthurian rather than
Italian). Like *Don Juan*, *Queen Hynde* was attacked as morally question-
able. And like *Don Juan*, in Hogg's poem the most significant element

is the narrator, though in *Queen Hynde* it is the bard's relationship to his audience that provides the cohesion.

In this context, *Queen Hynde* emerges as an original combination of old and new, though it is still decidedly a Romantic poem. In his adoption and revision of that Romantic symbol of poetic inspiration, the Eolian harp, Hogg follows the by then established poetic convention; but *his* music of nature is played on 'an uncouth harp of olden key':

> When an air of heaven, in passing by,
> Breathed on the mellow chords; and then
> I knew it was no earthly strain,
> But note of wild mysterious kind,
> From some blest land of unbodied mind.
> But whence it flew, or whether it came,
> From the sounding rock, or the solar beam,
> Or tuneful angels passing away
> O'er the bridge of the sky in the showery day,
> When the cloudy curtain pervaded the east,
> And the sunbeam kissed its humid breast,
> Invain I looked to the cloud overhead;
> To the echoing mountain dark and dread;  (p.179)

In his self-presentation as an inspired but misunderstood bard, Hogg adopts a popular contemporary persona. But while on the one hand he takes the role of the Romantic poet very seriously, on the other he critiques such self-importance. The bard of *Queen Hynde* is not the solitary, wandering, melancholy genius that Romantic poets had formed from the material of Macpherson's *Ossian*, Thomas Percy's and Thomas Gray's minstrel bard, James Beattie's Edwin, and the tragic life and death of Thomas Chatterton (1752–70). The eight-line invocation that Hogg puts in the mouth of Rimmon the bard of Turim to preface his advice to Donald Gorm is suitably, though exaggeratedly, poetic:

> "Thou lord of that romantic land,
> The winged isle, of steep and strand;
> And all the creeks of brake and fern,
> Those pathless piles so dark and dern
> That stretch from Sunart's sombre dell,
> To Duich's heights of moor and fell.
> Thou stem of royal seed—nay, more,
> Son of an hundred kings of yore!  (pp.106–07)

This grovelling, however, is followed by a warning to anyone who challenges the bard's importance: 'Unto thy servant deign regard; / Wo to the chief that slights his bard!' (p.107). Hogg's presentation of the bard—even of himself as bard—may thus be read in several ways, one of them ironic. When he declines to describe 'all the deeds of might' undertaken in the battles because it would distress his 'virgin patroness' and result in his song being classed 'mid fabulous lore', the reader must question his assertion that this is a 'folly' he will 'indulge no more' (p.209).

What seems to interest Hogg is not so much the solitary, prophetic, Romantic figure of the bard as the bard in relationship to an audience. The minstrel of *Queen Hynde* eschews the literariness of much poetry based on the bardic tradition. This is an *oral* performance to a specific audience, and as such Hogg's narrator is permitted to use language appropriate to an oral performance.[27] Hogg practically pulls the Maid of Dunedin herself into the poem, like the implied listener in one of Robert Browning's dramatic monologues. Exploring this dynamic—investigating the many functions of the bard and his audience in the poem—helps to clarify one key element of Hogg's and *Queen Hynde*'s relationship to Romanticism.

From the beginning, the audience is drawn into a contract with him, for 'secrets strange are on the wing, / Which you must list and I must sing' (p.134). In his first address to the 'Maids of Dunedin', he laments the cynicism of 'o'erpolished times' that would dismiss the pathos of his tale. He enlists women readers in particular, the major audience for sentimental novels, to share with him in Hynde's distress: 'If in such breast a heart may be, / Sure you must weep and wail with me!' (p.16). On the other hand, he also seems to mock them gently, and this reading is underscored by the increasingly extravagant language of his plea and by the tone of his other direct addresses to the 'Maids' or 'Maid'; he admonishes, ' if to wail thou can'st delay, / Have thou a bard's anathema' (p.16). The plea for the audience to empathise with Queen Hynde (and with the bard) rises to a climax when he breaks from the narrative of Hynde's sudden awakening from her nightmare:

> Maid of Dunedin, do not jeer,
> Nor lift that eye with jibing fleer;
> For well you wot, deny who dares,
> Such are the most of woman's cares;
> Nay if I durst I would them deem
> More trivial than a morning dream;
> Have I not seen thy deep distress,

> Thy tears for disregarded dress?
> Thy flush of pride, thy wrath intense,
> For slight and casual precedence?
> And I have heard thy tongue confess
> Most high offence and bitterness!
> Yet sooth thou still art dear to me,
> These very faults I love for thee,
> Then, why not all my freaks allow?
> I have a few and so hast thou. (p.18)

Thus, in a pattern that repeats throughout the poem, after recalling attention to the performer/audience relationship he returns to the story.

The bard sometimes acts as a tour guide, inviting the listener/reader into the scene. The most obvious instance of this is the opening lines of Book Third; it is the poetic version of the very specific directions Hogg provides in his endnote on 'Beregonium' (see p.218):

> O traveller, whomsoe'er thou art,
> Turn not aside with timid heart
> At Connel's tide, but journey on
> To the old site of Beregon;
> I pledge my word, whether thou love'st
> The poet's tale, or disaprove'st,
> So short, so easy is the way,
> The scene shall well thy pains repay.
> There shalt thou view, on rock sublime,
> The ruins gray of early time,
> Where, frowning o'er the foamy flood,
> The mighty halls of Selma stood.
> And mark a valley stretching wide,
> Inwalled by cliffs on either side,
> By curving shore where billows broke,
> And triple wall from rock to rock;
> Low in that strait, from bay to bay,
> The ancient Beregonium lay. (p.58)

Hogg goes on to point out specific features of the prospect, including the 'green sea-wave' of the bay, the cliff and ruins, the islands of Jura and Mull, the crests of Ben Nevis and Ben Cruachan, and Barvulen ridge (pp.58–59). Other instances of this function of the bard appear as interjections throughout the poem; for instance, describing Queen Hynde's entourage stepping onto the sacred shores of Iona, he beckons,

> Come view the barefoot group with me,
> Kneeling upon one bended knee,
> In two long files—a lane between,
> Where pass the maidens and their queen,
> Up to the sacred altar stone,
> Where good Columba stands alone. (p.22)

He calls on the reader's empathy at many points in the narrative, shifting in mood and person from narrative to direct address, drawing in the audience by encouraging personal, emotional associations:

> If thou didst e'er the affliction bear,
> Of having all thou valued'st here
> Placed in a frail & feeble bark,
> Exposed, upon the ocean dark;
> And when thy spirit yearned the most,
> The word arrived that all was lost;
> Then may'st thou guess the pains that stole
> Cold on the Caledonian's soul. (p.42)

Hogg constructs the past as an escape that enables him still to love the present, and in this context the bard is a conjurer of another world:

> I'll quit this jointured age and thee,
> This age of bond and bankruptcy,
> With all its sordid thirst of gold
> And conjure up the times of old,
> Raising from ancient days a queen,
> And maids that were, or might have been,
> That I may mould them as I will,
> And love thee froward trifler still. (p.56)

His positioning of the performing bard as central allows him to comment on and occasionally mock both periods of history. Though ancient Caledon is accorded great respect, as reflected in the opening lines of the poem, its authority is undercut by the tone of passages that humanise the heroes and spiritual leaders. Queen Hynde and her attendants manage the rough sea crossing to Iona with grace; the modern Maid in the same situation surely would become seasick:

> Maid of Dunedin, well I know
> Had'st thou been there there had been woe!
> Distress of body, and of mind,

> And qualms of most discourteous kind,
> < For I have seen on summer tide,
>  Where Forth's blue waters playful glide,
> Such paleness, and such dire alarms,
> Such dissarray of beauty's charms,
> As child within its nurse's arms!
> And, grieved for thy too dainty nature,
> I've deemed thee a most feeble creature.> (pp.19–20)

In the other world, however, Hogg also treats with humour the crossing of Columba and his sailor-monks with M‚Houston at the helm. In a scene designed to show the kingly potential of the savage M‚Houston, even 'that most holy man' Columba suffers indignity as he is 'washed from his hold' and 'Blinded with cowl of many a fold, / And wildly capering as he rolled' (pp.89–90). And the passages in which St Oran (perhaps a thinly-disguised John Knox) is discomfited by the antics of the wicked Wene capture the pious man in one of the poem's funniest moments, and align Wene with the Maid of Dunedin:

> Saint Oran was that very time
> Giving such picture of the crime
> Of woman's love, and woman's art,
> Of woman's mind, and woman's heart!
> If thou, dear maid, the same had'st heard,
> Thy blissful views had all been marred!
> For thou durst never more have been
> In robe of lightsome texture seen!
> Thy breast, soft heaving with the sigh,
> Arresting glance of vagrant eye,
> Love's fatal and exhaustless quiver,
> Must have been shrouded up for ever!
> The perfume—simper—look askance—
> The ready blush—the ogling glance—
> All all o'erthrown, ne'er to recover!
> Thy conquests and thy triumphs over!
> O breathe to heaven the grateful vow,
> That good Saint Oran lives not now! ( pp.20–21)

Hogg's attitude to the Highlands is complex, involving empathy but also bardic rivalry, with Hogg liable to assert the superiority of the Scots Border tradition over the Gaelic/Highland tradition. From this perspective Scots, the Borders, and Burns are aligned with nature, simplicity, and truth (telling it like it is), while the Gaelic and the

Highland tradition tends towards the inflated, laborious, and bombastical. The song offered by the minstrel Ila Glas is 'A lay full tiresome, stale and bare / As most of northern ditties are'. The speaker himself 'learned it from a bard of Mull, / Who deemed it high and wonderful', but he find it less impressive: ''Tis poor and vacant as the man, / I scorn to say it though I can' (p.29). Perhaps even the well-loved Ossian (like the well-loved Maid) is implied in this criticism.

Hogg writes himself into other roles within the narrative itself, sometimes more obviously than at others. Readers may see Hogg in the conflation of messenger, bard, and fool (a 'brown and breathless hind, / Whose habit and whose mein bespoke / A maniac from confinement broke'), who brings news of the Norse invasion (p.34), claiming, 'In artifice I ne'er was beat!' (p.39):

> O when that hind aside had laid
> His fool's attire, and was arrayed
> In belted plaid and broad claymore,
> And robes which once a chief had wore;
> And came with martial cap in hand
> Before the nobles of the land,
> It would have joyed your heart to 've seen
> His face of wisdom and his mein.
> And aye he stretched with careful fold
> His philabeg of tassled gold
> And tried with both hands to sleek down
> His locks all weatherbeat and brown;
> Then quite bewildered every sense
> With words of great magnifiscience;
> < Thro' every look and action ran
> The self-importance of the man: >
> The motley clown O do not blame,
> Few are his paths that lead to fame!
> One gained let him that path pursue
> For great and glorious is the view! (pp.39–40)

But perhaps most obvious is his identification with the 'low hind, M,Houston named' (p.200). The image (pp.162–63)of the 'burly peasant proud' who comes 'dashing through the heartless croud, / Shouldering both chief and vassal by, / As things of no utility' evokes another scene, of Hogg among his sophisticated Edinburgh contemporaries. Striding into the contests, M,Houston's ambiguous class standing proves to be his strength, for

> He had in various garbs appear'd,
> And gain'd, because he nothing fear'd;
> Having no title of renown,
> Nor line, to bring discredit on. (p.173)

Delighted with his hero, Hogg nonetheless (and characteristically) invites readers to be amused by M,Houston as well as with him:

> M,Houston grasp'd the treasure bright,
> And ran, and laugh'd with all his might,
> Loud jabbering something 'bout the sun,
> And kingly treasures fairly won; (p.174)

Frequently Hogg unequivocally claims the bard's voice for himself. In the long address that closes Book First, he takes centre stage:

> Maid of Dunedin, thou may'st see,
> Though long I strove to pleasure thee,
> That now I've changed my timid tone,
> And sing to please myself alone;
> And thou wilt read, when, well I wot,
> I care not whether you do or not. (p.30)

This passage is a complex mixture of performer teasing audience, self-mockery, plea for understanding, and declaration of poetic independence. He wants to be a 'sportive vagrant', to write about many themes, 'But only if, and when I will'. He compares himself to 'the meteor of the wild / Nature's unstaid erratick child', and asks, 'Can that be bound? can that be reined? / By cold ungenial rules restrained?' Emphatically he answers his (albeit rhetorical) question with 'No!' The meteor is 'nature's errour', he claims, and 'so am I!' His subsequent plea is to pity his faults 'but do not blame!'; instead, he urges, 'leave to all his fancies wild / Nature's own rude untutored child, / And should he forfeit that fond claim / Pity his loss but do not blame'. Instead of the 'regular and profuse' garden flowers, this natural poet offers the 'mountain gems' of the 'dell and lonely lea' which are 'By nature's hand at random sown'. The listener of poetry like this will be touched by 'sweeter strains [...] than are producible by art' (pp.30-31). His attitude toward the Maid shifts throughout the poem, but ultimately he claims her as his best ally:

> But yet, for all thy airs and whims,
> And lightsome love the froth that skims,
> I must acknowledge in the end
> To 've found thee still the poet's friend,

> His friend at heart; would jeer and blame,
> But aught degrading to his fame
> Would ne'er admit, nor join the gall
> Of slanderers mean and personal;
> Therefore, I bless thee, and engage
> To profit by thy patronage. (p.177)

In the closing sections of this book, Hogg strikes out at another group: his critics. He 'debars' from reading his poem 'all those who dare [...] To name the word INDELICATE!' (p.177). The poem becomes self-reflexive; Hogg's is the 'peasant's soul' (p.177) under attack:

> Then lower stoop'd they for a fee
> To poor and personal mockery;
> The gait, the garb, the rustic speech,
> All that could homely worth appeach,
> Unweariedly, time after time,
> In loathed and everlasting chime
> They vended forth [...] (p.178)

Given his history with the critical establishment that had overseen both his rise in reputation and his stereotyping as the vulgar Shepherd-Poet, Hogg's desire to preempt his critics may be understood. The audacity of his attack, however, merely fuelled the critical misunderstanding and rejection of this most strange of epic poems.

# 4. The Reception of Queen Hynde.

On completing *Queen Hynde*, Hogg certainly was pleased with what, as we have seen, he called 'the best epic poem that ever had been produced in Scotland'; and as time progressed he was surprised at the meagre sales of both *Queen Hynde* and the *Justified Sinner*. Writing to Blackwood (1 September 1825), he sought to shore up the publisher's confidence:

> I am very sorry and not a little surprised that the two works have not had a quick sale but I am conscious that they both deserved to have it and that they will ultimately do us all credit We must try to get Sir W Scott to review it in the Quarterly I mean Queen Hynde In the mean time you must give it a new round of advertisement with a short note from some favourable review If you want a splendid characteristic one I shall

give you one from Dr Burton's new work. "Modern times can furnish no example of native and exalted genius more truly astonishing than the Ettrick Shepherd. His pages are like the constellations of Taurus and Cerberus which seem to have usurped above their proportion of stars. His beauties are so thickly strewed almost on every page it would be difficult to say where such an amazing collection of highly poetical conceptions can be found." *Burton's Bardiad,* p. 118 [28]

This or any better thing that you know of would not cost much additional and would give the works a little stimulus among a certain class ere the reading season again begin. (NLS, MS 4014, fols 289–90)

Two years later in February 1827, Hogg complained to Blackwood that *Queen Hynde* had not been given every opportunity to succeed:

I am grieved as well as dissapointed that Queen Hynde should stick still. I cannot believe that she does not deserve notice and think some expedient should be fallen on to draw notice to her. A round through the papers perhaps with a small note of criticism You rejected Dr Burtons remark on the poem because it is too flattering I have sought out several others but none that pleases me so well and cannot help thinking it would do good alongst with an advertisement. (NLS, MS 4019, fols 185–86)

*Blackwood's* had played a role in the poem's reception, arguably complicating the image problem *Queen Hynde* faced soon after her public debut. Maga's first published reaction characteristically seems designed to present Hogg as the in-house, pet shepherd-poet, the 'old dog' incapable of learning the new trick of Blackwoodian 'tone and delicacy'. Couched in an article entitled 'Scotch Poets, Hogg and Campbell, Hynde and Theodric', the review sets up a comparison that favours Hogg as much for his tolerance of drink (he 'can drink eight-and-twenty tumblers of punch' whereas 'Campbell is hazy upon seven')[29] as for the strength of his poetry. In the *Noctes Ambrosianae* of the same number, while 'Hogg' ostensibly naps the others read out passages and discuss *Queen Hynde*. ODoherty enthuses, '''Tis really a good, bold, manly sort of production. There's a vigour about him, even in the bad passages, that absolutely surprises one. On he goes, splash, splash—By Jupiter, there's a real thundering energy about the affair'.[30] North approves that 'there is a more sustained vigour and force over the whole strain than he ever could hit before; and though, perhaps, there is nothing quite so charming as my Bonny

Kilmeny, that was but a ballad by himself—while here, sir, here we have a real workmanlike poem—a production regularly planned, and powerfully executed'. 'Hogg will go down as one of the true worthies of this age', North declares; though to Tickler's question 'Is the poem equal?', he retorts, 'Of course not. 'Tis Hogg's. There are many things in it as absurd as possible—some real monstrosities of stuff—but, on the whole, this, sir, is James Hogg's masterpiece, and that is saying something, I guess' (pp.126–27). When 'Hogg' awakens, he is portrayed in typical *Noctes* style, as a braggart. Hearing that his companions had been 'delighted with *Queen Hynde*', he boasts, 'Toots, man. Ay, I can make as braw poetry as ony ane o' them a', when I like to tak the fash' (p.128). And, after reciting a passage himself, 'Hogg' raves, 'There's a strain for you, lads. What say ye to that ane, Mr Tickler? Did Byron ever come that length, think ye? Deil a foot of him. Deil a foot of ane o' them. [...] if I did but really pit furth my strength! ye wad see something—' (p.130). But 'Hogg' is not allowed the last word; North chastises him as he would a child:

> Come, James, you must not talk thus where you go out into the town. It may pass here, but the public will laugh at you. You have no occasion for this sort of trumpetting neither, no, nor for any sort of trumpetting. Sir, you have produced an unequal, but, on the whole, a most spirited poem. Sir, there are passages in this volume, that will kindle the hearts of our children's children. James Hogg, I tell you honestly, I consider you to be a genuine poet. (p.130)

The 'Hogg' of the *Noctes*, of course, cannot handle this and begins to sob drunkenly, 'You're ower gude to me, sir, you're clean ower gude to me—I canna bide to expose mysell this way before ye a'—Gie me your haund, sir,—Gie me your haund too, Mr Tickler—Och, sirs! Och, sirs! (*weeps.*)' (p.130). As positive as *Blackwood's* seems to be about *Queen Hynde*, within the January 1825 review and *Noctes* piece may be found the germs of the generally more hostile reviews to appear later.

Neither *Blackwood's* nor Hogg (who shared a financial interest in seeing *Queen Hynde* succeed) foresaw the negative critical reaction to the poem that was to follow. Blackwood, in fact, seems to have judged the January strategy a success. On 22 January 1825, he wrote to Hogg,

> You will be I hope amused with the way Queen Hynde is served up after supper at the Noctes. This will produce a bet-

ter effect than regular review as it is a book published by me
You will I hope forgive the quiz upon yourself & Campbell
You are dragged in merely to heighten the effect of the hits
upon Theodric. You may be sure I would much rather on
every account have seen no notice of the Queen in this kind
of way But you know one is obliged to give way to such
wicked wit as Maginn who is not easy to deal with when he
has a favourite Joke in hand That you may not be laying this
wickedness at the door of any of our friends here I send you
his MS (NLS, MS 30308, pp.43–44)

Hogg wrote to Blackwood on 29 January that he had 'looked
over' the magazine's handling of the poem and was 'not only not
angry but highly satisfied and pleased':

I had forgot to mention to you that I was afraid terrified for
high praise in Maga because our connection considered it
would have been taken for *puffing* a thing of all things that I
detest and one that I think has ought but a good effect a bitter
good humoured thing like this was just what I wanted and I
wish from my heart it had been worse provided my compan-
ion had got tit-for-tat which I think *he* at least justly deserves.
You know very well that I never knew one M.S. from another
all my life not even my own from another man's so you were
quite safe in sending it. I think both articles are Wilsons as
indeed I do every clever and every bitter thing in all the Magas
of the kingdom. I have a strange indefinable sensation with
regard to him, made up of a mixture of terror admiration and
jealousy just such a sentiment as one deil might be supposed
to have of another (NLS, MS 4014, fols 287–88)

Hogg declines here to implicate *Blackwood's*; in his *Memoir of the Au-
thor's Life* ( p.41) he blames the poem's lack of sales on early reviews
in general and on one in particular: 'That malicious *deevil*, Jerdan,
first took it up and damned it with faint praise. The rest of the re-
viewers followed in his wake, so that, in short, the work sold heav-
ily and proved rather a failure'.[31] Of course, Hogg likely angered
his critical audience with his preemptive characterisation of review-
ers as 'Bald, brangling, brutal, insincere' ( p.176) within the very
poem submitted for their consideration. The *Westminster Review* noted
the passage, and its reviewer, after blasting the poem, quips, 'It is
very natural, that such a writer as Mr. Hogg should fear and hate
reviewers, and their readers'.[32] The *News of Literature and Fashion*
observes Hogg's apparent attack on critics and 'against those who

should presume to suspect any indelicacy in his work' and pronounces this 'a protest not altogether needless'.[33]

The preoccupations of contemporary reviewers have influenced readings of *Queen Hynde*, in 1825 and more recently. Most of these are familiar; a few are quite specific to the poem. As is the case with other Hogg works, many (if not most) reviews focus on Hogg's reputation as a man rather than as a poet; and certainly *Blackwood's* influence contributed to this trend. In the case of *Queen Hynde*, the *Literary Gazette's* early review (December 1824) set the tone, arguing that the 'many undoubted proofs of real genius' in *Queen Hynde* are inexorably linked to the fact that the poem is, first and last, 'the production of one who was bred a shepherd'.[34] Writing three years later in 1828, the *Athenaeum* defends Hogg by offering a lengthy account of his life.[35] In the 'heaven-taught shepherd' approach common to those writing about Hogg, the *Philomathic Journal and Literary Review* praises *Queen Hynde* but actually says little about it, instead giving a detailed, and romanticised, description of his life as the rustic mountain bard.[36] Ostensibly friendly critics intent on exonerating him were, perhaps through ignorance, as dangerous to his reputation as his worst enemies. The *Philomathic Journal*'s answer to a caustic article in the *Westminster Review*, for example, calls *Queen Hynde* 'wildly-beautiful and very original', 'not a faultless production,–but the production of a man of genius, and worthy of him and it' (pp.161, 205). The writer chastises the *Westminster Review*, but in so doing compounds the image problem that Hogg faced:

> The Westminster Review, indeed, has inserted a trumpery and unfeeling article respecting it, which, for its want of candour, and utter insensibility to the pure poetic merits of the piece, ought to put that periodical at once out of circulation, as a pseudo-critical work from which it is vain to expect either truth or taste. (p.161)

The reviewer, however, goes on to make an uninformed–and unfortunate–play on the name 'hogg':

> It is in truth a *hoggish* article, but has the misfortune of not grunting so musically as the famous porker against whom it is ignorantly obstreperous, and who "*grunts* you as sweet as any'– we would say–"nightingale," but that himself forbids it. He will be nothing but a lark–"a lark, lost in the heavens' blue." [...] And a lark he is too, for all his name, which, by some sly caprice of chance, was bestowed upon him as the opposite of his nature; perhaps by contrast, to heighten the charm of his

genial sweetness, or to surprise us into admiration by the prompt appearance of his native bearing, so different from the character of his announcement. We know he is a lark, but fortune called him Hogg in jest. Well, "A rose / By any other name would smell as sweet." But let us call the Westminster reviewer what we may, his article will remain a *swinish* one–a mere grunt.  (p.161)

Hogg's identity as shepherd-poet intrigued critics and sometimes provided them with a means of condescending to and writing off elements of his work that they did not understand. It also left him vulnerable to another kind of attack from critics, who warn, 'Don't quit your day job'. The *Monthly Review* provides a good example:

> Critical encouragement bestowed on such poems as 'Queen Hynde' would bring the literary taste of the country into just suspicion; and however deserving Mr. Hogg may be of the public patronage, it highly imports the interest of our literature, that any thing which is due to his misfortunes should not be confounded with that which is due to his productions. A man naturally well-gifted, who struggles in obscurity and indigence with the hardships of his lot, is justly an object of sympathy to all feeling and considerate minds:–but it is a question whether we really aid him by encouraging him in fruitless endeavors to attain poetic excellence, and thus diverting him from the more profitable and equally laudable avocations, to which he was originally destined. On the contrary, we decidedly think that the sooner a man thus situated is taught to descend from the airy elevations of poetry, and to renounce its idle hopes and deluding visions, (one of the worst effects of which is, that they unnerve him for a vigorous conflict with the difficulties of life,) the nearer will he approach to that sober and practicable happiness, which is always within the reach of those who do not suffer themselves to be cheated by the precarious and fitful flatteries of public favor.[37]

Another frequent target of commentary is Hogg's 'egotism', a judgment exacerbated by the *Noctes* portrayal of the Ettrick Shepherd. In its review of *Queen Hynde*, the *Monthly Critical Gazette* echoes the sentiment of many of Hogg's critics when it complains, 'He is babbling eternally, either of sorcery and diabolism, or–of himself. The present work contains as much of these primary elements of his writing, as any of its predecessors'.[38]

The poem itself suffered a different sort of critical blow. From a close study of *Queen Hynde*'s reception emerges a sense of the poem as puzzling, inexplicable, undecidable. The *Literary Gazette*'s early response epitomises the bewilderment:

> Is Queen Hynde the effusion of an unstudied shepherd, a natu-
> ral bard? there is a great deal of genius to admire in it. Is
> Queen Hynde the composition of a practised writer, one to be
> tried by the rules of all true poetry? there is as much to cen-
> sure as to praise. Though the story is interesting, it is made
> tiresomely long; and such is the manner of the author, that, at
> the end of it, it defies our penetration to tell whether he means
> to be serious or burlesque. (p.817)

And further,

> We have said that we could not tell whether the author in-
> tended to be grotesque or grave; and after perusing the sub-
> joined quotations, our readers, we dare presume, will be in
> our case. (p.818)

The *Monthly Critical Gazette* declines to explain the plot, which it describes as 'quite out of our reach', and claims that 'of the poetry of Queen Hynde, it is difficult to speak' (p.343). The *Westminster Review* echoes that sentiment regarding the story: 'from what we have been able to discover, it consists of the unintelligible adventures of sundry persons, who aspire to the hand of Queen Hynde, who reigned over Scotland, it seems, somewhere about 1,300 years ago' (p. 531). Even in *Blackwood's* sympathetic send-up, *Queen Hynde* proves baffling:

> we have read it over six times backward and forward, up and
> down, round and round—we have held the book in every pos-
> sible posture that can be conceived, sideways, angularly, topsy-
> turvy, upsides down, and downsides up; and yet, for the life
> of us, we have not been able to discover what it is about. A
> puzzling sense of unintelligibility came over us, yet was our
> pleasure not in the slightest degree diminished. We have at all
> times risen from the Shepherd and his Hynde delighted and
> instructed, without knowing why or wherefore. (p.111)

Expressions of confusion thus form a clear pattern in the recep-
tion of *Queen Hynde*, revealing something that twentieth-century read-
ers have lately recognised as important to understanding Hogg. Read-
ers' expectations figure prominently in their impressions of the poem;
those accustomed to Hogg's experimental approaches are less con-

fused when their expectations are not comfortably met. This response may be compared with the disparity between expectation and experience as expressed by the *Monthly Review*:

> Before we consent to a journey through such a poem, may we not reasonably bargain, even in the absence of sense and matter, for a little of that melodious and flowing versification, the smooth stream of which carries us gently along, and lulls and stills us with its murmurs;—or, if the numbers be broken and abrupt, for a higher compensation in those bold and towering conceptions, which, descending from the high heaven of invention, cast away, as incumbrances and restraints, the rules of rhythm and harmony;—or, if these be denied us, at any rate, for the humbler merit of interesting and awakening incidents? If 'Queen Hynde,' therefore, deludes all and each of these hopes;—if it be lamentably deficient in every requisite to render a book readable;—if its language be trivial and vulgar, its tale heavy, flat, and "signifying nothing," its versification inelegant and careless;—if, in short, it contains nothing to recompense us for the trouble of reading it;—surely Mr. Hogg, in sending forth so crude and negligent a performance, has shewn an inadequate return for the patronage which a benevolent public, never deaf to the appeals of obscure and indigent merit, has on other occasions awarded him. ( p.369)

Even in the most positive responses, the critics' view that the poem does not deliver the promised goods is frequently supported by evidence that it is 'uneven' or 'unequal'. The *Athenaeum* reviewer praises *Queen Hynde* for the 'many sparkling gems of poetry unequally spangled over' the last four books (p.146), and blames its shortcomings on haste. A general discussion in *Nepenthes* calls *Queen Hynde* 'a great work [...] which does honour to Hogg', but finds that 'it has the same fault as the Queen's Wake, it is very unequal': 'for with all its faults, it is a noble production, and contains passages eminently beautiful'.[39] Among the passages often cited favourably is what the *Monthly Critical Gazette* ( p.343) calls the 'rich and spirited' introduction, which establishes an epic subject and tone—an expectation of 'epicness'—which is then shattered when wicked Wene takes the stage.

The poem refuses to rest, and uneasiness caused by Hogg's shifts and contradictions reverberates throughout the reviews. The *Monthly Critical Gazette* deplores the poem's 'unseasonable mixture of the serious and the burlesque' ( p.343). The *Monthly Review* finds ridiculous Queen Hynde's sudden awakening from a prophetic dream in which she 'throws herself down a precipice' to escape the Black Bull of Norroway only to find that 'her leap was merely from a downy couch'; and the reviewer mockingly quotes the passage in which Hogg denigrates the Maid of Dunedin's sailing abilities 'as it may be edifying to learn how the sea-sickness, though a most unpoetical sensation, can be made a pleasing topic in a poem' ( pp.370, 371). In its review of new publications *La Belle Assemblee* comments:

> There is interest in the story of this virgin queen of Caledon, and there are occasional beauties in the diction; but the poem is sadly disfigured by quaintness and vulgarism, by a mixture of the pathetic and ludicrous, the sublime and the ridiculous.[40]

Continuing, the reviewer laments, 'It is a pity that, with the fine and vigorous genius which Mr. Hogg possesses—the sweetly poetical conceptions to which he at times gives birth—he should be so utterly void of taste and judgment' ( p.82). The *Lady's Magazine* remarks that Hogg is 'unquestionably a man of considerable talent; but, when he displays vigor, it is destitute of elegance'. Citing as its sole example the 'Hymn to Odin', the reviewer complains that Hogg's 'attempts to reach sublimity have sometimes a ludicrous air'.[41] The 'hymn' is also targeted by The *Westminster Review*, which offers the most overwhelmingly hostile review of *Queen Hynde*:

> THIS POEM, as it is called in the title-page, seems to have been inspired by insolence and whisky-punch: and is not so much a genuine effusion of raving dulness, like most of the former works of the author, as an experiment intended to ascertain how far the English public will allow itself to be insulted, and as an attempt to introduce into our language certain graces of diction and peculiarities of pronunciation, which have hitherto been confined to the polite gentlemen, who digest their lucubrations in the obscure pot-houses of the modern Athens. (p.531)

The reviewer systematically, and sarcastically, gives extracts as evidence of Hogg's failed 'experiment', blasting his delineation of character, his description, his song-writing, and his poetic craftsmanship. Targeted here is Hogg's rhyming[42] of words that 'no English mouth could transform [...] into rhymes: perhaps they may sound better in their native Doric' (p.535). The *Literary Gazette* reviewer painstakingly cites extracts, calling the poem a 'curious and original production—the work of unquestionable talent, but miserably deformed by want of taste and judgment' (p. 817); even the few passages that earn approval are undercut by footnotes. Hogg's seemingly contradictory presentation of women in *Queen Hynde* draws tremendous fire, with many critics citing it as the prime example of Hogg's inconsistency and, therefore, his poetic failure. Donald Gorm's murder of the priest of Odin provokes, for example, the *Literary Gazette* to remark, 'even massacre is not without its joke' (p.818).

A major objection raised in many reviews is Hogg's irreverence. According to the *Literary Gazette*, Hogg errs by his 'profane introduction of the most sacred things, which can offend even minds not over scrupulous on such points'; and the reviewer warns, 'such language we will plainly tell the author is most unfit to be used in such a place. It is a stain not to be effaced from his poem'. Hogg's errors, according to this reviewer, 'proceed from want of just perceptions and cultivation of mind, and not from a desire to outrage decorum by his familiar coarseness' (p.818). Hogg's portrayal of Columba's vision and the destruction of Beregon, then, violates sacred taboos. To the *Monthly Critical Gazette* reviewer, Hogg's use of the 'same levity in speaking and treating of subjects of the most awful nature [...] has the appearance of daring impiety':

> We are convinced that to a well regulated mind, many passages in Queen Hynde would be considered more reprehensible than any thing to be found in [Percy Shelley's] Queen Mab, and indeed, to deny a Deity altogether, seems scarcely so blasphemous, as to admit his existence, and lose sight of the reverence due to him. (p.343)

While the *Belfast Magazine* (April 1825) praises *Queen Hynde*'s poetic quality, the review expresses surprise that St Columba and his company 'are such tame and common-place beings', exciting 'none of the interest or enthusiasm which ought to be inspired, by the primitive Apostles and Professors of Christianity'; it complains that 'nothing is made of their purity and simplicity, as contrasted with the vices of later ages: nay they are sometimes introduced rather as objects of raillery'. In general, Hogg is accused of 'a want of proper sympathy for moral and religious worth':

> Mr. Hogg seldom throws fine moral colouring over his paintings; and in this poem interests us as much in the wildest superstitions of Paganism, as in the purer principles of Christianity, by which they were at that time gradually subverted. Occasionally, too, we must blame him for stepping out of his way to give unfavourable views of some religious principles of which he does not appear to have formed correct notions.[43]

A consideration of Hogg's alleged inconsistency and 'indelicacy' cannot be separated from the issue of his penchant for genre-bending. Here Hogg may have played into his critics' hands, setting particular (if narrow) expectations by calling the poem his 'Epic Song'. According to M. H. Abrams's definition of 'epic', *Queen Hynde* meets some but not all of the generic criteria (and, therefore, readers' expectations) associated with this form. Like the traditional epic, *Queen Hynde* is 'a long narrative poem on a serious subject', and it is 'centered on a heroic or quasi-divine figure on whose actions depends the fate of a tribe, a nation, or (in the instance of John Milton's *Paradise Lost*) the human race'.[44] But whereas Hogg sometimes adopts the 'formal and elevated' epic style, at other times he changes the language and tone radically, approximating instead to the 'mock epic' or 'mock heroic' style of Pope's *The Rape of the Lock* or Byron's *Don Juan*.

Seemingly Hogg is permitted to present himself as 'king o' the mountain and fairy school', but epic poetry is deemed out of his range. A review in *Literary Cynosure* makes this point quite clear:

> In the delightful illusions of Elfin-land, and in the picturing of the poetical superstitions of our forefathers, he stands, perhaps, unrivalled; but of those dark and stormy passions which agitate and agonise the human heart, he seems to have formed a very inadequate idea. An Epic poem was, therefore, to him a bold and rather an unhappy attempt; as so much of its interest must necessarily depend upon a thorough knowledge of mankind. The present work, although it abounds with striking and beautiful passages, is upon the whole deficient in that deep and thrilling interest which we look for in an Epic. The situations, though admirably conceived, are described with such an air of levity as in a great measure to destroy their effects; but he almost redeems this great deficiency by his beautiful and highly poetical descriptions of the face of nature. In this department he proves himself a master; and it is a pity he should have wandered into any other region with which he was not equally well acquainted.[45]

From this perspective, if the Shepherd is going to misbehave, he had best remain in the mountains where he belongs.

In an apparent allusion to Macpherson's epic Ossian poems, the *News of Literature and Fashion* complains that 'The Shepherd of Ettrich [sic] does not appear to agree with the general opinion, that it is too late in the day for ballads, four-hundred pages long, about Scotland, divided into six books' and that 'seriously speaking, it is hard work to get through *Queen Hynde*' (p.15).

More favourable responses come when the moniker of 'epic' is not invoked and when the multiple voices of the poem are appreciated rather than despised. Picking up on the poem's comic mode, the *Belfast Magazine* (April 1825) enthuses,

> Mr. Hogg shows great power of comic painting; reminding us occasionally, even of Ariosto, in a happy mixture of delicate satire, with good humoured raillery, and playfulness; especially towards the ladies—to whom the poem is addressed. (p.239)

In this estimation, Hogg is 'peculiarly the fairy poet', yet this time he 'has succeeded eminently in some of his human characters', including Queen Hynde, Wene, and M,Houston; the review invokes a comparison with Shakespeare's *A Midsummer Night's Dream*. It argues that 'the genuine lover of Poetry will find in many parts of this poem a rich intellectual repast' and that the dominant characteristic of his poetry is 'originality'. Approving of Hogg's crossing of boundaries between dream and reality, the review observes that Hynde's idyllic dream is portrayed as though it were an actual occurrence, whereas the waking moment that follows is full of 'fearful visions'. The 'comic humour [...] compensates in some degree for the improbability' of the trick that Wene plays on Eric and other far-fetched elements of the plot. The poem's 'defects' are 'connected with its length' (an understandable point if, as in this case, *Queen Hynde* is *not* considered an epic): 'the materials are too much spread out: in consequence of which, the blooming spots and picturesque objects are often separated by tame, if not bleak scenery'; and 'little is made of some of the most interesting objects and characters' (pp.239–42).

Hogg not only offers a new definition of epic, but he audaciously grafts onto it elements of the metrical romance, yet another genre. The romance, according to an established understanding articulated by Abrams, represents 'not a heroic age of tribal wars, but a courtly and chivalric age, often one of highly developed manners and civility'.

> Its standard plot is that of a quest undertaken by a single knight in order to gain a lady's favor; frequently its central interest is *courtly love*, together with tournaments fought and dragons and monsters slain for the damsel's sake; it stresses the chivalric ideals of courage, loyalty, honor, mercifulness to an opponent,

and exquisite and elaborate manners; and it delights in won-
ders and marvels. Supernatural events in the epic had their
causes in the will and actions of the gods; romance shifts the
supernatural to this world, and makes much of the mysteri-
ous effect of magic, spells, and enchantments.[46]

The romance genre is characterised, too, by the 'comic' ending,
in a marriage or marriages. Sense may be made of one critic's com-
plaint that Eric is too chivalric for an epic antagonist if *Queen Hynde* is
thought of as a complex combination of genres, weaving together
strands of Ossianic heroics and Arthurian romance, with Hogg the
performing bard offering a send-up of both. The darker side of *Queen
Hynde*'s narrative may be illuminated by its suggestion of the Shake-
spearean problem plays: 'bitter comedies' that 'explore dark and
ignoble aspects of human nature', and in which 'the resolution of the
plot seems to many readers to be problematic, in that it does not
settle or solve [...] the moral problems raised in the play'.[47] *The Three
Perils of Man*, which Hogg refers to as his 'border romance', also
involves a chivalric contest for a royal lady's hand in marriage. For
Hogg, then, what qualifies *Queen Hynde* as an epic is its preoccupa-
tion with the origins of Scotland; and about this he is most serious.

By the early years of the twentieth century, interest in *Queen Hynde*
had reached a low ebb. Edith Batho describes the poem as 'a weak
following of Scott'; and her remarks sum up the general view of
Hogg's epic in the 1920s:

> *Queen Hynde* is half as long again as *The Queen's Wake* and not
> half so amusing. The Shepherd tried to be humorous and tried
> to throw in moral reflections, and the humour is rather more
> tedious than the reflections.[48]

Recent years, however, have seen a growing willingness to take
*Queen Hynde* seriously; and particularly important contributions to
this process have been made by Douglas Gifford and Elaine Petrie.[49]
Because the present edition has returned to the manuscript, many
passages of which have never before been seen in print, it presents
a genuinely new opportunity to carry forward the process of reas-
sessing *Queen Hynde*. The new passages from the manuscript, we
believe, deliver even more of the poem's inherent energy: and the
very qualities that so disturbed early readers interest us today. As
with *The Three Perils of Woman*, *Queen Hynde* has had to wait for a long
time to find its audience; but, as with *The Three Perils of Woman*, its
time may now have come.

# 5. The Present Edition.

Apart from one small section that has not been preserved, Hogg's manuscript of *Queen Hynde* survives in the Huntington Library in San Marino, California. This document shows every sign of having been carefully prepared for the printer; and in this respect, the manuscript of *Queen Hynde* is similar to the manuscript of 'Ringan and May', a much shorter poem by Hogg. Peter Garside has offered an interesting speculation about the manuscript of 'Ringan and May'; and he introduces his suggestion by discussing some of the features of Scott's manuscripts.

> In his own manuscripts Scott offered guiding signs—some punctuation at crucial points, clearly spelt proper names on first appearance—but many of the more workaday aspects of transposing the text into print were left to intermediaries (who, of course, worked for a firm that Scott had the means of controlling). In contrast Hogg's manuscript has all the marks of a document which has been prepared for direct transference into print—indeed, considering indignities already suffered at the hands of the Edinburgh trade, it is tempting to imagine a deliberate ploy on the author's part to lure the compositor and/or copy editor into non-intervention by offering the most straightforward of jobs.[50]

If there was a ploy of this kind in the case of *Queen Hynde*, it was not destined to be successful: further 'indignities' lay in store.

In the manuscript of *Queen Hynde*, various alterations have been made to the text in a hand that is not Hogg's. These alterations are followed in the first edition; and it would therefore appear that they represent a copy-editing process carried out before the manuscript went to the compositor for typesetting. In general, it is not difficult to draw conclusions about the reasons why these changes were made: the motive normally seems to be a wish to make a correction when it is felt that Hogg has made an error of some kind—in taste, perhaps, or in grammar. For example, in Book Second Columba attempts to persuade King Eric to give up his intention to marry Queen Hynde, because her troth may already be pledged to a Scottish chief. In Hogg's original text, the invading king dismisses Columba's argument out of hand:

> "I'll fight him" was the short reply;
> "Let arms decide for he and I." (p.51)

The copy-editor, however, spots a grammatical error lurking in 'for he and I'; and these lines are altered, in a hand that is not Hogg's, to:

> "Let arms decide the right," said he;
> ["]The sword be judge 'twixt him and me."[51]

This change duly makes its way into the first edition. It certainly tidies up the Viking king's grammar; but perhaps it detracts somewhat from his impressively uncomplicated energy, as expressed in Hogg's original version.

A striking feature of the manuscript of *Queen Hynde* is that it contains several passages, some of them quite lengthy, through which double vertical lines have been drawn; and these passages are all omitted in the first edition. Questions arise: were these cuts perhaps made by Hogg himself before the manuscript left his hands; or were they made as part of the copy-editing process? All of the deleted passages might well have been felt to be liable to cause offence in the increasingly prim climate of public taste in the 1820s; and this suggests that the cuts were probably the work of the copy-editor. One such passage appears towards the end of Book First in Hogg's manuscript. Wicked Wene is having fun with some sleeping sailors on board ship; and the deleted passage includes these lines:

> While all was still around the queen,
> With slender reed and needle keen
> Wene so contrived to wound and wreak
> The slumbering sailors on the deck,
> That each on others threw the scath
> And all grew tumult, pride, and wrath.
> And just as rage began to cease,
> And dwindle into sullen peace,
> At one a steady aim she took,
> On place where pain he ill could brook,
> Which roused him sorely to disgrace
> With blows his weetless comerade's face.
> O how the elf enjoyed the strife,
> It was to her the balm of life;
> But when her laugh could not be drowned,
> She said 'twas thro' her sleep, and moaned!  (p.30)

No doubt *Queen Hynde* becomes more prim and respectable because of the absence of such passages in the first edition; but the poem also becomes tamer and less alive as a result of their removal. At all events, these passages were deleted, either by Hogg himself or (more probably) by another. They are restored in the present edition; but they are enclosed in angle brackets < thus >, in order to indicate the fact of their deletion in Hogg's manuscript.

The text of *Queen Hynde* underwent various other changes as it moved from the manuscript to the first edition: for example, Hogg's spelling and punctuation were tidied up. Further details of the differences between Hogg's manuscript and the first edition of *Queen Hynde* are given in the Note on the Text in the present edition; but the situation may be summarised here. It appears, then, that Hogg prepared his manuscript with some care; and he sent it off as a completed document, ready for publication. Unfortunately, however, respectable people regarded him with some suspicion: it was accepted that the Shepherd was a man of powerful natural talent; but he was not felt to be fully house-trained, as it were. There was therefore a perceived need to polish and tone down his text; and this was duly done as *Queen Hynde* was carefully prepared for her appearance in public.

After the publication of the first edition in December 1824, Hogg's epic was not reprinted during its author's lifetime; and the various nineteenth-century posthumous printings all follow the text of the first edition. There are thus two versions of *Queen Hynde*: the manuscript version and the printed version; and these two versions differ quite substantially.

Faced with this situation, what should a modern editor of *Queen Hynde* do? The great American editor Fredson Bowers and his followers argued that editors should almost always base their texts on an author's fair-copy manuscript, when such a document survives. This was for long the accepted view; and it was a view based on the Romantic assumption that the inspired utterance of the Poet-as-Prophet was progressively corrupted as it passed through the hands of rude mechanicals—publishers, copy-editors, printers, and the like. However, these old editorial certainties of the Bowers school have been undermined by Jerome McGann's *A Critique of Modern Textual Criticism* (1983). In this seminal book McGann argued that, as soon as an author's work begins its passage to publication,

> it undergoes a series of interventions which some textual critics see as a process of contamination, but which may equally well be seen as a process of training the poem for its appearances in the world.[52]

In this way, McGann opens up the possibility that a literary work is a product of an act of collaboration between the author and publishing institutions. It is thus a social document, the articulation of which is not fully completed until it has passed through all the processes involved in preparing a text for its public appearance. McGann's line of argument, then, would tend to suggest that the manuscript of *Queen Hynde* represents a mere stage in the production of the poem; while the first edition represents the finished article. This suggests that there is a case for a new edition of Hogg's poem to follow the first edition rather than the manuscript.

McGann's line of argument works well for authors like Lord Byron and Sir Walter Scott. Gentlemanly writers like the lord and the baronet could produce their manuscripts with freedom and élan, secure in the knowledge that bothersome details like spelling and punctuation would be tidied up by the competent professional activity of printers and publishers. Furthermore, writers like Byron and Scott were powerful enough to be able to feel confident that their professional assistants would not overstep the mark, and meddle destructively with the text by imposing alterations that involved matters of real substance.

Hogg, however, was in a much less powerful situation than Sir Walter and Lord Byron. The Ettrick Shepherd was perceived as being talented and inspired; but he was also perceived as being naive, incompetent, and boorishly unaware of the limits imposed by the delicacy of feeling of his well-bred female readers. What, after all, could a mere shepherd know of the refined feelings of a lady? So when *his* texts were knocked into shape for publication, something more radical than a tidying-up of punctuation and spelling was felt to be required. In short, wicked Wene had to be tamed: she could not possibly be allowed to poke a sailor 'on place where pain he ill could brook'. So out that passage went, along with many others. And this seems a pity.

A possible way forward for the editor of *Queen Hynde* is offered by recent discussions of the notion that literary texts can exist in different versions, each of which can have its own coherence and integrity. Several scholars, including Jerome McGann, have played a part in developing a new theory of versions, a new approach that involves a questioning of the traditional notion that, for every literary work, there is, as Jack Stillinger puts it, 'some *single* version that is best or most authoritative'. Stillinger continues:

> This is a belief that nowadays is being challenged, and gradually replaced, by a pluralistic concept first proposed by James Thorpe in the 1960s and then developed and championed more recently in Germany by Hans Zeller, in the United States

by Jerome McGann, Donald Reiman, Peter Shillingsburg, and me (among others), and in Britain by James McLaverty and the next serious editor of Coleridge's poems, J. C. C. Mays. This newest idea is that every individual version of a work is a distinct text in its own right, with unique aesthetic character and unique authorial intention.[53]

In a detailed and convincing argument, Stillinger suggests that, because Coleridge was an energetic reviser of his poems, 'we have eighteen different Coleridge-authored versions of *The Ancient Mariner*'. In this situation, Stillinger suggests,

> it simply does not make good sense to argue that the latest (only) or the earliest (only) or any other single version (only) is the "real" *Ancient Mariner*, or the most authoritative, or the one (above all others) that best embodies Coleridge's intentions in the work. If *The Ancient Mariner* is one poem, then in theory at least it *has* to be all its versions taken together. On the other hand, or simultaneously, *The Ancient Mariner* might theoretically be recognized as the title of eighteen different poems.[54]

Increasing sensitivity to the integrity of different versions of a text has been manifesting itself in various ways in recent years. One example has been the decision of the editors of the Oxford Shakespeare (1988) to print two separate versions of *King Lear*. The Oxford editors discuss this decision as follows:

> *King Lear* first appeared in print in a quarto of 1608. A substantially different text appeared in the 1623 Folio. Until now, editors, assuming that each of these early texts imperfectly represented a single play, have conflated them. But research conducted mainly during the 1970s and 1980s confirms an earlier view that the 1608 quarto represents the play as Shakespeare originally wrote it, and the 1623 Folio as he substantially revised it. [...] Conflation, as Harley Granville-Barker wrote, 'may make for redundancy or confusion', so we print an edited version of each text. The first [...] represents the play as Shakespeare first conceived it, probably before it was performed. [55]

The Oxford editors go on to suggest that the second version of *Lear* is a 'revision made probably two or three years after the first version had been written and performed'. The editors also take the view that the second version is 'a more obviously theatrical text' than the first, being a version that contains changes which 'stream-line the play's action'.[56]

Like *Lear*, *Queen Hynde* exists in two versions. One of these is the original version, the poem as Hogg first conceived it, the version prepared by its author for the printer. This is the poem as it stood when Hogg offered it to the publishing institutions of his own day and generation, no doubt hoping against hope that it would find its way into print without significant alteration. The later version of *Queen Hynde*, on the other hand, represents what the publishing institutions in fact offered to the public in December 1824, after they had made some very significant alterations to Hogg's epic while preparing it for its appearance in the market-place.

In the light of current theories about the integrity of different versions of literary works, a modern editor of *Queen Hynde* might reasonably choose to edit either version of the poem; or indeed both, separately. For the present volume, however, the most useful course seemed to be to edit the original version. The reasons for this decision are uncomplicated. The original version has never been published; but it appears on examination to be a poem of great sophistication, complexity, and energy. The revised version, however, is already accessible in libraries; and it is in effect a lobotomised version. In these circumstances, an edition of the original version of the poem seems to be what is most urgently required.

An edition of the later version of *Queen Hynde* also seems desirable, but less urgently so. The later version represents what the publishing institutions of the time made of Hogg's poem; and as such it is a version with its own kind of interest and coherence. The later version is of interest not only for students of publishing history, but also for students of the developing social conventions of the English-speaking world of the 1820s. In addition, it has the advantage of presenting *Queen Hynde* in the form in which it was read by Hogg's contemporaries. From a literary point of view, however, the later version of Hogg's epic seems distinctly tame when compared with Hogg's original. The present edition, therefore, is edited from the author's manuscript; and as a result it might fairly be described as the first printing of the unbowdlerised text of *Queen Hynde*.

# Notes

1. Edith C. Batho, *The Ettrick Shepherd* (Cambridge: Cambridge University Press, 1927) is still a useful biography of Hogg, although its literary judgments now look dated.

2. For details, see the 'Bibliography' in Batho, pp.183–221.

3. See Gillian H. Hughes, *Hogg's Verse and Drama: A Chronological Listing* (Stirling: James Hogg Society, 1990) for further details.

4. Hogg, *Memoir of the Author's Life* and *Familiar Anecdotes of Sir Walter Scott*, ed. by Douglas S. Mack (Edinburgh: Scottish Academic Press, 1972), pp. 40–41. Future page references to *Memoir of the Author's Life* are to this edition, and are given in the text.

5. The manuscript of *Queen Hynde* (Huntington Library Call No. HM 12412) falls into various sections: one section is made up of paper with leaves of one size; this is followed by another section made up of leaves of another size; and so on. The opening section includes the first two Books of the poem, together with the first 1071 lines of Book Third; and this section breaks off with a note in Hogg's hand reading 'The vol. 3$^d$ for continuation'. Some of the leaves in this first section carry a watermark date, 1813. Watermark dates also appear in some of the leaves of the later sections; but here the dates are 1820 and 1821. The various sections of the manuscript of *Queen Hynde* consist of sheets of hand-made paper; and the moulds on which such paper was made often carried a watermark date indicating the year in which the mould had been manufactured. Moulds wore out fairly quickly, and paper did not linger in warehouses for very long periods before being used. Typically, then, paper tended to be used approximately two or three years after the mould on which it was made was manufactured. Hogg's *Memoir of the Author's Life* suggests that the first section of *Queen Hynde* was written around the time of the publication of *Dramatic Tales* in 1817; and this seems very much in line with the watermark dates of 1813 to be found in the first section of the manuscript. Likewise, the watermark dates of 1820 and 1821 to be found in the later sections of the manuscript are consistent with Hogg's suggestion in the *Memoir* that the composition of his epic poem was completed in the months leading up to its publication in December 1824. For a discussion of the manufacture of hand-made paper, see Philip Gaskell, *A New Introduction to Bibliography* (Oxford: Clarendon Press, 1972), pp. 57–77.

6. National Library of Scotland (hereafter NLS), MS 2245, fols 84–85.

7. Hogg, *Anecdotes of Sir W. Scott*, ed. by Douglas S. Mack (Edinburgh: Scottish Academic Press, 1983), pp.29–30.

8. Longman Archive: Impression Book 8, fol. 54; and Divide Ledger D2, p. 267.

9. Claire Lamont, 'One Good Reason for Reading Scott: The Highland Works', *The Scott Newsletter*, 23/24 (Winter 1993/Spring 1994), 2–8 (pp. 7–8).

10. James Macpherson, *The Poems of Ossian and Related Works*, ed. by Howard Gaskill with an introduction by Fiona Stafford (Edinburgh: Edinburgh University Press, 1996), pp. ix–x.

11. *The Poems of Ossian*, pp. xiii–xiv.

12. For a discussion of Hogg's interest in Johnson, see Hogg, *A Series of Lay Sermons*, ed. by Gillian Hughes with Douglas S. Mack (Edinburgh: Edinburgh University

Press, 1997), p. xix. Hogg's account of his 1802 journey to the Highlands was published in instalments in the *Scots Magazine*, 64 (1802) and 65 (1803); his account of his 1804 journey was published in *The Scots Magazine*, 70 (1808) and 71 (1809); and *A Tour in the Highlands in 1803* was published posthumously in *Scottish Review*, 12 ( July 1888), 1–66. It was also published soon afterwards in book form (Paisley: Alexander Gardner, 1888).

13. Samuel Johnson and James Boswell, *Journey to the Hebrides: A Journey to the Western Islands of Scotland* and *The Journal of a Tour to the Hebrides with Samuel Johnson*, ed. by Ian McGowan (Edinburgh: Canongate, 1996), pp. 347–48. Further page references to Johnson's *Journey* and Boswell's *Journal* are to this edition, and are given in the text.

14. John Hill Burton, *The History of Scotland*, new edition, 8 vols (Edinburgh: Blackwood, 1897), I, 178–79.

15. In his *Jacobite Relics* (Edinburgh: William Blackwood, 1819 and 1821), a two-volume collection of traditional Jacobite song, Hogg provides copious notes which make it clear that he sometimes worked from Gaelic material in translation. Furthermore, many of Hogg's writings (for example *The Three Perils of Woman*) use Gaelic words and phrases frequently and fairly competently, but with a lack of idiomatic ease.

16. Quoted from *The Poetry of Scotland*, ed. by Roderick Watson (Edinburgh: Edinburgh University Press, 1995), pp. 271, 275.

17. Quoted from *The Poetry of Scotland*, pp. 319–21.

18. Iain Crichton Smith, 'Duncan Ban Macintyre', in *Discovering Scottish Writers*, ed. by Alan Reid and Brian D. Osborne (Hamilton and Edinburgh: Scottish Library Association and Scottish Cultural Press, 1997), p. 60 ( p.60).

19. Scott, *The Lord of the Isles* (Edinburgh: Constable, 1815), pp. 21–22. Future page references to *The Lord of the Isles* are to this edition, and are given in the text.

20. David Stevenson, *The Covenanters: The National Covenant and Scotland* (Edinburgh: Saltire Society, 1988), pp. 76–77.

21. Stevenson, *The Covenanters*, pp. 1, 33.

22. See, for example, Book Sixth at lines 130, 898, 974.

23. Hogg, *The Shepherd's Guide: Being a Practical Treatise on the Diseases of Sheep* (Edinburgh: Constable, 1807), p. 305. For the passage by Johnson to which Hogg refers, see *A Journey to the Western Islands of Scotland*, ed. by McGowan, p. 30.

24. *The Poems and Songs of Robert Burns*, ed. by James Kinsley, 3 vols (Oxford: Clarendon Press, 1968), II, 803.

25. James Hogg, *The Three Perils of Woman*, ed. by D. Groves, A. Hasler, and D. S. Mack (Edinburgh: Edinburgh University Press, 1995), p. 225.

26. The 'Voyage in the Lighthouse Yacht to Nova Zembla, and the Lord knows where' did not appear in print until it was included in Lockhart's *Memoirs of the Life of Sir Walter Scott, Bart.*, 7 vols (Edinburgh, 1837–38), III, 136–277. Scott's reference to 'Beregonium' [sic] appears on p. 258.

27. In '*Queen Hynde* and the Black Bull of Norroway', Elaine E. Petrie argues that Hogg 'loves to create [...] a narrative frame where one character relates the story to another as a fireside entertainment. [...] It is this Hogg, the storyteller with the love of traditional folk narrative, that we need to remember when we turn to *Queen Hynde*': see *Papers Given at the Second James Hogg Society Conference (Edinburgh 1985)*, ed. by Gillian Hughes (Aberdeen: Association for Scottish Literary Stud-

ies, 1988), pp. 128–39 (p.128).

28. Charles Burton, *The Bardiad: A Poem [...] with Copious Critical Notes* (London: Longman, 1823), pp. 118–19. Hogg here quotes extracts from one of Burton's 'critical notes'. The note in question is a discussion of Hogg's poetry in general, with particular emphasis being placed on *The Queen's Wake*. As *The Bardiad* was published before *Queen Hynde* Burton makes no mention of Hogg's epic.

29. 'Scotch Poets, Hogg and Campbell, Hynde and Theodric', *Blackwood's Edinburgh Magazine*, 17 (January 1825), 109–13 (p.110). For this and subsequent quotations from reviews of *Queen Hynde*, page references after the first are given in the text.

30. 'Noctes Ambrosianae. No. 18', *Blackwood's Edinburgh Magazine*, 17 (January 1825), 114–30 (p.123). Further page references to this number of the 'Noctes' are given in the text.

31. William Jerdan (1782–1869), a native of Kelso, was editor of the London-based *Literary Gazette*, which published on 25 December 1824 one of the first reviews of *Queen Hynde*.

32. *Westminster Review*, 3 (April 1825), 531–37 (p. 537).

33. *News of Literature and Fashion*, 1 January 1825, 15–16 (p. 15).

34. *Literary Gazette*, 25 December 1824, 817–19 (p. 819).

35. *Athenaeum*, 26 February 1828, 145–47.

36. *Philomatic Journal and Literary Review*, 3 (April 1825), 161–205.

37. *Monthly Review*, 2nd series no. 106 (April 1825), 368–72 (pp. 368–69).

38. *Monthly Critical Gazette*, 2 (March 1825), 343–47 (p. 343).

39. *Nepenthes; or, Liverpool Weekly Correspondent, and Journal of Fashionable Literature*, 43 (November 1825), 342–43 (p. 343).

40. *La Belle Assemblee*, 1 (February 1825), 81–82.

41. *Lady's Magazine*, n. s. 6 (February 1825), 97.

42. Disapproval of Hogg's rhyme appears in many reviews: thus the *Literary Gazette* (p. 819) lists examples culled from the poem's 'multitude of monstrous rhymes'.

43. *Belfast Magazine*, 1 (April 1825), 230–43 (pp. 241–242).

44. M. H. Abrams, *A Glossary of Literary Terms*, 6th edn (Fort Worth: Harcourt Brace Jovanovich, 1993), p. 53.

45. *Literary Cynosure*, 1 (January 1825) 12–16 (pp. 12–13).

46. Abrams, p. 25.

47. Abrams, p. 172.

48. Batho, *The Ettrick Shepherd*, p. 77. Douglas Mack (he is now embarrassed to remember) took a similar view of *Queen Hynde* in James Hogg, *Selected Poems*, ed. by Douglas S. Mack (Oxford: Clarendon Press, 1970), p. xxix.

49. Douglas Gifford, *James Hogg* (Edinburgh: Ramsay Head, 1976), pp. 219–22; and Elaine E. Petrie, '*Queen Hynde* and the Black Bull of Norroway', in *Papers Given at the Second James Hogg Society Conference (Edinburgh 1985)*, ed. by Gillian Hughes (Aberdeen: Association for Scottish Literary Studies, 1988), pp. 128–43.

50. P. D. Garside, 'Notes on Editing James Hogg's "Ringan and May" ', *The Bibliotheck* 16 (1989), 40–53 (pp. 40–41).

51. Huntington Library Call No. HM 12412, p. [76].

52. Jerome J. McGann, *A Critique of Modern Textual Criticism* (Chicago: University of Chicago Press, 1983), p. 51.

53. Jack Stillinger, *Coleridge and Textual Instability: The Multiple Versions of the Major Poems* (New York: Oxford University Press, 1994), pp. 120–21.

54. Stillinger, p. 121.
55. William Shakespeare, *The Complete Works*, ed. by Stanley Wells and Gary Taylor (Oxford: Clarendon Press, 1988), p. 909.
56. Shakespeare, *Complete Works*, ed. Wells and Taylor, p. 943.

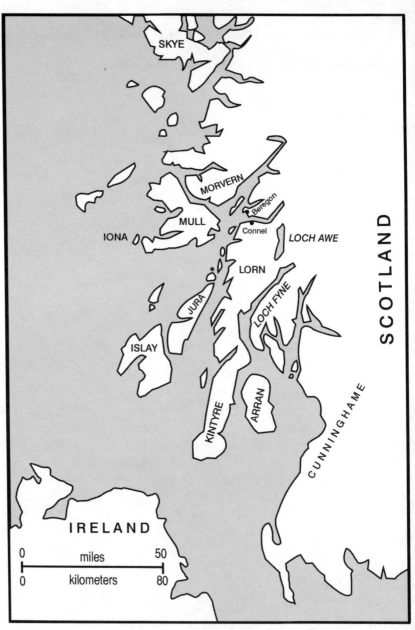

SKYE

MORVERN

Beregon

MULL

Connel

IONA

LOCH AWE

LORN

LOCH FYNE

JURA

ISLAY

ARRAN

KINTYRE

CUNNINGHAME

SCOTLAND

IRELAND

0        miles       50
0     kilometers     80

North-east Ireland and south-west Scotland.

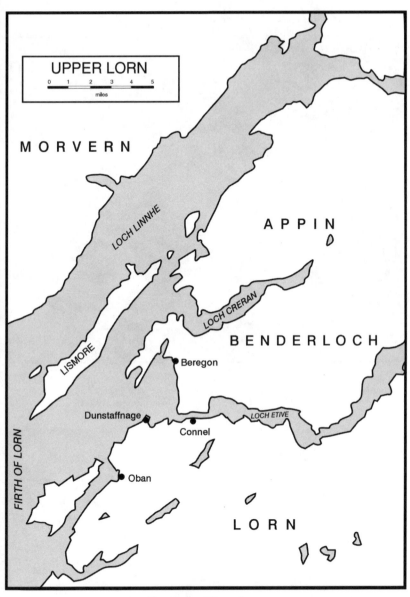

'Beregon' and Upper Lorn.

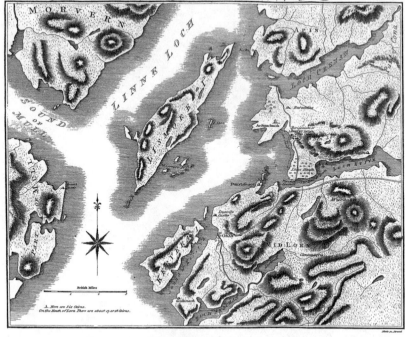

Map of the area around 'Selma' ('Beregon'), from Sir John Sinclair's edition of
*The Poems of Ossian in the Original Gaelic*, 3 vols (London, 1807).

Detail from the above map.

*Dun Mac Uisneachan from the shore S.W. fancifully called Beregonium, castle of Fergus and Selma.*

*Dun Bhaile an Righ or Dun Valanree - extremity of Ledaig.*

Sketches of 'Dun mhic Uisneachan' and 'Dun bhail an righ', from R. Angus Smith, 'Descriptive List of Antiquities near Loch Etive', *Proceedings of the Society of Antiquaries of Scotland*, 9 part 1 (1870–71). These sites are discussed in the Appendix: Beregonium (pp. 238–44).

[The hand-written titlepage of Hogg's manuscript is transcribed below.]

# Queen Hynde

A Poem in Six Books

By The Author of The Queen's Wake &c. &c.

Printed for

Longman Hurst Rees Orme Brown & Green

London

# Dedication

To the <virgin> daughters of Caledonia
This Poem is addressed throughout
And most humbly and respectfully inscribed
By their obliged and devoted serv[t]

## The Author

# Queen Hynde

## Book First

There was a time—but it is gone!
When he that sat on Albyn's throne,
Over his kindred Scots alone
    Upheld a father's sway;
Unmixed and unalloyed they stood          5
With plodding Pict of Cimbrian brood,
Or sullen Saxon's pampered blood,
    Their bane on future day.
Nations arose, and nations fell,
But still his sacred citadel          10
Of Grampian cliff and trackless dell
    The Caledonian held;
Grim as the wolf that guards his young,
Above the dark defile he hung,
With targe and claymore forward flung;     15
The stoutest heart, the proudest tongue,
    Of foeman there was quelled!
The plumed chief, the plaided clan,
Mocked at the might of mortal man,
Even those the world who over-ran     20
    Were from that bourn expelled.

Then stood the Scot unmoved and free,
Walled by his hills and sounding sea;
Child of the ocean and the wood,
The frith, the forest, gave him food;     25
His couch the heath on summer even,
His coverlet the cloud of heaven,
While, from the winter wind and sleet,
The bothy was a shelter meet.
His home was in the desart rude,     30
His range the mountain solitude;
The sward beneath the forest tree
His revel-hall, his sanctuary;

His court of equity and right,
His tabernacle, was the height;                                35
The field of fame his death-bed stern,
His cemetry the lonely cairn.
     Such was the age, and such the day,
When young queen Hynde, with gentle sway,
Ruled o'er a people bold and free                              40
From vale of Clyde to Orcady.
The tale is old, but the event
Confirmed by dreadful monument.
Her sire had eastern vales laid waste,
The Pict subdued the Saxon chased,                             45
And dying old and loved, resigned
The sceptre to his lovely Hynde.
     Each warrior chief of name was there,
Each bard, and gray-haired minister,
When the old king, in accents mild,                            50
Commended to their love his child.
     "My friends your faith has oft been sealed
In counsel tried, and bloody field;
For Scotland's right, by foes o'er-run,
We pledged our lives—we fought and won;                        55
Now every Scot can wander free
From hill to hill, from sea to sea,
Thanks to your worth—the throne is fast;
Now list my suit, it is the last.
     "One child I have, and one alone,                          60
To fill my father's antient throne;
Your virgin sovereign you behold;
I speak not of her beauteous mould,
But if affection do not blind,
I vouch her energy of mind;                                    65
Here pledge your honours, still to be
To her what you have been to me."
     Each warrior vowed upon his brand,
And kneeling kissed the maiden's hand;
Each gray-haired sire, with moistened eye,                     70
Swore by his country's liberty.
     The king then rose upon his bed,
And, leaning forward, bent his head;
His silver locks waved o'er his cheek
Like winter clouds on mountain bleak,                          75

And like that mountain's hoary form,
All blenched and withered by the storm,
Was every feature's grizly cast,
Pale but majestic to the last!
   "Grieve not my gallant friends," he said,      80
"That by a queen the land is swayed;
When woman rules without controul,
Her generous but dependant soul
To worth and wisdom gives command,
And then 'tis man that rules the land.      85
   But when in second place she sits,
Then all her cunning—all her wits
Are on the stretch with knaves to league,
And rule the king by court intrigue.
Trust me 'tis truth to you I tell,      90
I have been tried, and know it well!
A queen by men of wisdom rules,
A king by mistresses and fools.
   Now note my will—My daughter Hynde
Must wed the knight that suits her mind;      95
Her choice no interest let revoke
Be it as free as bird on oak;
Or the gray eagle of the rock;
But suffer not, on any plea,
A lover to her privacy;      100
No breathings of extatic bliss;
No fond caress, or burning kiss,
May be allowed, else all is done,
A coxcomb shall the lady won;
And Albyn's ancient royal blood      105
Run to a weak and spurious brood.
Forbid it God!—In time to be,
Should my unbodied spirit see,
A son of mine to sloth betake,
Or sleep while warriors toil and wake,      110
On such my soul shall never tend,
As guardian angel or as friend!
< I'll leave the nation to its fate,
And every ill subordinate. >
   These woes and failings to prevent,      115
Let young queen Hynde, in royal tent,
Hear chiefs debate on government;

Mark all their feats in bold tourney,
And list their love or warrior lay,
And thus, her keen and piercing sight,                    120
Will hardly fail to judge aright.
    Think of this charge—much it portends.
I go—but not resign my friends;
No home I'll seek within the sky;
My patriot soul shall hover nigh,                         125
To watch your actions, mark your deeds,
In battle-field where glory leads,
And o'er the counsel group, reclined
Upon the eddy of the wind,
I'll list how truth your counsel brooks,                  130
And read your spirits in your looks.
    Woe be to him whom I observe
Daring from loyalty to swerve!
Though neither blood nor bone invest
The living flame within this breast,                      135
That flame shall sear his palsied sight;
With shades of horror strew the night;
Load with disgust the light of day;
His motions cross, his path belay;
Each warden spirit's arm controul,                        140
And whisper vengeance to his soul,
Till down the miscreant shall be driven,
The hate of man, the scorn of heaven!
    Be thou my child upright as fair,
And thou shalt be my special care;                        145
And O should power's temptations try,
Think of thy father's spirit nigh;
Be that thy stay on ruin's brink!—
Nor tongue may frame, nor heart may think,
How distant far such crime will spurn                     150
The kindred minds that round thee burn.
    I may not warn thee face to face,
But still, when danger, or disgrace,
Unseen approaches, I'll be nigh,
Therefore my child on dreams rely.                        155
Then to thy spirit's eye unfurled
I'll hold, in shadowy courses hurled,
The motions of the moving world.
Farewell—be calm—my time is nigh;

Would that the parting thrust were bye!"            160
    He stretched him on his couch resigned;
The ruthless foe of human kind,
Whom he had met mid fire and storm,
And braved in every heideous form,
Now unresisting found his arm,                      165
And stopped the tide that scarce was warm.
    No plaint—no groan hung on his breath,
To gratify the ear of death;
Steady and dauntless was his look,
As one a bitter draught who took,                   170
Or, for the sake of health to be,
Suffered a transient agony;
Yea that pale face when turned to clay,
When lifeless on the couch he lay,
A bold defiance still was blent,                    175
Uncancelled, with each lineament.
    The cross was o'er the body hung,
The royal coronach was sung,
And paid each rite, each honour due,
To sire beloved and sovereign true;                 180
And young queen Hynde holds the command
O'er Caledon's unconquered land.
    High were the hopes her chiefs among,
Their emulation great and strong;
Before their queen, in circle set,                  185
When for deliberate counsel met,
Never was heard such manly sense,
Such high and moving eloquence.
Never did armed list present
Such bold and rapid tournament;                     190
And when the festal days came on,
Such gallant splendor never shone
In royal halls of Caledon.
    Then did the towers with echoes ring,
For every knight his song would sing                195
Whether his voice to music's tone
Had note of harmony or none;
And strange though seems the incident,
Those who sung worst were most intent.
    No smile—no marvel let arise,                   200
That such the strife, when such the prize,

A flower in Albyn never shone,
Like Hynde the queen of Caledon.
    The lord of Moray famed in war,
Proud Gaul of Ross, and lordly Mar,         205
Were first in rank and wide controul,
And others shrank before their scowl.
Young Allan Bane was brave and bold,
And Sutherland of manly mould;
And Donald Gorm, of lion eye,         210
Chief of the kindred tribes of Skye,
Was such a knight in heart and mein
As Skye again hath never seen;
Yet after year and day was past,
It was not trowed from glances cast,         215
Who would be chosen king at last.
    Once on a day—a day it seemed
When more than earthly splendor beamed
On Appin hills, that towered on high,
Like golden columns to the sky,         220
Bathed in the glories of the morn
That west on airy rivers borne,
Streamed over all the woods of Lorn.
    Queen Hynde upon the mountain leant,
She wist not how or why she went;         225
But there she sat by old grey stone,
Upon the flowery sward alone;
The day-breeze played in eddies weak,
And waved the rock-rose to her cheek;
The little ewe-flower starred the lea,         230
The hare-bell nodded at her knee,
While all the sward in summer prime
Was woven with the moreland thyme.
    Blithe was her bosom's guileless core,
Unthoughtful all of woes before!         235
With nature's beauties glowed her mind,
She breathed a prayer for all mankind,
Pondering of nought but onward bliss,
And peace, and love, and happiness.
    How transient all we here enjoy!         240
How short our bliss without alloy!
While thus she lay with heart elate,
In nature's purest blissful state;

She heard a voice rise from the ground
With hollow, soft, and moving sound;                     245
Fixed was her eye and mute her tongue,
While thus some viewless being sung.

## Song.

"The black bull of Norway has broken his band,
"He's down through the links of fair Scotland;
"And the flower of the land shall be lost and won,     250
"Ere ever he turn his tail to the sun."

She looked around with eyes intent,
In breathless dumb astonishment;
No living thing she could espy,
Yet still a sound was murmured nigh!                    255
It sunk into a mournful tone,
And flitted like a passing groan.
    She deemed she lay on fairy ground
By some unearthly fetters bound;
For why she came so far astray,                          260
Or why she did not haste away
She nothing knew.–The East grew dun,
A cloud came floating o'er the sun,
And down the hills of Appin rolled
In many a dim and darksome fold;                         265
The scene was mingled shades of night,
With dim with pale and dazzling light.
    Still was the mighty ocean seen
A boundless field of dazzling sheen,
For west the morning beam withdrew                       270
To bask upon the shelvy blue,
And on its bosom went and came
In thousand shreds of shivery flame.
    But O between the east and north
Came moving on a veil so swarth,                         275
From earth to heaven one solid wave,
Like pall upon creation's grave;
As if the lord of nature furled
Up like a scroll the smouldering world.
    The virgin sovereign looked aghast,                  280
And weened each breath would be her last;
For denser grew the vapour's coil

And backward seemed to whirl and boil;
At length stood fixed from earth to sky
A wall of gloomy ebony;                                    285
Save that when wreaths of downy gray
Turned their pale bosoms to the day,
Like fillets of empyrean white
Circling the funeral brow of night.
　　It seemed as if the world from thence          290
Was severed by Omnipotence,
One part in light and life to bloom,
The other grope in murky gloom;
As all behind were left in wrath
A gloomy wilderness of death,                             295
And all before rejoice for aye
In starry night and sun-shine day.
　　Conscious of innocence the while,
The queen looked on that heideous veil
With awe, but yet with such an eye                       300
As virtue turns unto the sky;
Expecting every glance she cast
To see forth bursting from its breast
The hail, the thunder, or the flame,
Or something without form or name.                      305
　　The virgin looked not long invain,
The cloud began to move amain;
Inward like whirlpool of the ocean,
It rolled with dark and troubled motion;
And sometimes like that ocean's foam,                   310
Waving on its unstable home,
The silvery verges tossing bye
Were swallowed in obscurity.
　　Still as it opened on the sight,
The gauzy linings met the light;                         315
And far within its bosom grew
A human form of face she knew;
No earthly thought it did convey,
It was not formed like face of clay,
But in the cloudy dome was seen                          320
Like image of a thing had been.
As if on canvass heavenly fair,
A reverend face was formed of air,
On texture of celestial land,

And pencilled by an angel's hand.                         325
    Yet every line was there approved,
And every feature once beloved;
The silence as she gazed was broke,
Aloud the hoary vision spoke;
But yet no motion it addrest;                             330
Lip unto lip was never pressed;
It moved no feature, tongue, nor eye,
Yet this was uttered solemnly.

"Queen of green Albyn liest thou alone?
"Look to thy honour, and look to thy throne!          335
"The ravisher comes on his car of the wind,
"The sea is before thee, the spoiler behind;
"Queen of green Albyn, dare not to roam!
"There's rapine approaching, and treason at home!
"Trust not the sea-maid with laurel in hand;          340
"Trust not the leopard, or woe to the land!
"The falcon shall fail, and the oak of Loch-Orn,
"The eagle of Mar, and the lion of Lorn;
"But trust to the roe-buck with antler of gray
"In the halls of Temora! or woe to the day!"          345

    Up closed the cloud dark as before,
But chilling terror was not o'er;
Just where the maiden's eye was set,
Where cloud and land and ocean met,
A bull came forth, of monstrous frame,               350
With wreathy mane and eyes of flame;
Slowly he pawed the yielding ground,
Then stood and madly gazed around;
His white horns flickering in the light
Like boreal streamers o'er the night.                 355
    Soon as he fixed his savage look
On young Queen Hynde, the mountains shook
With bellowings of unearthly tone,
As wild and furious he came on;
She tried to fly—her sight grew dim,                  360
A numbness seized on every limb,
And nought remained in such a place
Save meeting danger face to face;
For she had heard that maiden's eye

Had some commanding majesty,     365
At which, if bold and fearless cast,
All earthly things would stand agast.
Other expedient there was none;
Mighty the motive!—all alone
She turned, and with as dauntless look     370
As eye of beauty well might brook,
Beheld the monster as he came
Roaring and foaming on his aim.
     He eyed her moveless as she stood,
And all at once, in raving mood,     375
Halted abashed, and 'gan aloof
To tear the ground with horn and hoof,
Uttering such horrid sounds of wrath,
As hell had bellowed from beneath.
The mountains caught the clamours loud,     380
And groaned in echoes from the cloud.
     Proud of her virtue's power displayed,
And homage by creation paid,
High glowed the beauties kindly given
As maiden's shield by favouring heaven;     385
So strong the fence, that savage fierce
Was baulked, and could not thro' it pierce.
But, mad at such a viewless toil,
He kneeled he groveled in the soil:
Shortened by fury broke his roar,     390
Not in long bellow as before,
But with loud rending bursts of breath
He vomited forth smoke and wrath;
< His tufted tail, at every blare
Writhing like serpent in the air. >     395
     I've heard it said by reverend sage,
And why should youth discredit age,
That maiden's form, when pure, and free,
Had something of divinity.
That furious ban-dog changed his eye,     400
And fawned and whined as she drew nigh;
That elfin spear, or serpent's sting,
Or pestilence on mortal wing,
To her was harmless as the dew;
That crockodile and lion knew     405
The virgin frame, which had a charm

They would not, or they could not harm.
That even the thunder-bolt of heaven,
Poured in resistless liquid levin,
Would turn aside before her eye,                410
Or part and fleet unhurtful bye.
Because she formed, in nature's reign,
That link of the eternal chain,
Which earth unto the heavens combined,
And angels joined to human kind.                415
From worth this adage I recieved,
I love it, and in part believe't.
   Well might Queen Hynde have stood unmoved
Trusting a power so fairly proved,
For o'er her memory stealing came               420
That old and wonderous apothegm;
And she had stood, save for the eye
Of virgin's only enemy.
   Across the hill swift as the deer,
Fierce Mar approached with shield and spear,    425
To save his beauteous sovereign bent,
And claim the due acknowledgement;
Aloud his threat and clamour grew
Daring the savage as he flew.
   Soon as the monster saw advance               430
The chieftain with his threatening lance,
Away he rushed in vengeance dire,
And met him with redoubled ire;
The chieftain bawled and braved amain
To cow the savage, but invain,                  435
Onward he drove with stayless shock,
The rested lance in splinters broke,
And down to earth the chief was borne,
Struggling to ward the ruthless horn;
But all invain!—Queen Hynde beheld             440
Him gored and tossed along the field,
She saw him swathed in bloody red,
And torfelled on the monster's head.
   Appalled, and shocked, her faith withdrew;
She turned and off in horror flew,              445
But soon all hopes of life resigned
As the loud bellowings neared behind!
Upon a rough and rocky steep

That overhangs the restless deep
She was o'erhied, and tossed in air,                    450
Loud were her shrieks of wild despair;
Oh! for the covert of the grave!
No refuge!—None at hand to save!
    Maids of Dunedin, in despair
Will ye not weep and rend your hair?                    455
Ye who in these o'erpolished times,
Can shed the tear o'er woeful rhymes;
O'er plot of novel sore repine,
And cry for hapless heroine.
O ye dear maids of forms so fair,                    460
That scarce the wandering western air
May kiss the breast so sweetly slim,
Or mould the drapery on the limb;
If in such breast a heart may be,
Sure you must weep and wail with me!                    465
    That full set eye, that peachen chin,
Bespeaks the comely void within;
But sure that vacancy is blent
With fuming flaming sentiment!
Then can you read ye maidens fair,                    470
And neither weep nor rend your hair?
    Think of a lady all alone!
The beauteous Hynde of Caledon!
Tossed up the air a heideous height,
On point of blood-stained horn to light!                    475
And if to wail thou can'st delay,
Have thou a bard's anathema.
    Still is there one resource in view;
For life one effort still is due;
It is, to plunge with desperate leap                    480
Into the far resounding deep,
And in the pure and yielding wave
To seek a refuge or a grave.
    The leap is made, the monster foiled,
Adown the air the virgin toiled;                    485
But in cold tremor crept her blood,
For far short of the yielding flood,
Her fall descends with deathful blow,
Sheer on the pointed rocks below.
    Oh can'st thou view the scene with me,                    490

The scene of ruth and misery?
Yes, thou shalt go, and thou shalt view,
Such scene as artist never drew.
      In western lands there is a hall,
With spire, and tower, and turret tall;                    495
And in that tower a chamber fair.—
Is that a mortal triad there?
For sure such beauty, such array,
Such moveless eye of wild dismay,
Such attitude, was never given                             500
To being underneath the heaven.
Yes there are two most fair I ween,
But she whom they support between,
In symmetry of form and face,
In comely yet majestic grace,                              505
Statue or vision she would seem
Chose from celestial cherubim!
      Come modalist thy toil renew,
Such scene shall never meet thy view!
See how the raven tresses flow,                            510
And lace that mould of purest snow;
The night-robe from one shoulder flung,
In silken folds so careless hung;
The face half-turned, the eagle eye
Fixed rayless on the morning sky;                          515
That neck—that bosom, ill at rest,
White as the sea-mew's downy breast;
And that pure lip was ne'er outdone
By rose-leaf folding to the sun.
      And note that still and stedfast eye,                520
That look of wild sublimity,
As dawning memory wakes, the while
Soft fading to a virgin smile;
O modalist! thy toil renew,
Such scene shall never greet thy view!                     525
      High looks that chamber o'er the sea,
And firth, and vale, and promontry;
From dark Cruachan pours the day,
The lattice drinks the golden ray;
And that fair form you there behold,                       530
That statue of majestic mould,
Leaning two beauteous maids upon,

Is Hynde the Queen of Caledon!
The leap was from a couch of down,
The rest a dream for ever flown!                          535
      Maid of Dunedin, do not jeer,
Nor lift that eye with jibing fleer;
For well you wot, deny who dares,
Such are the most of woman's cares;
Nay if I durst I would them deem                          540
More trivial than a morning dream;
Have I not seen thy deep distress,
Thy tears for disregarded dress?
Thy flush of pride, thy wrath intense,
For slight and casual precedence?                         545
And I have heard thy tongue confess
Most high offence and bitterness!
Yet sooth thou still art dear to me,
These very faults I love for thee,
Then, why not all my freaks allow?                        550
I have a few and so hast thou.
      It was a dream—but it was one,
The more the virgin pondered on,
The deeper on her heart it fell,
Her sire's last words remembering well,                   555
"When danger threatens I'll be nigh,
"Therefore my child on dreams rely;"
And she believed each incident
Was by her father's spirit sent,
To warn of treason, or of blood,                          560
Or danger all misunderstood.
      A load upon her heart it weighed,
And on her youthful spirits preyed;
At length she left her royal pile,
To visit, and consult the while,                          565
Columba of the holy isle;
A seer and priest of God was he,
A saint of spotless purity,
And then held in such high regard,
That Scotish sovereign nothing dared,                     570
Of war, religion, or of law,
Without consulting Columba.
      Queen Hynde embarks in Uan bay,
Brisk was the breeze and bright the day;

Before the tide, before the gale, 575
The gilded barge, with silken sail,
Adown the narrow channel run
Like meteor in the morning sun.
So swiftly swept the flying keel,
The woods and islands seemed to wheel; 580
And distant peaks of freckly gray,
Were winding to the north away.
    The sea-gull rose as she drew nigh,
And tried before her speed to fly;
But after toilsome travelling, 585
With beating breast and flapping wing,
Was forced to turn aside outworn,
For shelter in the creeks of Lorn.
    But Ila Glas the minstrel gray,
Well noted as they sped away, 590
That sea-fowls flocked from isle and steep,
To view that wonder of the deep;
And well they might, for never more
Such bark shall glide from Scotland's shore.
    The sailors were as chiefs bedight, 595
The queen and virgins all in white;
The prow was formed in curious mould,
The top-mast stem of beaten gold;
The sails were white, the sails were blue,
And every dye the rainbow knew; 600
And then the pennons red and pale
So far were fluttering in the gale,
She was not like an earthly thing,
But some sweet meteor on the wing.
I may not say (and if I might 605
Man never has beheld the sight)
That all were like pure angels, driven
By living breeze, in barge of heaven.
    When westward from the sound she fell,
She met the ocean's mighty swell; 610
Yet bounded on in all her pride,
Breasting the billow's mountain side,
Or downward with delireous sweep
From dizzy verge into the deep.
    Maid of Dunedin, well I know 615
Had'st thou been there there had been woe!

Distress of body, and of mind,
And qualms of most discourteous kind,
< For I have seen on summer tide,
Where Forth's blue waters playful glide, 620
Such paleness, and such dire alarms,
Such dissarray of beauty's charms,
As child within its nurse's arms!
And, grieved for thy too dainty nature,
I've deemed thee a most feeble creature. > 625
    But here, in days of yore, were seen
Young Hynde the Caledonian queen
With all her maids enjoy the motion
Blyth as the bird that skims the ocean.
O to have been the soaring gull, 630
Perched on the headland cliff of Mull,
There to have watched, with raptured eye,
That royal bark go bounding bye,
Casting a tiny rainbow shade
O'er every hill the ocean made! 635
    Iona bay is gained at last,
The barge is moored, the anchor cast;
And though no woman might come nigh
That consecrated land of I,
The queen, presuming on her sway, 640
Went right ashore without delay.
Her sire that isle had gifted free,
And reared that sacred monastry;
The doctrine of the cross he heard,
Believed, and paid it high regard; 645
For he percieved that simple plan
A band twixt God and sinful man,
Befitting well his nature weak,
That would not loose and could not break;
And with his child and kinsmen came, 650
And was baptized in Jesus' name.
    When Ila Glas, in holy fane,
Announced his queen and virgin train,
Saint Oran was that very time
Giving such picture of the crime 655
Of woman's love, and woman's art,
Of woman's mind, and woman's heart!
If thou, dear maid, the same had'st heard,

Thy blissful views had all been marred!
For thou durst never more have been                    660
In robe of lightsome texture seen!
Thy breast, soft heaving with the sigh,
Arresting glance of vagrant eye,
Love's fatal and exhaustless quiver,
Must have been shrouded up for ever!                   665
The perfume—simper—look askance—
The ready blush—the ogling glance—
All all o'erthrown, ne'er to recover!
Thy conquests and thy triumphs over!
O breathe to heaven the grateful vow,                  670
That good Saint Oran lives not now!
    When he of such intrusion heard,
Around in holy wrath he stared;
"What?"—said the Saint—"What, even here
Must these unrighteous pests appear!                   675
Though even the rough surrounding sea
Could not protect our sanctuary;
Nor maiden modesty, nor pride,
Can keep them from where men reside,
I should have weened that thus retired                 680
The frame of mind the place required,
The frame of holy penitence,
Had been enough to keep them hence.
    I know them well, and much I fear
No good intent has brought them here.                  685
E'er since that day deplored the most,
When Adam sinned, and man was lost,
By woman tempted to the deed,
Mischief to man has been their meed.
Rise holy brethren—rise with me,                       690
And drive them back into the sea;
Should they risist, do them no harm,
But bear them back by force of arm."
    Up sprung the bearded group amain,
Who to be first each nerve they strain;                695
Whether to save the holy isle
From woman's snare and witching wile,
Or once again to fold the charms
Of beauty in their idle arms
I nothing wot—but all was vain,                        700

For in the chancel of the fane,
Columba rose before the band,
With crosier stretched in his right hand.
"Hold my loved brethren—is it best
Thus to expel a royal guest?                              705
We not as woman her recieve
But Scotland's representative;
And meet it is that maids should be
Tending on virgin royalty."
    That word was law—the rage was o'er,      710
The stern Saint Oran said no more.
< But when of *maids* Columba spoke,
And *virgins*, with such serious look, >
He sat down on his chair of stone,
Shook his grey head and gave a groan.                     715
    Come view the barefoot group with me,
Kneeling upon one bended knee,
In two long files—a lane between,
Where pass the maidens and their queen,
Up to the sacred altar stone,                             720
Where good Columba stands alone.
    There was one maiden of the train
Known by the name of wicked Wene;
A lovely thing, of slender make,
Who mischief wrought for mischief's sake,                 725
And never was her heart so pleased
As when a man she vexed or teased.
By few at court she was approved,
And yet by all too well beloved;
So dark, so powerful was her eye,                         730
Her mein so witching and so sly,
That every youth, as she inclined,
Was mortified, reserved, or kind,
This day would curse her in disdain,
And next would sigh for wicked Wene.                      735
    No sooner had this fairy eyed
The looks demure on either side,
Than all her spirits 'gan to play
With keen desire to work deray.
Whene'er a face she could espy                            740
Of more than meet solemnity,
Then would she tramp his crumpled toes,

Or with sharp fillip on the nose,
Make the poor brother start and stare,
With watery eyes and bristling hair.                    745
And yet this wayward elf the while
Inflicted all with such a smile,
That every monk, for all his pain,
Looked as he wished it done again.
 Saint Oran scarce the coil could brook,        750
With holy anger glowed his look;
But judging still the imp would cease,
He knit his brows and held his peace.
 At length the little demon strode
Up to a huge dark man of God,                          755
Her soft hand on his temple laid
To feel how fair his pulses played,
Then by the beard his face she raised,
And on th' astonished bedes-man gazed
With such enchantment, such address,                   760
Such sly insidious wickedness,
That, spite of insult and amaze,
Softer and softer waxed his gaze,
Till all his stupid face was blent
With smile of awkward languishment.                    765
 Saint Oran saw—In trumpet tone,
He cried—"Satan avoid!—Begone!
Hence!—all away!—for, by the rood!
Ye're fiends in form of flesh and blood!"
 Columba beckoned; all was still.                 770
Hynde knew the mover of the ill,
And instant turning looked for Wene;
"I told thee girl, and tell again
For once remember where thou art,
And be due reverence thy part."                        775
 Low bowed the imp with seemly grace,
And humbly showed to acquiesce;
But mischief on that lip did lie,
And sly dissemblage in the eye!
Scarce had her mistress ceased to speak,               780
When formed the dimple on her cheek,
And her keen glance did well bewray
Who next should fall the jackall's prey.
Saint Oran—woe be to the time

She marked thy purity sublime!           785
O never was her heart so fain!
'Twas a new fund for wicked Wene.
     Meantime the queen most courteously
Addressed the seer and priest of I,
And told her latent fears at large,         790
Her aged father's dying charge,
And finally, with earnest mein,
Of the late vision she had seen;
And that for counsel she had come
Thus on a pilgrimage from home.         795
     "Yet reverend sires—the truth to say,
Though I have pondered night and day
On this strange vision—yet, so tossed
Hath been my mind, that much is lost;
And now I only can present         800
You with its startling lineament."
     "Oh!" cried Saint Oran—"here forsooth
Is sample fair of woman's truth!
Here she pretends to ask her lot
From dream, yet owns that dream forgot!     805
Out on you all!—your whole intent
Is on some devilish purpose bent!"
     The queen was utterly astounded;
Even Saint Columba was confounded
At such outrageous frowardness;       810
The real cause they did not guess.
     Ere that time Wene, full silently,
Had slid up to Saint Oran's knee,
And ogled him with look so bland
That all his efforts could not stand;      815
Such language hung on every glance;
Such sweet provoking impudence.
     At first he tried, with look severe,
That silent eloquence to sear,
But little weened the fairy's skill,      820
He tried what was impossible!
His flush of wrath, and glance unkind,
Were anodynes unto her mind.
Then she would look demure and sigh,
And sink in graceful courtesy;       825
Press both her hands on her fair breast,

And look what could not be exprest!
When o'er his frame her glance would stray,
He wist not what to do or say!
No one percieved the elf's despight,          830
Nor good Saint Oran's awkward plight.
So quick the motion of her eye,
All things at once she seemed to spy;
For Hynde, who loved her, wont to say,
For all her freaks by night and day,          835
Though mischief was her hourly meed,
She ne'er could catch her in the deed.
So instantly she wrought the harm,
Then as by momentary charm,
Stood all composed, with simplest grace,      840
With look demure and thoughtful face,
As if unconscious of offence,
The statue of meek innocense!
Of Oran's wrath none saw the root,
The queen went on and all were mute.          845
    "Now Sires to you I have appealed,
To know what's nature what revealed;
And that you may discern aright,
I'll tell you how I passed the night;
What feelings on my fancy crept,              850
And all my thoughts before I slept."
    "Now for the virgin's sake, I pray
Spare the recital if you may!"
Cried Oran with distempered mein
And stretched his hands forth to the queen.   855
"My liege whate'er the train denotes,
O spare the feelings and the thoughts!
We know them well—too well forsee
Their tenor and their tendency.
Heavens! how we're bearded and belaid!        860
Would that the dream itself were said!"
    Columba poignantly reproved
The rudeness of the man he loved;
Though all were shocked at that he said,
None saw how the poor priest was bayed.       865
O Wene! for many a wild uproar,
Much much hast thou to answer for!
    Scarce had the queen again begun,

When something Wene had looked or done
Enraged the saint to such excess, 870
He cried with desperate bitterness,
"Avoid thee Satan!—off! away!
Thou piece of demon-painted clay!
Thy arts are vain! thy efforts lost!—"
All looked astounded, Wene the most, 875
So sad—so sweet—so innocent,
That all supposed the queen was meant.
Between the fathers strife arose
And words were like to end in blows.
    "Sooth" said Saint Oran "is it fit 880
That you or I should calmly sit
Listening to tale, in which the theme
Is woman's thought and woman's dream?
Out on them all!"—And forth he strode,
Groaning as one beneath a load; 885
And muttering words, they heard not well,
Of limbs of Satan, sin, and hell!
Straight to his little cell he wended
Where loud th' impassioned prayer ascended;
Peace was restored and Wene was left 890
Of every cue to ill bereft.
    Columba listened to the queen
With deep regard and troubled mein;
And conscious many dreams were sent
By spirits kind and provident. 895
The more he thought and pondered o'er
That wonderous vision, still the more
He was confirmed it did portend
Some evil wisdom might forefend;
And he resolved to journey straight 900
Home with the queen th' event to wait
For well he knew, the christian cause
Rested on Scotland's throne and laws.
    The vow was sealed, the host was laid,
The hymn was sung, the mass was said, 905
And after gifts of value high,
The royal Hynde withdrew from I.
Columba went her guide to be,
In rule, in truth, and purity.
    They halted on the shore a while, 910

And ere they left the sacred isle,
Oran with holy garments on
Bestowed on each his benison.
Yet all with half an eye could see,
He deemed it did nought signify;                        915
He seemed as if with heaven he strove,
And more in anger than in love.
    Scarce had he said the word *Amen*
When petulent and pesterous Wene
Kneeled on the sand and clasped his knee,               920
And thus addressed her earnest plea.
    "O holy sire, be it my meed
With thee a heavenly life to lead;
Here do I crave to sojourn still,
A nun, or abbess, which you will,                       925
For much I long to taste with thee
A life of peace and purity.
Nay think not me to drive away,
For here I am, and here I'll stay,
To teach my sex the right to scan,                      930
And point the path of truth to man."
    "The path of truth"!! Saint Oran cried
His mouth and eyes distended wide.
It was not said, it was not spoke,
'Twas like a groan from prison broke,                   935
With such a burst of rushing breath
As if the pure and holy faith
Had by that maiden's fond intent
Been wholly by the roots uprent.
"The path of truth!!! O God of heaven!                  940
Be my indignant oath forgiven!
For by thy vales of light I swear,
And all the saints that sojourn there,
If ever again a female eye,
That pole-star of iniquity,                             945
Shed its dire influence thro' our fane
In it no longer I remain.
    Were God for trial here to throw
Man's ruthless and eternal foe;
And ask with which I would contend,                     950
I'd drive thee hence and take the fiend!
The devil man may hold at bay,

With book, and bead, and holy lay;
But from the snare of woman's wile,
Her breath, and sin-uplighted smile,                        955
No power of man may scape that gin,
His foe is in the soul within.
    O if beside the walks of men,
In green-wood glade and mountain glen,
Rise weeds so fair to look upon,                            960
Woe to the land of Caledon!
Its strength shall waste, its vitals burn,
And all its honours overturn.
Go, get thee from our coast away,
Thou flowret of a scorching day;                           965
Thou art, if mein not thee belies,
A demon in an angel's guise."
    "Angels indeed!" said Lauchlan Du,
As from the strand the boat withdrew.
Lauchlan was he whom Wene addrest,                         970
Whose temple her soft hand had prest;
Whose beard she caught with flippant grace,
And smiled upon his sluggish face.
A burning sigh his bosom drew!
"Angels indeed!!" said Lauchlan Du.                        975
    "Lauchlan," the father cried with heat,
"Thou art a man of thoughts unmeet!
For that same sigh, and utterance too,
Thou shalt a grievous penance do.
Angels forsooth!—O God, I pray,                            980
Such blooming angels keep away!"
Lauchlan turned round in seeming pain,
Looked up to heaven, and sighed again!
    From that time forth it doth appear
Saint Oran's penance was severe;                           985
He fasted, prayed, and wept outright,
Slept on the cold stone all the night;
And then as if for error gross
He caused them bind him to the cross,
Unclothe his back, and man by man,                         990
To lash him till the red blood ran.
But then—nor yet in after time,
No one could ever learn his crime;
Each keen enquiry proved invain,

Though all supposed he dreamed of Wene.  995
Alas what woes her mischief drew,
On Oran and on Lauchlan Du!
  Sweet maiden, I thy verdict claim;
Was not Saint Oran sore to blame
For so inflicting pains condign?   1000
O think, if such a doom were thine!
Of thy day-thoughts I nothing know,
Nor of thy dreams—and were it so,
They would but speak thy guileless core
And I should love thee still the more.  1005
But Ah! if I were scourged to be
For every time I dream of thee,
Full hardly would thy poet thrive!
Harsh is his song that's flayed alive!
Then let us breathe the grateful vow,  1010
That stern Saint Oran lives not now!
  The sun went down, the bark went slow,
The tide was high, the wind was low;
And ere they won the Sound of Mull,
The beauteous group grew mute and dull.  1015
Silent they leaned against the prow
And heard the gurgling waves below,
Playing so near with chuckling freak,
They almost weened it wet the cheek;
One single inch 'twixt them and death  1020
They wondered at their cordial faith!
  During this silent eiry dream,
This tedious toiling with the stream,
Old Ila Glas his harp-strings rung
With hand elate, and puled and sung  1025
A direful tale of woe and weir,
Of bold unearthly mountaineer;
A lay full tiresome, stale and bare
As most of northern ditties are:
I learned it from a bard of Mull,   1030
Who deemed it high and wonderful;
'Tis poor and vacant as the man,
I scorn to say it though I can.
  < No more of high important things,
Which hap'd that night, my legend brings;  1035
Save that, with harping and with motion,

Thus cradled on the heaving ocean,
The queen and maidens slept full sound
Then waked and told their dreams around;
And Wene, whom other joys possest,                1040
*Made* one that far outdid the rest.
(I must each trifle turn t' avail
Remember 'tis a highland tale.)
    While all was still around the queen,
With slender reed and needle keen                 1045
Wene so contrived to wound and wreak
The slumbering sailors on the deck,
That each on others threw the scath
And all grew tumult, pride, and wrath.
And just as rage began to cease,                  1050
And dwindle into sullen peace,
At one a steady aim she took,
On place where pain he ill could brook,
Which roused him sorely to disgrace
With blows his weetless comerade's face.          1055
O how the elf enjoyed the strife,
It was to her the balm of life;
But when her laugh could not be drowned,
She said 'twas thro' her sleep, and moaned! >
    Maid of Dunedin, thou may'st see,             1060
Though long I strove to pleasure thee,
That now I've changed my timid tone,
And sing to please myself alone;
And thou wilt read, when, well I wot,
I care not whether you do or not.                 1065
    Yes I'll be querulous, or boon,
Flow with the tide, change with the moon,
For what am I, or what art thou,
Or what the cloud and radiant bow,
Or what are waters winds and seas,                1070
But elemental energies?
The sea must flow, the cloud descend,
The thunder burst, the rainbow bend,
Not when they would, but when they can;
Fit emblems of the soul of man!                   1075
Then let me frolic while I may,
The sportive vagrant of a day;
Yield to the impulse of the time,

Be it a toy, or theme sublime,
Wing the thin air or starry sheen,                    1080
Sport with the child upon the green,
Dive to the sea-maid's coral dome,
Or fairy's visionary home,
Sail on the whirlwind or the storm
Or trifle with the maiden's form,                     1085
Or raise up spirits of the hill—
But only if, and when I will.
    Say may the meteor of the wild
Nature's unstaid erratick child,
That glimmers o'er the forest fen,                    1090
Or twinkles in the darksome glen,
Can that be bound? can that be reined?
By cold ungenial rules restrained?
No!—leave it o'er its ample home
The boundless wilderness to roam!                     1095
To gleam, to tremble, and to die,
'Tis nature's errour, so am I!
    Then O forgive my wandering theme!
Pity my faults, but do not blame!
Short my advantage, small my lore,                    1100
I have one only monitor,
Whose precepts to an ardent brain
Can better kindle than restrain.
Then leave to all his fancies wild
Nature's own rude untutored child,                    1105
And should he forfeit that fond claim
Pity his loss but do not blame.
    Let those who list, the garden chuse,
Where flowers are regular and profuse;
Come thou to dell and lonely lea,                     1110
And cull the mountain gems with me;
And sweeter blooms may be thine own,
By nature's hand at random sown;
And sweeter strains may touch thy heart
Than are producible by art.                           1115
The nightingale may give delight,
A while, 'mid silence of the night,
But th' lark lost in the heavens blue,
O her wild strain is ever new!

End of Book the first

# Queen Hynde

## Book Second

When Hynde returned to her royal hall
    With Saint Columba she withdrew,
Who told her much that would befal,
    For of the future much he knew.

He solved the eagle, and the oak,        5
    The hawk, and maiden of the sea,
(Of whom the hoary vision spoke)
    To chiefs defined by heraldry.

But who would fight, or who would fly,
    Or who their sovereign would betray;     10
Or what the roe-buck could imply,
    With all his gifts he could not say.

But there was trouble and suspense,
    For though they knew that woe would come,
The seer could not divine from whence,     15
    If from abroad, or rise at home.

Much sorrow woman's bosom bears
    Which oft she braves with courage high;
But to that ardent soul of hers
    Suspense is utter misery.     20

Hynde could not hunt, she could not play,
    She could not revel in the ring,
She could not fast, she could not pray,
    Nor yet disclose her languishing.

One day as, in her topmost tower,     25
    Upon her lattice she reclined,

Her eyes to mountain, sea, and shore,
    Roving all restless as her mind,

She spied a hind stand at her gate
    With face of mystery and despair;                30
But when he came before her seat
    He told her with a troubled air,

That fairies were to Morven come,
    In thousand thousands there to dwell;
That the wild correi was their home,                35
    Watched by a grizly sentinel!

That with his eyes he had them seen,
    In countless myriads on the hill,
Clad in their downy robes of green,
    Rising and vanishing at will!                   40

When Hynde had heard the story wild,
    And saw the teller quake amain;
She looked unto the man and smiled,
    And bade him say his tale again.


Again the wonderous tale was said,                  45
But nothing could of that be made,
It was so unallied and odd.—
Again she cast her eyes abroad,
And spied on green Barcaldine lea
A horseman posting furiously;                       50
His steed, outspent, was clotted o'er
His neck with foam, his sides with gore;
Though great his speed, at every strain,
He seemed to eye the verdant plain,
With look most haggard and agast,                   55
As if for spot to breathe his last;
Yet still he strained, leaving behind,
A stream of smoke upon the wind.
    The rider waved his bonnet high,
And cried aloud as he drew nigh,                    60
"Open your gates and let me on,

Throw wide the gates of Beregon!
Clear, clear the way, and let me fly,
The messenger of wonder I!"
    Down dropt his steed the gate before,    65
His breath was spent his efforts o'er,
While the rath herald of dismay,
Cursed him and urged on foot his way.
He saw the queen at casement high,
"Tidings"! he bawled with tremulous cry;    70
The queen grew red—the queen grew wan,
From lattice to the door she ran,
Then back—then hurried down the stair
To meet that vehement messenger,
But when his sounding step drew nigh    75
She fled back to her turret high,
And 'mid her maids, with feverish mind,
Listened the brown and breathless hind,
Whose habit and whose mein bespoke
A maniac from confinement broke,    80
But when his accents met the ear
They showed him fervent and sincere.
    "Which is the queen of fair Scotland?
Pardon—I need not make demand.
O haste, my liege, and raise afar    85
The beacon and the flag of war;
Warn all your chiefs to tend you here,
For high your peril is and near.
Let this be done without delay,
And then I have a tale to say!"    90
    The flag of blood was raised anon,
The war-blast from the tower was blown;
The battle whoop aloud began,
The henchmen rode, the pages ran,
The beacon which from Uock shone,    95
Was answered soon on Bede-na-boan,
And that from every mountain hoar,
From Melforvony to Ben-More,
Uttering afar, o'er firth and flood,
The voice of battle and of blood.    100
    When this the peasant saw prevail,
He proffered to the queen his tale;
Showing the while he had a sense

Of his own mighty consequence;
Three times he drank his thirst t' allay,                105
Pledging the dames in courteous way;
Thrice forth his seemly leg did show,
And sleeked the brown hair down his brow;
Then thus in hurried earnest way
Began his wonderous tale to say.                         110
    "Last eve upon the height I stood,
Where Ardnamurchan bays the flood;
The northern breeze sung on the tree,
Wrinkling the dark and purple sea,
Yet not a cloudlet was in view,                          115
For heaven was deepening into blue.
    I thought I saw, without the bay,
Just in the line where Canay lay,
Somewhat that did the ocean shroud,
It seemed a living moving cloud.                         120
I turned mine eyes from off the sea,
Deeming it was some fantasy;
But still when turning round again,
I saw that vision of the main.
Nay once I thought white foam arose,                    125
Rolling before un-numbered prows.
    While thus I stood in deep surprise,
The vision vanished from my eyes.
But whether it melted into air
Or sunk beneath, or lingered there,                     130
I could not tell, for fall of night
Shaded the spectre fleet from sight
And though to fear not much inclined,
A kind of terror seized my mind.
All reasoning but increased my dread,                   135
I rose at midnight from my bed,
And heard a din upon the ocean,
As if the world had been in motion;
Voices repressed along the shores
And lashes from a thousand oars.                        140
    I heard them—yet confess I must,
I scarcely could my senses trust
But deemed some trouble swayed my blood
Or on enchanted ground I stood;
For all was calm at break of day,                       145

Nor ship nor boat was in the bay.
Along the shore and heathy hill
No whisper moved save from the rill;
Yet I could note the roaming deer
Turn from that mountain's side in fear;     150
No snowy flocks were straggling there,
The kid had left its wonted lair,
And the dull heifer paused to gaze,
And ruminate in deep amaze!
    From what I saw at even tide,     155
I deemed that something there did hide;
If so, I knew all was not well,
But how, or why, I could not tell.
So I resolved my life to stake,
For my fair queen and country's sake.     160
    I clothed me in this fool's array,
I launched my shallop in the bay;
I crossed Loch-Sunart to the east,
And strayed along the mountain's breast,
Jabbering and singing as I went,     165
Like ideot mean and indigent.
    At first one warrior crossed my way,
Resting his lance to make me stay;
A man he was of rugged mein,
Such arms or robes I ne'er had seen.     170
My hands were clasped my back behind,
My eyes wide open to the wind,
I did not once these hands divide,
But, with my elbow, turned aside
His lance, with wide unaltered stare,     175
As if such man had not been there.
Rough words he spoke in unknown tongue,
But still I jabbered and I sung,
And onward past, resolved to spy
The mystery out, though doomed to die.     180
The warrior smiled and laid him down;
I sauntered, sung, and wandered on.
    At length an armed file I spied,
Hid in the heath all side by side!
I made no motion of surprise,     185
But trudged, and sung, in ideot wise;
Then stretched me down amid the throng,

And pulled the grass, and crooned my song.
They seemed amused, and smiled to see
My deep unmoved stupidity;                                190
My ears on all their accents hung,
But all was in an unknown tongue.
    I next went to a rising ground,
Where I could see all round and round,
And uttered such a horrid yell,                           195
That rocks and hills rang out the knell.
But never since I viewed the day
Saw I such vision of dismay!
Thousands of warriors grim and swarth,
Upraised their heads out of the earth,                    200
Then softly like a fairy scene
They crept into the earth again;
Each brake was lined above the strand,
With warriors of a foreign land.
    This brought me many an angry look,                   205
And chastisement and stern rebuke;
I bore them all full patiently,
And scaped to bring the word to thee.
O'er Morven hills I ran with speed,
I swam the Coran on my steed,                             210
And I have ridden the Appin o'er
As never mortal rode before.
This is my tale, I vouch it true;
Much it imports, my liege, to you;
The foe is strong, the danger nigh;                       215
My steed I've lost! and here am I."
    "If that be truth," Queen Hynde replied,
"A truth in nothing falsified;
Of thy lost steed have no regard,
For ample shall be thy reward,                            220
In gifted lands and honours high,
For thou hast acted gallantly;
If false, then of thyself take heed,
The highest tree shall be thy meed.
To prove thee honest as thou seem'st,                    225
Say all thou saw'st and all thou deem'st."
    "I've braved the Briton on the field,
I've met the Roman, shield to shield;
Of many a foe I've seen the face;

But such a rough and warlike race                    230
As they who lie on Morven's shore,
In sooth I ne'er beheld before.
    If there are nations north away,
As I have heard old minstrels say,
Who live by land, or live by sea,                    235
As suits the time or casualty;
Who o'er the wave on summer tide,
Along the wastes of ocean glide,
Or in the deep indented bay
Like pellochs dive to pick their prey,               240
< Then float in rings their meals to sup,
And craunch the filthy lobster up >
And when the seasons 'gin to turn,
Amid the forests they sojourn,
Hunting the great deer to and fro,                   245
Or burrowing 'neath eternal snow,
Deep in the bowels of the ground,
With their unlovesome mates around,
Howling the songs of other spheres,
And feasting on lank wolves and bears.               250
If such there are, a countless host
Of such now lies on Scotland's coast:
For all their robes are from the wood,
Or seal-skin of the northern flood;
Their beards are long, their arms unclean,           255
Their food the hateful haberdine.
    Farther I saw that to the sea
Their eyes reverted constantly,
There still they looked, though not aware,
As if their hopes were anchored there;               260
And thence I judge, from Barra's shore,
This night will bring as many more;
And that before the break of day,
Their fleet may ride in Creran bay.
    Nay more, I dread, that to their side     265
Some Scots have turned, and been their guide;
For not in all our western bound,
Could such a landing place be found;
Such solitude in bay and hill,
So deep, so lonely, and so still.                    270
    One passenger while I was there,

Came up the shore with lightsome air;
He sung he whistled and he ran;
I deemed him one of Moidart's clan.
But as he passed, with luckless eye,                    275
He saw the beach all trodden lie;
He marked the footsteps and stood still,
Looked to the sea, and to the hill,
Still lingering on the tainted brink,
As if he wist not what to think.                        280
    A chief arose, with ill intent,
Out of the brake, and to him went;
And with one stroke and little din
Clove the poor traveller to the chin,
Then hid him in the clustering brake.                   285
O how my heart began to quake!
I thought of death, and 'gan to con
The prayer that would be soonest done.
I 'scaped them all, though sore beset!
In artifice I ne'er was beat!                           290
< No—nor in length of wind, nor speed;
Nor yet in urging on a steed! >
None else could thus have cautioned you,
Though I who should not say it, do."
    O when that hind aside had laid                      295
His fool's attire, and was arrayed
In belted plaid and broad claymore,
And robes which once a chief had wore;
And came with martial cap in hand
Before the nobles of the land,                          300
It would have joyed your heart to 've seen
His face of wisdom and his mein.
And aye he stretched with careful fold
His philabeg of tasseled gold
And tried with both hands to sleek down                 305
His locks all weatherbeat and brown;
Then quite bewildered every sense
With words of great magnifiscience;
< Thro' every look and action ran
The self-importance of the man: >                       310
The motley clown O do not blame,
Few are his paths that lead to fame!
One gained let him that path pursue

For great and glorious is the view!
   High on a rock the palace stood 315
Looking afar o'er vale and flood,
Amid a mighty citadel,
To force of man impregnable.
Seven towers it had of ample space
Which still the stranger well may trace 320
And these in legendary lore
Was Selma in the days of yore.
But East and north the city lay,
On ridge and vale, from bay to bay,
And many a stately building shone 325
Within the ancient Beregon,
And many a fair and comely breast
Heaved in that jewel of the west.
While round it cliffs and walls arose
Impassible to friends and foes. 330
   The Caledonians lay at ease,
Beleaguered by their hills and seas.
They knew no force by land could won
Their old imperial Beregon;
But hostile navies were their dread, 335
To which a thousand bays were spread,
Round every peopled vale and hill,
Where they might ravage at their will;
And never news so fraught with fear
E'er met the Caledonian's ear. 340
   Benderiloch and Appin men,
From Etive bay, to Cona glen,
Led by old Connal of Lismore,
Appeared the first on Creran shore.
Gillian of Lorn, at close of eve, 345
Crossed over Connel's boisterous wave,
With seven score yeomen in his train,
Well baited on the battle plain.
All these, with other armed men,
Knight, squire, and serf, and citizen, 350
Assembled were at evening fall,
Scarcely a thousand men in all.
But where the watch to keep o'ernight,
Or where the danger would alight,
What foe was nigh, or what would be, 355

All was in dim uncertainty!
   On every height and headland steep
Wardens were placed the watch to keep,
By shores of Appin and of Lorn,
With pipe, and call, and bugle horn,        360
In various notes to give alarms,
To warriors resting on their arms.
   The autumn eve closed on the hill;
The north was breathing brisk and chill;
The stars were sprinkled o'er the night,      365
With goggling and uncertain light,
As if eventful watch to keep,
Over these reavers of the deep.
What with the roar of Connel's stream;
The cormorant's awakening scream;       370
The constant whistling of the gale;
The dead-lights glimmering in the dale;
The shadowy mountains, bored and riven,
That seemed to gap the eastern heaven;
It was by sages truly hight,         375
An ominous and aweful night!
   High beat the heart of many a maid,
And many a ear was open laid,
Deep listening with suspended breath
To hear the signal sound of death.       380
Each casual clang, and breathing boom,
And voice that wandered thro' the gloom,
Sent to the heart a thrilling knell.
And when the morrow's sentinel
The cock, his midnight larum blew,      385
A thousand cheeks were changed of hue;
Ten thousand heads, stunned and amazed,
Were from green moss and pillow raised.
   The midnight came and past away,
And silence hung o'er keep and bay;     390
Save that three watchers on Loch-Linhe
Above Glen-hendal's groves of pine,
Just in the midnight's deepest reign,
When Orion with his golden chain
Had measured from the moors of Tay     395
To keystone of the milky way,
Heard a soft lay of sorrow given

Somewhere from out the skirts of heaven,
Much like the funeral song of pain
Which minstrel pours o'er warrior slain.                    400
And well the strains to sorrow true
Of Ossian's airy harp they knew,
Which his rapt spirit from the sky
Gave to the breeze that journeyed bye;
And well they knew, the omen drear                          405
Boded of danger death and weir.
    The first watch of the morning past,
Dark was the shade o'er nature cast!
And o'er the eyes that watch had kept
The short and dreamy slumber crept!                         410
When all at once from centinel
Burst on the air the bugle's swell!
And never did note from bugle blown,
Congeal so many hearts to stone!
    If thou didst e'er the affliction bear,       415
Of having all thou valued'st here
Placed in a frail & feeble bark,
Exposed, upon the ocean dark;
And when thy spirit yearned the most,
The word arrived that all was lost;                         420
Then may'st thou guess the pains that stole
Cold on the Caledonian's soul.
    Unto the first alarm that broke,
No answer came save from the rock,
For all sat listening in suspense,                          425
And doubting every mortal sense;
But soon repeated was the roar,
Longer and louder than before.
    Then one o'erwhelming flood of sound
Burst over Scotland round and round;                        430
Away, away! by mountain hoar,
By moated peel, by isle, and shore,
Far eastward to the break of morn,
And o'er the thousand glens of Lorn;
Slow down the links of Spey it flew,                        435
On Lomond waked the slumbering mew,
Till down Cantire, with rolling sweep,
It died along the southern deep.
The matron said her holiest prayer;

The household dog rose from his lair, 440
Turned up his snout, and howled amain,
The fox and eagle joined the strain;
The capperkailzie scorned to flee
But gallowed on the forest tree;
The hill-wolf turned him to the wind, 445
And licked his bloody flew and whined.
How shook the foemen at the noise,
They deemed it was the land of voice!
   By every mountain lake and glen,
By forest firth and shaking fen, 450
Came rows of men in arms bedight,
Panting and hurrying thro' the night.
And aye as from the mountain's head,
Beside the bealfire blazing red,
The watcher's warning note was blown, 455
Faster they strode, and posted on.
Yet all those lines afar and near
Straight inward to one goal did steer,
As to the lake the streamlets run,
Or rays point to the morning sun: 460
Or like the lines of silvery foam
Around the ocean's aweful tomb,
Where grim Lofodden's thirsty cave
Swallows adown the living wave;
Around around the whirlpool's brink 465
To that they point, and run, and sink.
So poured the warriors of the land,
Around their queen and throne to stand;
Too late they came! ere rose the sun
The bloody fight was lost and won! 470
   Where sounded first the watcher's horn,
Rushed to the shore the men of Lorn,
And saw, as to the strand they pressed,
Upon the ocean's groaning breast,
As if the forest of Lismore 475
Came struggling on to Appin's shore.
So far that moving wood was spread,
The sound so wholly covered,
That all along its level sheen
No image of a star was seen; 480
Such fleet no Scot had ever hailed,

Nor e'er on Albyn's seas had sailed.
   Onward it came like moving wood,
Loaded, and lipping with the flood,
Till every keel refused the oar,                 485
And stranded leaned on Appin shore;
Each warrior there had pledged his faith,
To win a home for life or death.
   The barks were moored all side by side,
Then plunged the warriors in the tide.       490
"Now!"—cried old Conal in a tone
Of extacy—"On, warriors! on!"
And as the hail-cloud hanging swarth
Bursts with the thunder on the earth,
So rushed on death our warriors brave,      495
With shout that deadened every wave.
The plunge of horses and the neigh,
The broken and uncertain bay,
Where floundering warriors fought and fell,
The utter darkness, and the knell          500
Of battle still that louder grew,
The flashes from the swords that flew,
Formed altogether such a scene
As warrior scarce shall view again.
   In sooth when first these warriors met,    505
When every sword to sword was set,
You would have weened some meteor's ray,
Or curve of flame hung o'er the bay,
So flew the fire from weapons keen,
While all was noise and rage between,      510
But nothing save that fire was seen.
   Where Lorn with his brave horsemen came,
The coast was firm, the beach the same;
But where the gallies lay, they knew
Abrupt and deep at once it grew.          515
Into the wave they rode amain,
The foe withstood them, but invain.
They drove them backward in the strife
To plunge amid their ships for life.
But too intrepid in their wrath,          520
And too intent on foemen's death,
Over the beach, into the deep,
They rushed like flock of weetless sheep,

That headlong plunge with flurried mind,
While dogs and shepherds whoop behind.          525
Or like the cumberous herd that goes
(Of panting thirsty buffaloes)
From deep Missouri's wave to drink,
Fast press they to the stayless brink,
Pushing the foremost from the shore,            530
Till thousands sink to rise no more;
So plunged our yeomen over head,
Till scarce a remnant turned and fled,
While rocked the gallies to and fro,
With struggling parting life below.             535
    This error muse may scarce define,
A breach was made in Scotia's line;
The foe in thousands gained the strand,
And stretched in files to either hand,
So that the footmen were beset,                 540
Who still the foe had backward beat;
For when they first met in the sea,
They scarcely fought unto the knee;
Now all the waving crescent line,
Toiled to the breasts in smoking brine,         545
Which round them thick and clammy grew,
A waveless tide of crimson hue;
But still they fought, though coiled in gore,
With foes behind and foes before.
No son of Albyn held at ought                   550
His life, or harboured once a thought,
That on his coast might step a foe
Who first not o'er his breast should go.
    Their perilous case hid from their view
Amid the morning's murky hue,                   555
Each warrior fought for country's sake
As if his all had been at stake,
As if the saftey of the land
Lay in the force of his right hand.
No groan of hero's death could tell,            560
As mid the thickening wave they fell;
Warriors on shivering warriors stood,
Choaked in that tide of briny blood.
    O when the sun thro' morning rime
Looked over Cana's cliffs sublime,              565

Never on Appin's shore was spread
Such files of blenched and mangled dead!
The tide, receding, left a stain
Of crimson ever to remain,
(For since that day no tempest's shock                570
Can bleach the colour from the rock)
And left in woful guise the while
Troops of pale warriors rank and file,
Stretched on the strand in lines uneven,
With their cold eye-balls fixed on heaven!            575
Their bodies swathed in bloody foam,
Their heads turned to their native home!
    And every corse of Albyn's race,
Had marks of gloom in his dead face;
As still for life and force he gasped,                580
And in his hand his sword was grasped.
Each visage seemed to interchange
With others grin of stern revenge,
But nigher viewed, it wore an air
Of gloom, of sorrow, and despair.                     585
As the last feelings of the heart
Had been a pang of grief, to part
From Caledon when needed most,
And that his powerful aid was lost.
    Columba with his sovereign fair,        590
Had spent the latter hours in prayer,
E'er since the time the bugle rung,
And many a holy hymn they sung.
They never knew till break of day
That Scotia's host had waned away,                    595
They knew of battle on the coast
But little weened that all was lost.
And when the morning's purple beam
On Beregon began to gleam,
O what a scene for sovereign's eye                    600
Was opened slow and gradually!
The bay all fringed with glistening gore;
The human wreck along the shore;
A thousand masts from bark and barge
Pointing to the horizon's verge,                      605
For all around the Keila bay
The fleet was moored and leaning lay;

And dreadful hosts of warriors grim
The plains beyond the gate bedim,
All crouding, gathering, bearing on 610
To hapless hopeless Beregon!
  Old Conal Bawn, and wounded Lorn,
With handful of brave men outworn,
Borne inch by inch back from the strand,
Now took their last and latest stand 615
Within the porch, with full intent
To fall or entrance there prevent.
  Too plain it was that all was lost;
But what astounded Hynde the most,
Was the broad banner of the foe, 620
High streaming on the morning's brow;
For on it flashed in dreadful wise
A sable bull of monstrous size,
His horns, his colour, and his frame,
His furious mood the very same 625
As that, remembered still with awe,
Which in her heideous dream she saw.
The close of that when she thought on,
Her heart grew cold and turned to stone!
  She saw a foresight had been given 630
To her of future things by heaven,
But yet so shadowy and so dim,
On reason's surf it seemed to swim,
And all the struggling of the mind,
Its form and substance could not find. 635
But plain it was to every sense,
That some sublime intelligence,
Beyond the power of mind to scan
Existed between God and man.
  Distempered thoughts her bosom stirred, 640
Her father's words again recurred:
And Ah! the thought that there could be
A thing of immortallity,
A spirit that had past away,
Of one in dust and death that lay 645
Still by her side, to smile, or frown,
Converse, and mingle with her own,
Was one so deeply pondered on,
That reason wavered on her throne.

Message on message posting came,                    650
Which so perplexed the youthful dame,
That all her mind's exertion fled,
A stupor on her brain was shed.
Her royal city of command,
The great emporium of the land,                      655
She saw exposed to foemen's ire,
To sword, to ravage, and to fire.
Her nobles gone to fetch supply,
One leader wounded mortally,
The other brave, but hard beset,                     660
Herself with holy anchoret
Surrounded by a ruthless foe,
Alas! what could the virgin do?
No human stay or succour near,
She looked to heaven, and dropt a tear!              665
    "My honoured liege," Columba said,
"Suffer your servant, thus arrayed,
Forth to the foe in peace to fare,
And learn from whence and who they are;
Their purpose, and their dire intent,                670
And why on war with maiden bent.
We haply thus may stay the war,
Till Lennox come, and rapid Mar;
I'll wend unaided and alone,
For every tongue to me is known."                    675
The queen approved the wise appeal,
And lauded high his honest zeal.
    Forth stepped the sire the hosts between,
Bearing a bough of holly green;
The marshalled foe his journey sped,                 680
And to their king the seer was led.
A prince he seemed of courage high,
Of mighty frame and lion eye,
With something generous in his face,
A shade of noble courteousness                       685
Mixed with a stern and jealous part,
Th' effect of caution not of heart;
And by him stood a prince most fair,
Haco, his sister's son, and heir.
    Before the king Columba stood,                   690
Nor bowed he head, nor lifted hood;

Erect he stood with tranquil ease,
Looking the monarch in the face,
Loth to avale, if it might be,
One jot of Scotland's dignity;                              695
And lother still to bring the blame
Of cringing on the Christian name;
Serene he stood, like one prepared
To answer, rather than be heard.
     One surly glance the monarch threw,          700
But momently that glance withdrew,
For well his eye had learned to trace
The human soul from human face.
But such a face! and such an eye!
Of tranquil equanimity!                                     705
He had not viewed in all his reign
O'er Scania's stormy wild domain;
'Mong all the dark and stern compeers
Of Odin's rueful worshippers.
     "Man who art thou, that thus arrayed         710
In frock of gray and cowled head,
Approachest on unbending knee
The face of sovereign majesty?"
     "I wist not king to whom I came,
What rank he claimed, or what his name,                     715
Else I had rendered honours due,
For to th' awards of heaven I bow;
And well I know the mighty hand
That rules the ocean and the land,
O'er mankind, his peculiar care,                            720
Places the sovereign powers that are;
If such thou art I'll honours pay;
But first thy name and lineage say.
< And more, I must thy motive know,
If thou art Scotland's friend or foe, >                     725
That thus thou comest in armour sheen;
The vicar I of Scotland's queen;
< My name's Columba, my degree,
Is deep professed humility." >
     "As suits you friend or foe I am,            730
Eric of Norway is my name;
My lineage is supreme and high,
Of Odin's race that rules the sky;

All Scandinavia owns my reign,
From Finmark to the northern main;                    735
My errand is, I frankly own,
To win your queen, and wear your crown;
That all the northern world may be
One huge resistless monarchy.
If young queen Hynde, of fair renown,                 740
Will yield to me herself and crown,
Our flag of war shall soon be furled,
I'll make her mistress of the world;
If not, to me it seems as nought,
I'll take her and her land to boot.                   745
I and my warriors value less
Your forces than one bitter mess;
I'll crush them like a moth, and must
Lay ancient Beregon in dust,
My soldier's prey it needs must be,                   750
Though I regret it grievously.
      Go tell your queen I proffer her
My hand, my love, my crown to wear;
And would she save her land from scathe,
Her warriors and her chiefs from death,               755
Her maids from brunt of rude desire,
Her capital from sword and fire,
Let her be sure her choice to make
Of that per-force she needs must take.
Eric of Norway is not wont,                           760
Of deeds he cannot do to vaunt."
      "Forsooth King Eric, I must say,
Such wooer comes not every day,
So frank to ask, and free to give,
So downright and so positive.                         765
So brief a courtship ne'er was known
Within the bounds of Caledon.
How it may end I little wot,
But the beginning has been hot!
And hence I pray that God may keep                    770
Such northern wooers north the deep.
      However I shall well agree,
I not dislike your policy;
For should your high designs succeed
The holy faith it needs must spread.                  775

As aiding counsellor, and guide,
And messenger of heaven beside,
I may not, and I will not cease
To cultivate eternal peace.
But should—as 'tis my firm belief,                    780
Her troth be pledged to Scotish chief,
What then remains?—She can't revoke,
A sovereign's word may not be broke."
    "I'll fight him" was the short reply;
"Let arms decide for he and I."                        785
This said he in so stern a tone,
The saint stood mute, reply was none.
"Whoe'er thou art" the king rejoined
"As vicar of the royal Hynde
I thee respect, and make appeal                        790
If I not fair and frankly deal.
My sovereignty I lay aside
From subject wight to win my bride
If vanquished I request no more,
I yield her to the conqueror;                          795
Better one man than thousands die,
Thou hast my answer;—homeward hie;
If not ere noon your seal returns,
You yield perforce, your city burns;
I'll leave nor pile nor standing stone                 800
In all your boasted Beregon."
    "Most gallant sovereign, I implore
One other word and then no more.
What if my queen have pledged her troth
By royal word or solemn oath                           805
To sundry chiefs, in their degrees
Bound to particular services?
< And who shall first his task fulfil
And prove completion to her will >
And most avails his native land                        810
To share her throne and win her hand.
I pledge no word that this I know,
But sooth, I deem, and judge it so."
    Then "Bring them all" king Eric cried
"Bring one, bring two upon your side,                  815
Princes or peasants let them be,
Bring ten it is the same to me!

Men to your men I will produce,
If Hynde from 'mong the victors chuse."
    "In thee king Eric I percieve 820
A noble foe or friend we have;
Forthwith before my queen I'll lay
Your gallant suit for yea or nay."
    Much was the stir, when this was known,
In palace of old Beregon. 825
Sore they demurred, yet it did seem
A respite in a great extreme,
A respite from a deadening blow
By an o'erpowering reckless foe.
Proud Gaul of Ross, and lordly Mar, 830
And Donald Gorm were distant far;
For Sutherland they looked invain
From verges of the northern main;
Lochorn was nigh, and Allan Bane,
Lochaber's fair and goodly thane, 835
But all uncertain was their power;
Argyle was looked for every hour,
And when he came to aid the war
They knew, that neither he, nor Mar,
Nor any Scotish chief, would bear 840
King Eric's brag in deeds of weir.
They weened that warriors there were none
Could match the chiefs of Caledon,
Yet such a stake as queen and crown
On such a die was never known. 845
    While thus they sat, in counsel slow,
And wist not how or what to do;
While fears were high, and feelings strong,
While words were few, and pauses long,
Queen Hynde from off her royal seat 850
Thus spoke in words and mood elate.
    "My ancient friends full well I see
Your kind concern and fears for me.
No more your risk—no more your stake
Than Albyn chuses that to make. 855
I'm a mere woman, and my crown
With your support is great I own,
Without it 'tis but sordid dust,
Let Eric take us if he must!

Though both are won, and I constrained,                860
The soul of Albyn is not chained,
By hard constraint whate'er I do
Be to your independance true.
    I'm great or small at your behest,
A queen, a trifle, or a jest;                          865
I rule because you will it so,
No more can mighty Eric do.
I take his offer—three to three
His claim shall straight decided be,
From out the number that subdues                       870
My husband and my lord I chuse.
    Were there a dread—as there is none—
That chosen chiefs of Caledon
Can e'er to barbarous foemen yield,
Or fainting quit the combat field,                     875
Then let king Eric take his all,
His queen and kingdom nominal!
    Whereas, should we this pause forego,
And baulk a proud and powerful foe,
Our wealth and crown ere falls the night               880
Must yield to his resistless might.
I take his offer without dread;
Be this proviso only made,
That as a queen and crown may go
From nation by a single blow,                          885
Whoever wins, on yonder plain
In seven days shall fight again,
That day shall all decisive be
The victors gain my crown and me.
But in the interim I shall claim,                      890
In whose soever power I am,
Such honours, deference, and esteem,
As may a virgin queen beseem."
    Consent was full, applause was high,
For why no better meed was nigh.                       895
Columba and old Connal went,
Forth to king Eric's royal tent,
Which now a wonder rose to view,
Spangled with furs of every hue.
The clause was joyfully approved                       900
For Eric blood and battery loved.

The day was set, the hour, the field,
The brief agreement signed and sealed,
And all the Norse to music's tone
Entered the gates of Beregon. 905
Friendly they were, and madly gay,
And sooth such revel and deray,
Such wassailing and noiance vast
Had not been seen for ages past.
The maids of Beregon were pleased 910
For they were flattered wooed and teased
And well 'tis known that woman's mind
Is still to noise and stir inclined,
She would be marked and wooed withal
Rather to ill than not at all, 915
< Constraint or ravishment was none
But deeds were done in Beregon
If ancient dames may be believed
That would Saint Oran sore have grieved.
   Fair Scotish maid why that grimace 920
Such frown but ill becomes thy face
Fresh is thy memory of the day
When here degraded foemen lay
Men of a nation void by will
Of honour and of principle 925
Men the broad bounds of Europe through
Hated and scorned by all but you.
Whose holiest oaths as for a meed
Were never mouth'd but to mislead.
All this thou knew'st, and well wast told, 930
And oft wast warned by parent old:
Though shame and ruin were foreseen,
Though language could not pass between,
By look and sign thou wast undone,
Short was the siege till thou wast won; 935
An alien and a captive foe
Could all thine honours overthrow.
When this so late, so well is known,
O it befits thee ill to frown!
If I from courtesy have swerved 940
I may be blamed, and may deserv't,
I oft have been, and oft will be.
—It may not, shall not be by thee.

How shall I tell of that I rue?
Or sing my mountain maids of you? 945
I thought—but oh I was beguiled!
The maids where Ettrick wanders wild,
Chaste as her snow in winter storms,
Or stream that bathes their lovely forms;
I weened them pure as they were fair; 950
So weened we all, and so they were.
The sycophants among them came,
To woo and win was all the same!
Now many a maid and maiden's son,
Proclaims the deeds that erst were done. 955
How shall I sing of that I rue?
How shall I think fair dames of you? >
   O I have thought and thought again,
And still the memory gives me pain!
For can I deem that beauty's glow, 960
The liquid eye and radiant brow,
The smile that like the morning dew
Sheds gladness on the gazer's view,
The graceful form, the gliding tread,
Too light to bruise the daisy's head, 965
The downy locks with roses twined
Or wanton waving in the wind,
The mantling blush so sweetly spread
Changing the pale rose to the red,
All but a gloss in kindness given 970
To woman's youth by pitying heaven
For glories lost by primal sin
To veil unsanctitude within?
   O that such thoughts I could consign
To darkness distant and condign! 975
If broods the soul on such alloy,
Then where is mine and nature's joy?
Still let me love thee as thou art,
Though passions rankle at thy heart;
Though chroniclers point thee for ill 980
I'll ween thee pure and gentle still:
I'll say, when thousand faults combine,
My sex has dross as well as thine;
And in my last and utmost need
I'll fly to Calvin's sweeping creed, 985

And say of crimes of deepest hue
They were predestined thee to do
Ere thou wast born, though thine the ill,
What is our lot we must fulfil!!
    Nay rather than to thousands yield,       990
Or fly defeated from the field,
I'll quit this jointured age and thee,
This age of bond and bankruptcy,
With all its sordid thirst of gold
And conjure up the times of old,           995
Raising from ancient days a queen,
And maids that were, or might have been,
That I may mould them as I will,
And love thee froward trifler still.
Only—though light I hold thy jeer—     1000
None of thy prudery let me hear,
I know thee well—too well to feign,
And have my way as thou hast thine;
If bards and maids must disagree
Woe to the fair! and woe to me!        1005
    I've sung of Wake and roundelay
In beauteous Mary's early day;
Of charms that could all hearts command;
Of maiden borne to fairyland;
Of worlds of love, and virgins bright;    1010
Of pilgrims to the land of light;
And I have sung to those who know,
Of Maiden's guilt and failings too;
And all in love, to point to thee
The charms of perfect purity.        1015
    Now I've called forth a patriot queen,
Of generous soul and courtly mein;
And I've upraised a wayward elf
With faults and foibles like thyself.
And these as women thou shalt see     1020
More as they are, than they should be.
Then wrangle not with one whose skill
Is short and laggard to his will;
Who yet can hope, and brow the heaven,
Of God and man to be forgiven       1025
For every strain he dared essay,
For every line of every lay,

That would to purity impart
One stain, or wound the virtuous heart.

---

### End of Book Second

### Note

On pages 54–55 above, lines 916–57 are enclosed in angle brackets. These lines are deleted in the manuscript, no doubt because they were regarded as an example of the kind of 'indelicacy' to which Hogg was prone. Hogg has supplied a shorter replacement passage on a small piece of paper, now bound in with the manuscript. This piece of paper has been addressed and sealed for delivery by post or by hand: however, almost all of the address has now been cut away. The replacement lines supplied by Hogg are as follows.

> Ah loveliest of the lovely throng!
> Why darts that frown my page along?
> If I from courtesy have swerved,
> I may be blamed, and may deserve't;
> I oft have been, and oft will be,
> It may not, shall not be by thee.
>   Why should I tell of that I rue,
> Or sing deluded flowers of you?
> Of seven fair sisters in a bower,
> Each lovelier than the opening flower,
> Chaste as the snow of winter storms,
> Or stream that bathed their lovely forms;
> And they were pure as they were fair—
> So deemed we all—and so they were
> The spoilers came—their toils were few!
> How can I sing of that I rue?

# Queen Hynde

## Book Third

Whoe'er in future time shall stray
O'er these wild vallies west away,
Where first, by many a trackless strand,
The Caledonian held command;
Where ancient Lorn, from northern shores     5
Of Clyde to where Glen-Connel roars,
Presents in frowning majesty,
Her thousand headlands to the sea:
O traveller, whomsoe'er thou art,
Turn not aside with timid heart     10
At Connel's tide, but journey on
To the old site of Beregon;
I pledge my word, whether thou love'st
The poet's tale, or disaprove'st,
So short, so easy is the way,     15
The scene shall well thy pains repay.
There shalt thou view, on rock sublime,
The ruins gray of early time,
Where, frowning o'er the foamy flood,
The mighty halls of Selma stood.     20
And mark a valley stretching wide,
Inwalled by cliffs on either side,
By curving shore where billows broke,
And triple wall from rock to rock;
Low in that strait, from bay to bay,     25
The ancient Beregonium lay.
    Old Beregon! what soul so tame
Of Scot that warms not at thy name?
Or where the Bard, of northern clime,
That loves not songs of Selma's time?     30
Yes, while so many legends tell,
Of deeds, and woes, that there befel,
These ruins shall be dear to fame,
And brook the loved, the sacred name.
    Nay look around, on green sea-wave;     35

On cliff, and shelve, which breakers lave;
On stately towers and ruins gray,
On mote, on island, glen and bay,
On remnants of the forest pine,
Old tenants of that mountain reign,                40
On cataract and shaggy mound,
On mighty mountains far around
Jura's fair bosom, formed and full,
The dark and shapeless groups of Mull;
Others far north, in haze that sink;               45
Proud Nevis on Lochaber's brink,
And blue Cruachan bold and riven,
In everlasting coil with heaven
    View all the scene, and view it well,
Consult thy memory, and tell                       50
If on the earth exists the same,
Or one so well deserves the name.*
    Thou still may'st see on looking round,
That saving from the northern bound,
Where stretched the suburbs to the muir,           55
The city stood from foes secure.
North on Bornëan height was placed
King Eric's camp, o'er heathery waste;
And on Barvulen ridge behind,
Rocked his pavilion to the wind,                   60
Where royal banners floating high,
Like meteors streamed along the sky.
    Within the palace he had been,
And converse held with Scotland's queen;
And the north tower, of strong defence,            65
Was given him for his residence.
There over night he would not stay,
But there he sojourned day by day;
For sooth to say, as well he might,
King Eric was in woeful plight;                    70
For ne'er was heart of monarch laid,
Nor stripling fair, nor rosy maid,
So wholly under love's arrest,
As was king Eric's noble breast.

---

* — *Selma* signifies The beautiful view *Beregon*, or *Perecon*, as
pronounced, The serpent of the strait

Queen Hynde was his perpetual theme,                    75
His hourly thought, his nightly dream;
And no discourse could chance to be
Of war, or peace, or policy,
In which, with fondness archly seen,
He introduced not Albyn's queen.                        80
It was a theme beloved so well,
He longed and loved on it to dwell.
　　She met him, but his presence thence
She shunned, as not to give offence;
She had no thought, no pride, no aim,                    85
But what her country's rights became;
And in the converse them between,
Such majesty was in her mein,
Such dignity with sweetness mixed,
The soul of Eric was transfixed;                        90
From former, ruder joys estranged,
His very nature seemed exchanged.
　　The comliest youth of northern name,
Prince Haco, marked the growing flame,
And wild impatience fired his mind,                     95
To see that fair, that wonderous Hynde,
That thus could raise in warrior's core,
Feelings unknown, unfelt before.
Oft watched he round the tower alone,
But word or intercourse was none,                       100
Till feigning tale of import high,
He gained admittance artfully.
Hynde to Columba's aisle had gone,
An hour with him to spend alone,
Just as the prince was introduced                       105
As messenger of secret trust.
　　By wayward chance it hap'd just then,
That frolicsome and restless Wene,
In all the royal robes of state
Arrayed, on throne of ivory sate,                       110
Aping a queen with such a face,
Such majesty, and proud grimace,
That all the noble maids around
With laughter sunk upon the ground.
One personated haughty Mar,                             115
One Norway's boisterous brand of war,

One Allan Bane, one Coulan Brande,
And one the lord of Sutherland;
And each addressed the suit to Wene,
In wooer terms as Scotland's queen.                    120
    To one the imp, with simpering grin,
Turned up her nose, and tiny chin;
Her scarf of tissued gold flung bye,
And raised her shapely arm on high,
Saying, in act most gracefully,                        125
"Have done, good friend! I'll none of thee!"—
Another she apart would eye,
With piercing glance or ogle sly;
Another flatter—then again
Turn to king Eric of the main;                         130
And all the patriot queen display,
In dignified and generous way.
    While this high game was at the height,
And all were wrapt in wild delight,
A gentle *rap* was at the door;                        135
"Come in," said Wene;  and on the floor
A bowing page these words address'd,
"A messenger in speechless haste
From Royal Eric craves thine ear."—
" 'Tis well," said Wene; "let him appear               140
Before OUR throne."—These words she said
So like the queen, the page obeyed.
Each maid looked to the throne on high
With dimpling cheek and pregnant eye,
And scarce from laughter could refrain                 145
At the effrontery of Wene,
But dreading sore that such a jest
Would lead to scorn and wrath at least.
    No time was now these fears to state,
To reason or expostulate;                              150
For, momently, in royal hall,
Prince Haco bowed amid them all.
His courtly form so tall and fair,
His flowing curls of flaxen hair,
His amorous look, and princely gear,                   155
Soon made him general favourite there.
    "Pardon illustrious queen," he cried
"Flower of the world and Albyn's pride;

For this intrusion on your court:
I tidings bring of strange report.                    160
Haco's my name, King Eric's heir,
My message suits your private ear."
    With sovereign air, and motion dumb,
Wene pointed with her queenly thumb
Unto the door—then in a tone                          165
Soft yet majestic cried "Begone
WE wish with him to be alone;
Shortly your counsels WE may crave,
To Scotland's weal WE are the slave."
Forth step'd the dames with court'sey low;            170
To each the Prince returned a bow;
But as the hindmost dissappeared,
A tittering sound of mirth he heard;
And in his brilliant eye was blent
Shame, anger, and astonishment.                       175
    "Regard not prince a court-dame's fleer,
To you they mean no scoff or jeer;
'Tis at their mistress, and their queen,
And she must bear't!" said Wicked Wene.
"Prince, when misfortune's at the door,               180
It looses tongues were mute before!
They jeer that thus their queen should be
In hall alone with prince like thee;
Nor is it meet, but I must bow
To things unfitting virgin now."                      185
    "And sooth" said Haco, "much I fear
The queen will turn on me the jeer,
When she shall hear, as now she must,
My message of important trust.
Forgive thy servant I intreat,                        190
'Tis love that brings me to thy feet;
To see thy face, thy words to hear,
Was the intent that brought me here."
    "Love!—" said the urchin, with a frown
Such as from eye was never thrown                     195
"Love darest thou name to Albyn's queen,
Whose face before thou hast not seen?
Such theme WE list not to discuss;
WE must not yet be toyed with thus."
    "Forgive my youth, angelic dame,                  200

And glowing heart of moulded flame.
Thou shalt not need one word to check,
Nor hear ought but with due respect.
I've set my head upon a die,
To pay this homage to thine eye;                    205
For of thy form of matchless grace,
Thy cherub eye, and lovely face,
So much I heard, that heavenly bliss
Seemed less to me than hour like this;
But all was short that I heard told               210
To beauty that I now behold."
    I've said before, and must repeat,
That Wene had beauty, archness, wit;
No young man on her face could look
Who felt not pang he ill could brook,             215
He loved, or in his bosom strove
With something similar to love;
And when she tried her witching skill,
Her eye with certainty could kill.
Now in the royal robes arrayed,                   220
With gold and jewels overlaid,
She seemed a being of romance,
A thing of perfect elegance;
And Haco, trembling, scarcely trowed
Before an earthly maid he bowed;                  225
Such dignity in mein and eye
A man beholds in Majesty!
    O titled rank, long be it thine
From common gaze remote to shine!
And long be nursed thy speech refined             230
From scrutiny of vulgar mind!
That thing, in robes of state attired,
The closer seen, the less admired,
Kept at a distance still may draw
The homage of respect and awe.                    235
Therefore most humbly do I sue,
In name of rank, and reverence due,
Subordination, manners prim,
And all that keeps a land in trim,
To keep thy sphere, whate'er it be,               240
From scar of scoundrel scrutiny.
This thing did Wene, for honour's sake,

Upholding rank she chanced to take;
And Wene knew more, as you'll espy,
Of men and things than you or I.    245
    As Haco spoke the elf the while
Lighted her visage with a smile,
And gave him look that thrill'd each vein;
For who could stand the eye of Wene?
The prince took heart, and blushing said,    250
"Here at thy feet O royal maid,
One moment list th' unwelcome theme,
And hear thy servant's simple scheme."
    "Not at OUR feet" queen Wene replied
With voice and air most dignified,    255
"A prince thou art—a foe 'tis true—
Yet—Rise—that honour is thy due.
No good from this can WE divine;
But let us hear that scheme of thine."
    "O say not foe!—If in this heart    260
One atom acted foeman's part,
I'd dig it from its latent goal,
The sanguine fountain of the soul!
What I will do thou yet shalt see,
For peace, for Scotland, and for thee.    265
My uncle Eric loves thee more
Than ever king did queen before,
I know it—but he's old—whil'st thou
Hast all that loved and living glow
Which youth on virgin can bestow.    270
Now since I've seen thee, and approve,
And feel, to see thee is to love;
Might Haco but thy heart engage
No deadly wars the Norse might wage.
For take my word, if here they stay,    275
War there must be do as you may;
In spite of truce or treaties made,
Their breaking forth is but delayed;
As certain as the wind must blow
Cold o'er their polar wastes of snow,    280
So where the chiefs of Scania are
Must there be ravage, waste, and war.
    This to prevent, and Scotland free,
Might you transfer your troth to me

Here might we reign on stable throne,                285
In old imperial Beregon;
And to your Albyn's present bound
Unite our islands all around.
And when the time comes, as it may,
That Scandinavia owns my sway,                       290
O'er these thy towers, shall wave unfurld
The ensigns of the northern world,
And Scotia's free unyielding land
To all these regions give command.
These things I deemed, O beauteous Hynde!             295
Worthy the counsel of your mind.
To do them all I pledge my troth—
No son of Odin breaks his oath."
    "Prince" said queen Wene "you pledge too high;
Even sanguine maid may not rely                       300
On such great priv'lege and command,
And 'vantage to her native land.
But yet the eye would be severe,
And heart, that judged you insincere.
Yet all the answer I can deign,                       305
As tis—(to those o'er whom I reign
The slave and vassal, subject still
To what they feel and what they will—)
Is thus, to thank you, and take leave;
This hand, in friendship, please recieve;            310
And, as thou lovest my peace and bliss,
Venture no more on scheme like this."
    Haco kneeled down in rapture bland,
And took the elfin's queenly hand,
Impress'd it with a kiss sincere,                    315
And wet the bracelet with a tear;
Whil'st Wene, with all her shrewd address,
Could scarce her merriment suppress.
The prince upraised his humid eye,
And noting well her aspect sly                        320
Turned half away with mimic flush,
With dimple and with fairy blush,
Fled all at once his humble air,
And but the lover nought was there.
Light as the bound of roe-buck young                 325
To footstool of the throne he sprung;

Put one arm round the royal neck;
The other, with all due respect,
Her jewelled bosom did enfold
The gentle form and arms to hold;       330
And then did lips in silence tell
Where lover's lip delights to dwell.
Full oft can maid, with frowning brows,
Reprove the act she well allows,
Though dear, as now, th' empassioned scene—   335
And action was the soul of Wene!
    Prince Haco's youthful heart o'erflowed
And turned to wax that liquid glowed;
And that fond kiss a seal has set
Of female form and coronet       340
On it, so deep, that from its core
That form was ne'er erased more;
For every thought his mind pursued
The dear the treacherous form renewed.
    True, though queen Wene her squire beloved   345
With sharp and cutting words reproved,
Yet in her radiant eye was seen
No proud offence nor pointed spleen;
And as he left her throne supreme,
His ardent spirit to inflame,       350
She cast that look of matchless art,
That never failed on young man's heart;
And said with sigh—"Hard is my lot!
Had I my will—as *I have* not!"
Then bent she down her brow sublime,     355
And wiped her cheek of beauty's prime.
The winding stair had steps a score,
Prince Haco made them only four;
And when he reached the outer gate
That led from Selma's halls of state,     360
Adown the steep from rock to stone,
Light as a kid he bounded on,
And won the street of Beregon;
Pleased to the soul with his address,
His courage and his bold success.      365
    Vain simple youth! thy bosom's queen,
The lovely and mischievous Wene,
On tassel'd footstool of the throne

In powerless laughter hath sunk down;
And prince, 'tis all at thy expense,                    370
Thy ardor, truth, and impudence.
    Loth would Dunedin's daughter be
T' admit such license Wene as thee!
Even though a prince, or general came,
Or Poet, a much greater name!                           375
< Or else, be sure that human eye
Must ne'er the granted boon espy;
Or else, be sure that human mouth
Must never breathe the shameful truth! >
For I have seen the mincing thing                       380
As dancing round the gleesome ring,
A gap leave in our saraband,
And shrink from poet's gloveless hand;
As if the touch of sun-burnt palm,
Could discompose the level calm                         385
Of virgin blood, or sacred core,
Or make thee guiltless so no more.
    O shame! O shame that such a blot
Should e'er attach to lovely Scot!
Oft have I mark'd the rueful flaw,                       390
And blush'd at what I heard and saw.
No book, however pure each thought,
Though by divine or matron wrote,
Dar'st thou essay aloud to read,
Till every page is duly weighed;                        395
And each equivocation eyed,
And con'd, and all constructions tried,
And then thou skip'st whole pages o'er
Of Galt, of Byron, and of Moore.
This have I seen, and grieved anew                      400
At thy constructions so untrue.
    Would'st thou this cherish'd frippery weigh
In reason's scale, tis plain as day,
That fishing, hunting on the scent
For what thou know'st was never meant,                  405
Of all indelicacies framed
By heart impure, or folly named,
This sure the worst, the most confest!
O such discoveries well attest
To what research thy thoughts are led,                  410

In what a school thy mind was bred!
   In Selma's halls much laughter grew,
And many queries Wene forth drew;
But not one word would she unfold,
Till to the queen the whole she told,      415
Who smiled, half in delight and pain,
At the unbridled freaks of Wene.
From that day forth, right carefully
She shunn'd the glance of Haco's eye;
No more as queen he her could see,      420
And less she did not chuse to be;
But some supposed her thoughts were given
To him, at least, as much as heaven;
While he, most blest illustrious wight!
Was crazed, was drunken with delight.      425
A queen's own lover! Yes forsooth–
And such a queen!–O happy youth!
His step grew lighter than the wind,
Aye when he thought of beauteous Hynde;
And often to himself he talk'd,      430
Smiling and swaggering as he walked,
"Well done Prince Haco! say who can
Thou hast not quit thee like a man!"
   Now every day and every hour
Brought new supplies of Scottish power.      435
Lochaber's Thane came down the coast,
With full seven hundred in his host:
And on the eve of that same day
Came all the motely tribes of Spey,
Led by a chief of eastern fame,      440
Mordun Moravius by name.
And from the Dee's wild branching flood,
The rapid Mar, of Royal blood,
Brought his grim files to battle bred;
Against the Pict and Saxon led,      445
Till for high deeds they were renowned
The bravest troops on British ground.
   Then came old Diarmid of Argyle,
With men from many a Southern isle,
Round whose domains the waters flow,      450
From far Cantyre to dark Lochow;
Two thousand men, a hardy train,

Rose from these margins of the main.
　　Then Donald Gorm the lord of Sky,
Came down attended gallantly,                          455
With pagan standards broad unfurled,
The remnants of a heathen world.
And last, but steadiest of the band,
The loyal lord of Sutherland
Came with his clans from firth and glen;               460
And Harold with his Caithness men.
These then the names of highest worth,
That ruled the land from south to north.
　　But long ere this the holy seer
Had failed at counsel to appear;                       465
Matins were said, and vespers sung
In Royal hall, by old and young;
But Columba was gone, yet how,
Or when, or where, they did not know;
While sadness, solemn and resigned,                    470
Sat on the brow of lovely Hynde.
　　In counsel there was deep surmise
Why he had gone in secret guise;
Some blamed him for a coward's part,
And some of deep and monkish art;                      475
And all the chiefs arrived of late,
Convened in fiery fierce debate,
Arraigned his counsels to the last,
The armistice—all that had passed!
What shame, they said, to risk with foe                480
Their queen and country at a blow!
As who could answer for his might
Or skill, or courage, in the fight;
While the high stakes for which he stood
Sufficient were to chill the blood,                    485
The highest soul the most to alarm,
And wrest the nerve from hero's arm.
In short, one feeling there prevailed,
A wayward one to be bewailed;
It was that, maugre dangers deep,                      490
That shameful truce they would not keep!
　　"List me my lords" said rapid Mar,
That whirlwind in the field of war,
And at the counsel board the same,

A very wreathe of mounting flame;                      495
While all too many fierce, austere,
Congenial souls of his were there—
"List me. Who was it made the vow
To keep this peace?—Was't I or you?—
Or who this foolish combat set?                         500
Who but a peevish anchoret,
Who knew not of our high command,
Or the resources of the land?
    The queen, you say, in counsel high
Approved the truce. I that deny.                        505
Who is there that our queen should sway
To such a deed when we're away?
We are the land, we'll let them know,
The people and the sovereign too.
Arouse, then, lords, and let us rush                    510
On these rude bears their force to crush,
O'erwhelm them in their bloated den,
That loathsome sty of living men,
And leave them neither root nor stem,
Nor tongue to howl their requiem."—                    515
"Here is the sword and warrior form
Shall lead the fray!" cried Donald Gorm.
    Then rose old Diarmid of Argyle,
With brow serene and placid smile,
Upraised his hand amid the rage,                        520
The wild commotion to asswage,
And thus began. "My lords, I deem
This truce made in a great extreme,
When none were nigh the foe to check,
Or crown or city to protect;                            525
And by its breach, would we not draw
Disgrace on Albyn's throne and law?
Would it not be more courteous plan
To fight their champions man to man?
And if the issue falls aright,                          530
As fall it must to Scottish might,
Then all is well. But should the Norse
Put Albyn's heros to the worse,
Then be the vigour of our host
Strained to the height, else all is lost;              535
For ne'er to proud presumptuous foe

Must we our queen and crown forego.
I say not how we shall proceed,
Each day's events must rule the deed;
But in one point we'll all agree,                       540
Of foreign thraldom to be free.
I thank you, chiefs, for this regard,
And pray no gasconade be heard
Till once the important lists be set,
And champions hand to hand have met;                    545
And then, let that eventful day
Our future deeds and counsels sway."
    Assent ensued, but some there were
Who looked with discontented air.
The chief of these, the lord of Sky                     550
Bit his proud lip, and bent his eye,
And muttered some impatient say
Of the intolerance of delay.
With right or wrong, he longed for blows
With Albyn's fierce invading foes,                      555
Who long, on prey and havock keen,
To him had pesterous neighbours been;
But voices bore it, and the while
The suffrages were for Argyle.
    That ancient chief again addressed          560
His stern compeers, and warmly pressed
Of peace the strong necessity;
Mixed with their foes as would be—
And farther said, "I grieve to hear
Dishonour cast on Albyn's seer;                         565
A man, the most upright and true,
That e'er our sinful nation knew:
Whose warmest prayers, and highest zeal,
Are all for Scotland's worth and weal.
Where he is gone, I can't divine,                       570
But for this truth the pledge be mine
Of word and honour, that the saint
On scheme for our behoof is bent.
Either on secret mission sped
To Christian prince for timely aid,                     575
Or else in fasting day and night
Before his God, in piteous plight;
For all our sins imploring heaven

That they in mercy be forgiven;
And that this land, within whose bound                    580
The cross of Christ a rest hath found,
May 'scape this overwhelming snare,
And still be God's peculiar care.
      Nor deem this naught. In olden time,
In writings holy and sublime,                             585
Strong instances stand on record
Of times unnumbered, when the Lord,
At the requests of prophets rent
The floors of heaven, and succour sent.
      There stands one record, never lost,                590
Of Captain of the Lord's own host,
Who prayed on Gilgal's plain by night
Against the invading Amorite;
And lo! the heav'n's dark breast distended,
And from it's heideous folds descended                    595
Hailstones of such enormous frame,
Like broken pillars down they came,
Or fragments, splintered and uneven,
Of rocks shook from the hills of heaven.
Upon the Amorite's marshalled power                       600
Was cast down this appalling shower,
Till thousands of their proud array,
Deformed and shattered corses lay.
      Still God's dread work was but begun,
At man's behest he staid the sun                          605
Arrested, fixed in heaven he shone,
And the moon paused o'er Ajalon;
Until the arm of man had done
What arm of angel had begun.
Then let no sinner, old or young,                         610
Against a prophet wag his tongue,
Lest vengeance on his head befall,
And bring down wrath upon us all.
      At holy Samuel's sacrifice,
Fierce lightenings issued from the skies,                 615
In streams so rapid and so dire,
The firmament seemed all on fire.
And then such thunders rolled abroad
As ne'er burst from the throne of God;
Till Mispeh hill, in terrors wild,                        620

Rocked like the cradle of a child,
Then yawned, and swallowed quick to hell
The enemies of Israel.
The remnant turned and fled away,
In utter horror and dismay; 625
Without a blow they were cut down,
And all their country overthrown.—
There is but one thing on the earth
I hold as unexcelled in worth;
It is (and who its scope may scan!) 630
The prayer of a righteous man.
And firmly as I trust in this,
That I've a spirit made for bliss,
I do, that this divine of ours
Is trusted by the heavenly powers." 635
  The lord of Sky sprung from his chair,
And, waving both his arms in air,
Thus said in loud impassioned twang,
"What boots this starched and stale harangue?
Has this old driveller of the Isle 640
Made canting monk of old Argyle?
If so, I boldly would suggest
To shun their counsel as a pest.
Who deems the chiefs of Albyn's reign
Of dogged churl can bear the chain, 645
Or stoop their lineage to disgrace?
Let bedesman keep to bedesman's place!
Stick to his bedework and his beads,
His crosiers and his canting creeds;
For should he more, or say I wis 650
That Donald Gorm is that, or this
Or small, or great, or weak, or strong,
Or meek, or proud, or right or wrong,
By the dread soul of Selma's king,
The dotard from the rock I'll fling!" 655
The nobles answered with a smile,
And sided all with old Argyle.
  "But where is good Columba gone?
Why has he left the tottering throne
In time of trial and of wo?" 660
I hear thee ask, and thou must know,
Fair maiden patroness of mine,

As far as I of his design.
    That very night the truce was made,
After the saint his prayers had said,                    665
In lonely cell his couch he chose,
Not for the slumbers of repose,
But that no worldly listening ear
His communings with God might hear;
And there he hymns to Jesus sung,                    670
Till utterance died upon his tongue,
And sleep her genial unguent shed
Soft round the good man's hoary head.
Then all his visions were of bliss,
In other climes and worlds than this.                    675
    That night to him a vision came;
Like form of elemental flame,
That seemed some messenger of grace,
But yet it wore a human face,
With lineaments the saint had seen,                    680
But in what land he could not ween.
"Dost thou remember me?" It said.
Columba raised his reverend head,
And sore his memory did strain
At recollection, but invain.                    685
But the bright shadow, he could see,
Some semblage bore of royalty.
    The phantom form of lambent flame
Waited a while then nigher came,
And said, with deep and hollow moan,                    690
In sorrow's most subduing tone,
"Wo's me, that thou remember'st not
Thy early friend! and hast forgot
That once to him thou vow'd'st a vow.
'Twas for a child.—Where is he now?                    695
The first of Albyn's race supreme
Thou first baptized in Jesus name.—
Where is he now? Thou must him find;
For he of all the human kind
Is rightful heir, and he alone                    700
To Caledonia's ancient throne,
In which 'tis destined he must reign,
Else it is lost to Albyn's line.
Think of my words; the time is now;

Sacred and solemn was thy vow.                         705
If he appears not on this coast,
The nation's liberty is lost."–
   "Yes I remember word and time,"
Columba said, in tone sublime;
"And sacred vow I made to thee,                         710
And straight performed that vow shall be.
My early friend! And art thou come,
From thy far off eternal home,
To warn me of the times to be,
And of thy people's destiny?                            715
I'll treasure up thy words and go,
And do what arm of flesh can do
To bring that prince back to the land
Where he is destined to command.
To keep that vow I'll not decline;                      720
But say, my friend, what fate is thine?
Where hast thou sojourned since thy death?
In heaven above, or hell beneath?
Oft have I dared of God to crave
Some tidings from beyond the grave;                     725
Now they are come. For love of heaven,
Be this unto thy servant given.
Tell me of all that thou hast seen
In heaven, or hell, or place between!"
   "No!" said the spirit, raising high            730
His brow sublime, with kindling eye,
And shaking locks that streamed as bright
As the first rays of morning light–
"No!–Who to mortal thing would send
Tidings he cannot comprehend?                           735
When once the bourn of death is passed,
A veil o'er all beyond is cast,
That future things concealed may lie,
Hid from the glance of sinful eye;
For mortal tongue may never name,                       740
Nor human soul presume to frame,
The scenes beyond the grave that lie
In shadows of Eternity.
Concealment suits thy being best.
Then O in darkness let them rest!                       745
When thou and I shall meet again,

Whether in land of living pain,
Or in the vales above the sky,
Then thou shalt know as much as I."
    Columba, listening, paused in dread;      750
He looked again, the form was fled!
'Twas that of christian Conran gone,
Who once had sat on Albyn's throne.
A king of mighty name was he,
And famed for grace and piety.      755
He died.  His brother seized his crown;
Eugene, a king of great renown,
And left it, as before defined,
Unto his daughter, lovely Hynde.
When Conran died, Columba then      760
Bore his young son across the main,
As he had sworn, with pious breath,
To Conran on his bed of death;
And gave the infant to the hand
Of Colmar, King of Erin's land.      765
    That king, who ruled a people wild,
Was grandsire to the comely child;
And trained that stem of Royal name
To every thing a prince became;
With fixed resolve, at his own death,      770
To him his kingdom to bequeath.
Thus both the realms contented were,
With laws, with government, and heir;
And good Columba thought no more
Of vow that exile to restore;      775
For peace he cherished—peace alone—
'Mong all who bowed at Jesus' throne.
    But now this message from the dead,
New light upon the future shed;
It was a dream; but it was truth;      780
A vow had issued from his mouth,
A sacred vow that child to guard,
And use his influence revered,
Again to bring him to his own
And father's long descended crown.      785
    Columba rose at midnight deep,
And roused his followers from their sleep,
Sailors and monks, a motely corps,

And straight they hastened to the shore,
Upheaved the anchor silently, 790
Unfurled the sails, and put to sea;
"For Erin straight," Columba cried,
"At Colmar's court, whate'er betide,
I needs must be without delay.
No time be lost!—speed we away!"— 795
His word was law; the vessel flew
Across the waters, waving blue,
With her dark sails, and darker train,
Like mournful meteor of the main.
Albyn's apostle's fervent pray'r 800
With heaven prevailed; the winds were fair.
These, with the tides, and billows prone,
Seemed all combined to bear her on.
With swiftness of the soaring swan,
She foamed, she murmured, and she ran, 805
Till safe within Temora bay,
Like thing outworn, she leaning lay.
    King Colmar, at an early hour,
Was looking from his topmost tower,
And saw the bark before the gale, 810
Speeding her course with oar and sail.
"This visit bodes no good," said he.
"What brings these truant monks to me?
Either they come for some supply
To their new founded sanctuary, 815
Or warlike force, to cross the main,
And prop their young usurper's reign.
They shall have neither, by yon sun!
Small good to Erin have they done.
For though this father bears a name 820
Of sanctitude and reverend fame,
I've always found that horde a pest,
An ulcer, and a hornet's nest.
Their cause is lost ere they appear;
I'm quite in mood their suit to hear." 825
    Columba came—his message said—
Old Colmar smiled, and shook his head.
"The Prince," said he, "is far from this,
Fighting my enemies and his.
But as well might you ask of me 830

My crown and kingdom seriously.
Whom have I now my foes to quell?
Or tame my subjects that rebel?
Or who at last my crown to wear
But he, my kinsman and my heir?"—                   835
    "O, King of Erin, hear me speak,
And see the tears on my wan cheek.
I seek the prince, his own to gain;
In Albyn he's the right to reign.
And well thou know'st I made a vow              840
Ere I consigned the child to you,
All my poor influence to strain
To bring him to his own domain.
Now, such the crisis on our coast,
There's not one instant to be lost.               845
The powerful Eric of the north
Has drawn his heathen myriads forth,
Who, at this moment, lie around
Old Beregonium's sacred ground.
He beat our warriors on the coast,               850
And braves them as a nerveless host,
Threatening their force to overgo,
And lay the towers of Selma low
Unless he's granted, without frown,
To wed their queen and wear their crown.         855
A transient truce is signed and sealed,
Till adverse champions, on the field
Shall meet, and strive in mortal game,
Each for his own and country's fame;
And whosoe'er the victory gains                  860
Wins Albyn's queen and her domains."
    Old Colmar paused and turned him round,
His dim eye fixed upon the ground,
And thrice he stroked his bearded chin,
While voices murmured him within.                865
His face was like a winter eve,
When clouds arise and billows heave,
And hinds look to the western skies,
Uncertain where the storm shall rise,
Or whether, mixing with the main,                870
It may not all subside again.
    So stood the king, with ardor fraught,

The model of suspence and thought;
Then crossed his arms upon his breast,
And thus the yearning sire addressed. 875
"Now by my father's sword and sheild,
If this be true thou hast revealed,
The prize hath in its scope a charm
That well befits a hero's arm.
There was a day, but it is past, 880
When this arm had not been the last
In such a high and martial play;
Though it had led my steps away
Through flood and fire, o'er shore and main,
To wastes beneath the polar wain, 885
Or lands that warrior never won
Beyond the rising of the sun.
Gods how the high and glorious theme
Lights this old heart with living flame!
　　"For some few days remain with me, 890
And as thou lists thy cheer shall be.
Of wine and feasting have thy fill;
But if perchance it be thy will
To fast and pray; by heaven I'll not
Baulk such devotion–Not a jot! 895
With prince and nobles of my court
I must have speech of high import,
Of your demand; and then expect
An answer downright and direct."
　　"O sovereign liege, great is the need 900
For answer most direct indeed:
Else, ere we reach the Scottish shore,
The eventful combat may be o'er,
And I had message from the grave,
That he alone our land could save." 905
　　"What? From the grave? Pray thee relate
How–Where–And why this fact so late?
Came there a voice direct from God?
Or came it oozing through the sod
Where purple flowrets weep and bloom 910
Above the warrior's bloody tomb?
Say was it so? For if it came
From grave of monk 'tis scarce the same."
　　"'Twas in a dream the spirit spoke–"

"Ha? In a dream? 'Tis all a joke!                    915
I've had such dreams—such visions seen
But what an ideot I had been
If I had dared on them rely!
But had'st thou seen, as oft have I,
Thy father's soul rise in his shroud,                920
From out the waste like livid cloud,
In awful guise without control
To wax, and wane, and writhe, and roll;
Approaching thee like giant grim,
With locks of mist and eyeballs dim;                 925
And while the hairs crept on thy head,
And all thy frame shook like a reed,
If thou had'st heard a language run
Into thy soul as I have done,
Then had I deemed thy message sent                   930
By some great power benificent,
That rules around, above, below,
One whom I dread but do not know.
But as it is—It goes for nought.
I hope I hold it as I ought."                        935
    King Colmar turned him round, and left
The seer well nigh of hope bereft,
Grieving with tears for Albyn's fate,
Her destiny, and perilous state.
But leave we him, by rock and wood                   940
To kneel, and pray, and kiss the rood,
And follow Colmar to his hall,
Where stood the prince and nobles all.
    He told them all full sullenly.
Prince Eiden danced in youthful glee                 945
And shouted till the armour rung
Against the wall, and sounding swung.
"Come let us go. Come my Cuithone,
And Parlan, put your armour on;
If men on earth can beat us three,                   950
Mightier than mortals they must be.
My heart is burning in my breast
To meet King Eric in the list;
Yes, brand to brand, and face to face—
Down goes the boast of Odin's race!                  955
Come let us haste;  the time is near,

For sake of all to warriors dear!"
    King Colmar's lip with anger dumb
Stiffened beneath his toothless gum;
And his white eye-brows scowled as deep          960
As snow-cloud o'er the wintery steep,
As up he strode to Eiden's eye,
Shaking his palsied hand on high.
"Thou babbler's brood of bounce and bang!
Thou lion's cub without the fang!                965
Think'st thou thy weetless warrior rage
Can be endured by sober age,
Well versed in deep affairs of state,
And by experience made sedate?
I tell thee prince, in speech downright,         970
One foot thou goest not from my sight,
On such a raffle made for fools,
The lowest of ambition's tools.
    Dost thou not see tis all intrigue?
A cursed and formidable league,                  975
To wile thee hence and take thy life,
On wild pretence of warrior strife?
There is no lord in Caledon
Who does not hope to fill thy throne,
And from high interest sure to be                980
Thy sworn and mortal enemy.
    Then go not to that fatal strand;
Nor leave thy old protector's hand,
Who has no hope but in thy sway,
Nor comfort when thou art away.                  985
Were it to fight our common foe,
As prince of Erin thou should'st go,
With such an army in thy rear
That force or guile I should not fear.
But to this game of fools to go,                 990
And combat with thou know'st not who;
I make a vow was never broke,
A promise that I'll not revoke,
By the great spirit I adore,
One foot thou mov'st not from this shore."       995
    The prince a low obeisance made,
But his fair face was flushed with red;
Which Colmar saw, and still his ire

The hotter blazed like spreading fire,
And sore he threatened in his rage                    1000
To chain the prince in iron cage,
Rather than suffer him to roam
Blustering about another home,
And raving of a thing so low,
A war of pedantry and show.                           1005
    Straight to the seer then Colmar went,
Part of his jealousy to vent;
And neither sanctity of name,
Nor mein revered, could ward the same.
He told him roundly he was sent                       1010
On base intrigue; to circumvent
The prince's progress to the throne,
And cut him off by guile alone.
Then talked in haughtiness and wrath,
Of renegades from ancient faith;                      1015
Who, maugre all their humble airs,
Were ne'er to trust in state affairs.
    Columba smiled, and with an eye
That shone through tears, said fervently.
"O Sire withold thy rash resolve,                     1020
And make no vow thou can'st not dissolve;
Say nought thy saviour to agrieve.
In him dost thou not yet believe?"
    "No, not one jot!" king Colmar said,
"I worship, as my fathers did,                        1025
The king of heaven armipotent,
And yon bright sun his vicegerent;
And when HE hides his face from me,
I kneel beneath the green oak tree.
But thou hast made the prince a fool                  1030
By the weak tenets of thy school,
All founded on a woman's words,
Which ill with sovereignty accords.
I'll none of them! And, once for all,
Leave thou my shore, lest worse befal.                1035
Nor ask thou that which is not fit;
To see the prince I'll not permit;
And if thou art not under weigh
Before the noontide of the day,
Perhaps a bed and sleep thou'lt find                  1040

Ill suiting thy ambitious mind."
   Columba for forgiveness prayed
On the old heathen's hoary head,
Then fled his fierce and angry glance,
Groaning in heart for the mischance                    1045
That thus of hope his soul bereft,
And Albyn to destruction left.
   The sable bark went out to sea
Lashing and leaning to the lee;
But northward when she turned her prow,               1050
She met the tide in adverse flow;
And the north breeze, in boastful sough,
Told them in language plain enough,
That all their force of sail and oar
Would fail in making Albyn's shore.                    1055
   To brave the king they had no mind,
But northward toiled against the wind
Till midnight, then at change of tide,
To a small creek they turned aside.
Of sailor monks there were but few;                    1060
And the dull lazy rower crew
Declared no farther they could wend,
Though that should prove their journey's end.
   Unless in time of utmost need,
Columba held it high misdeed                           1065
To weary heaven with earnest suit.
But danger now, and want to boot,
Obliged him humbly to apply
To his kind maker, presently
Help to afford, by tides or wind,                      1070
Or by the hand of human kind.

The vol. 3ᵈ for continuation

# Continuation of Book 3ᵈ

   The creek was all retired and bare;
Nor hamlet, hall, nor cot, was there,
Yet one approaching they could see,
Ere the good man rose from his knee.                   1075
Down from the cliff the being strode,

Like angel sent direct from God,
To guide the father and his train
Back to their home amid the main.
    The sun had just begun to flame        1080
Above the coast of Cunninghame,
When this strange guest, with caution drew
Toward our cowled and motely crew.
His step was firm, his stature tall;
Cunning and strength, combined with all       1085
The rudeness of the savage kern,
Kithed in his heideous face altern.
His feet were sandalled, and his coat
Made of the hide of mountain goat.
His dark locks, matted and unshorn,        1090
Had ne'er been combed since he was born;
A russet plaid hung to his knee
In sooth a fearful wight was he.
    Few were his words, when words were said;
But ah! his looks compensement made;      1095
Where terror, wonder, fierceness, rose
By turns, on youthful face morose.
The monks at times upon him smiled,
Then trembled at his gestures wild.
    Columba wist not what to do;        1100
To ask his aid, or let him go.
He saw his followers ill inclined
Towards the rude uncourtly hind;
And some even whispered in his ear,
He was some fiend of other sphere.        1105
Still he at such a time was given,
Just while imploring aid from heaven,
The sire concieved, that duty pressed
Some further knowledge of his guest.
    He called him in before his face.       1110
The youth advanced with giant pace;
While his elf-locks, of dew to dry,
He wildly shook above his eye;
Folded his rude plaid o'er his knee;
Looked at his leg of symmetry;        1115
Next at his sword that trailed behind,
An oaken club without the rhynde;
Then stood in half averted way,

To listen what the sire would say.
    He told his name, his age, his wit;      1120
And all for which his strength was fit.
But in such terms, the sire was moved
To mirth, which ill his frame behoved.
M,Houston was the varlet's name;
He could not say from whence he came,      1125
But he was born beyond the sea,
And there again he longed to be.
"What sea?" was asked. He looked askance;
And O what pride was in his glance,
As he returned in giggling tone.      1130
"Who ever heard of sea but one?"
O he could row, and he could sail;
And guide the rudder in the gale;
And he could make the vessel glide
Wriggling against the wind and tide.      1135
By his own tale, he was such man
As ne'er from jib to rudder ran;
But all their proffers of reward
He scorned, and held of no regard,
Till once they mentioned warrior brand,      1140
When they arrived on Scotia's strand.
Then kindled the barbarian's eye,
He flew on board with rapturous cry;
And from his side his club he flung,
That in the fold of mantle swung,      1145
Like sheathed sword. Then, with a shock,
He wrenched the hawser from the rock,
And ere the monkish crew had time
The virgin's sacred name to chime,
The bark had rocked upon her keel,      1150
And from the beech began to heel.
    "Do this!–Do that!" the savage roared.
And, heaving high his oaken sword,
He threatened sore, with growl and frown,
Whoe'er refused to cleave him down.      1155
The crew at first began to wink,
And from their posts assayed to shrink,
But blows from tall M,Houston's tree
Made them apply most strenuously.
Close by the helm his post he took;      1160

All shrunk from his offended look;
Whene'er he deigned to sing, or speak,
A smile would dimple rower's cheek,
But yet so gruffly and so grim,
It showed how much they dreaded him.                    1165
For lazier train no leader knew
Than good Columba's sailor crew.

    M,Houston by the helm stood fast,
And oft upon the sky he cast
A troubled look, and then again                          1170
Would fix it on the heaving main;
Then shake his black and matted hair,
And sing aloud some savage air.

    At length he said, with careless joke,
And aye he stuttered as he spoke.                        1175
"My masters we shall have a gale;
Stand by the beam, and reef the sail;
And he who fails, or handles slack,
Here's for the dastard vassal's back.

    Where art thou gone thou angry sun?      1180
What crime hath poor M,Houston done,
That thus thou hid'st thy radiant form
Behind the darkness of the storm,
And leav'st thy servant to the sway
Of tempest on his wildered way?                          1185
No friend in whom he can confide;
No little star his path to guide;
No parent dear to say adieu.
Such poor M,Houston never knew!
Nothing but weak and feeble men,                         1190
Some darksome slaves from downward den.
But if O Sun thy will it be,
I'll sacrifice them all to thee,
If thou thy servant's life wilt save
From bursting cloud and breaking wave.                   1195
Or show thy glorious face above,
If these are objects of thy love."

    By chance, the words were scarcely spoke,
When through the louring darkness broke
A ray of sunshine wanly bright,                          1200
A transient gleam of livid light,
Like the last smile from beauty's eye,

Resigned, and laid in peace to die;
That farewell glance, of smile and shiver,
Ere darkness seals the orb for ever.            1205
So passed the sun-beam o'er the deck;
The savage then, with due respect,
Kneeled down and bowed his matted head,
Then looked around with awful dread.
    "Now friends," he cried "for friends we are;   1210
For toil, or death, let all prepare.
See where the hurricane comes on
With violence dreadful and unknown.
The western world is in commotion;
See how the clouds oppress the ocean;          1215
And ocean, into vengeance driven,
With foamy billow scourges heaven.
Our bark will prove before it's swing
Like fern upon the whirlwind's wing.
Wake the old carl you call the seer,           1220
And ask him whereto we shall steer.
For toward sunrise we must fly,
With stern right in the tempest's eye;
A weather shore we needs must make,
It is our last, our only stake."               1225
    They ran the holy man to warn,
And told him of the hedious kern,
That prayed to heathen deity,
And brought the storm along the sea;
And every monk, in language strong,            1230
Declared the arch-fiend them among.
    Columba left his books and prayer,
With something of a timid air,
And moved his head above the deck,
Just as the masts began to creak.              1235
He cast his eye before, behind;
Then cried, with troubled voice and mind,
"To Isla sound, then we're at home."
And pointed out the path of foam.
    " 'Twould be as wise to gaze and ponder    1240
Upon the sky, and point us yonder."
The savage said "but here is land,
Which we might win if you command."
To east by south he turned her prow;

The rattling hail and pelting snow,                     1245
Just then in furious guise began;
Loud gusts along the ocean ran;
And every sob the tempest gave
Spoke language of a watery grave.
        "Stand by the beam, the main-sail under,"    1250
M,Houston cried, in voice of thunder.
"Pull in—Let go—You dastard knaves!
Down with your beads into the waves.
If cross, or bead, I note again,
I'll hurl the holder in the main.                       1255
O, king of heaven! such furious storm,
Did ne'er the ocean's breast deform!"
        The bark flew on before the wind,
So like a thing of soul and mind,
It made the savage shout with glee.                     1260
"There goes the jewel of the sea!
Speed on! speed on, my bonny bark!
Behind the storm is rolling dark;
But if such glorious speed thou mak'st,
Swift is the storm thee overtak'st.                     1265
O, speed thou on, thou blessed thing,
Swift as the solan on the wing!
And if behind yon headland blue,
Safely thou bear'st this feind-like crew,
Then poor M,Houston, on his knee,                       1270
Shall offer sacrifice to thee;
For God's own blessed oak I know,
His only emblem here below."
        The monks quaked like the aspin slim,
And their dark looks grew deadly dim;                   1275
They deemed each wave would them o'erwhelm.
With savage heathen at the helm,
Or fiend arrived from burning hell!
Their woful plight what tongue could tell?
        Yet still the bark her speed did strain,        1280
For better never plowed the main;
Till at the last, amid the roar
Of waves behind, and waves before,
By cataract and swell o'erthrown,
Adown she went with clash and groan.                    1285
        "Hold by the cords—" M,Houston yelled.

(Gods how the monks and rowers held!)
"To see the bottom of the main
We but descend to rise again."
Down went the bark, with stern upright,                    1290
Down many fathoms from the light.
As sea-bird, mid the breakers tossed,
Screaming and fluttering off the coast,
Dives from the surf of belch and foam,
To seek a milder calmer home,                              1295
So sought the bark her downward way,
From meeting waves and mounting spray.
      "Hold by the cords!" M,Houston called.
The monks obeyed, full sore appalled.
Here rose a groan, and there a scream,                     1300
As down they bore into the stream;
But these were stiffled in the brine,
As dived the sable brigandine;
And all was silent, save the gull
That mounted from the stormy mull.                         1305
      'Twas but a trice of lash and lave,
Till, on the top of mountain wave
The bark appeared with flapping sail,
And dripping monks, and rowers pale,
Hanging on ropes all here and there,                       1310
Deaf, blind, and blurting with despair.
Again they heard M,Houston's tongue,
As loud he hollo'd out and sung,
"Stand to your tackle manfully;
Hold fast, and leave the rest to me!"                      1315
      Again the waves rolled o'er the deck;
But, be it told with due respect,
At this dire moment, who should call
From ridge of wave and tossing fall,
But the good seer! Not seen till now;                      1320
Washed from his hold, they knew not how,
Blinded with cowl of many a fold,
And wildly capering as he rolled.
M,Houston caught him by the frock,
And held him stedfast as a rock;                           1325
Yet not one moment quitted post,
Though fearfully 'mong breakers tossed,
Nor once turned round his eye, to scan

The plight of that most holy man,
But sung and shouted o'er the swell,                  1330
With maniac laugh and demon yell.
    He saw, what other's saw at last,
That all the danger was o'erpast;
For this turmoil, this uproar dire,
Was at the point of low Kintyre,                      1335
Where breaking waves, and stormy stir,
Still fright the coasting mariner.
Now were they breasting mountain steep;
Now plunging 'mid the foamy deep;
Anon they wheeled from out the roar,                  1340
And swept along a weather shore,
Beneath the bank of brake and tree,
Upon a smooth and tranquil sea.
    Columba stared in dread amaze;
The pallid monks returned the gaze.                   1345
For he whose tall and giant form
Seem'd late the demon of the storm,
They now weened angel in disguise,
Sent down, to save them, from the skies;
And knew not how their guest to greet,                1350
Or if to worship at his feet.
    "Who *art* thou?" said Columba then.
"Thou best of angels or of men!
For if commissioned from above,
By the dear Saviour whom I love,                      1355
As guardian spirit of the sea,
I'll kneel and pay my vows to thee."
    The savage laughed with such good will,
That eagles answered on the hill,
Sailed on the bosom of the cloud,                     1360
And neighed as fiercely and as loud.
    "Ha? Worship me? That would be brave!
A homeless vagrant and a slave.
Worship the sun; whose glorious road
Along'st the heaven was never trode;                  1365
Who frowns, and men are in distress;
Who smiles, and all is loveliness!
But if of better god you know,
In heaven above, or earth below,
Or seraph, saint, or demon grim,                      1370

Tell me, and I will worship him."–
    The holy sire, to tears constrained,
The doctrine of the cross explained:
The fall–The covenant above;
And wonders of redeeming love. 1375
M,Houston listened silently,
His dark locks trembling o'er his eye,
Then said, It was his good belief
That Jesus was a noble chief;
For none could more for vassals' good, 1380
Than for their sakes to shed his blood;
And for that cause, it was his mind
To follow prince so brave and kind.
    "But yet the sun of heaven," said he,
"Has been benignant god to me. 1385
'Twas he who reared the roe-deer's brood,
And the young bristler of the wood;
The sprightly fawn, with dappled sides,
And leveret in the fern that hides;
The kid, so playful and so spruce; 1390
And all for poor M,Houston's use.
'Tis he that makes the well to spring,
The dew to fall, the bird to sing;
And gives the berry of the waste
It's ripeness, and it's savoury taste. 1395
Oft with the rook and crow I've striven
For that delicious gift of heaven;
Not elsewhere knowing, when I first
Could quench my hunger or my thirst.
    'Tis he that rears the racy pea, 1400
And spreads the crowfoot on the lea,
And makes the holy acorn grow,
The highest gift to man below.
'Tis he that mars the summer's prime,
The rabid storm, and wreathy rime, 1405
Makes seas to roll, and rivers run.
M,Houston still must *love* the sun!"–
    Columba answered with a sigh
To that barbarian's language high;
And wondered at his strength of mind, 1410
In such low rank of human kind,
That, like his frame, seemed thing elate,

Far o'er the peasant's lowly state.
Thence he resolved to win the youth
Unto the holy christian truth.                                    1415
When, in Dalrudhain's lonely bay,
They rendered thanks to God that day,
Than he, none showed more humble frame,
Nor lowlier bowed at Jesus' name.
    Loud and more loud the tempest blew;          1420
On high the fleeting lightenings flew;
The rain and sleet poured down so fierce,
As if the concave universe
Had been upset, or rolled awry,
And oceans tumbled from the sky;                                  1425
The heaven was swathed in sheets of gray,
And thunders gallowed far away.
    The seer impatient to proceed
Knowing his virgin sovereign's need,
Bade up that narrow firth to wend,                                1430
(Now called Loch-Fyne) unto its end;
Resolved to cross the mountains dark,
And leave the sailors with the bark.
For a long night and stormy day,
They sailed that long and narrow bay;                             1435
And the next day, at dawn of morn,
Mounted the pathless wastes of Lorn.
    Columba and the savage rude
Entered alone that solitude;
For now he so admired the wight,                                  1440
He scarce could bear him from his sight.
A dangerous path they had to scan,
For every petty torrent ran
Pelting and foaming furiously,
As if to say, "Who dares come nigh?"                              1445
Then proved the kern a trusty guide,
And many a time his strength was tried,
O'er rugged steep, and rapid river,
Bearing the old man safely ever.
    But when to Orchay's vale they came,        1450
So mighty was that moorland stream,
'Twas like an ocean rolling on,
Resistless, dreadful, and alone!
It's path with desolation traced,

The valley all one watery waste, 1455
One foamy wave, thundering and smoking,
And mighty pines rending and rocking.
   Columba gazed upon the scene
So wild, terrific, and immane,
Until his lip grew pale as clay. 1460
Said he, "I've journeyed many a day,
From hill of Zion to the shore
Beyond which there is land no more;
But never looked, in all my time,
On aught so marvellous and sublime. 1465
That day the storm was at it's height,
Was trial 'twixt the wrong and right;
The wrong has triumphed, now I know,
And Albyn's rights are lying low.
Her chosen chiefs are fallen and gone; 1470
For it was destined, one alone
Could save the land that fateful day,
And he was kept by heaven away.
It's will be done, for well or wo!
We now must bend before the foe; 1475
The Christian banner's in the toil,
The heathen riots in our spoil.
   I may be wrong, as grant I may;
But it is plain, that on that day
The storm hath all unequalled been, 1480
Such as no living man hath seen.
These are the signs of sinful deed,
And these are tokens that I dread.
The demons of the fiery reign
Have been abroad in Christ's domain, 1485
Roused, by some powerful heathen spell,
From out the lurid vales of hell,
The face of earth and heaven to mar,
And hurl the elements in war.
   But note me youth. The time will come 1490
That men shall stand, in terror dumb,
And see the Almighty's arm of power
Stretched forth in the avenging hour.
Yes HE will show to heaven, and hell,
And all that in the earth do dwell, 1495
From babe, to prince upon the throne,

That HE is God and HE alone!"–
    But trust not all that prophets say;
The best may err, and so may they.
Predictions are but ticklish gear,             1500
Though specious, logical, and clear,
Condensed, and penned in language strong,
Where once aright, they're ten times wrong.
This sage experience hath me taught,
Whilest thou hast hooted, railed, and laughed.   1505
Alak! the credit due to seers,
Too well is known to my compeers!
    Our travellers gained the farther shore
Of dark Loch-Ow, by dint of oar;
And there the tidings met their ear,          1510
Of deeds of darkness, and of weir,
Which made the holy father weep,
And the rude boor to laugh and leap,
And shout with joy, and clamour vast,
"M,Houston finds a home at last!          1515
A vagrant outcast though he be,
This is the land he loves to see!"
    By Connel's tide they journeyed then,
And met whole multitudes of men;
Some fleeing to the forest land,          1520
Some guarding firm, with sword in hand,
Each path, and ford, that lay between
Their fierce invaders and their queen.
For much had hap'd, that I must tell,
And you must read, if you do well.          1525


End of Book The Third

# Queen Hynde

## Book Fourth

O fain would I borrow the harp of that land
Where the dark sullen eagle broods over the strand,
Afar in his correi where shrub never grew;–
Or mounts on bold pinion away from the view,
On beams of the morning to journey alone,       5
And peal his loud matin where echos are none.
The harp of that region of storm and of calm,
To mount with the eagle, or sport with the lamb;
To warble in sunshine; in discord to jar,
And roar in the tempest of nature or war.       10
Of that have I need, and but that I'll have none,
To sound the memorial of old Beregon.
    The city is crouded, each alley, and hall;
Loud rattle's the scabbard on pavement and wall.
The bow and broad arrow of Scythia are there,       15
And files of bright lances gleam high in the air;
They flash and they flicker, so dazzling, and high,
Like streamers of steel on the fields of the sky;
But nigher survey them, how deep is their stain!
That redness is not with the drops of the rain;       20
Proud badges of battle depart they must never–
But there as memorials fester for ever.
Our clans and the Norse-men, nor beckon, nor smile,
As file meets with column, and column with file;
Yet still there was bustle by night and by day;       25
And ne'er were the maids of green Albyn so gay;
But many a sad mother to heaven appeals;
And from the old warrior the groan often steals,
As from his high turrets he sees with despair
The Black Bull of Norroway pawing the air.       30
Queen Hynde waits the issue submissive and dumb;
And noble king Eric with love is o'ercome.
    King Eric came over a conqueror proved;
A kingdom he wanted, a kingdom beloved;
The queen was an item he did not imply,       35

But the conqueror fell at the glance of her eye.
His proffer was made as a lure to the land,
For woman he loved not, nor woman's command;
The name of a hero was all his delight;
His sword was a meteor unmatched in the fight;                40
The north he had conquered, and governed the whole
From Dwina's dark flood to the waves of the pole;
And ne'er in his course had he vanquished been,
Till now, by a young Caledonian Queen.
But thou, gentle maiden, to whom I appeal,                    45
Who never hast felt, what thou could'st not conceal,
Love's dearest remembrance, that brought with the sigh
The stound to the heart, and the tear to the eye;
Oh ill can'st thou judge of the mighty turmoil
In the warrior's bosom thus caught in the toil.              50
     For the queen kept the words of her father in view,
Who charged, that, in secret, no lover should sue;
And therefore bold Eric was still kept at bay,
For all his impatience, and all he could say;
And this was his answer both early and late.                 55
"The time is at hand that determines my fate;
Then he whose arm in battle is strongest,
Whose shield is broadest, or falchion longest,
And twice in the lists shall win the day,
I am his to claim and carry away.                            60
But till that day all suit is vain;
In strick retirement I remain."
     Ah princely Haco, wo for thee!
What hop'st thou round these towers to see?
Which still thou circlest morn and even,                     65
With cheek and eye upturned to heaven;
Or rather to each casement high
In Selma's towers for answering eye.
And thou hast seen it, though at more
Than fifty fathoms from the shore;                           70
And who can eye of maiden fair
Read, more than halfway up the air?
The glance of love, the blushing hue,
Are lost amid the hazy blue,
But other signs—As, snowy veil                               75
Reared high aloft like streamer pale;
A helmet waved in queenly hand;

A dazzling glance from gilded brand,
Whose point is turned north away
Where Eric's camp like city lay. 80
    These signals boded nothing good,
And scarce could be misunderstood.
A thousand times prince Haco bowed,
And humblest gratitude avowed;
He kissed his hand, then kneeled profound, 85
And thrust his sword's point in the ground
In homage to that virgin queen,
For such he deemed capricious Wene,
And *she* it was. But what she knew
That thus such signals out she threw; 90
Or if 'twas all a freakish jest,
Nor friend, nor foeman ever wist.
    But as it was, it gave the alarm
Unto the prince to watch and arm.
His was a brave and goodly train, 95
The pride of Norway's stormy reign;
All youths on fame and honour bent;
And all of noble proud descent;
Who the high heir of Eric's crown,
As path to fortune and renown, 100
Had followed with supreme good will,
Claiming the post of honour still;
And, sooth, a comelier warrior train
Ne'er mounted wave of northern main.
    To these he said, in secret guise, 105
With looks profound and shrewdly wise,
"I dread these coward Scots for ill;
There has been bustling on that hill,
As if some treachery were designed,
Or some misprision in the wind; 110
Scouts have been running up and down,
From town to camp, from camp to town."
( For an encampment strong and high
The Scots had formed on Valon-Righ. )
" 'Tis meet that we should arm and watch, 115
Such violators first to catch,
If such there be. If I am wrong,
Our silent watch will not be long;
While, should we baulk some foul surprise,

Our fame to Odin's throne will rise."          120
His warriors armed with youthful pride;
But laughed full mirthfully aside;
And wondered where their gallant prince
Caught such enormous sapience.
    Meantime the troops of various climes          125
Met in the city lanes betimes;
And there they crouded, trading, bustling
Till eventide, full rudely justling.
They met, they scowled, then rushing mingled,
While their rude weapons jarred and jingled.          130
Few words were changed for ill or good;
For why? they were not understood;
But many brazen looks said plain.
"Friend, you and I may meet again!"
    In short, throughout each highland clan,          135
A spirit most indignant ran.
They could not brook their foes to see
Parade their streets unawed and free;
And from their cliff-borne camp they viewed
The march of these barbarians rude,          140
Beneath their feet from day to day,
Like tygers growling o'er their prey.
    Nor wanted there, the chiefs among,
Some fiery heads, that, right or wrong,
Would blow this breeze into a storm.          145
First of these fiends was Donald Gorm,
Whose spirit, like the waves that roar
For ever on his stormy shore,
Was ne'er at ease by night or day,
But restless and perturb'd as they.          150
Among the clansmen of his name
Revenge was his perpetual theme,
Until so fierce his fury burned,
His sovereign's faith aside was spurned;
And, if to join him there was none,          155
He'd break the truce and fight alone.
    "We'll go," said Donald, "in the night,
And seize this king of boasted might;
And first we'll bind *him* heel to head,
And bear him to our rock with speed;          160
And then we'll turn, and kill, and kill,

And spoil, and ravage, at our will!
That cumberous host we well may dread,
With doughty Eric at its head;
But, rend that moving spring away, 165
And down it falls the spoiler's prey.
What boots it me, a maiden's vow?
Vouchsafed I see not why, nor how;
If Donald this atchievement grand
Performs by dint of sheild and brand, 170
He reigns the king of fair Scotland!"
"God bless the mark!" said every tongue,
And every sword on buckler rung.
    King Eric's camp was scanned with care,
For sundry spies went sauntering there. 175
But so it hap'd, that Haco's tent
Surpassed the king's in ornament.
The prince's proud batallions lay
Round his with streamers soaring gay,
And golden crests, and herald show; 180
So that the spies went to and fro
Staring aghast. Then back they sped,
And, with sagacity inbred,
Declared, and swore, with gaping wonder,
"That all the kings of the earth were yonder!" 185
    This was a prize, we may suppose,
Too rich for Donald Gorm to lose;
So straight was passed the order high,
That all the men of Mull, and Skye,
And Moidart too, themselves should dight 190
In arms at dead hour of the night,
And follow where their chief should lead
To enterprize of glorious meed.
    The harp had ceased in Selma's hall;
And from her towers, and turrets tall, 195
No glimmering torch or taper shone,
For they had died out one by one
Like fading stars, whose time was spent,
Above the airy firmament.
    Many a bard on Valon-Righ, 200
Had sung his song of victory
And gone to rest—or converse hold
With spirits of the bards of old.

The cymbal's clang, the bugle's swell,
The trumpet's blare, the bagpipe's yell,                205
Had ceased, and silence reigned alone
Around the skirts of Beregon;
Where thousands lay, stretched on the soil,
Panting for battle and for broil.
  But Donald Gorm had other scheme,                      210
Than thus on battle clang to dream;
He panted for the waking fight,
The blood and havock of the night;
The silent rush on prostrate foe;
The stroke, the stab, the overthrow;                     215
Their mortal terror, flight, and thrall,
And captive king—the best of all!
A thousand times, with grin and growl,
Did Donald curse the minstrel's howl;
Then rolled him on his russet floor,                     220
And railed against the lagging hour.
For every minute in its flight,
From evening till the noon of night,
Was fetter laid on Donald's might.
  The hour arrived, as hour must come                    225
To him that dreads it as his doom,
As well as they who for it long.
And Donald's men, in phalanx strong,
Moved from the cliff around the steep
With swiftness, and in silence deep.                     230
Then Haco's watcher by the tarn,
Straight ran his wonderous prince to warn;
And found him and his troop prepared,
Couched on their arms and keeping guard,
Hid in the heather and the brake,                        235
Along'st the road the Scots must take.
  Down came the Skye men like a torrent,
Foaming and muttering terms abhorrent;
Furious they came, with whirl and crush,
As midnight tides through narrows rush.                  240
Or, when the storm is at the sorest,
Like wild bulls rushing from the forest,
With grinding hoof, and clattering horn,
And hollow humming as in scorn,
So rushed this phalanx multiform,                        245

Led by the headlong Donald Gorm.
    The front bore on swift as the wind,
But Haco's gallants closed behind;
And Donald's rear, was levelled low,
As fast as blow could follow blow. 250
His front poured on from tent to tent,
And robbed and romaged as they went,
While those behind, without a blow,
Were chased and routed by the foe.
Right over ditch, and foss, and fen, 255
Was Donald borne by his own men;
For all his boast of warrior deed,
He neer got blow at foeman's head.
    O Donald Gorm, hard fate is thine!
Exposed to punishment condign. 260
The truce is broke; and thou hast lost
One fifth of all thy gallant host.
The daring deed thou canst not hide;
Thy kinsmen vanished from thy side,
And shame imprinted on thy brow. 265
Ha Donald Gorm! what think'st thou now?
    To morrow all will be in flame,
And only thou must bear the blame;
For thou hast dared, thy country's troth,
Thy sovereign's honour, and her oath 270
Thus rashly, rudely, to deface;
And all for nought but deep disgrace.
Over thy head there broods a storm
Will blast thy honours, Donald Gorm!
    But one thing yet thou dost not know; 275
Thou had'st to deal with generous foe,
Who sorrowed at thy rash ado,
A hero, and a lover too;
Who feared if once thy deed got wind,
The blame would fall on royal Hynde. 280
    When past was all the hasty fray,
And Donald Gorm thus chased away;
And not one son of Norway miss'd,
Excepting Odin's sacred priest,
Whom Donald's men had caught asleep, 285
And hurried off unto the steep,
They deem'd him chief of high command,

Some ancient lord of Scania's land.
When fled I say that headlong force,
Prince Haco called his counsellors.                    290
"My gallant friends" said he "I must
Rejoice to find in whom I trust.
This night you've shown, with courage true,
What youths of noble blood can do,
Have saved our sovereign's sacred life,                295
And crushed at once a dangerous strife.
Now, trust me, we'll more credit win
By hushing this with little din,
Than by ostent, and fulsome boast,
To break the truce with Albyn's host,                  300
And lose at once the glorious right
Of gaining all by heros' might.
By secret trust full well I know
The treachery bred with private foe,
That gave us chance thus to debel.                     305
This thing I know, but dare not tell.
     Then let us strip these savage slain,
And sink their bodies in the main;
And pass the whole with answer brief,
As enterprize of robber chief;                         310
A trivial thing, of no regard,
Unsuiting honours or reward."
Each gallant thought as Haco did,
Although his motives still were hid.
     The slain were heaped upon a team,                315
And in the sea, to sink or swim,
Their bodies hurled without delay,
And all was o'er by break of day.
Then such a stir arose at dawn;
Torrents of blood like rivers ran;                     320
But none could tell who was to blame,
Or whence the purple deluge came.
Amazement filled the Norway men,
They gathered round in thousands ten,
Until the king all patience lost,                      325
And called a muster of his host.
No one was missed in all the lists,
Save one of Odin's sacred priests!
     King Eric as a monarch brave,

Of priestcraft was the very slave; 330
This omen dire his soul oppress'd;
He caught the terror of the rest,
And orders gave, in sullen mood,
For sacrifice of human blood,
< To appease the mighty Odin's ire, 335
And Thor's, the gods of war, and fire;
Who thus had shown their gracious love,
By portent of the wrath above;
And caused, without a prayer or spell,
Rivers of blood from earth to well. > 340
    Haco was grieved; for in that rite
He had no comfort or delight;
And therefore told all that had pass'd
Unto the king from first to last;
But chiefly dwelt on signal, seen 345
From casement of the Scottish queen.
    Now hushed were Eric's false alarms;
He caught his nephew in his arms;
For his big heart impetuous strove
With throes of glory and of love; 350
And thrice he bless'd his hero young,
Who thus withheld the blabbing tongue
From telling of a deed of fame,
That added lustre to his name.
Then said, "No favour he could crave 355
That as reward he should not have."
    The prince of this laid hold, and said.
"My king and uncle, then I plead
That I to morrow be allowed
The honour and distinction proud, 360
Within the lists with thee to stand,
A champion for my native land.
And thou in Haco's deeds shalt trace
The might of Odin's heavenly race."
    The king nor frowned in sullen mood, 365
Nor tried his promise to elude.
Generous, as absolute in sway,
And downright as the light of day,
He all at once, in terms uncouth,
Reproved the madness of the youth. 370
    "Thou tendril of a rampant plant!

Dar'st thou to ask, or I to grant
A thing that throws from my right hand,
The glory of my native land?
What would my well-tried champions say          375
Were I to fling such prize away,
And all our soaring hopes destroy
For the wild frenzy of a boy?
Thy rath, fond aim full well I see;
Thou think'st the choice will fall on thee.     380
Dare not to raise such lofty looks;
Eric but ill a rival brooks;
And thus to sacrifice his all
He may not, and he never shall!"
        "My liege I had your sacred word,        385
Giv'n freely of your own accord;
I ween'd on that I might rely.
Can Odin's son his troth deny?
I claim it. And to morrow stand,
To win, or fall, at thy right hand.             390
Thy word is giv'n; if broke it be
By Thor, the breaker fights with me!"
        "Haco thou art a noble stem,
That well should brook the diadem.
My sacred word I must fulfil,                    395
Though grieveously against my will.
By one rash promise I am crossed,
And all my fame in battle lost.
How dare I in myself confide
With such a stripling by my side?               400
For should'st thou fall, or wounded be,
Farewell to Eric's victory!
But at the hour the heralds name,
Come, and the post of honour claim
As right of thy illustrious line.               405
My word is past, and it is thine."
        Turn we to Donald of the Isle,
In sad dilemma placed the while;
To censure subject, for th' abuse
Of sovereign's faith, and broken truce.         410
He kept his place in outer ward,
To fight with friend or foe prepared;
And much he wondered, when he saw

The armies mix, as if no flaw
Or breach of contract had been known.            415
Still Donald kept his hold alone,
Till Eric's muster roll was o'er,
And freedom reigned as theretofore.
    "'Tis strange" said Donald "should this breach
And foul defeat the throne not reach.             420
It would appear there is no blame
Attached to queen's or liegeman's name.
Therefore I judge it best, at once
The daring outrage to renounce;
And prove it, swear it, though they should,      425
Deny it all through fire and blood."
    "Dear master, know, your gallant men
Amid king Eric's camp lie slain."
    "There let them lie; I'll flatly swear
They are not mine, nor ever were."                430
    "Your clan is short. What will you say
When called out on the muster-day?"
    "I'll say the men of Mull are gone
To fetch supplies of venison;
To see their dames, and shun the strife;          435
And all have forfeited their life."
    "The priest of Odin in our thrall
Will broad disclosure make of all."
    "Were he the devil's priest arrayed,
One whom I more than Odin dread,                  440
I'd let him blood, and make his bed
Full fifty feet below my tread,
Rather than he should blab disgrace
On great M,Ola's royal race.
My fathers had one liberal form,                  445
Which stands unbroke by Donald Gorm;
It is, that neither old nor young,
Nor oath pronounced by human tongue,
Shall e'er a rest, or bearing, find
Between his honour and the wind.                   450
Come, and the secret thou shalt know
How the old dotard brooks the blow."
    The chief and bard together went
In to the priest, with foul intent.
The old man rested on the floor,                  455

With lip of scorn and look demure;
His ankles were by withe entwined;
His arms were crossed, and bound behind;
His grizly beard seemed scarce terrene,
It flowed like centaur's shaggy mane                    460
Far o'er his girdle crimosin,
And quivered to his palsied chin.
A portrait of majestic scorn,
Was that old heathen priest forlorn,
With eye fixed on his galling yoke,                     465
And leaning calmly to the rock.
    "Father full froward was the fate
That cast thee in this captive state."
Said Donald with affected grief
"But here comes one to bring relief;                    470
Since mighty Odin hides his face,
And there's no other eye of grace,
This is the boon thy god sends thee,
A thirsty brand to set thee free."—
        "Beware, thou sanguine, savage chief,            475
Slave to a new and fond belief!
Beware how thou upliftest sword,
Or utter'st rash or ruthless word
Against the lowest holy guide
To Odin's service sanctified.                           480
Know'st thou who measures mortal age?
Who loves the battle's lofty rage?
And riots mid the overthrow,
In wreaking vengeance on each foe?
Even HE whose servant for his sin                       485
Lies chained thy hateful power within.
Then be thou ware the crime eschew
Nor do a deed thou sore shalt rue."
    "Speak, Rimmon, bard of Turim's hall;
What think'st thou of this heathen's fall?"—            490
    "Thou lord of that romantic land,
The winged isle, of steep and strand;
And all the creeks of brake and fern,
Those pathless piles so dark and dern
That stretch from Sunart's sombre dell,                 495
To Duich's heights of moor and fell.
Thou stem of royal seed—nay, more,

Son of an hundred kings of yore!
Unto thy servant deign regard;
Wo to the chief that slights his bard! 500
    I've heard an adage in my time,
A simple old Milesian rhyme,
Which bore, that, whatsoever god
Was worship'd all the world abroad,
From him that reigns in heaven alone, 505
Unto the gods of wood and stone,
That, still among each erring crew
These gods should have a reverence due;
Because, in offering insult there,
A nation's feelings injured are; 510
And man's deep curse, when insults move
His sacred feelings to disprove,
Is next to that of God's above.
I say no more; but that I've found
These ancient sayings often sound"— 515
    Donald looked down with dark grimace,
And primm'd his mouth, and held his peace;
And rather seemed disposed to show
Relenting heart o'er prostrate foe.
But as imprudence in th' extreme, 520
Or dire mischance, (a gentler name,)
Suggested, the old priest began
To brave the spirit of the man;
And his o'erbearing pride defy,
By brief and threatening prophecy. 525
    " 'Tis known," said he, "o'er all the lands
Where Odin's heavenly sway expands,
That whosoever dares enthrall
The meanest guide unto his hall,
Or move a tongue his faith to upbraid, 530
Or hand against his sacred head,
That sinner's blood shall first be spilt
Of all his kindred's, for his guilt.
Therefore I dare the whole degrees
Of those who bow to oaken trees; 535
Or to the dazzling god of day;
Or moon that climbs the milky way;
Or to that god, mysterious, mild,
That died and lived, the virgin's child.

I dare you all, by curse unheard,      540
To wrong a hair of this grey beard;
Or down to Loke the caitiff goes,
The first of Odin's fated foes."—
    "So be the offence and the reward!
Thou speak'st to one that ne'er was dared;"      545
Said Donald, as he rose amain,
Trembling with anger and disdain;
And ere his bard a word could say
His master's vengeance to allay,
Cursing and foaming in his rage,      550
Sheer to the belt he clove the sage;
To either side one half did bow,
His head and breast were cleft in two;
An eye was left on either cheek,
And half a tongue, to see, and speak.      555
O never was so vile a blow,
Or such a bloody wreck of wo!
    Old Rimmon bowed upon his knee;
And, that such sight he might not see,
Shaded his eyes with his right hand,      560
And poured forth coronach so grand,
Oer the old stranger's mournful fate,
That Donald Gorm became sedate;
And softened was his frown severe,
To stern regret and sorrow drear;      565
But his stout heart not to belie,
He dashed the round tear from his eye;
Then turned and wiped his bloody glave,
And bade to dig the heathen's grave;
Far in the bowels of the hill,      570
And with huge rocks the crevice fill,
That forth he might not win at all,
To blab in Odin's heavenly hall;
For, sooth, whate'er was doomed to be,
He would that boisterous deity      575
Might lay his bloody guerdons by
For those who owned his sovereignty.
Sore trembled Turim's ancient bard,
For the rash deed his lord had dared;
And, the transgression to redeem,      580
Sung a most solemn requiem.

Of Donald's nightly overthrow
No note was taken by the foe;
For, yeilding to the generous prince,
King Eric slyly blink'd th' offence.                                     585
Those strangers both were swayed by love;
And hoped, before the queen to prove
Their heroism and matchless might,
And claim unto her hand by right.
But either mighty Odin heard                                             590
His dying servant's last award,
Or some all-seeing righteous eye
Beheld the ancient father die.
   To Eric's tent that night were call'd,
Priest, prophet, patriarch, and scald;                                   595
And thence were heard, in thundering jar,
Loud anthems to the god of war.
And when the orisons were said,
And victims on the altar laid,
And rose the frenzy to the full,                                         600
With cup drunk from an enemy's skull;
Then blood was dashed on all around,
As text, or omen to expound;
And that surveyed with much grimace,
The victory given to Odin's race.                                        605
   Again the frenzied song of war
On the night breeze was borne afar,
Till, on the dark and gelid rock,
The drowsy cormorant awoke,
And, moved by wonder and dismay,                                         610
Scream'd out in concert with the lay.
Some sentinels that watched nigh,
On the north cliff of Valon-Righ,
Descended softly to the plain,
And overheard the closing strain;                                        615
And thus it ran, the roundelay,
As near as Scottish tongue could say.

     \*   \*   \*   \*

   Veil up thy heaven
   From morning till even,
With darkness, thy throne surrounding,                                   620

Whenever thy wrath
At the foes of our faith,
Thou showest in gloom confounding.

   Roll up the thunder,
   Thy right hand under,       625
And the snow and the hail up treasure;
   And gather behind
   Thy tempest of wind;
All weapons of thy displeasure.

   Dreadfully pouring,       630
   Rending and roaring,
Send them with vengeance loaden,
   That all below
   May tremble to know,
There's none so mighty as Odin!       635
There's none so mighty as Odin!
There's none so mighty as Odin!
   That all below
   May tremble and know
There's none so mighty as Odin! &c.       640


   The combat day arrived at last,
And with it congregations vast
Of maidens, youths, and aged men,
From isle, from dale, and highland glen;
All panting, burning, to survey       645
The deeds of that eventful day.
And every group disputing came,
Who were the warriors first in fame.
For every clan avowed its head
Unmatched in might and warrior deed;       650
One 'gainst a world to throw the gage,
The master spirit of the age!
Full plain it was to eye and ear,
That chose to see, and chose to hear,
That no three lords the land could call       655
Would satisfaction give to all.
   That morning rose in ruddy hue,
So bright, that all the fields of dew,

The gleaming mountain, and the wood,
Appeared one mighty waste of blood;                660
Even the slow billow of the main
Appeared to heave and roll in pain—
A clammy, viscous, purple tide,
That murmured to the mountain side,
And broke, with harsh and heavy groan,             665
Upon the beach of Beregon.
The sages looked with wistful eye
Upon the flushed and frowning sky;
Then on the purpled earth and sea,
And sighed a pray'r internally.                    670
        But scarcely had the morning's prime
Flamed o'er the mountain's top sublime,
Ere sable shades began to spread,
And mingle with the murky red;
The sun glared through a curtain gray              675
With broadened face and blunted ray,
And short way had he left the rath
Upon his high and gloomy path,
Till nought appeared to human sight
But a small speck of watery light,                 680
That seemed above the rack to fly,
Carreering through a troubled sky.
        Dark and more dark the morning frown'd;
At length the shadows closed around,
Until the noontide of the day                      685
Looked like a twilight in dismay.
'Twas like that interval of gloom
'Twixt death and everlasting doom,
When the lorn spirit, reft away
From it's frail tenement of clay,                  690
And forced through wastes of night to roam,
In search of an eternal home—
That space of terror, hope, and dole,
The awful twilight of the soul.
        Alas! what earthly anxiousness               695
Resembles such a pause as this?
But mortal tremor and alarm,
For the success of foeman's arm,
And for the congregating gloom,
That almost threatened nature's doom,              700

Were never moved to wilder scope
Than on that day of fear and hope.
    In Eric's council was no flaw,
His will was rule, his word was law;
But in the Scottish camp there grew          705
A furious general interview.
There was no lord, nor chief of name,
Who put not in conclusive claim
As his the right, the brand to wield
Upon the glorious combat field.              710
After great heat in proud deport,
With stern arraignment and retort,
Resource or remedy was none,
But that of casting lots alone;
A base alternative, 'twas true,              715
But that, or battle, nought would do.
The lots were cast with proper form,
And fell on Mar, and Donald Gorm,
And Allan Bane, of wide command,
The goodliest knight in fair Scotland.       720
    Mar's name was called throughout the croud;
The men of Dee hurra'd aloud;
But those of Athol and Argyle
Looked to the earth, with hem, and smile;
While Moray lads, with envy stung,           725
Cursed in a broad unfashioned tongue.
    Brave Donald Gorm was next proclaimed.
Gods how the men of Morven flamed!
And those of Rannoch, and Lochow,
Pulled the blue bonnet o'er the brow,        730
And muttered words of scorn and hate,
Lamenting Albyn's hapless fate;
While through the clans of Ross there pass'd
A murmur like the mountain blast.
    Each neighbouring clan was moved to scorn, 735
That such a chance from it was torn
Of royal sway, and warrior boast,
And given to those they hated most.
While distant tribes forbore to foam,
Pleased that it came no nigher home.         740
    But when the name of Allan Bane,
Lochaber's calm and mighty thane,

Was called, there was no grumbling sound,
Nor aught but plaudits floated round.
The gathered thousands seemed to feel, 745
That heaven had chosen for their weal;
For neither lord, in sway, or name,
Equalled that chief in martial fame.
    The ring was form'd above the bay,
Where Eric's ships incumbent lay; 750
Its circle measured furlongs ten,
One half inclosed by Norwaymen,
While all the Scots rank'd on the lea,
Between the city gate and sea;
And 'twixt the hosts, from east to west, 755
Strong ramparts, lined with guards, were placed.
    The seven towers of Beregon
Were clothed and crouded every one.
High soaring o'er the sordid strife,
Unmeasured piles of mortal life, 760
Breathing, and moving, frowned they there,
Like cloudy pyramids of air.
    Both friends and foemen turned their eyes
To these pilasters of the skies,
And almost weened the living towers, 765
The altars of the heavenly powers,
The tabernacles of the skies,
Where angels offered sacrifice,
With victims heaped of shadowy forms;
Above the pathway of the storms 770
Up rendered, from some dread abode,
The foes of men and foes of God;
And there piled for some dire cremation,
Some final, horrid immolation.
    The whole of that momentuous scene 775
Was such as ne'er on earth again
The eye of man can ever see,
On this side of Eternity.
The various nations armed and filed;
The thousands round on summits piled, 780
Of rock, of ravelin, and mast;
The sky with darkness overcast;
And when the trumpet's rending blare
Bade champions to their posts repair,

Ten times ten thousand panting breasts          785
Were quaking, yearning, o'er the lists;
Ten thousand hearts with ardor burn'd;
Ten thousand eyes were upward turned,
Trying to pierce the fields of air;
But there was nought but darkness there!          790
What could they do, but mutter vow,
And turn their eyes again below?
    King Eric, and his champions twain,
Entered the lists the first. And then
Appeared the Scottish heros three,          795
Arm'd and accoutred gallantly.
But when they met to measure swords,
And change salute in courteous words,
From the Scots files there rose a groan;
For far, in stature, and in bone,          800
The Norse excelled; so far, indeed,
That their's appeared of pigmy breed.
    The heros measured sword and sheild;
Then to their various stations wheeled;
And just when ready to begin,          805
Prince Haco sprung like lightening in,
Kneeled to the king, and made demand
To fight that day at his right hand,
As his by right and heritage.
The champions boded Eric's rage,          810
And gazed at Haco. But anon
King Eric bade the knight begone
From his right hand, with kingly grace,
And the young hero took his place.
A mighty clamour rent the air,          815
And shook the loaded atmosphere;
He was, forsooth, a comely sight,
In golden armour burnished bright,
And raiment white, all glittering sheen
With gems of purple and of green.          820
With face so fair, and form so tall,
So courteous, and so young withal,
He seem'd, amid the multitude,
Like sun beam through a darksome cloud.
    Among the shouts that scaled the shower,          825
A shreik was heard from Selma's tower.

Far upward Haco turned his eye,
And saw, far in the hollow sky,
A female form of radiant white
Upheld, and fainting with affright;                    830
But soon she waved a snowy veil,
The prince's cheek grew red, and pale;
Then with rash hand, and streaming eye,
He heaved his golden helmet high.
King Eric gave him stern reproof,                      835
And warned him to his post aloof;
But his fond heart, with burning glow,
Was roused to more than man might do;
He trode on air; he grasped at fame;
His sword a meteor seemed of flame.                    840
  The King was matched with lordly Mar;
And Allan Bane with Osnagar,
A Dane of most gigantic form;
And the brave prince with Donald Gorm.
The marshals walked the circle round,                  845
Surveyed the lists, and vantage ground;
Then raised a signal over head,
The baleful flag of bloody red.
The trumpet sounded once; and then
Bugle and tabour rolled amain                          850
O'er all the host with rending swell;
Till slumbering echos caught the knell
And, calling to the mountain side,
Proclaimed the combat far and wide.
  The trumpet gave the second boom;            855
Again the clamour rent the gloom!
It gave the third.–No murmur ran!
No sound moved by the breath of man
O'er all that collied, countless throng;
For trembling feelings, fierce, and strong,            860
Oppressed them all.–Blench'd was each cheek,
And lip; that moved, but durst not speak.
  The triple combat then began;
That instant man was matched to man;
And at that very moment flew                           865
From out the cloud the lightening blue;
The thunder followed, and the hail
Came like a torrent with the peal,

Straight in the faces of the three
Who fought for Albyn's liberty.                        870
The priests and scalds of Scania raised
The stormy hymn, and Odin praised;
But Albyn's thousands, blinded quite
With hail, and sleet, and glancing light,
To covert fled in dire dismay,                         875
Trembling and faultering by the way;
All ignorant of what befel,
And asking news which none could tell.
  But not the wrath of angry heaven;
The storm with tenfold fury driven;                    880
The forked flames, with flash, and quiver;
The thunder that made earth to shiver,
Could daunt the courage of the brave
Who fought for glory or the grave.
  No stately marshall was allowed,                     885
Nor umpire, verging from the croud,
To meddle with the mortal strife;
Each hero fought for death or life.
Few words on either side were spoke,
To daunt oppounent, or provoke.                        890
For why? The storm so fiercely jarr'd,
They neither could be said, nor heard.
Their weapons met with clanging blows,
And high from helm and buckler rose.
Mar lost his ground, as Eric press'd;                  895
But calmly still the king regressed.
With foe before, and foe behind,
To quit his line he had no mind,
And vantage of the rain and wind.
  'Tween Osnagar and Allan Bane                         900
The fight was dreadful. But the Dane,
With every vantage of the field,
Eluded Allan's oval shield,
And pierced his shoulder to the bone,
Reddening his arm and hacqueton.                       905
This roused the Scottish hero so,
That back he bore his giant foe;
And it was plain to every eye,
Though few there were that could espy,
That Albyn, in her Allan Bane,                         910

Would suffer no dishonest stain.
　　Ha, mighty Donald of the main,
Why flag'st thou on the battle plain?
Why is thy bronzed cheek aghast?
And thy fierce visage overcast? 915
Can thunder's roar, or fire, or storm,
Appal the heart of Donald Gorm,
Who, till this hour, at danger spurned,
Whose sword in battle ne'er was turned?
No.–But there had been boding sight! 920
Some dreadful visitant o'ernight!
And now the hero powerless seemed,
And fought as if he slept and dreamed.
　　When Haco first met eye to eye
With the impetuous lord of Skye, 925
One thought alone possessed the host.
Even Eric deemed his nephew lost;
And only kept proud Mar at bay,
To watch the issue of the day.
Haco strode up with giddy pace, 930
And shook his brand in Donald's face.
The day had shortly been, forsooth!
If such a fair and flexile youth
Had shook a gilded sword or spear
At that imperious islander, 935
Heavens how the tempest's howling breath
Had heightened been by Donald's wrath!
Whereas, he now to battle fared,
As if he neither saw nor heard.
　　Haco made play; and joined, and sprung 940
From side to side, like galliard young.
Now on his golden shield he clang'd;
Now on his foeman's buckler bang'd;
Now back, now forward would he fly,
In hopes to catch a royal eye. 945
But all the feints he could perform
Were lost on drowsy Donald Gorm;
Though life and death were laid in stake,
He held his guard as scarce awake.
　　The prince grew reckless, and surprised, 950
Thinking his foeman him despised;
And, pressing down that sluggish brand,

He closed with Donald, hand to hand.
Then did a furious course ensue,
Of push, and parry; hack, and hew;          955
Until the prince, in sidelong bound,
Gave Donald's thigh a ghastly wound.
Then burst the chief's inherent ire
Forth like the blaze of smother'd fire.
Alas! 'twas bravery's parting qualm;          960
The rending blast before the calm:
The last swoln billow in the bay,
When winds have turn'd another way.
     "Curse on thy wanton slight!" he cried
"Thou gossip for a maiden's side!          965
And curse upon the wizard charm,
That thus hath chained M,Ola's arm,
Whose pristine might and majesty
Was framed to punish ten like thee.
Here's to thy foppish heart abhorred!          970
Ward if thou may'st this noble sword.
Hence to thy ghostly charlatan,
And bear him back his curse and ban;
And say, that I'll requite it well,
In whate'er place he dares to dwell,          975
In earth, in cloud, in heaven, or hell."
     Thus saying, Donald forward flung,
And at the prince his weapon swung
With back and forward sweep amain;
But only fought the wind and rain,          980
Or thing invisible to man.
He toiled, he wheeled, and forward ran;
But not one stroke, for all his fume,
So much as levelled Haco's plume;
Or downward on his buckler rang;          985
Or made his golden helmet clang.
His rage seem'd madness in th' extreme,
The struggle of a frenzied dream.
     The prince kept guard, but smiled to see
The wildness of his enemy.          990
At length, with flourish, and with spring
Forward like falcon on the wing,
He pierced the raving maniac's side.
Forth welled the warm and purple tide;

And like an oak before the storm, 995
Down crashed the might of Donald Gorm.
A shout from Norway's files, too well
Proclaimed the loss Scot dared not tell.
    "True son of Odin!" Eric cried
And rushed on Mar with madden'd stride 1000
"Presumptuous lord! What thing art thou
That com'st king Eric's ire to brow?
Would that I had (if such there be)
A score of Scottish lords like thee!
With dint of this good sword of mine 1005
I'd heap them all on Odin's shrine!"
So saying, at one dreadful blow,
He shore the warriors helm in two,
With lightening's force.–The Scottish lord
Lies prostrate o'er his bloodless sword. 1010
    By this time giant Osnagar
Was from his station borne afar,
And sore by Allan Bane oppress'd;
Heaved like the sea his ample chest.
His hand unto his weapon clave, 1015
Scarce could he weild that weighty glave.
He in his targe to trust began,
For blood o'er all his armour ran;
And as he wore from side to side,
Most bitterly to Odin cried. 1020
One other minute in the strife,
And Osnagar had yielded life;
But to that goal when Allan press'd,
Two other swords met at his breast!
"Yield!" cried King Eric "Yield, or fall." 1025
"I never did, and never shall!"
The chief replied. But Eric's arm
Waved back his friends from farther harm.
    "Most generous king, I will not yield,
Nor living quit the combat field; 1030
Come one, come all, this arm to try,
Here do I stand to win or die.
Shall it be told on Lochy's side,
That Allan Bane for rescue cried?"
    King Eric smiled, and made reply. 1035
"Thou bear'st thyself most gallantly;

We're three to one, and doubly strong;
But none shall gallant foeman wrong;
Then yield thee to a king this day,
Whose sword in battle ne'er gave way."          1040
    "For once it shall!" Bold Allan cried
And made a blow at Eric's side.
"Hurra!" cried Eric joyfully.
"I'll trust this wight with none but me.
Keep all aloof, both friend and foe,          1045
Till we two change a single blow.
His wayward will he needs must have,
Though he is one I fain would save."
        Clash went the swords, the bucklers clashed,
And 'gainst each other soon were dashed;          1050
But short the strife, ere Allan Bane
Lay stunned upon the slippery plain,
Bereft of buckler, and of brand,
But without wound from Eric's hand.
He was no more in Eric's clasp          1055
Than leopard in the lion's grasp.
        The king up raised the wondering thane,
With soothing words and smiling mein;
Returned his sword, and, as a charm,
Bound golden bracelet round his arm;          1060
Then, in a bold impatient strain,
These words addressed to Allan Bane.
        "Thou art as stout and staunch a knight
As ever braved our northern might;
But know thou this, and when thou dost,          1065
Thou know'st it to thy nation's cost.
In youth, before this beard was brown,
Or only waved a golden down,
From childhood I to battle bred,
Was then to single combat led.          1070
Before my eighteenth year, I say,
Had clothed this chin, which now is gray,
Within the lists I had to fight
For life, before my father's sight.
I won—and of applause was vain.          1075
I've fought a thousand times since then;
In southern climes have laurels won,
Beyond the seasons and the sun;

I've journeyed all the world around,
Wherever fame was to be found;                    1080
Have fought with Frank, and Turcoman,
With prince, with visier, and with khan;
And though their painim creed I spurn'd,
This sword was ne'er in combat turned.
    "The seventh day we fight again              1085
In triple combat on the plain;
But as well may you challenge then
Great Odin, prince of gods and men,
Or brave that liquid fiery levin,
Red streaming from the forge of heaven,          1090
Trying his power to countercharm,
As brave the force of Eric's arm.
    "This tell the nobles of your land;
And say, I make sincere demand
Of them, ere more deray is done,                 1095
To yield the queen. I have her won.
I flinch not from my royal seal,
It is in friendship I appeal;
But should they wish again to just,
And in the second combat trust,                  1100
'Tis well. Then henceforth I must claim
The guardship of the royal dame.
They have but choice, 'twixt bad, and worse;
I claim but what I'll take perforce;
One hour I wait return discreet,                 1105
The next I do as I think meet."
    By that time Mar had breathed his last;
And Donald Gorm approached fast
The bourn of all the human race;
Yet in his stern and rugged face                 1110
There seemed no terror, wrath, or teen,
Save at some being all unseen.
When Haco raised him to his knee,
He look'd aside most movingly,
And to the wind these words addressed;           1115
He saw nought but the slaughtered priest!
    "Ay, thou may'st stand, and smile, and beck,
With thy half head on half a neck!
M,Ola soon shall be with thee,
His sworn, and subtile enemy!                     1120

Thou basilisk of burning spheres!
Thou, and thy hellish, damn'd compeers,
With dreams, and visions of dismay,
And terrors of a future day;
With dreadful darkness, fire, and storm,          1125
At last have vanquished Donald Gorm!
But some shall rue, since so it be!
Go to. Go to. I'll be with thee."
　　The hero turned his beamless eye
Toward the grizzly peaks of Skye          1130
Some thought unfathom'd seem'd to hover
His dark departing spirit over,
Of roaming on his mountain wind
Swifter than hawk or dappled hind;
Of staghound's bay, and bugles swelling,          1135
And answering echos bravely yelling;
But all was one distorted scene,
The vision of a soul in pain,
That trembled, neither bound nor free,
'Twixt time & immortality.          1140
With that wild look it fled for ever,
From hollow groan, and rigid shiver,
From clenched hand, and writhing brow.–
Eternal God! What is it now?

　　　　End of Book the fourth

# Queen Hynde

## Book Fifth

O come, gentle maiden  
    Of queenly Dunedin  
Arrayed in thy beauty and gladdening smiles;  
    Thine the control I list,  
    Lovely mythologist!                5  
Thine the monition that never beguiles.

    Over the mountain wave;  
    Over the hero's grave;  
Over the darkness of ages gone bye,  
    Be thou my enquirer,             10  
    And holy inspirer;  
And keenly I'll follow the glance of thine eye.

    But, bowing before thee,  
    Far most I implore thee,  
When rapt in the strain that I love beyond measure;   15  
    That theme so ecstatic,  
    Sublime, and erratic,  
The love of a maiden, the magnet of pleasure!

    What were the sailor's joy,  
    Roll'd in his bavaroy,             20  
Far in the gloom of the dark polar sea;  
    What were the warrior's deed,  
    Minstrel, or Monarch's meed,  
What, without hope of approval from thee?

    Thou gem of creation,             25  
    The world's admiration,  
Thy mind is a mystery I cannot explore;  
    I'll love and caress thee,  
    Admonish and bless thee,  
But sound the high tone of thy feelings no more.     30

The grey hairs of sorrow,
And dread of to morrow,
Have bow'd down thy bard on his cold native lea;
Then list the last lay
Of the green braken brae,                                    35
The song is a medley and model of thee.

---

Queen Hynde's in her tower,
For the storm and the shower
Had driven the maidens within;
And shrouded the view                                        40
Of the anxious few
That yearned o'er the fates of their kin.
All trembling and pining
The queen sat reclining,
She knew not what was befalling;                             45
But she boded deep dismay,
For the shouts were far away,
And each sound through the storm was appalling.
One after one to the field she sent,
Who hasted away incontinent;                                 50
But out of the throng, the mire, and the rain,
No one return'd with the tidings again;
And the first that arrived was Allan Bane.
All sheeted in blood appeared he there,
And his looks and his words were all despair.               55
King Eric's message in full he told,
And of his claim, the queen to hold;
Then vouched the boast of his warrior sleight,
As far inferior to his might;
For he said, that "enchanter's mighty charm                 60
Had given that force into his arm.
The combat was lost; no power to deliver!
And so would the next, and the next for ever."
Perplexity reign'd in every face,
As every rankling pang kept place                           65
In various breasts; one there might see
Anger, regret, temerity,
Hope, fear, contempt, elation, shame,

And every passion tongue can name,
All crouded on a darksome scene, 70
With scarce a ray of light between.
   As ever you saw, on winter eve,
When the sun takes a joyless leave,
Descending on some distant coast,
Beyond the waste of waters lost, 75
The ocean's breast all overspread
With shades of green, and murky red,
With distant fields of sackcloth hue,
With pale, with purple, and with blue,
And every shade defined and strong, 80
Without one cheerful ray among,
And knew'st these spectres multiform,
The heralds of approaching storm.
   So was it here. Proud Albyn's blood
Began to boil, the storm to brood; 85
Some blamed the preference by lot;
Nor were old jealousies forgot.
Some blamed the brave and wounded thane
Of brangle, hurtful, and inane;
And said, a thousand might be found 90
Would Eric beat in Albyn's bound.
It was a scene of feud and dare,
As feudal councils always were.
   Old Diarmid rose this feud to check;
His reverend age insured respect. 95
And thus he spoke:–"My sovereign dame,
And noble maids, and chiefs of fame,
Hard is our fate; whate'er the worth
Of this bold wooer of the north.
This city of our fathers' names 100
In one short hour may be in flames,
And with the thousands of our kin,
That now are crouded it within,
Of every age, sex, and degree,
How dreadful would the sequel be? 105
King Eric's claim, confess I must,
Can scarcely be pronounced unjust;
'Tis only that for which he fought,
Else he has staked his all for nought.
And should he win again, 'tis clear, 110

(And likely too from all we hear,)
If we such claim should dissallow,
He has no more than he has now.
Therefore I deem, in such a case,
To save our gathered populace,                               115
We must to Eric straight present
Some pledge, some great equivalent,
If such there be; but as for more,
I say but as I said before,
The moment with our queen we part,                           120
Our country's freedom we desert."
        "Forbid it heaven!" Queen Hynde replied,
"For me no warrior's hand be tied.
When I am gone, as go I must,
I in your patriot ardor trust,                               125
That by your country's rights you stand,
Nor lose one jot for maiden's hand.
This hour I go, ere worse arrives,
To save my people's sacred lives."
        One buzz of dissaproval ran                          130
Around the hall, from man to man;
And all prepared to take the field;
To sell their lives, but not to yield
Their youthful queen; as, doing so,
They stoop'd unto a foreign foe.                             135
        As wilder still the uproar grew,
And nought but havoc was in view;
The city crouded perilously,
No room to fight nor yet to flee;
Confusion, ruin, crouds aghast,                              140
Defeat, and conflagration vast,
The certain consequence to be
Of this their fierce fidelity.
        In this dilemma came relief;
Not from the clan of distant chief,                          145
From friendly prince, nor subject isle,
But from a maiden's witching wile!
The restless Wene, since she had seen
Prince Haco, sore perplexed had been;
And much she longed for some deray,                          150
To throw her in that hero's way,
Whose youthful arm, and sprightly form,

Had cowed the might of Donald Gorm:
And hence her mind was wholly bent
On being with her mistress sent,                    155
An hostage to king Eric's tent.
    Now when she saw the proud resolve
Of Albyn's chiefs, would straight involve
The land in trouble, toil, and wo,
And all her measures overthrow;                    160
Forthwith she rose with seemly grace,
And all her majesty of face,
And proffered, for her mistress' sake,
Her place of royalty to take;
And on the instant to go thence,                    165
In such an adverse exigence.
    "Send me to Eric straight!" said she,
"In all the pomp of royalty;
With maids and pages at my beck,
Kneeling, and bowing with respect;                    170
And loads of comfits, and of dress
Blazing in eastern sumptuousness.
His forward claim he may repent,
I'll queen it to his heart's content!
One only claim to make I chuse,                    175
Which as a king he can't refuse;
It is, that, as a virgin queen,
My face by man may not be seen,
Until the seven days are outrun,
And Albyn's chiefs have lost or won.                    180
This for my country's sake I crave,
Now trembling o'er her freedom's grave;
And then I yield me to his hand,
An hostage for my native land.
To plague that king I have a mind,                    185
If he's not sick of woman kind;
And, ere the seventh day, driven insane,
My name no more is wicked Wene!"
    The courtiers smiled, as well they might,
And lauded much the maiden's sleight;                    190
But sore they feared the plot would fail,
And do more mischief, than avail.
Wene's form was slight, her stature small,
The queen's majestically tall;

And, worst of all, the king had seen,                    195
And held some converse with the queen.
    Wene smiled, and bade them nothing dread,
She should be taller by a head
Than Eric could of queenship guess;
She'd add one inch of wickedness,                    200
And three of beauty, pride, and mind,
Should dazzle mighty Eric blind.
She'd swath the braggart in amaze,
If not drive mad in seven days.
    Queen Hynde embraced the elf, and said,                    205
No mistress e'er had such a maid;
And if success this effort crowned,
She would for ever be renowned;
For future bards, in many a strain,
Would sing the deeds of beauteous Wene.                    210
And when a lover she should chuse,
Her sovereign would no boon refuse;
While all her interest she might claim
To win a lord of noble fame.
    "Ohon an Banrigh!" sighed the elf;                    215
"Preserve your interest for yourself,
My generous queen; for you may need
That and some more in marriage speed.
For me, henceforth I'll use mankind
As I would do the passing wind,                    220
To breathe upon, and bid it fly
Away from great important I!
Or to supply this ardent breast
With cooling laughter and with jest.
Interest! The proffer is sublime!                    225
Come let us go, we lose but time.
When from this presence I depart
In all the pomp of female art,
'Mid grandeur and respect to move,
I'll queen it mortal queens above!"                    230
    All present owned with earnestness,
There was no mode so safe as this,
Save for the danger of the maid,
Of which she nothing seem'd afraid.
The queen assured them, that she knew                    235
The cunning of the lively shrew

Too well from trial, to suspect
That what she said she'd not effect.
Forthwith a herald went with speed,
To Eric at his army's head,                     240
Prepared to bathe their weapons' rust,
And lay old Beregon in dust.
Eric, with generous love inspired,
Conceded all the queen desired,
And straight made preparation high,             245
For this most lovely prodigy;
This queen, of frame and soul refined,
Surpassing all of human kind!
    Eastward the storm it's course had traced,
To roar amid the Grampian waste,                250
In one dark elemental stole
These everlasting hills to roll;
And in that deep impervious cloud
Were rolled, as in a hellish shroud,
The hail, the thunder, and the flame;           255
And ghastly shades without a name,
Holding them all in order due,
Prepared the outrage to renew;
To sport them all in wild excess,
And riot in the wilderness.                      260
    Soon as that cloud had pass'd away,
Forth issued Wene like meteor gay,
With music pealing on the wind,
And troops before, and troops behind;
Twelve pages, glancing all in green,            265
Twelve maidens in their tartans sheen;
Twelve bards, who sung in strains intense,
Their sovereign's great magnificence;
And deeds her ancestors had done,
Surpassing all beneath the sun.                 270
All were sincere, you may believe't.
How oft poor minstrels are deceived!
    In all the splendor of the morn,
The beauteous dame herself was borne,
On high, a gilded throne within,                275
A lightsome yielding palanquin;
Her form begirt with many a gem;
Her head with sparkling diadem;

A gauzy veil of snowy white,
Befringed with gold and silver bright,                    280
Floated around her on the air,
Circling a form so passing fair,
So pure, so lovely, so benign,
It almost seemed a thing divine.
    Eric, arrayed in warrior trim,                    285
Surrounded by his nobles grim,
Came forth the royal dame to meet,
And with kind salutations greet.
Behind him shone a goodlier view
Prince Haco and his retinue;                    290
And he himself that train before,
Robed in the armour which he wore
That morn upon the sanguine field,
The golden helmet, and the shield;
And in his youthful hand displayed                    295
The golden hilt and bloody blade,
All saying, with full fond regard,
"See for your sake what I have dared."
O how his ardent bosom pined
For one sweet glance, approving, kind,                    300
Of the dear being he had seen,
And now his bosom's only queen.
    Queen Wene approached with colours streaming,
Music sounding, lances gleaming,
Borne on high by gallant yeomen                    305
Slowly forth to Albyn's foemen;
There stood Eric, smiling, bowing;
What a form for youthful wooing!
Bearded, dark, robust, and vigorous,
Stern, gigantic, blunt, and rigorous,                    310
All his youthful manner over;
Such a man to play the lover!
Mid such array, and such a scene,
And to such elf as wicked Wene!
    Wene, from her gilded chair on high,                    315
Returned king Eric's courtesy
With grace so courteous, and so kind,
It quite deranged the hero's mind.
He kissed his brown and brawny fist,
And laid it on his ample breast;                    320

Then grinned with most afflicting leer,
And from his visage wiped the tear!
His nobles blench'd and fretted sore,
And so did Eric when 'twas o'er.
His face was like a winter day                    325
Aping the summer's glancing ray,
With sunbeam low, and rainbow high,
Arching a frigid boreal sky,
Shaded with cloud so darkly bleak;
Like pall upon creation's cheek                   330
Rather than summer's youthful hue,
And cloudlets weeping balmy dew.
    A herald then with verge and sword,
And many a pompous swelling word,
Approached king Eric, and, at large,              335
Delivered o'er the sacred charge,
A charge in value and esteem,
Ne'er trusted to a king but him.
Eric, with nodding burgonet,
Returned an answer most discreet,                 340
With sacred promise to neglect
No kind of homage or respect.
Wene court'seyed with commanding air,
And motioned him behind her chair.
    The king look'd up, the king looked down,     345
Uncertain if to laugh or frown;
But when he saw the flimsy fair
Moving like angel through the air
With such a glittering gaudy show
Of flounce, and frill, and furbelow,              350
His eyes descended from the jilt,
Slowly upon his weapon's hilt,
And something that he muttered there
Made all his warriors stern to stare.
    When Haco met the elfin's eye,                 355
Her little heart ne'er beat so high;
Full well she noted, as she pass'd,
His eager glances upward cast,
And, turning by her snowy veil,
With such a glance, and such a smile,             360
And such a transport of delight,
Prince Haco's heart was ravished quite!

Straight to king Eric's royal tent
Wene and her retinue were sent,
And strick commands were left therein,                365
To Frotho, the old chamberlain,
That Albyn's queen and suit should have
Whate'er their utmost thoughts could crave;
To that the king had bound him fast,
And he would keep it to the last.                     370
    Alas! invain the high behest!
He little wist what vixen guest
Under his guardship he had ta'en,
But found it nothing to his gain.
Ere half an hour had overpast,                        375
Frotho had applications vast
For things so rare, and unforeseen,
He cursed his chance, the truce, the queen.
At first the old man did not miss
To bustle round, and answer, "yes."                   380
But ere the fall of night, he stood
More like a chamberlain of wood
Than living thing of flesh and blood;
His senses utterly confounded,
With pages and with maids surrounded,                 385
Calling for this, for that, for more
Than the old man with all his lore
Had e'er heard specified, or knew
In what abundant clime they grew.
    Three times, in uttermost despair,                390
To Eric's presence did he fare,
With face that told how hard his lot,
And eyes that spoke what tongue could not,
Begging his master on his knee,
Of that dire charge his slave to free.                395
But the fourth time he came outright;
And then his straits were at the height!
The king on homelier couch was laid,
For sake of this illustrious maid,
And when aroused from deep repose,                    400
Full high his pride and choler rose.
"Frotho, begone! By heaven's light,
I'll hear no more of queens to night!"
    "O king, my message I must tell;

I've served thee long, and served thee well;          405
But such a task as I have had
For one day more will put me mad.
My heathbell beer, and cyder good,
—And two such browsts were never brewed,—
They've poured all forth; and now they whine      410
And yawn, and weep, and cry for wine.
My fish they say is food for hogs;
My hams they cast unto the dogs;
And seem united in one plot,
Of calling for what I have not.                       415
And now, to crown these insults high,
The queen desires respectfully,
Her royal Ally straight to send
Orders their treatment to amend;
And that 'tis meet, her maids and she              420
Have night apartments seperately
Yet all conjoined, for their repose.
What's to be done great Odin knows!
      "She says your tent's not meet for men,
Nor better than a lion's den,                         425
And highborn dames can't make them lairs
On hides of badgers and of bears.
And therefore, she intreats you, grant
Them chambers, which they greatly want.
For sake of heaven, my master kind,               430
Return that pestilence Queen Hynde."
      " 'Tis what she wants," king Eric said,
"A plot among'st her nobles laid
To win their sacred pledge again;
Such stratagems are my disdain!                      435
No crime to me shall one impute;
I'll keep her, and my word to boot;
And if I fail, all men shall see
From fault of mine it shall not be.
I'll keep her till the time be run,                     440
And the last combat lost or won,
Else she is more to reason blind,
Than all the rest of womankind."
      "Reason my liege? God bless the word!
She's free of that as of a sword."                    445
      King Eric rose in growling mood,

And, hurrying on his cloak and hood,
Went forth at midnight gallantly,
Beds for these maidens to supply.
A fair arrangement soon was made;                    450
Queen Wene in Haco's tent was laid,
The very spot on earth where she
Wished that her residence might be;
Her sprightly lover, and his train,
Her guards, all rudeness to restrain.                455
O ne'er was maid so blest as Wene!
    To tell the wiles of loving pairs;
And all the coquetry and airs
Of blooming maids, I do not deign,
Such theme is no delight of mine;                    460
But Haco was in love sincere,
As most of youthful warriors are;
And Wene held hers of higher worth
Than e'er did maiden of the north.
    Sooth, they for one another's sake        465
Were kept for days and nights awake;
And there was fretting, toying, whining,
Jealousies, and inward pining,
Fears what others might discover,
All the joys that bless the lover!                   470
< All but those which most they crave,
Which for their souls they cannot have. >
    Nor can I half the projects sing
Which Wene contrived to plague the king;
So much she drove him from his wit,                  475
No suit from her he would admit;
He spent his days mid thousands round;
His nights where he could not be found;
And thus the lovers had their leisure
For grief, for strife, for pain, or pleasure.       480
But darker paths are to be trode,
For darker doings are abroad;
And secrets strange are on the wing,
Which you must list and I must sing.
    King Eric sat concealed, and free          485
Of woman's importunity,
And to the nobles of his land
Pass'd round the cup with ready hand;

When lo, the captain of the ward,
Brought in a stranger under guard!                   490
"My liege, here is a churlish wight,
Who craves admission to your sight;
But neither will his name disclose,
Nor whether of our friends or foes;
But so important is his suit,                        495
He will no other tongue depute."
      "Ay captain; doubtless one of those,
Who, thrusting his officious nose,
Into the affairs of other men,
Presumes their notice to obtain.                     500
Speak out intruder. Say at once
Thy name, thy business? and from whence?
If thou'rt a cotquean, by my soul,
I'll split thy pruriginious noul!"
      "My name, or business, few shall hear;         505
They're for king Eric's private ear;
If thou art he, I deem it fit
That these gruff carls who round thee sit
Should be dismissed, for I have theme
Of which you could not even dream                    510
It is so base. Perhaps I'll sue
For matters touching maidens too;
That's as I chuse; but must request
Your private ear, if so you list."
      "It is not difficult to guess,                 515
From thy presuming sauciness,
From whom thou comest; but perchance
Thy errand thou shalt miss for once.
Drag forth the knave without the line;
This is no business hour of mine."                   520
      The captain seized the plaided breast
Of this austere and stubborn guest,
But better had his hand withheld,
The stranger's haughty blood rebelled;
He aimed a blow so fierce and full                   525
On that rude captain's burly skull,
That down he dropp'd with growlings deep,
Mumbling out oaths as in a sleep.
      "Curse on thy petulance and thee!"
The stranger cried indignantly.                      530

"I stand unarmed, as knight should do
Who comes before a king to bow,
Else I had given thee, for thy meed,
That which should have laid low thy head
In peace from insult or affray 535
Until the final judgement day.
Here do I stand in Eric's sight,
A messenger in my own right,
Who tidings bring you to your cost;
Refuse them, and your army's lost. 540
Unless you'd stand as stocks or poles,
A horde of brainless jobbernoles,
A byword ever to remain,
Dismiss me at your peril and pain."
King Eric stood amazed to see 545
The stranger's bold effrontery,
And to a chamber led the way,
To listen what such guest would say.
    The stranger doffed his deep disguise,
And showed to Eric's wondering eyes 550
A chief he formerly had known,
A traitor to the Scottish throne,
With whom he secret league had framed.
That chief in song must not be named!
Such shame it is to move a hand, 555
Or utter word, or lift a brand
Against our sacred native land.
Such cursed laurels, and such fame
Shall blur the face of heaven with shame.
    "I come to thee, my sovereign lord, 560
According to my pledged word"
The traitor said. "In enmity
I fought against thy sway and thee;
My life by thee was saved, and all
My people from Norwegian thrall; 565
I will requite it if I may.
Eric; with all thy proud array,
With all thy might, and valour wild,
Thou art as simple as a child.
Thou think'st thou hast within thy tent 570
A pledge the most magnificient;
The jewel of all earthly things,

The daughter of an hundred kings!
Eric. (To Albyn's shame be't said!)
Thou nothing hast but waiting maid;                        575
And some few giglets of the court,
Sent forth of thee to make their sport.
    The queen is fled, with her the crown,
And all the riches of the town;
Each thing of value is defaced,                            580
Or safely in Dunstaffnage placed.
The guards are set at ford and pier,
And now at thee they laugh and jeer.
The queen by night was borne away;
I bore a hand across the bay,                              585
And viewed the works; the huge fascines,
The fosse, the bridge, the martial lines
And must confess, ere them you win,
You'll buy all dear that is within."
    King Eric's rage was too severe                 590
His indignation to declare
In human speech. He look'd around,
And smiled with eyes cast on the ground;
But when again those eyes were raised
A flame unearthly in them blazed,                          595
Which, from a face of generous light,
Had something dreadful to the sight.
It was as if the lightening's gleam
Had mingled with the noonday beam,
As ray of heaven and flash of hell                         600
Together upon mortals fell.
    No word the king had yet expressed,
When other message on him press'd;
Odin's high priest it was who came,
With bloody hands and bloated frame;                       605
A man, who Eric more enchained,
Than he the serfs o'er whom he reigned.
And thus he spoke "O mighty king,
Some dire events are gathering
Around our heads. The heavenly host                        610
Is wroth, and Norway's army's lost,
Unless these tyrants of the skies
Are straight appeased by sacrifice.
    "I've sacrificed on Odin's shrine,

And Thor's, and Freya's, nine times nine          615
Of living creatures, one and all
On which they feast in Odin's hall;
But all my omens are of death,
And all my answers given in wrath.
Now mighty king, there's but one meed;          620
A human sacrifice must bleed.
A solemn offering there must be,
Of stainless virgins three times three;
Though all the bounds of Caledon
In search of them should be outgone,          625
They must be had—whate'er the cost,
Else thou, and I, and all are lost.
If these are found, in beauty's prime,
And to Valhala sent in time,
To join the galliardise and noise,          630
And reap Valhala's boisterous joys;
I pledge my word, and faith in heaven,
Ample success shall yet be given
Unto your arms. But sure as thou
And I are living creatures now,          635
That rite neglected, all is done,
And mighty Eric's race is run."
    "Sire, I attend thy hest sublime,
Thou ne'er could'st come in better time;
I now have under my controul          640
Twelve virgins, pure of frame and soul,
And thou as freely them shalt have
As e'er thou had'st a worthless slave.
Without the light of Odin's eye
We're less than nought, and vanity;          645
Then take them all, without debate,
And on thy altars immolate.
Captain, attend my strick behest,
Go forth with Odin's ancient priest,
And guard the altar of the sun,          650
Until this great oblation's done;
And whosoever dares controul
This high command, or fret, or growl—
Straight cut him off, whate'er he be
Regardless of his high degree!"          655
    The priest let fall his gastful jaw,

When Eric's ireful looks he saw.
He deem'd the order given in jest,
If not in mockery of a priest.
To immolate a sovereign dame,                          660
And hostage maidens without blame,
Was act so ruthless and severe,
As Scania's annals did not bear.
But when he heard the closing threat,
His bloodshot eye became elate;                        665
And through his soul of dark alloy
There darted stern and bloody joy.
      As when, in ages long agone,
The sons of God before the throne
Of their Almighty father came,                         670
To pay their vows, and name his name;
And there came one, the rest among,
In hopes, that in the glorious throng,
A skulking vagabond and spy
Might 'scape his lord's omniscient eye.                675
Think how that felon would appear
When these dread words fell on his ear.
"WHENCE COMEST THOU?" Sure then, that eye
That once had beamed in heaven high,
Would be up raised, in terror, fierce,                 680
Towards the lord of the universe.
If that great God had added then,
"Go seize that righteous, best of men
My servant Job, with all his kin,
And close them up thy den within                       685
For evermore." Think of the air,
The savage joy, the dark despair,
That would have mingled in the mein
Of face that once had angel's been;
And think too of this look below,                      690
From antitype of mankind's foe.
I love to draw a scene to thee
Where misconstruction cannot be,
And spread it to thy spirit's view,
In hopes the mental glass is true.                     695
      Eric went forth without delay;
The war note rang from brake and brae
And Norway's warriors rushed with joy

To reave, to ravish, and destroy.  
The priest of Odin likewise went      700  
Up to prince Haco's gaudy tent,  
And laid the splendid Wene in thrall,  
With her attendant maidens all.  
Their feet with silken bonds they tied,  
Their lily hands down by each side;      705  
Then bathed their bodies in the milk,  
And robed them in the damask silk;  
While every flower of lovely bloom,  
And all that shed the sweet perfume,  
In wreaths and fillets richly bound,      710  
Bedeck'd their heads, and bodies round.  
The red rose of Damascus shed  
Down from the brow the tints of red,  
O'er faces, late in beauty's glow,  
But now as pale as winter snow.      715  
    They were, in sooth, a lovely sight,  
Stretched side by side in bridal white;  
Their lips praying to be forgiven;  
Their streaming eyes turn'd towards heaven;  
While Odin's priest and suffragan      720  
The consecration work began.  
    The bloated heathen cast his eyes  
On that benignant sacrifice,  
And, lifting up his hands on high,  
The briny tear drop'd from his eye;      725  
It was not for the grievous doom  
Of beauty blasted in the bloom,  
But at the triumph and delight  
Would be in Odin's halls that night.  
He thought how his great god would laugh,      730  
And how his warrior ghosts would quaff  
Their skull-cups, filled unto the brim,  
In long and generous healths to him,  
Who sent them such a lovely store  
As warrior ghosts ne'er saw before;      735  
And then he thought, how welcome he  
In high Valhala's dome would be.  
    Great God! 'tis thou alone can'st scan  
Thy lingering, longing creature—man;  
Who, from the time that reason's ray      740

Beams from his eye on nature's sway,
Still onward must insatiate press
To unknown state of blissfulness.
One summit gain'd; how many more!
Before! before! Tis still before! 745
But must be reach'd; till, grasping far
Beyond the range of sun and star,
He rears himself a heavenly home,
In glory's everlasting dome.
　　Still must that state, to be believed, 750
Be something dark and unconcieved;
And distant far, involved must be
In shadows of futurity.
Our Caledonian sires of yore
Looked upward to their mountains hoar, 755
As to the place they loved the best
For home of everlasting rest;
And there, within his shroud of mist,
The rude, romantic sciolist,
Hoped with the souls of friends to meet, 760
And roam in conversation sweet;
Or on his downy bark to sail,
High oer the billows of the gale.
　　The Scandinavian look'd before
For wine, and wassail, ramp and roar; 765
For virgins radiant as the sun,
And triumphs ever, ever won.
For revels on the fields above,
And maddening joys which warriors love.
　　But now; where rests the morbid eye 770
Of sceptical philosophy?
On the cold grave; and only this—
Worms, dust, and final nothingness!
Great God! within this world of thine,
Is there a human soul divine, 775
That hopes no farther bliss to scan?
How dark the question, "What is man?"
What *he hath been*, the world can see.
Thou only know'st *what he shall be*!
　　While this extatic rite went on, 780
The battle raged in Beregon.
With Eric's host the day went hard,

Which caused the holy altar's guard
To be withdrawn. A virgin's pray'r
No passing gale can waft in air                           785
From it's high aim. The gods are kind,
And lovers' eyes are ill to blind.
　　Prince Haco, from the battle field,
The stir within the camp beheld;
For still his eyes unconcious moved                       790
Toward the treasure which he loved,
And sore he feared mischance might fall
To Albyn's queen and maidens all.
He sent a friend, whose truth he knew,
That scene of bustle to review                            795
And bring him word. Short then the space
Ere Haco vanished from his place,
And more with him; for there was need
For ardent lover's utmost speed.
　　Wene in life's bustle took delight,                   800
Whether in frolic or despite;
And even this splendid sacrifice
Held some enchantment to her eyes;
The robes, the flowers, the proud display,
The pallid forms that round her lay,                      805
Whom Wene from year to year had known
To frolic prone, and that alone;
Though sore beset, she felt delight,
Some sly enjoyment at their plight;
For still she deemed that honour's law                    810
So dire a warrant would withdraw.
　　But when the priests their hymns had sung,
And their white robes aside had flung;
When from long words they came to deeds,
Had laid their hands on victims' heads,                   815
And sacred fire deposed the while,
To set on flame that lofty pile,
Good sooth but Wene thought it was time
For her best wits to be in prime;
And straight to bring them to the test,                   820
They ne'er could be in more request!
Soon as the rapt and ruthless priest
Had strewed the deathdew on her breast,
(An ointment rich in heavenly worth!

And fragrance of the flowery north)                    825
And said the words that they were all
To say on entering Odin's hall;
Wene thus, with sharp and cutting speech,
Presumed the pedagogues to teach.
    "List me, thou priest of Scania's land,    830
And dolts that drudge at his command;
If you dare christian maidens send
To Odin's hall, 'tis at an end.
Valhalla falls! And, take my word,
His godship of the shield and sword          835
From heaven descends with all his crew,
Driv'n headlong from yon vales of blue;
A banished, branded, broken corps,
Doomed to disturb the heavens no more.
    A sacred sovereign, you'll allow,        840
Should better know these things than you;
For God's vicegerent must have wit,
What the supreme approves as fit;
And this is truth. If you would please
Great Odin, and his wrath appease,           845
Preserve us lovely living things,
An offering to your king of kings.
For should you dare suppose that he
A god so brutalized could be,
As in dead virgin to delight                 850
More than in living beauty bright,
You shall stand beacons of his scorn,
And rue the time that you were born!
    But what is more; though Eric now,
In anger, hath consigned to you              855
Me and my maidens, to disgrace
The faith of Odin's kingly race;
On this rely; his ire and hate
Will turn on you when 'tis too late;
For on his name you fix a stain              860
That ne'er can be washed out again.
Think of a sovereign's sacred blood;
And for a word in churlish mood
Dare not to break through law divine,
And bring a curse on all your line;          865
That curse that rends from heaven's grace,

Pronounced by all the human race."
   At the first part of Wene's address
The priesthood smiled in scornfulness,
But the last part appeared too true        870
Even to their own distorted view.
They paused and whisper'd round the pile,
Keeping the flame subdued the while.
The virgins cried aloud to God
To look down from his blest abode,        875
And for his sake, who took the scorn
Of earthly virgin to be born,
Regard their peril and their grief,
And in his mercy send relief.
The priest of Odin was distress'd,        880
But to proceed he judged it best;
Though reason showed the thing unjust,
These Christian prayers were ne'er to trust.
   The flame unto the pile was set,
But seemed to mount in slow regret;        885
Reluctantly, from spray to spray,
It crackled, hissed, and crept away.
The smoke arose in writhing pain,
Then bent its course to earth again,
As if affrightened to bedim        890
The snowy robe and tender limb;
A throe of hesitation dumb
Seem'd struggling not to be o'ercome.
   Bless'd be the power of maiden's tongue!
Aye, in the lovely and the young        895
Supreme. And blest the shrewd surmise
That marr'd this odious sacrifice!
Before the prayer of rueful Wene
Had half way reached the last *Amen*;
Before the blaze had half way won        900
Around the altar of the sun,
The gods, or men contrived so well,
(For which the priests could never tell,)
To send relief, that at one bound
It seem'd to spring out of the ground.        905
A rapid rush of clansmen true,
In tartans dark, and bonnets blue,
Sprang on the pile as on a prey,

And bore the sacrifice away.
The priests were hurtled to a side,                              910
And with the fetters firmly tied;
Then up the flame rose to the sky,
Without a human groan or cry;
While Odin's servants lay amazed,
And on the bloodless offering gazed.                             915
    Within the tents, or them behind,
Swift as an image of the mind,
The clansmen vanished from the scene,
As quickly as their rise had been;
Each bearing virgin on his arm,                                  920
Panting with joy and wild alarm,
Their forms bedecked with many a wreath,
And all the bridal robes of death.
    The men were arm'd with sword and shield;
And, as the priests lay on the field,                            925
Full sore they wondered how they fared
So well; and why their lives were spared;
And how it hap'd their enemies
Had not made them the sacrifice.
But there they lay, safe and alone,                              930
And the mysterious troop was gone
Without a word of threat or dare;
They could not tell from whence they were!
If by the sea or air they went,
Or if by man or angel sent!                                      935
But this most shrewd conjecture rose,
On priest's conception comatose,
That these gods of the christian crew
Somewhat of earthly matters knew.
    But all this while, from side to side,            940
The battle rolled like swelling tide;
Now southward bearing all before,
Now north, with eddy, and with roar.
It raged in every lane and street,
And space where foemen chanced to meet.                          945
There was no foot of hallowed ground,
The regal Beregonium round,
That, ere the setting of the sun,
Was, inch by inch, not lost and won.
    The men of Moray, cautious still,                 950

Kept by the rampart of the hill,
And hurl'd their javelins afar,
Sore galling the Norwegian war;
But the fierce clansmen of the north,
And western tribes, of equal worth, 955
Rush'd to the fight withouten awe
Whene'er a foeman's face they saw,
And grievous was the slaughter then,
Among the bravest Scottish men.
   O what a waste of mortal life! 960
And what a stern and stormy strife
Prevailed around, as far it spread,
Reeling as warriors fought or fled;
Not then, as now, met mortal foes
In phalanx firm, to wheel, and close, 965
Trying to win by warrior sleight,
Manuevring by the left or right.
In those rude days they closed amain,
Fought shield to shield upon the plain;
And the more hot the battle glowed, 970
The farther was it shed abroad;
Till every warrior, as might be,
Fought one with one, with two, or three;
And one resistless hero's hand
Oft bore the honours from a land. 975
  So was it there; the battle's roar
Spread all along the level shore;
The city lanes were too confined,
Men had not scope unto their mind;
And forth they issued, west around 980
The citadel, on level ground;
And there, in motely mortal coil,
Went on the battle's bloody toil.
  Gods, how king Eric's sovereign wrath
Peopled the ghostly vales of death! 985
Where'er his rapid course he turned,
With deadlier heat the combat burned;
Forward, around, where Eric came,
There roared the vortex of the flame.
'Twas like the whirlwind's rolling ire 990
Carreering through a field of fire,
Rending and tossing as in play

The thundering element away!
    There was a chief of Albyn's land,
Of proud renown, hight Coulan Brande,       995
Who held his sway by forest stern,
And many a mountain dark and dern,
From where the Lwin meets the tide,
To proud Ben-Airley's shaggy side;
That land of red deer and of roe,       1000
Possessed by the great Gordon now.
    That chief had borne his honours far;
Amid the waning southern war;
And his red balachs* of the hill
The foremost in the broil were still.       1005
Ill brooked he the degrading sight
Of that deray, by Eric's might;
The vortex came like rolling tide;
Brande called his followers to his side,
And bade them open and give ground       1010
Till Eric passed, then wheel around,
And close upon his giant train,
Their ruthless ravage to restrain.
    "Press on them hard; retreat be none.
Be work like that of warrior's done.       1015
Let me behold no broad claymore
That is not stained with foeman's gore.
Let me behold no buckler's face,
That is not cloured with sword or mace,
And could you sever from his train       1020
That hector of the northern main,
Then, by my Ciothar's lofty crest,
That props the heaven's own holy breast;
And by that heaven's uplifted dome,
The warrior's everlasting home!       1025
This sword shall make that hero's brow
Stoop lowlier than his footstep now.
    Alongst the field king Eric flew,
The boldest from his brand withdrew;
Red desolation marked his track;       1030
For his fierce veterans, at his back,
On either side were hard bestead,

---

*Balachs.* Rude peasantry, boors.

Where gallant foemen fought and bled,
Along the midst of Coulan's train.
O dreadful grew the conflict then! 1035
For the red balachs of the fell,
With shout, with clangor, and with yell,
Rushed on the Norse from either hill,
And sore with broadsword and with bill,
Galled the array of that fierce train, 1040
Who, back to back, could scarce sustain,
Upon their long outlengthened line,
The claymore and the brigandine;
For every man that Coulan led,
Had his broad breast with bull's hide clad. 1045
    But Eric, reckless oft of life,
Pressed forward in the bloody strife,
Till so it hap'd, his train outgone,
There was he left to fight alone.
Coulan perceived, with throbbing breast, 1050
The chance had come for which he wished;
Longer the strife he could not shun,
Something illustrious must be done;
Either his life he must lay down,
Or raise his name to great renown; 1055
Then rousing all his energies
To this momentuous enterprize,
Shaking his javelin and claymore,
He took his stand the king before.
    "Oppressor of a guiltless land! 1060
Presumptuous spoiler! Stay thy hand."
He cried, "and hear the truth severe
That shall not quail for monarch's ear.
Say is thy soul not darker now
Than e'er was Ethiop's sable brow? 1065
Distained with every human crime
That blotted has the rolls of time?
Detested persecutor! Who
But thee would manhoods claim forego
By raising war, and breaking sooth 1070
With beauty, innocence, and youth?
And if no lies are on the wind
With sacrifice of dreadful kind?
Thou monster! Loathed be thy name

By all that bear the human frame! 1075
Thy race is run, thy hour at hand.
God speed the shaft of Coulan Brande!"
    With that his brazen javelin true,
With all his mountain might he threw,
And steady aim that might to tell, 1080
But short the winged weapon fell;
For to his left wrist it was tied
With plaited thong of badger's hide;
And swifter than a mind can frame,
Unpracticed in that warlike game, 1085
He hauled it back, and threw, and threw
With force increased, as nigh he drew.
    Eric was galled, his ire arose,
For faster, fiercer, came the blows,
Without impediment or let, 1090
From that aerial dragonet.
It pierced his gorget and his gear,
Stunning his brow and sovereign ear;
Yet farther durst he not advance,
But checked his own precipitance; 1095
For all his valour and his rage
Were tempered by reflection sage.
He foamed with ire, and plunged amain,
Like restiff steed that scorns the rein,
But saw if once his men he left, 1100
An hundred balachs, stern and deft,
Watching with keen and eager eye,
Unto their leader's aid to fly;
And with a smile of fierce disdain,
He drew back to his lines again. 1105
    Loud shouted Brande's obstreporous horde,
Lauding their brave and matchless lord,
Who, in the splendor of his might,
In single combat had outright
Put the great northern king to flight! 1110
    What vengeance Eric poured around!
Where'er a combatant he found
That dared the strife, and many a brave
And gallant knight found timeless grave.
Oft did his glance embrace the strand 1115
In search of haughty Coulan Brande;

Who on his name had cast a stain
That would not well wash out again;
Alas! he knew not, nor could see
How much more deep that stain would be!        1120
    Brande of his fortune was so proud,
The very ground on which he stood
He seem'd to spurn, as o'er the war
His eye rolled loftily afar.
This Donald Bane, his neighbour sly,        1125
Beheld, and strode up hastily,
And said these words, for clansmen near,
Each other's pride could never bear:—
    "O, Gallant Brande, make haste, advance;
For none, save thee, with sword or lance        1130
Can check yon scourge of Scotia's host;
Advance, or Albyn's banner's lost!
Gillespick's down; Clan-Gillan's broke;
Lochourn leans o'er his tarnished oak;
My brother Allan keeps aloof,        1135
Trustless of arm, and armour's proof;
The field's laid waste!—O Brande, there's none
Can turn that tide but thee alone."
    "Reptiles!" cried Brande, and forth he flew,
Curling his lip, and eke his brow,        1140
Straight onward, Eric to amate,
Yet there was something in his gait
That showed reluctance to the way;
A hurry, mingled with delay,
Perhaps an omen ill defined,        1145
A darksome boding of the mind.
    As ever you saw a fiery steed
Eying the path with wistful dread,
And eyes with gleams of fury glancing,
Wheeling, snorting, rearing, prancing;        1150
Till lashed amain, away he breaks,
The steep ascent with fury takes,
And panting, foaming, flounders on,
Until his strength and spirits gone,
Straining to do more than he can;        1155
Down rushes chariot, horse, and man.
    So was it now with Coulan Brande,
The lord of Lwin's forest land,

The hunter proud of Garnachoy,
Of Laggan, Lurich, and Glen-Roy,                    1160
Goaded along, he crossed the field,
Upreared his sword, advanced his shield,
And straight in front of Eric ran,
And thus addressed the godlike man:—
    "Traitor, me thought that I had once          1165
Given thee to know thy puissance
Not matchless was. Why wilt thou then
Come fuming 'mid ignoble men,
Staining thy brand with boorish blood?
Tyrant, this braggart lustihood                    1170
Becomes thee not. Desist, for shame!
Here stands thy conqueror, thee to tame."
    Eric laughed loud; both cliff and shaw
Made answer to his keen ha, ha!
No more he said, but sword in hand                 1175
He ruthless rushed on Coulan Brand;
Furious upon the chief he came,
Trowing his mountain might to tame
At the first blow; but tale he lost,
And reckoned once without his host.                1180
    Brand his broad buckler managed so,
That Eric's furious rush and blow
Were borne aside with science yare,
And Eric spent his force in air,
So freely spent, that, on the strand,              1185
Forward he stumbled o'er his brand;
And, since his restless life began,
Such perilous risk it never ran.
    Brand was too brave of soul and mind
To strike a prostrate foe behind;                  1190
Else doubt is none, that, in that strife,
Low at his steps lay Eric's life;
And kinsmen ever blamed the hand
That nailed him not to Scotia's strand.
    Eric arose, his cheek was flushed,            1195
With shame the mighty monarch blushed
In such an onset thus to be
Outdone, and more in courtesy.
The pangs he felt were so severe,
They were too much for him to bear;                1200

And wish from these his heart to free,
Had nearly brought him to his knee;
But pride of rank, and pride of name
His brilliant and untarnished fame,
Mustered around without controul,                    1205
And whispered vengeance to his soul.
He rose and turned upon his foe;
Brand all undaunted met the blow;
And in the scuffle that ensued,
Showed equal might and fortitude.                    1210
    The king rushed in, with guard and clasp,
And, trusting to his powerful grasp,
From which no single force could free,
He closed with Brand impetuouslye;
And seizing on his gorget fast,                      1215
With wrench that giant force surpassed,
He snapp'd the clasps of burnished steel,
And casque and cuirass, to his heel,
Came off with jangle and with clang,
And on the level rolled and rang.                    1220
    Brande turned to fly, for in a word,
His buckler, too, if not his sword,
Had in that struggle fallen or broke;
He turned to fly; but, at a stroke,
Eric, while at his utmost speed,                     1225
Sheer from his body hewed his head.
Far rolled the bloody pate away;
The body ran without a stay,
A furlong in that guise uncouth;
So said the Norse, and swore it truth!               1230
    The shouts of subjects from each side,
Aroused the hero's warrior pride—
A moment roused it; but anon
On his brown cheek the tear-drop shone
And throbs that in his bosom's cell                  1235
Heaved like an earthquake, told too well
How sore he rued the ruthless blow,
Inflicted on so brave a foe,
To whose high generous soul he owed
A life most haplessly bestowed,                      1240
And, as if from a dream awoke,
These words he rather groaned than spoke.

"Ah! How this laurel galls my brow!
Eric ne'er vanquished was till now."
    The battle now had spread away      1245
Round all the friths of Keila bay;
Parties with adverse parties meeting,
And both sides losing and defeating.
Where chief 'gainst adverse chief prevailed,
There partial success never failed;      1250
And braver feats were never done,
Than were that day round Beregon,
Nor more illustrious were the slain,
No not on Illium's classic plain.
    The chiefs that most distinguished shone    1255
In that dire day's confusion,
Were Allan Bane, who, mid the war,
O'erthrew the giant Osnagar,
Despite the monster's might in weir,
And execrations dread to hear;      1260
Roaring and cursing his decay,
He foamed his savage soul away.
    And the brave lord of Sutherland,
Of dauntless heart, and steady hand,
Who ne'er in all that bloody coil      1265
Engaged with foe he did not foil:
A Finnish prince, and Danish lord,
Both sunk beneath his heavy sword,
And all their buskin'd followers fierce,
Dismayed at such a stern reverse,      1270
Before the men of Navern dale,
Fled like the chaff before the gale.
    Intrepid Gaul, the lord of Tain,
And Ross's wild and wide domain,
Bore on with unresisted sway;      1275
He seemed some demon of dismay,
That through the ranks of Scania's war
Bore desolation fierce and far.
His heideous face was grisly grim,
His form distorted every limb,      1280
Yet his robust and nervous arm
Laid warriors low as by a charm;
For that rude form contained a mind
Above the rest of human kind.

Distressed by Brande's unworthy fate, 1285
Eric drew off ere it was late,
Scowling and sobbing by the way,
Like warrior that had lost the day;
And oft repeating as before,
These words, that grieved his captains sore. 1290
"Eric is conquered at the last!
His day of victory is o'erpast!
A conquest ne'er to be believed,
Reversed, remitted, nor retrieved!"
  The gathering trumpet's lordly sound 1295
Gathered his scattered bands around,
And from a fiercer bloodier fray
That note ne'er called his troops away,
For though the vantage they had won,
Never was Eric so outdone. 1300
  The pride of Albyn's mountain strand,
The great emporium of the land,
The royal city now was lost,
And occupied by Eric's host.
The seven towers of Selma too, 1305
Alas, were all abandoned now!
That for a thousand years had stood,
Circled by mountain, cliff, and flood,
And ne'er had oped at foe's behest,
Except to captive or to guest. 1310
  For why, this landing unawares
Placed Hynde amid a thousand snares;
Her throne, her city, and her state,
Beleaguered by a force so great
That the least turn of fortune might 1315
Place all at Eric's steps outright;
Her nobles, this to countervail,
Bore her away by oar and sail
In dead of night, and not alone;
Her court, her treasures, and her throne 1320
Safe in Dunstaffnage they did place,
Where they had vantage-ground, and space
To place their guards by ford and mere,
That none should come their treasure near.
  Their queen thus safe, it was not strange 1325
That they, with coolness and revenge,

Fought out the field, from early noon
Until the rising of the moon;
And then drew off, from pursuit free,
In still and sullen enmity.                              1330
    Though concious that a fraud full low
They had practiced upon the foe,
They knew not yet on what pretence
Eric had dared this bold offence,
Breaking his faith without regard,                       1335
And rushing on them unprepared.
Their loss was great, without defeat;
Yet still their queen, and coronet,
And sacred chair, they all the three
Had placed in full security;                             1340
Hence they resolved to suffer dumb
The good, or ill, as each should come.
    Outposts and watchers not afew
They placed around in order due,
And straight prepared, with rueful speed,                1345
To pay due honours to the dead.
At dawn a messenger was sent
With all dispatch to Eric's tent,
To ask of him one peaceful day,
Due honours to their slain to pay.                       1350
    The king at first declined discourse;
O'erwhelmed with sorrow and remorse
He sat alone, and neither foe
Nor friend durst nigh his presence go.
His ruthless and ungenerous deed,                        1355
Gnawed his great soul without remede;
And the brave youth he loved the most,
Prince Haco, was in battle lost,
With all the chief men of his train,
And were not found among the slain.                      1360
If these were captives; what avail
Had fallen into his enemy's scale!
If they deserted had the land,
The sceptre wriggled in his hand.
    But worst of all, the sacrifice                1365
In which he trusted from the skies
Support to win; the god's command
Seemed to have reft from his right hand.

And now his priests, in deep despair,
Foreboded nought but dole and care.                    1370
    Eric sat wondering all alone,
Into what land these maids had gone.
If some intrepid chief's array
Had come and stol'n his pledge away,
Or Odin had upborne them all                           1375
Alive into Valhala's hall.
At all events, that hope was cross'd,
The mighty sacrifice was lost,
And Eric was assured too well,
Of more mishap than tongue could tell;                 1380
In such a toilsome mood he flounced
When Albyn's herald was announced.
And this was all the answer brief
He deigned unto the Scottish chief.
    "Go tell him to speed home apace;                  1385
With son of that decietful race
No speech I hold; no, not a word,
Save o'er the gauntlet or the sword."
    "Sire he is sent express, to say
The Scots request one peaceful day                     1390
To bury those in battle slain,
Which, if refused, they come again
Over their carcasses to fight,
And God in heaven support the right!
For that dear privilege they'll stand                  1395
While living man is in the land."
    "The Scot's request is bold and high;"
King Eric said with kindling eye.
"And straight I grant it, with demand
That at the bier of Coulan Brande                      1400
I as chief mourner may appear;
Then all the obsequies so dear
To kindred souls, shall mingled be,
Without offence or frown from me.
In feast, and sport, we all combine;                   1405
No answer—Let the charge be mine."
    Next morn, by mutual consent,
The arms of either host were pent
In heaps within each camp, and all
Flocked to the mingled festival.                       1410

At Coulan's bier king Eric took
Chief place, with attitude and look
That struck both friend and foeman's eye
As fraught with dread solemnity.
High on the hill of Kiel were laid                    1415
The ashes of the mighty dead,
Hence called, with all its cairns so gray,
"Hill of the slain" until this day.
There over Coulan's lowly urn,
The mighty Eric deigned to mourn;                     1420
Bowed his imperial head full low;
Wiped his red eye and burning brow;
And thus address'd the gaping croud,
That motely, moving multitude.
      "Soldiers and denizens give ear;                1425
I say the words, that all may hear;
Here o'er the dust of chief I bow,
That conquered him who speaks to you;
He owns it. Eric of the north,
Who ne'er before acknowledged worth                   1430
Superior to his own, avows
That Coulan Brande has shorn his brows
Of all the honours there that grew,
So long untarnish'd, bright, and new.
      This chief, in battle's deadliest hour,         1435
A forfeit life held in his power;
That life was mine; it lay full low
Beneath his lifted, threatened blow:
But, scorning vantage and reward,
High honour only his regard,                          1440
His hand withheld the blow intended.
Would to the gods it had descended!
And cleft this heart, whose festering core
Feels pangs it never felt before.
      Fortune gave me such chance again.              1445
Where was thine honour Eric then?
In heat of ire I struck the blow
That laid this injured hero low;
But that this stroke I did not stay
I'll rue until my dying day,                          1450
And to the world this truth proclaim;
Eric, with all his martial fame,

For once acknowledges compeer;
Vanquished in that he held most dear,
He shrouds the palm can ne'er return    1455
Within this low and sacred urn.
    Warriors from shores of either main,
In honour of this hero slain
Contend in every manly game,
To be memorial of his name,    1460
And theirs, upon that fatal field,
Who rather chose to die than yield,
Prizes I grant, of warrior store,
Such as were never giv'n before.
    As is the wont in Albyn's land,    1465
For the chief hero's shield and brand
The trial first, of skill, must be,
Who throws the dart as well as he;
For in that art he could outdo
All men that ever javelin threw.    1470
Hie to the contest. Every throw
Be steady as at breast of foe."
    Each chief, each prince, and petty king,
Prepared the javelin to fling;
But of them all, the steadiest hand    1475
And eye, were those of Olaf Brande,
Who bore in triumph from the field
His honoured brother's sword and shield,
Though it was ween'd, superior skill
Could well have won, but had not will.    1480
    The prize that next was heaved in sight
Was golden bracelet burnished bright,
To him that in the race should won
And chief, and hind, and all outrun.
For there no preference was to be    1485
Confered on lineage or degree.
Nor was it needful, in that age,
The low estate of vassalage
Withheld the peasant from the bound
Of high exploit, or deed renowned.    1490
A being mean of mind and frame,
The creature of a chief supreme,
No heart had he, no towering hope
With proud Milesian might to cope;

And of these casts, as legends say, 1495
The traits remain until this day.
 Eager the golden prize to win,
The light of heart came pouring in,
All noble youths of agile make,
Who loved the race for running's sake; 1500
And hoped, at least, to mar the way
Of the superiors in the play,
But chiefly, if they saw the Norse
Would Albyn's youths put to the worse.
 No fewer wights than twenty two, 1505
All rank'd in one continuous row,
Stood strip'd and belted for the fun,
And panting for the word to run.
The bugle sounded short and low;
A paleness glittered on each brow! 1510
The bugle sounded loud and long,
And every chest, with heavings strong,
And mouth, seemed gasping, breath to gain,
More than their circuits could contain.
The bugle's third note was a yell, 1515
A piercing, momentary knell;
O what relief to every heart!
It was the warning note to start.
Then, like a flock of sheep new shorn,
Or startled roes at break of morn, 1520
Away they sprung mid whoop and hollo,
And light of foot were those could follow.
 For three good furlongs of the space
All was confusion in the race;
For there was jostling, jumping, fretting, 1525
And breasts with elbows rudely meeting.
One luckless youth, who took the van,
Had overstrained him as he ran;
His ardent breast had borne him so
Much faster than his wont to go, 1530
That his untoward limbs declined
To strike as fast as he'd amind,
Refused the effort with disdain,
And down he stumbled on the plain.
Before one could have uttered cry, 1535
Or sworn an oath, or closed an eye,

A dozen flagrant youths and more
Were heaped and tumbling on the shore,
Each muttering terms uncouth to tell,
And cursing aye the last that fell.            1540
    Some rose and ran, though far behind;
Some joined the laugh, and lay reclined;
But now the interest grew extreme;
Feldborg the Dane, like lightening's gleam,
Shot far ahead, and still askance         1545
Backward he threw his comely glance,
Which said full plainly, "I opine,
Most worthy sirs, the prize is mine."
And still, as straining in the race,
A smile played on his courteous face;      1550
For who in courtly form and air,
With Danish Feldborg could compare?
    The farthest goal is won and past,
And Feldborg still is gaining fast;
Aloud the joyous clamour grew          1555
From Eric's grim and boisterous crew,
While one small voice alone could cry
From Albyn's host, "Fie, kinsmen! fie!"
Eon of Elry heard that word
Called by a loved and honoured lord,      1560
And straight the bold athletic bard
Was after Feldborg straining hard,
Skimming the sandy level plain
With swiftness man could not sustain.
    Feldborg of Denmark, now the time    1565
To weave thy name in lofty rhyme!
To rank thee with the seraphim
Depends but on thy strength of limb!
But well thou knew'st, that chief, nor king,
Nor living creature without wing,         1570
To scale the heaven might try as well,
As run with thee and thee excel;
All this thou knew'st; it was thy boast,
And so did many to their cost.
    Eon M,Eon, do not flinch,          1575
For thou art gaining inch by inch;
Strain thy whole frame and soul to boot;
Nay thou art gaining foot by foot;

The croud percieves it with acclaim,
And every accent breathes thy name.        1580
Eon of Elry, God thee speed!
One other stretch and thou'rt ahead.
    Feldborg? what's that which thee doth gall?
What does thy look equivocal,
Note by thy side glittering so bright?        1585
A bracelet clasp! By Odin's might!
And that proud slieve in verity,
Eon of Elry forces by.
Strain, Feldborg, strain, or thou shalt lose;
His elbow kithes, and eke his nose!—        1590
Where are they now? In moment gone!
And Feldborg gains the goal alone!
Elry lies prostrate, on the plain,
Laughing aloud, in breathless pain,
Spurning the Land with fitful scream;        1595
While his bright eye's unearthly gleam
Bespoke full well how ill content
His heart was with the incident.
With curling lip, and brow of flame,
And cheek that runkled half for shame,        1600
He laughing rose, and wiped his brow,
"By heaven, sir, I no more could do!"
    The golden gem of potent charm
Glitters on Feldborg's swarthy arm,
While he surveyed the trophy grand,        1605
With countenance as proudly bland,
As every bard in Albyn green
An eulogist to him had been,
And given to him a fulsome lay,
The dearest pledge e'er came his way.        1610
    Feldborg, thou hast effected feat,
That stamps thee consummately great;
For thou hast vanquished one whose name
Stands highest on the list of fame.
Although an enemy and a Dane,        1615
I hold thy victory immane;
Laud to thy noble visage swart!
Illustrious man of tale and chart!
Proffessor of the running art!
    The game that followed next the race        1620

Was pitching of an iron mace,
From buskin'd foot, which made it wheel,
With whirling motion like a reel
Aloft in air—I not pretend
This ancient game to comprehend;                    1625
But yet th' expert could pitch it straight,
Like arrow at convenient height,
And lodge it at the farthest goal,
Fixed in the earth like upright pole.
A Danish game it was; therefore,                     1630
The Danish chiefs the mastery bore;
As for the Scots, they toiled invain;
Like coursers without curb or rein,
They spent their spirits and their might
In efforts without rule or sleight.                  1635
       King Eric, grimly smiling, came
As if in sport to share the game;
He heaved the mace like stager's poy,
And twirled it like a lady's toy;
Then from his buskin's brazen toe,                   1640
Like arching meteor made it go;
Till far beyond the utmost cast,
Deep in the soil it lodged fast.
No clamour rose, as one might trow,
From such a monarch's master-throw;                  1645
But through the host, from man to man,
A buzz of admiration ran,
And no one judged it for his thrift,
The mighty mace again to lift.
       "Come princes! Captains!" Eric cried,         1650
With voice as though he meant to chide;
"Come. To the sport! It is confest
You're playing with it for a jest,
Pitch all again. I gave that throw
As earnest of what more I'll do."                    1655
       Each chief disclaimed the fruitless deed,
Or hem'd, and smiled, and shook the head;
And all prepared the prize to yield,
And rush into some other field.
When lo! a burly peasant proud                        1660
Came dashing through the heartless croud,
Shouldering both chief and vassal by,

As things of no utility;
Straight to th' avoided mace he broke,
And aye he stuttered as he spoke;                    1665
Fast from his tongue the threatenings fell,
Though what they were no man could tell;
Up from its hold he tore the mace,
And ran unto the footing place;
But lo his sinewy foot was bare,                     1670
Nor sandal, hoe, nor brog was there!
To pitch the iron club from thence,
Surpassed even savage trucculence.
    The laugh was loud, while, in his need,
The kerne looked round for some remede,             1675
And for a bonnet grasped his hair,
But a red snood alone was there.
With grasp of power he seized the bent,
A sod from the earth's surface rent;
Which, placing on his foot with care,               1680
The massive club he rested there;
Then his strong limb behind him drew,
And grinned and goggled as he threw,
But with such force he made it fly,
It swithered through the air on high,                1685
Soughing with harsh and heavy ring,
Like sound of angry condor's wing.
Till far beyond king Eric's throw
It delved the earth with awkward blow.
    "Beshrew the knave!" king Eric cried;             1690
His nobles with a curse replied,
And crouded to the spot outright,
To wonder at the peasant's might.
"Who, or what is the savage young?"
Was ask'd by every flippant tongue;                 1695
But to make answer there was none,
Nor one could tell where he was gone;
The golden prize on high was reared,
But claimant there was none appeared.
    "It is the giant Loke, I know,                     1700
Sent by the gods from hell below,
Against my growing power to plot,
And vanquish might which man could not,"
With look demure king Eric cried.—

" 'Tis Loke!" each Scanian tongue replied.        1705
The victor was not found, nor came
His prize of lofty worth to claim;
And all the Norse believed, and said,
Their king by Loke was vanquished.
  The leaping, wrenching, fencing, all,        1710
Were won by youth's of Diarmid's hall;
While Eric's soldiers took their loss
With manners quarrelsome and cross.
But of the boat-race these made sure;
The gilded barge was their's secure;        1715
On that they reckoned, and prepared
To row with skill and strength unspared.
  Fourteen fair barges in a row,
Started at once, with heaving prow;
With colors, flags, and plumes bedight;        1720
It was forsooth a comely sight!
King Eric's seven rowers swarth,
Chosen from all the sinewy north,
Were men of such gigantic parts,
And science in the naval arts,        1725
And with such force their flashes hurled,
They feared no rowers of this world.
  King Eric, crowned with many a gem,
Took station on his barge's stem;
Secure of victory, and proud        1730
To shoot before the toiling croud,
And spring the first upon the shore;
Full oft he'd done the same before.
  Seven boats of either nation bore,
In proud array from Keila's shore,        1735
With equal confidence endowed;
To each seven rowers were allowed;
But by the way they spy'd, with glee,
That one Scots barge had only three,
And she was bobbing far behind,        1740
As toiling with the tide and wind;
The rowers laughed till all the firth
Resounded with the boisterous mirth.
Around an isle the race was set,
A nameless isle, and nameless yet;        1745
And when they turned its southern mull,

The wind and tide were fair and full;
Then 'twas a cheering sight to view
How swift they skimmed the ocean blue,
How lightly o'er the wave they scooped,                1750
Then down into the hollow swooped;
Like flock of sea-birds gliding home,
They scarcely touched the floating foam,
But like dim shadows through the rain,
They swept across the heaving main;                    1755
While in the spray, that flurr'd and gleamed,
A thousand little rainbows beamed.
    King Eric's bark, like pilot swan,
Aright before the centre ran,
Stemming the current and the wind                      1760
For all his cygnet fleet behind,
And proudly looked he back the while,
With lofty and imperial smile.
O mariners, why all that strife?
Why plash and plunge 'twixt death and life?            1765
When 'tis as plain as plain can be
That barge is mistress of the sea.
    Pray not so fast, sir minstrel rath!
Look back upon that foamy path,
As Eric does with doubtful eye,                        1770
On little boat, that gallantly
Escapes from out the flashing coil,
And presses on with eager toil,
Full briskly stemming tide and wind,
And following Eric hard behind;                        1775
And worst of all for kingly lot,
Three rowers only man the boat!
    "Ply rowers ply! We're still ahead.
Lean from your oars—shall it be said
That the seven champions of the sea                    1780
Were beat outright by random three?
Ply rowers ply! She gains so fast,
I hear their flouts upon us cast.
'Tis the small boat, as I'm on earth!
That gave so much untimely mirth."                     1785
    "Curse on her speed! Strain rowers strain!"
Impatient Eric cried again,
"See how she cleaves the billow proud,

Like eagle through a wreathy cloud;
Strain, vassals, strain! If we're outrun          1790
By moving thing below the sun,
I swear by Odin's mighty hand,
I'll sink the boat and swim to land."
    Hard toiled king Eric's giant crew;
Their faces grim to purple grew.          1795
At last their cheering loud *ye-ho*
Was changed into a grunt of wo.
For she, the little bark despised,
And foully at the first misprised,
Came breasting up with skimming motion,          1800
Scarce gurgling in the liquid ocean;
And by, and by, and by she bore,
With whoop of joy, and dash of oar!
The foremost rower plied his strength
On two oars of tremendeous length,          1805
Which boards on further end revealed,
Broader than Eric's gilded shield;
The monarch trembled and looked grave
To see the strokes that rower gave.
    Just then he heaved his oars behind,          1810
Like falcon's wings leaned to the wind,
As passed his little pinnace plain
The monarch's meteor of the main;
And as he bent his might to row,
He struck king Eric's gilded prow          1815
With such a bounce, and such a heave,
That back she toppled o'er the wave,
And nigh had thrown as nigh could be
Her king and champions in the sea.
"Ho! Oar-room, friends! Your distance keep"          1820
Cried that rude hector of the deep.
    "Ye-ho! Ye-ho!
    How well we go!
Our's is the bark that fears no foe!"
    Then, not till then, king Eric saw          1825
A sight that struck him dumb with awe;
He saw that wight the very same
In the last sport who overcame,
And now, by Odin's dread decree,
Had vanquished him most ominously.          1830

"'Tis Loke the giant! Loke again!"
King Eric cried in thrilling pain
"How flourish can our sovereign sway
If gods and demons both gainsay?"
"'Tis Loke!" responsed each rower grim,                1835
"Too oft I've thwarted been by him!"
    With sullen prow and lagging oar
The vanquished barges reached the shore,
But there the conquerors could not see,
The boat stood leaning to the lee;                     1840
An ancient boat with wale and wem,
And gilded mermaid on her stem;
Then great the press and bustle grew,
That wonderous boat of hell to view,
Till an old man of Isla came,                          1845
And of the marvel made a claim;
He'd lent his boat for trivial fare,
But knew not who the hirers were.
That poor man got the prize prepared,
Or in its stead a meet reward.                         1850
    The tossing of the ponderous mall
Was won by Ross of Armidell;
And he who farthest threw the stone
Was from the Spey, his name unknown.
But when the rival archers came,                       1855
At target hung afar to aim,
The Scandinavians bore the gree,
For ages trained to archery.
No bard can now detail those games,
Nor modern tongue express their names,                 1860
But at the setting of the sun,
Nor Scot, nor Norse, had lost or won;
The rival nations equal stood,
In feats of skill and lustihood;
One prize remained—one and no more,                    1865
To stamp one side THE CONQUEROR!
And now, no living can concieve
The ardor that prevailed that eve;
It was as if each nation's fate
Hung on the scale, it was so great.                    1870
    The prize was one of high avail,
A Roman sword, and coat of mail;

A sword most dazzling to behold,
Its basket was of burnished gold;
Such blade no Briton ever drew, 1875
A two edged blade of glancing blue,
Five feet from point to bandelet;
And yet when bent they fairly met,
A mighty Roman general wore
That sword and armour both of yore; 1880
The feat of wrestling was the game,
On which each nation's pride or shame
As on a balance heaving hung,
While every patriot heart was wrung
With feelings of such poignant sway, 1885
As none can rate this latter day.
    A level field was fenced around
With palisades, mid rising ground;
And after proclamation due,
Into that field the wrestlers drew; 1890
But that no vantage one might gain,
The Norse and Scot went twain by twain.
Each prince and chief of note was there,
Threescore and four came pair by pair;
Eric among the rest appeared, 1895
Who never man at wrestling feared.
    The bugle sounded to begin,
And two by two, as they came in,
The wrestlers joined most orderly,
With toe to toe, and knee to knee. 1900
And there each stood with parched throat,
Waiting the bugle's warning note;
Then fiercely heel on heel 'gan dashing,
And bones and sinews rudely crashing,
And ere the heart of keenest throes 1905
Had beat on breast an hundred blows;
Or three short minutes were outgone,
Thirty and two were overthrown.
    They counted heads of Dane and Scot,
And wrestled till the end by lot; 1910
And after many a strain and twist,
And many a bruised antagonist,
Two conquerors there stood revealed,
One at each corner of the field.

Eric was one in trial true;                          1915
The belted plaid and bonnet blue
Bespoke the country and degree
Of his tall comely enemy;
From his high bearing and his mein,
He seemed some chief in manhood green;               1920
All knew him as he forward came,
They said, though none could say his name;
But many an anxious eye was bent
On this decisive throw intent.
    Slowly they neared, the stranger's air     1925
Was sauntering stately void of care,
But Eric's eye had fiery glow,
Like that of planet rising low;
His brows the while projecting far,
Like dark cloud over rising star,                    1930
And once he started and upreared
His form, as if he treachery feared,
Or marked a feature undefined
That brought some guilty deed to mind.
    The youth, too, paused, and still as death,   1935
Like statue without blood or breath
He stood with hands half raised and bent,
And face fixed on the firmament,
As if he wrestled had with heaven,
Or with some strong enchantment striven.             1940
Men were afraid, and Eric's jaw
Descended as oppressed with awe;
For Loke across his memory came,
Like thrill of an electric flame;
But wheth'r the youth the powers unblest             1945
And adverse to the gods addressed,
Or looked with suppliant's humble eye
To Odin's stern divinity,
Bowed to the glorious god of day
Or owned the son of David's sway                     1950
No one could guess for in those times
These were the gods of northern climes.
This wild and solemn revery o'er,
Eric stood up the youth before,
And words of wonderment express'd,                   1955
How he had vanquish'd all the rest;

For that some champions had been thrown,
Who ne'er in prowess had been known
To yield to man, save one alone.
        The youth no answer deign'd, or heed,          1960
To this sly boast of matchless deed,
But moveless stood as form of stone,
And turn'd his eye to Beregon.
"Come, art thou ready?" Eric said.
The youth a slight obeysance made,          1965
With due respect, as it behoved;
But neither hand nor foot he moved,
Till Eric laid his arms around,
And in his iron-grasp him bound;
Then lithely did he square each limb,          1970
And set his joints in proper trim.
        The king that day had thrown his men
By heaving them aloft; and then,
With foot advanced, and ready knee,
Twisting them down full dexterously.          1975
But when he tried that youth to foil,
He seem'd to grow unto the soil;
Despite the force of Eric's frame,
Which might of man could never maim,
That stranger wight, with careless air,          1980
Preserved his footing firm and fair,
And circumvented with such sleight
His great opponent's perilous might,
That even the monarch's breathless jest
Began his doubts to manifest.          1985
        "Ay, ay! so thou refusest even
To make one movement towards heaven?
Doesn't this bespeak a perverse mind,
And heart most sordidly inclined?
Well, some new mode we then must press          1990
To suit thy taste of daintiness."–
        With that the hero nerved his might,
And roused his spirit to the height;
That force that (save by wizard's charm)
Had never blench'd at mortal arm,          1995
That so by one resistless throw
He might o'erpower this haughty foe,
And in the lists the highest place

Might still pertain to Odin's race.
    The effort's past; the trip, the strain,    2000
All given full sway, and given in vain!
And ne'er before had human eye
Beheld such dazzling energy,
Without all surliness or wrath;
But now King Eric gasp'd for breath    2005
So sore, that every Danish eye
Saw double; many a heart beat high,
While ears sang out the torrent's lay,
Dreading the issue of the day.
    The doughty youth had all this while    2010
Nor utter'd word, nor deign'd a smile;
On the defensive kept he shy,
The monarch's utmost skill to try;
But now, with such an agile pace
That eye his motions scarce could trace,    2015
He wheel'd and sprang from side to side,
And sundry feints and amblings tried;
Till, ere onlooker was aware,
He struck King Eric's heels in air.
Yet to the game inured so well,    2020
He caught the monarch as he fell,
And, as supporting him he stood,
These words nigh chill'd King Eric's blood:–
"Ah! God forbid that king renown'd,
And head with sacred honours crown'd,    2025
Should fall degraded to the ground!"–
    Although the faltering cluck was gone,
At once the tongue and voice's tone
Assured King Eric of the sway
That twice had vanquish'd him that day.    2030
And to be thus within the clasp
Of giant Lok's own hellish grasp,
(Whom Scania's priests, a thing full odd!
Hold both a demon and a god,)
O that was such a direful case,    2035
It spoke the end of Odin's race!
    "Down with immortal rivalship!"
King Eric cried, with quivering lip;
"This is unfair! Let mortal man
Vanquish King Eric if he can;    2040

But with the Eternal's rival he
Presumes no chance of mastery.
I know thee, fiend! thy dreadful name,
Thy malice, and thy power supreme!
And, for one punishment condign,   2045
Thy hate to Odin's heavenly line.
Though of the race of gods, thou art
A deadly demon at the heart!
And though in various forms this day
Thou hast o'ercome me in the play,   2050
Be't known to all the world abroad,
To man I yield not, but a god.
For thou art Lok, that being stern,
Whom reason's eye can ill discern;
A god—yet virtue's deadliest foe,   2055
And ruler of the realms below."–
  The youth laugh'd a derisive peal,
And lightly turn'd upon his heel,
To work his way throughout the list,
And aye he mumbled as he press'd   2060
Some scraps of high contempt, that spoke
Of "mongrel gods, and fabulous Lok."
And he had vanish'd in a trice,
As was his wont; but every voice
Call'd out to stop him, friend or foe,   2065
That Albyn might her champion know.
"Stop him!" cried Eric; " 'tis my mind
You may as well oppose the wind;
Or try to stop, by mortal force,
The lightning in its vengeful course."–   2070
  The youth was staid and brought to task;
All came to listen, few to ask;
And there they heard, without reserve,
From tongue, they deem'd, that could not swerve
From native truth, for there stood he,   2075
Telling, in flush'd simplicity,
How he was all unknown to fame;
That poor M,Houston was his name,
Though some there were, on Erin's shore,
Call'd him M,Righ, and Eiden More,   2080
He knew not why; but he had come
Of late to seek his native home,

And there had first that self-same day
Beheld his country's proud array.
That, eager in the lists to try 2085
His youthful strength with princes high,
He had in various garbs appear'd,
And gain'd, because he nothing fear'd;
Having no title of renown,
Nor line, to bring discredit on. 2090
  With shouts that echoed far away,
And hush'd the waves on Keila Bay,
The sons of Albyn gather'd round,
And heaved their champion from the ground;
And with obstreperous acclaim, 2095
Lauded M,Houston's humble name.
The Norsemen's looks were all dismay,
And dark as gloom of winter day,
As well they might; for he whose worth
They eyed as pole-star of the north, 2100
By a Scots peasant overcome,
Stood sullen, mortified, and dumb!
  The sword was brought, of magic mold,
And armour glittering all with gold,
And proffer'd to this wond'rous guest, 2105
Whom Eric mildly thus address'd:–
  "This is thy prize, and fairly won;
But, as no man beneath the sun
Can this enormous weapon wield,
Or prove the armour and the shield, 2110
Let them by friends appraised be,
And I'll pay down that sum to thee.
They are an old bequest. I may
Not part with them in sportive way."–
  "No, sire; exchange there can be none; 2115
The prize I claim, and that alone."–
  "I'll pay it thee in warrior store,
In silver, brass, or golden ore;
So they be valued, here in sight
I'll pay thee triple for thy right."– 2120
  "No, I have said it; and I swear
By the great God whom I revere,
If proffer me thy royal throne,
The prize I'd have, and that alone."–

"Then take it thee; and be thou first          2125
He that repents the claim accursed!
If I had ween'd that human might
Could e'er have reft them from my right,
I would have staked a kingdom's worth,
Ere that I valued most on earth.          2130
Ah, hind! thou little art aware
Of what hath fall'n unto thy share!
Curse on these feats of youthful play,
Unmeet for men whose heads are grey!"—

    M,Houston grasp'd the treasure bright,          2135
And ran, and laugh'd with all his might,
Loud jabbering something 'bout the sun,
And kingly treasures fairly won;
While many a youth of Albyn's land,
Follow'd the wight along the strand,          2140
With clamour vast, and song combined,
Till far upon the wavy wind,
Within the Connel's winding coast,
The loud and jarring sounds were lost.

    Fair maid of Albyn's latter day,          2145
How brook'st thou now thy shepherd's lay?
Dost thou not grieve that royal blood
Should yield to vassal's dogged brood?
And griev'st thou not that beauteous Hynde
Should in old fortress be confined,          2150
And ne'er appear in martial show,
In proud defiance of her foe?
And worst of all, the wayward Wene,
That thing of whim, caprice, and bane,
Is lost! transported to the skies,          2155
To Odin's barbarous paradise;
Or borne to place, unknown to man,
Save some uncouth outlandish clan;
While he, the premier of the brave,
For maiden's love or warrior's glaive,          2160
Prince Haco of the northern main,
Is lost upon the battle plain.
Full sorely art thou cross'd, I ween,
In what thou wished'st to have been;
The amends lies not within my power,          2165
But in thine own, beloved flower!

Be this thy lesson; pause, and think,
Fair seraph, leaning o'er the brink
Of sublunary joy and bliss,
The pale of human happiness.                          2170
Stretch not too far the boundary o'er,
To prove the sweets that float before,
Or certain is thy virgin meed
To shed the tear and rue the deed!
    Can nought allay that burning thirst,          2175
That hath annoyed thee from the first,
That fluttering hope that spurns controul,
That yearning of the aspiring soul,
Which gilds the future with a ray,
Still brighter than thy present day,                  2180
And onward urges thee to strain,
For what 'tis ruin to obtain?
    Ah! that inherent fault in thee
Has ruin'd worlds, thyself, and me!
While yet thy lovely mold was new,                    2185
And pure as dawning's orient dew,
Bright as an angel's form could be,
A flower of immortality!
Alas! when then thy sacred core
The germs of this impatience bore,                    2190
Which ill thy tongue can disavow;
What has thy bard to hope for now?
    One grace he asks, a trivial suit,
That thou for once this flame acute
Wilt conquer, and peruse along,                       2195
Straight to the end, his epic song,
Else he shall rue it to his cost;
His hope, his little charm is lost.
And can'st thou tarnish by a look
The treasures of his valued book?                     2200
Valued alone, when it hath proved
Itself by Scotia's maids beloved.
    He once was crown'd by virgin's hand
The laureate of his native land,
While many a noble lady's voice                       2205
Lauded aloud the fond caprice.
By virtue of that office now,
Which maiden dares not disallow,

He hereby, in the sacred names
Of reason, right, and regal claims,                      2210
Debars, with due and stern regard,
The following characters unspared,
From the plain banquet here prepared:–
     First, he debars, without redress,
All those of so much frowardness                          2215
As yield them to the subtile sway
Of their great foe on primal day,
And, without waiting to contend,
Begin the book at the wrong end,
And read it backward! By his crook,                       2220
This is a mode he will not brook!
     Next, he debars all those who sew
Their faith unto some stale review;
That ulcer of our mental store,
The very dregs of manly lore;                             2225
Bald, brangling, brutal, insincere;
The bookman's venal gazetteer;
Down with the trash, and every gull
That gloats upon their garbage dull!
He next debars (God save the mark!)                       2230
All those who read when it is dark,
Boastful of eyesight, harping on,
Page after page in maukish tone,
And roll the flowing words off hand,
Yet neither feel nor understand;                          2235
All those who read and doze by day,
To while the weary time away;
All maids in love; all jealous wives,
Plague of their own and husbands' lives!
All who have balls and routs to give                      2240
Within a fortnight; all who live
In open breach of any rule
Imposed by Calvin's rigid school;
All such as sit alone and weep;
All those who lisp, or talk in sleep;                     2245
Who simper o'er a fading flower,
Or sing before the breakfast hour;–
All such have more whereof to think
Than pages marbled o'er with ink;
And I beseech them keep the tone                          2250

Of their own thoughts—let mine alone.
   All those must next excluded be
Who feel no charm in melody;
That dogged, cold, slow-blooded set,
Who scarce know jig from minuet;          2255
And, what is worse, pretend to love
Some foreign monstrous thing above
Their native measures, sweetly sung
By Scottish maid in Scottish tongue.
   He next debars all those who dare,       2260
Whether with proud and pompous air,
With simpering frown, or nose elate,
To name the word INDELICATE!
For such may harp be never strung,
Nor warbling strain of Scotia sung;       2265
But worst of guerdons be her meed,
The garret, poll, and apes to lead:
Such word or term should never be
In maiden's mind of modesty.
   Oft hast thou grieved my heart full sore   2270
With thy sly chat and flippant lore;
Thy emphasis on error small,
And smile, more cutting far than all;
The praise, half compliment, half mock,
The minstrel's name itself a joke!        2275
But yet, for all thy airs and whims,
And lightsome love the froth that skims,
I must acknowledge in the end
To 've found thee still the poet's friend,
His friend at heart; would jeer and blame,   2280
But aught degrading to his fame
Would ne'er admit, nor join the gall
Of slanderers mean and personal;
Therefore, I bless thee, and engage
To profit by thy patronage.          2285
   Ah, how unlike art thou to those
Warm friends profest, yet covert foes!
Who witness'd, grinding with despite,
A peasant's soul assume its right,
Rise from the dust, and, mounting o'er    2290
Their classic toils and boasted lore,
Take its aerial seat on high

Above their buckram fulgency.
In vain each venom'd shaft they tried,
The impartial world was on his side;      2295
Their sport was marr'd—lost was the game—
The halloo hush'd—and, eke the name!
    Then lower stoop'd they for a fee
To poor and personal mockery;
The gait, the garb, the rustic speech,      2300
All that could homely worth appeach,
Unweariedly, time after time,
In loathed and everlasting chime
They vended forth. Who would believe
There were such men? and who not grieve      2305
That they should stoop by ruthless game,
To stamp their own eternal shame?
While he, the butt of all their mocks,
Sits throned amid his native rocks
Above their reach, and grieves alone      2310
For their unmanly malison.
    And so dost thou—the base and mean
Will gloat, and scorn, and scoff, I ween.
So be it. We must now pursue
Our theme, for we have much to do;      2315
And if before the closing measure,
I yield thee not the promised pleasure,
Then must I from my patrons sever,
And give my darlings up for ever.

END OF BOOK FIFTH.

# Queen Hynde

## Book Sixth

No muse was ever invoked by me,
But an uncouth harp of olden key;
And with her have I ranged the Border green,
The Grampians stern, and the starry sheen;
With my grey plaid flapping around the strings,     5
And ragged coat, with its waving wings.
Yet aye my heart beat light and high
When an air of heaven, in passing by,
Breathed on the mellow chords; and then
I knew it was no earthly strain,     10
But note of wild mysterious kind,
From some blest land of unbodied mind.
But whence it flew, or whether it came,
From the sounding rock, or the solar beam,
Or tuneful angels passing away     15
O'er the bridge of the sky in the showery day,
When the cloudy curtain pervaded the east,
And the sunbeam kissed its humid breast,
Invain I looked to the cloud overhead;
To the echoing mountain dark and dread;     20
To the sun-fawn fleet, or aerial bow;
I knew not whence were the strains till now.
    They were from thee, thou radiant dame,
O'er fancy's region that reign'st supreme;
Thou lovely queen of beauty, most bright,     25
And of everlasting new delight,
Of foible, of freak, of gambol and glee,
      Of all that pleases,
      And all that teases;
All that we fret at, yet love to see!     30
In petulance, pity, and love refined,
Thou emblem extreme of the female mind!
    O come to my bower, here deep in the dell,
Thou queen of the land 'twixt heaven and hell;
Even now thou seest, and smil'st to see,     35

A shepherd kneel on his sward to thee;
But sure thou wilt come with thy gleesome train,
To assist in his last and lingering strain:
O come from thy halls of the emerald bright,
Thy bowers of the green, and the mellow light,                    40
That shrink from the blaze of the summer noon,
And ope to the light of the modest moon.
O well I know the enchanting mein
Of my loved muse, my Fairy Queen!
Her rokelay of green, with its sparry hue,                        45
Its warp of the moonbeam and weft of the dew;
Her smile where a thousand witcheries play,
And her eye that steals the soul away;
The strains that tell they were never mundane;
And the bells of her palfrey's flowing mane;                      50
For oft have I heard their tinklings light;
And oft have I seen her at noon of the night,
With her beauteous elves in the pale moonlight.
      Then thou who raised old Edmunds lay
Above the strains of the olden day,                               55
And waked the bard of Avon's theme
To the visions of his Midnight Dream;
Yea even the harp that rang abroad
Through all the paradise of God,
And the sons of the morning with it drew,                         60
By thee was remodelled and strung anew.
Then come on thy path of the starry ray,
Thou Queen of the land of the gloaming gray,
And the dawning's mild and pallid hue,
From thy vallies beyond the land of the dew,                      65
The realm of a thousand gilded domes,
The richest region that fancy roams.
      I have sought for thee in the blue harebell,
And deep in the foxglove's silken cell;
For I fear'd thou had'st drunk of its potion deep,                70
And the breeze of the world had rocked thee asleep.
Then into the wild rose I cast mine eye,
And trembled because the prickles were nigh,
And deem'd the specks on its foliage green
Might be the blood of my Fairy Queen;                             75
Then gazing, wondered if blood might be
In an immortal thing like thee!

I have opened the woodbine's velvet vest,
And sought the hyacinth's virgin breast;
Then anxious lain on the dewy lea,                         80
And looked to a twinkling star for thee,
That nightly mounted the orient sheen,
Streaming in purple and glowing in green;
And thought, as I eyed its changing sphere,
My Fairy Queen might sojourn there.                        85
   Then would I sigh and turn me around,
And lay my ear to the hollow ground,
To the little air-springs of central birth,
That bring, low murmurs out of the earth;
And there would I listen, in breathless way,               90
Till I heard the worm creep through the clay,
And the little blackamoor pioneer,
A grubbing his way in darkness drear;
Naught cheered me on which the daylight shone,
For the children of darkness moved alone!                  95
Yet neither in field, nor in flowery heath,
In heaven above, nor in earth beneath,
In star, nor in moon, nor in midnight wind,
His elvish queen could her minstrel find.
   But now I have found thee, thou vagrant thing,          100
Though where I neither dare say nor sing;
For it was in a home, so passing fair,
That an angel of light might have lingered there;
I found thee playing thy freakish spell,
Where the sun never shone, and the rain never fell,        105
Where the ruddy cheek of youth ne'er lay,
And never was kissed by the breeze of day.
It was sweet as the woodland breeze of even,
And pure as the star of the western heaven,
As fair as the dawn of the sunny east,                     110
And soft as the down of the solan's breast.
   Yes, now have I found thee, and thee will I keep,
Though thy spirits yell on the midnight steep;
Though the earth should quake when nature is still,
And the thunders growl in the breast of the hill;          115
Though the moon should frown through a pall of gray,
And the stars fling blood on the milky-way;
Since now I have found thee, I'll hold thee fast,
Till thou garnish my song, it is the last!

Then a maiden's gift that song shall be,                    120
And I'll call it a Queen for the sake of thee.

———————————

Sing of the dreary gloom, that hung
Clouding the brows of old and young
Through all the Scandinavian host,
And on the monarch pressed the most,                       125
Who was of direful dreams the prey;
Some bodings of an olden day,
That told of trouble and of teen,
Of late fulfilled had darkly been;
Foiled by a hind before his host,                          130
His consecrated armor lost,
That held a charm he valued more
Than ought his ample kingdom bore.
His scowl bespoke his heart's dismay,
And bore with it an ample sway;                            135
For when in temper he was crossed,
His was the mood of all his host.
Captain passed brother captain by,
Paused, beckon'd waiting some reply,
But there was none; save look that spoke                   140
Of direful deed; no hint was broke;
But all percieved the armie's mood
Forboded tumult, reif, and blood.
Well did they bode; the order flew;
King Eric out his legions drew,                            145
Ranging his grim and hardy files
Around old Selma's stately piles.
In armor bright he walked alone
Before his host, and bade lead on
To force the Connel and the Croy,                          150
To waste to ravage and destroy
With fire and sword, and foray keen,
And none to save but Albyn's Queen.
Then waked his trumpets' brazen throat
With such a copious rending note,                          155
That rocks and doons began to pant;
The grey and solid adamant
Travailed in anguish with the noise,
With the first throes of thunder voice,

And issued sounds that shook the spheres, 160
And silence of a thousand years.
 Short was the march along the coast
Till, lo, an herald met the host!
The same that first it's rage appeased,
Now came to have his bond released; 165
Scotland's apostle there once more
Opposed king Eric on the shore.
 The king at first in high disdain
Answered the sage, and scarce would deign
Exchange of speech; but such a grace 170
Shone in Columba's saintly face,
That Eric calmed, and stayed his van
To listen to the reverend man.
 "Sire, I was called to distant shore,
Which caused the breach we all deplore; 175
On Gods own mission forth I went,
To save this christian throne intent,
My purpose failed, but then as now
I trust in heaven, and must avow
Our nobles' fraud, fearful I ween 180
Of parting with their youthful queen,
They have done that which monarch must
Declare right generous, though unjust.
They knew not Eric's honour high,
And now regret it grieviously, 185
But must be pardoned. List then me.
You've fought and conquered three to three;
But still your victory is not won,
Nor can be, ere to morrow's sun
See Albyn's champions once more beat, 190
And then we yield us to our fate.
Our queen with Scotia's coronet,
Shall on the combat field be set,
And whoso wins shall wear that crown,
And claim the wearer as his own: 195
She cannot wed all three, tis true,
But to her choice the three must bow."
 The king grinned in derision proud,
And shook his beard and said aloud
"Thou say'st? Then shall my champions be 200
Men not endowed to cope with me

In maiden's love. Of monsterous form
I've plenty, thanks to clime and storm!
That are, for all their spurious brood,
A match for aught of Albyn's blood.                    205
But, carping wizard as thou art!
Com'st thou again to act a part
Of wheedling fraud, to chaunt and chime,
And gain a blink of lothsome time?
To practice some unholy scheme?                        210
Some low and servile stratagem?
I say it boldly to thy face;
There is no chief of Albyns race
Dares for his soul presume to stand
And brave again this deadly brand.                     215
Thou know'st it churl as well as I.
Vile christian! I thy power defy!
Thee and thy gods I hold as dust,
And in this arm and Odin's trust."

　　"Say'st thou we dare not sire? Why then        220
Came I thus forth from Scotia's queen
These words to say? Hath she as thou
Swerved from her holy plighted vow,
And without warning or pretence,
In savage stormy insolence                             225
Broke on thy ranks with havoc red?
No! such is not the christian's creed!
Thou'rt the agressor, doubly so,
This thou hast done, and ere I go
I'll say, if 'twere my latest breath,                  230
*Thou darest* not fight and keep thy faith!"
　　"Worm! reptile! dolt! What dost thou say?
Thou clod of cold presumptuous clay!
Dare such a being, seared and knurl'd,
Beard Eric of the northern world,                      235
Whose arm has quenched the Saxon's light,
And broke the German's iron might,
The Pole and Painim overrun,
And beat the blue and bloody Hun?
Darest thou, in name of christian cur                  240
Or female prig, these honours blur?
He tells thee once again, and swears
By Odin's self who sees and hears

This lifted hand, and solemn vow,
He'll fight your champions brow to brow;                245
And if none dares his arm withstand
He'll fight the two best of your land.
Chiefs, kinsmen, sheathe your swords to day
In peace, and measure back the way
Straight to the camp. If Odin speed,                    250
To morrow sees your sovereign's head
Circled by Albyn's ancient crown,
And honours of supreme renown!"
    Columba bowed as it behoved,
But smiled to see the monarch moved                     255
To such a towering tempest pride
Which scarce to reason seem'd allied;
And as he gazed in Eric's face,
Some thoughts like these his mind did trace.
    I've touched the proper peg that winds  260
That mounting flame of mortal minds
Up to the height! O God of life,
Why mad'st thou man a thing of strife?
Of pride, and lust of power so high
That scarcely quails beneath the sky;                   265
Yet a poor pin, a scratch, a thrust,
Can bring his honours to the dust,
And lay the haughty godlike form
A fellow to the crawling worm!
I've sped; but thou alone can'st know                   270
Whether I've sped for well or wo.
O thou To Morrow! who can see
What joy or sorrow waits on thee!
    The seer retired, but quickly stayed,
And turning short, to Eric said;                        275
"Sire I request before I go
From thy own lips this thing to know,
Where be the maidens that were sent
As hostages unto thy tent?
For they were noble maids each one;                     280
Then say without evasion
Where they are now, for words are said
Which tend thy honour to upbraid,
And manhood too. Then pray thee tell
Where be the maids we love so well?"                    285

Eric looked grave; his towering pride
'Gan in an moment to subside;
His speech sank to a hollow calm,
And his pale lip bespoke a qualm
Of conscience, whil'st these words he spoke.    290
"By all the gods, and pesterous Lok,
I know not—dare not hint a dread
Into what clime their fate is sped.
They are where they are called to be
By the great king of heaven's decree!"    295
    "Sire, I have nothing from this speech,
Vague as the voice on ocean's beach,
Of sounding billow bursting in
With harsh unmodulated din.
If thou has dared such foul offence    300
As injure virgin innocence,
The curse of heaven be on thy head!
Be hence thy valour siderated,
And all thy pride and power decay—"
    "Withhold thy dread anathema"    305
King Eric cried. "I'd rather brave
The rage of Albyn's winter wave,
Her tempests wild, her headlands stern,
Her friths so crooked dark and dern,
Her nation's force in rear and van,    310
Than the vile curse of christian man!
    "Bring forth these champions of your land,
That mine may meet them brand to brand;
I dare them—If that will not do,
I'll fight the cravens one to two.    315
Thou hast my answer—speed thee hence;
And for thy nation's best defence
Be thou prepared; for if the Queen
To grace the combat is not seen,
I swear by Odin's warlike name,    320
And Thor's, the god of fire and flame,
No lists shall be, nor warrior boast;
I'll pour my vengeance on your host,
And neither leave you root nor stem,
Memorial, name, nor diadem."    325
    Columba raised his hand on high,
About to make sublime reply,

But Eric, to his trumpet's blare,
Wheeled off, and left the father there
Like statue raised by wizard charm,                    330
With open mouth, outstretched arm,
Forehead uplifted to the sky,
And beard projecting potently.
There stood the seer, with breath drawn in,
And features bended to begin;                          335
But lo! ere he a word could say,
The king had wheeled and sped away!
The sire relaxed his form the while,
His features softening to a smile;
And back he strode in thoughtfulness,                  340
To tell the Queen of his success.

    He found her decked in youthful pride,
And blithesome as a maiden bride,
Resolved to trust her royal right
Unto her doughty kinsmen's might;                      345
Despite of all her lords could say,
Who urged her from the lists to stay,
She vowed the combat she should see,
And trust in heaven's ascendancy.

    Columba's prayers and counsels wise            350
Had from despondence cleared her eyes;
While something he had said, or done,
Unto all living else unknown,
Had raised her hopes to such a height,
They almost wriggled with the right;                   355
For aught her court could see or deem,
They were even froward in the extreme.
No matter! Hynde felt no annoy,
But of the combat talked with joy;
And of the manner she would greet                      360
King Eric kneeling at her feet,
Or raise the chief that should him slay,
Unto her throne that self same day.

    These rash resolves could not be lost
To any part of Albyn's host;                           365
For all were summoned to appear,
That dared to stand the test severe;
While highest honours were decreed,
To those whose valour should succeed

In saving Albyn's rights and laws;                          370
That highest, most momentuous cause
For which a hero ever fought,
Or sovereign hero's aid besought.
    The evening came, and still no knight
Had proffered life for Scotia's right.                      375
The morning rose in shroud of gray
That ushered in the pregnant day,
Big with the germs of future fame,
Of Albyn's glory or her shame!
And still no champion made demand                           380
Of fighting for his sovereign's hand!
    Just as the morn began to shower
Its radiance on Dunstaffnage tower,
Queen Hynde, arrayed in robes of state,
Descended by the southern gate,                             385
With face that owned no hid distress,
But smiled in angel loveliness;
And there amid the assembled croud,
An herald thus proclaimed aloud.
    "Here stands our virgin queen alone,         390
The sole support of Albyn's throne,
Craving the aid of hero's might
To guard her, and her sacred right.
If any here dares wield a sword
'Gainst Scandinavia's sovereign lord,                       395
Or champions of his giant band,
Let such approach our sovereign's hand,
And tender here his envied claim,
That so enrolled may be his name;
And Scotia's banners may not fly                            400
O'er lists where none dares for her die;
The right, and left, and post between,
Must fall by lot—God save the Queen!"
    Still there was none that forward pressed!
Then first Queen Hynde's wan looks confessed  405
An inward pang allied to fear,
A dissapointment hard to bear;
Till Saint Columba by her side,
With locks of silver waving wide,
And spread hands quivering in the air,                      410
Thus to the heavens preferred his prayer.

"O thou Almighty one whose throne
O'erlooks Eternity alone;
Who once in deep humility
Lay cradled on a virgin's knee,                          415
Turn here thine eyes on one, whose face
Bespeaks the virtues of her race,
Who in this time of dire alarm
Puts not her trust in human arm,
But in thy mercy and thy truth.                          420
Then O! in pity to her youth,
Preserve her to her native land;
Save the dear maid of thy right hand,
And rouse up heros that may quell
The pride of braggart infidel.                           425
    Yes, thou wilt grant thy aid divine
To those who stand for thee and thine
Wilt steel their hearts, and guard their heads,
Till of their high and glorious deeds
Their everlasting rocks shall ring,                      430
And bards unborn their honours sing."
    Then bowed the saint his brow serene,
And tens of thousands said, AMEN!
    The bugle's note and herald's voice,
Proffered again the exalted choice                       435
To every youth of noble mind,
To chief, to yeoman, and to hind,
Of fighting in his country's name
For royalty and deathless fame.
Then up came courteous Sutherland,                       440
And, kneeling, kissed his sovereign's hand,
Proffering his arm, his sword, his life,
To combat in the glorious strife;
Saying, he delayed the honour dear
In hopes that better would appear.                       445
Then drew his lot, and fell the right,
To fight with Eric's left hand knight.
    Red Gaul of Ross came up the next,
And said these words with voice perplex'd.
"My beauteous liege, I stood aloof,                       450
In hopes some lord of more approof
Would eagerly rush forth to throw
The gauntlet to our reckless foe;

But as I am, for Albyn's good,
I dedicate my sword and blood."                          455
        "I know full well my generous lord
No braver chief e'er drew a sword,"
The Queen replied. "To such as thee
I well can trust my throne and me.
Now to the test the final lot                            460
Whether you fight the king or not."
He drew the left and thereupon
To fight king Eric there was none.
        From Hynde's dark eye, that glistened clear,
Was seen to drop the briny tear;                         465
While yet a softened smile of pain,
Like sunbeam through the morning rain,
Unto her lords seemed to confess
Their want of noble generousness.
Still good Columba cheered her on,                       470
And bade her trust in Christ alone;
Who could his sacred pledge redeem
Even in their last and great extreme.
        But time there was no more to stay,
The boats were gathered in the bay,                      475
And the decisive hour drew near,
When Hynde must in the lists appear;
On board she went in joyless mood;
An hundred barges plowed the flood;
While many a bold and warlike strain                     480
Of music pealed along the main,
That seemed to say in daring tone,
"Here comes the Queen of Caledon!
Who dares her royal rights gainsay?
Hie braggarts, to your wastes away!                      485
For, fume and banter as you will,
Old Albyn shall be Albyn still!"
Alas! what variance God hath seen
Between man's heart and outward mein!
        It was a gorgeous sight that day,                490
When Hynde arrived in Keila bay;
On high above her maidens borne,
Like radiant streamer of the morn;
A ray of pure and heavenly light,
Shining in gold and diamonds bright;                     495

A lovelier thing, of human frame,
From armies never drew acclaim,
Or looked more queenly and serene,
As heaving o'er the billow's mane.
An hundred barges her behind,                        500
Came rippling on before the wind;
And as they sunk the waves between,
Seem'd paying homage to their queen.
Such freight ne'er sailed on western sea;
A thousand dames of high degree,                     505
With lords and gallants many a one,
Came with the queen of Caledon.
      The lists were framed and fenced around
With pallisades on level ground,
And these again were lined the while                 510
With warriors, rank'd in triple file;
Upon the east was raised a throne,
Where Hynde in all her beauty shone,
And dames unnumbered, on each side,
Shone o'er the lists in blooming pride;              515
Their tartans streaming row on row,
Bright as the tints of heavenly bow.
      Sure 'twas a fair and goodly view!
Even Eric's dull and swarthy crew,
Whose minds had been bred up in broil,               520
Innured to blood and battle toil,
Acknowledged beauty's power supreme,
By looks of wonder's last extreme.
There one with half a glance might spy
The gaping mouth and gazing eye,                     525
The turgid blink, the scowl askance,
The sterile stare, the amorous glance;
The thousand looks that utterance found
In language mightier than in sound.
Ah BEAUTY! but for woman's mein                      530
And form, thy name had never been!
      When all the wonted forms were past,
The judges' rules, the warning blast,
King Eric and his champions twain,
Entered the lists the first again;                   535
And there, in daring martial pride,
Walked round the ring with stately stride.

Brave Sutherland appeared at length,
And Gaul, a burly mass of strength,
Knarled and misshaped from toe to chin;                540
But ah! the soul that frame within
Was pure, and brave, and calm, and just;
A pearl amid a coil of dust.
    There was a pause; the champions eyed
Each other well, and talked aside;                     545
Queen Hynde grew wan as winter snows,
Then ruddy as the damask rose,
As far she cast her humid eye,
O'er serried thousands crouding nigh;
But none rushed in—(O hour of shame!)                  550
To save his queen from foreign claim.
    'Twas said, the bugle blasts between,
Columba's lips were moving seen,
And his dim eyes to heaven up cast,
As that dumb prayer had been his last.                 555
O read not dumb! What speech can feign
The language of a soul in pain!
That pray'r, though made in deep distress,
Was not by creature succourless,
For, beaming from his faded eye,                       560
There shot a ray of hope on high.
    First to the queen King Eric kneeled;
Then to the judges of the field
He turned, and said, " 'Tis past the hour;
I claim my mistress and her dower.                     565
Produce three champions of your land,
Or give my bride into my hand.
The pledge is forfeited. Think'st thou
We three will shed the blood of two?
No, by the gods!—But I alone                           570
Shall fight that couple one by one;
Grant this, and I by it abide;
If not, then bring me forth my bride;
Or by yon heaven, and burning hell,
And all that in the twain do dwell,                    575
In carnage red I'll pen a law,
Such as your nation never saw!"
    "Hold, sire!" cried one of Scottish blood,
"This hasty challenge is not good.

The hour's not sped by half at least; 580
The shadow falls not to the east;
Yon arched oriel casement mark,
When its armorial rim grows dark,
The hour is past; till then tis meet
That thou should'st wait in mode discreet, 585
Since Albyn's hero's bold intent,
Is thwarted by some strange event;
So it would seem; remain a while,
Till once the shadow from the pile
Falls eastward; then, with woful heart, 590
Old Albyn from her queen must part."
    To Selma's tower looked one and all;
The sun-beam strayed aslant the wall,
In scattered fragments, pointed bright,
Though scarce one hundred'th part was light; 595
But still the casement's carved frame
Shone with a bright and yellow flame.
Each Scottish eye, as by a charm,
Fixed on that tower in wild alarm,
Till every little gilded mark 600
Vanished amid the shadow dark;
Save that the casement's arch alone,
With dim and fading lustre shone.
The last ray of the lingering sun
Is verging thence.—The prize is won! 605
    Columba rose, but not alone,
To lead the queen down from her throne,
And give her to the imperious hand
Of the oppressor of the land;
The tears streamed o'er her pallid cheek, 610
She looked abroad, but could not speak.
Then many a stiffled groan was heard,
From breasts that were but ill prepared
To yield their queen to such a fate;
Ten thousand swords were drawn too late; 615
One moment, and the prize is won
'Tis past!—The will of God be done!
    What gathering shout is that begun?
Toward the list it seems to run!
It heightens, gains, and swells around, 620
The skies are shaken with the sound;

While dancing swords and plumes give way,
Bespeaking tumult or deray,
Queen Hynde in middle step stood still,
Her sponsors paused with right good will,      625
And Eric step'd aside to see
What meant that loud temerity.
That moment through the lists there sprung
A warrior, stalwart, lithe, and young,
Covered with foam and ocean brine,            630
And blood upon his brigantine;
Then pointing to the oriel frame,
That still was tinged with fading flame,
He cried, "Behold, all is not lost!
I make appeal to Eric's host."—              635
     "No! to himself thou shall appeal,
To him who never yet did fail
On such request to yield a foe,
Or friend, or kinsman, blow for blow!"
King Eric said, "Here's fame for thee         640
To win. Thou art the man for me
To match! for rarely have I seen
A comelier warrior tread the green!
Wo's me, for such a blooming spray,
Which I must level with the clay!"            645
     "Yes, I'm for thee!" that warrior said,
And threw away his belted plaid;
And lo! his panoply was braced
With belts of gold, and interlaced
With many a fringe and mottled hem,           650
Where lurk'd the ruby's burning gem.
Such princely champion ne'er before
Had gauntlet thrown on Albyn's shore!
     Out through the host a whisper ran,
Which said, he was no earthly man!            655
But angel sent from God on high,
To help in great extremity.
Others there were, who said, he bore
Semblance to Haco, now no more;
So lithe, so brisk, so void of fear,          660
So brilliant in his warlike gear:
A ray of hope, like wildfire's gleam,
From Maidens' eyes began to beam;

But in the eye of warrior grim
That ray of hope was deadly dim.                665
Ah! how could youth, whate'er his worth
Excel great Eric of the north,
Whose arm had spread through human kind,
Dismay before, and death behind?
    Forthwith the deadly strife began;          670
Clash went the weapons man to man.
Harold of Elle, a Danish knight,
Was matched with Gaul on Eric's right;
And Hildemor from Bothnia's strand,
Was matched with seemly Sutherland;             675
Gigantic heros, bred to strife,
And combat yearly for their life.
    In that fierce onset to the fray
There was no flout nor giving way;
To work they fell, with blow and thrust,        680
And strokes that shore the level dust
From shields descending. Then, anon,
Flickering in air their weapons shone,
With crossing clang so fierce and high,
As if the javelins of the sky                   685
The livid lightenings at their speed,
Had met and quivered o'er each head.
    But soon both wings, as with assent,
Paused, and stood still, to gaze intent
On the tremendeous strife that grew             690
'Twixt Eric and his foeman new.
Such rabid rage on combat field,
No human eye had e'er beheld;
They tried to wound, but ne'er below,
Round, round they battled toe to toe,           695
But not one inch would either flee;
They fought on foot, they fought on knee,
Against each other fiercely flung;
They clang'd, they grappled, and they swung;
They fought ev'n stretched upon the green,      700
Though streams of blood ran them between.
    Thou ne'er hast seen the combat grand
Of two wild steeds of southern land,
Rivals in love? How grows their rage
And shakes the fen when they engage!            705

Or two wild bulls of bison brood,
The milk-white sovereigns of the wood
And the dire echos that outyell
The grovelling bellowing sounds of hell?
To view these savages aloof,                         710
Rending the ground with horn and hoof,
Or meet to gore, and foam, and die,
Is scarce a sight for maiden's eye!
Or two huge monsters of the wave
Rearing their forms, with lash and lave,             715
Far up the air; there snort, and howl,
Then grappling sink with groan and growl,
While bloody Ocean boils ahight,
And nature sickens at the sight?
    Such wars have been since Eden's day,     720
When thou first erred, and peace gave way;
Yes, such dread scenes have daily been,
Though such thine eye hath never seen;
And if thou had'st, as nought they were
Unto the mortal combat there,                        725
Where heros toiled in deadly strife,
For love, for empire, and for life.
    It was as if two Alpine hills,
Lords of a thousand rocks and rills,
And sovereigns of the cloudy clime                   730
Had once in battle joined sublime;
Together dashed their mighty heads,
Those gray and grizly pyramids,
The footstools to the gates of heaven;
Think of them shattered, torn, and riven!            735
And down the shrieking steeps beneath
Red rolling o'er a waste of death.
    Such was the strife, while every heart
Around them bore a trembling part.
Ah many an eye was dimmed of sight,                  740
When, in the terrors of their might,
They saw the heros grappling fast,
And deemed each struggle was the last;
But no! They seemed two beings framed
Not to be wounded, foiled, or maimed.                745
    Three times they closed within the shield;
Twice rolled they down upon the field;

But then, 'gainst Eric were the odds,
They heard him cursing by his gods!
And when they parted for a space,          750
A wildness glared in Eric's face;
A haggard rage not to be told,
A something dreadful to behold.
    Twas as if spirit from the earth,
Proud of its righteousness and worth,    755
Had hurried to the gates on high,
Passing poor pensive journeyers bye;
But lo! when at the gates above,
The paradise of peace and love,
He finds all entrance there denied,      760
And the poor ghost is thrust aside;
Barred from the presence of his god,
And banished to some drear abode,
In darkness and in chains to lie
Through ages of Eternity!         765
Think of that spirit's rueful case;
The lines of his deploring face,
And livid hues twixt black and wan,
And think of Eric if you can.
    This dread expression was not miss'd    770
By th' eye of his antagonist,
Who without wooing strength or breath,
Rushed in for victory or death.
But Eric still withstood his shock;
He fought a tower, a strength, a rock,    775
That ne'er had bowed unto the blast,
And knew no yielding till the last.
    At length their motions grew more slow,
Their swords fell lighter every blow;
And all percieved they neared the last,    780
And th' bitterness of death was past.
On swords that bent and streamed with blood,
They leaned, and staggered as they stood,
Yet grimly levelled eye to eye,
And not one inch would either fly.    785
The conflict's o'er—wild tremor reigns,
And stilness for a space remains.
    King Eric was the first that fell!
Down like a tower with groan and knell

The prince of heros falls supine! 790
A shudder pass'd through Norway's line,
Yet none durst enter in the list,
Although upon the monarch's breast
The foot of conquering foe was set,
And sword upraised, in vengeful threat, 795
His royal head and trunk to sever,
And close his conquests up for ever.
None interfered, nor called it crime,
Such were the statutes of the time.

But fate withheld the stroke designed, 800
For like the willow in the wind
The conqueror's plume began to bow,
And nod and totter to and fro;
Then back he staggered on the field,
Low bending o'er his sword and shield, 805
And ere his panting breath was gone,
He reach'd the rail and leaned thereon;
Then hands were stretched (why should they not)
That loosed his gorget from his throat,
His helm and corslet they untie, 810
And all his belted panoply;
And though no mortal wound they saw,
The blood oozed through at every flaw.

The champions on the field that stood,
Still gazing on the deadly feud, 815
Now, without langour or remark,
Flew to the combat stern and stark.
When, strange to tell! the lord of Ross,
The warrior shapeless, gnarled, and gross,
So hardly pressed the giant Dane, 820
That round and round upon the plain
He made him shift and shun the strife,
Then fairly turn and fly for life.
Gaul followed; but as well he might
Have chased the red deer on the height, 825
As his tall enemy, that strode
Slow round the field with taunt and nod;
Gaul waddling after sword in hand,
Puffing and cursing him to stand;
Loud rang the shouts around the pale, 830
And laughter gibbered on the gale.

On th' other hand the strife was sore
'Twixt Sutherland and Hildemore;
It was a combat to be seen!
If former combat had not been,                                835
To which all others when compared
Sank to a thing of no regard.
Keen was the strife–the Scot gave way,
Either in need or galliard play;
And as he wore across the field,                              840
They reached a spot of blood congealed,
Where, as the Swede rushed on his foe,
He slid, and stumbled with the blow,
When Sutherland, with ready sleight,
Met in his fall the hapless wight,                            845
And pierced the corslet and the core
Of the redoubted Hildemore.
He rolled in blood, and aptly tried
To stem the red and rushing tide;
Then feebly at his foeman struck,                             850
And cursed his gods for his misluck.
The accents gurgled in his throat;
Still moved the tongue, but speech was not,
And with a spurn and heideous growl,
Out fled the giant's murky soul.                              855
    Now, two to one, the flying Dane
In gnashing terror scowered the plain;
His king and his companion gone,
A madness seized the knight upon;
He tried to leap the circling piles,                          860
For shelter mid the Danish files,
But was repulsed with fierce disdain,
And thrown back headlong on the plain;
No hope thus left him in the strife,
He kneeled to Gaul and begg'd for life.                       865
    "No," said the chief; "it may not be!
The devil waits dinner for the three!
Henceforth with earth thou hast no tie,
The man is damn'd that dreads to die.
But one relief for thee is left,                              870
And here it is." With that he cleft
The stalwart craven to the brow,
Severing his ample brain in two.

"Beshrew thee for a bloody Scot,
If thou'st not done what I could not!"          875
Said Sutherland as turning bye,
But seeing the tear in Ross's eye
And sorrow on his nut-brown cheek,
So deep that word he could not speak,
The burly chief he kindly press'd,          880
Unto his bold and kindred breast.

     The day now won! a wild dismay
Blenched every cheek of Norroway!
The list now oped to Odin's priest,
Who ran to have his king released,          885
Upraised his huge and fainting frame,
And comfort spoke in Odin's name;
While leeches plied with license brief,
But ah! the case was past relief!
Seven deadly wounds, and all before,          890
Told them great Eric's reign was o'er.
Still not one sentence he had spoke,
But whispered o'er the name of Lok.
Lok! Lok! That name of terror hung
Alone upon his dying tongue.          895

     One told him, that, on Albyn's side,
Detraction had a tale supplied,
Of a low hind, M,Houston named,
Who not ev'n birth or lineage claimed;
When all refused had done this deed,          900
Laid low in dust that royal head,
And dared, even on his great acquest,
To set his foot on Éric's breast!

     When this the hero heard, he rolled
And writhed, as if in serpent's hold;          905
And from his motions it was plain
He deemed he fought the field again;
While, from his eye's impassioned gleam,
And smile of fury, it did seem
He thought his fame he could redeem.          910

     At length with throbbings long and deep,
Calm as a child about to sleep,
That softly lifts imploring eye
Unto the face of parent nigh,
So lay, so looked, in piteous case,          915

That terror of the human race!
And so must all the achievements vast
Of this poor world come to at last!
He stretched the priest his hand to hold;
That hand was bloody, glewed, and cold!                920
While these last words hung on his breath,
"Appease the gods!–Revenge my death!"
    Leave we the uproar and distress,
Which Norway's chiefs could ill suppress;
And pass we over, for a while,                         925
To Hynde, the flower of Albyn's isle,
Who saw, with joy ne'er felt before,
Her gallant champion Eiden More,
Upraise his pale and wounded head,
Like beauteous phantom from the dead,                  930
And wipe his bloody brow, and say
The faintness quite had passed away;
For untried armor wrought the harm,
And not the force of Eric's arm.
    The nobles now with clamorous glee,        935
Brought to the queen the conquering three,
And bade her choose a sovereign lord,
With whom they all should well accord;
So was she bound in her distress,
And in th' event could not do less.                    940
The courtly Sutherland looked down,
As guessing well to whom the crown
Was destined.  As for Eiden More
(Or poor M,Houston, called before,)
Leaning and pale he took his stand,                    945
And turned his eyes on Sutherland,
As one his sovereign soon to be:
But burly Gaul fell on his knee,
And said, with sly and waggish whine,
"My liege, I hope the chance is mine?"                 950
    The queen descended to the green
With lightsome step, but solemn mein;
And passing Ross and Sutherland,
She took M,Houston by the hand,
And with a firm unaltered voice,                       955
Said, "Here I make my maiden choice.
Since thou hast come without a meed

To save me in my utmost need;
And since, though humbly born, thou art
A prince and hero at the heart,                     960
So, next my saviour that's above,
Hence thee I'll honour, bless, and love."
    M,Houston's cheek grew pale as snow,
And the cold drops fell from his brow;
He raised his blood-stained hand, and seemed   965
About to speak; and, as they deemed,
He meant his sovereign to disswade,
And dissaprove of all was said.
But ere a word his tongue could frame,
Forward rushed lord, and noble dame,                970
And chief, and squire, in courteous way,
Due homage to their king to pay.
For all extolled with ready tongue,
The bravery of a hind so young;
And vowed by such a hero's hand,                    975
In death and danger aye to stand.
With prayers, and vows, and blessings said,
The crown was set upon his head;
Then shouts ascended on the wind,
"Long live King Eiden, and Queen Hynde!"            980
    Need was there for a leader brave,
For Norway's host, like wave on wave,
Began to move with backward motion,
Like tide receding on the ocean;
Only to come with double sway,                      985
Resistless on its sounding way.
    The king's last words had moved the host
To grief and rage the uttermost;
And without head to rule the whole,
The tumult grew without control;                    990
Distant from home, and in command
Of the great bulwark of the land,
The soldiers swore that land to have,
Or of green Albyn make a grave:
Ev'n Odin's priest approved the choice,             995
And only asked for sacrifice!
    "Now is the time!" the soldiers cried,
"While Albyn's army is employed
In joyful rite, and must repass

Yon straits with all their force a mass!"                1000
The chiefs gave way, and joined the flame,
For why, their natures were the same;
And thus their army moved away
To set the battle in array.

    Eiden, the new made king, beheld              1005
The movements on the adverse field;
And cried, in firm commanding tone,
"Each Scottish leader straight begone,
And range your clans these columns under,
For lo, a storm is gathering yonder!                     1010
And if maturely I foresee,
Dreadful the breaking out will be!

    Meantime, let all the dames of birth
Speed to the boats and cross the firth;
For in such dangers, woman still                         1015
Is a dead weight on warrior's will.
Dread not our strength, though some may scoff,
There's help at hand you wot not of;
Mine be the chance to lead the van,
And fight on foot the foremost man;                      1020
Stranger, I am to take command;
But, as my guardians on each hand,
I choose forth Ross and Sutherland.

    Haste! There is not a moment's speed
To lose, else we shall rue the deed.                     1025
See that these orders be obeyed,
And promptly. If they are delayed
By any here, better his head
Had been laid low among the dead!"

    The lords were stunned almost to death:      1030
They stared and gasped as if for breath.
"What's this?" said they. "A peasant's son
Speak thus to chiefs of Caledon!
Better we had our deed revoke,
Than bow our necks to such a yoke!"                      1035

    Eiden percieved that they demurred,
And, heaving high his mighty sword,
Which token gave of lustihood,
Bestained with Eric's royal blood.
"My lords," said he, "the danger's nigh.                 1040
Who's to command?–Is't you or I?–

By your award the right is mine;
When you ordain it, I resign.
But my commands are given to day
And he that dares to disobey!—                          1045
I *say* no more—submission's best—
If more must be, I'll *do* the rest."
    One of M,Ola's haughty race,
Who held and ruled the forest chace,
Along the lofty hills that lie                          1050
'Twixt Lochy's side and Kyle-an-righ,
By sad mischance a speech began
To this supreme impatient man;
A speech that tended more t' inflame
Proud opposition than to tame.                          1055
    King Eiden step'd across the space,
With scowl portentous in his face;
And in the midst of all his kin
He clove the chieftain to the chin.
"If more such speeches be to say,                       1060
We'll hear them out some other day.
This moment's ours—the next I wis
Is his who best improveth this,"
He said, and, heaving his claymore,
Resumed the stand he held before.                       1065
    The chiefs were awed at such control;
Such energy of frame and soul
They ne'er had witnessed among men,
Far less in upstart denizen;
Still there were some aloof that stood,                 1070
Unused to yield to vassal blood.
    Just at that instant, thro' th' array
A troop of strangers burst their way;
Led by an ancient chief, who rode
A stately steed with silver shod.                       1075
And O that chief was stern to view!
His robe was crimson set with blue,
While on his head, like spheral crown,
Stood broad and belted chaperoon;
His face was bent like curve of bow;                    1080
His hair as white as alpine snow;
His grey beard, quivering with disdain,
Hung mingled with his horse's mane.

Soon as he spied king Eiden stand
With bloody sword reared in his hand, 1085
He cried, "Ah, varlet! Do I see
Thee where I swore thou should'st not be?
How dar'st thou rear that bloody glaive
Before my face, thou saucy knave?
Hast thou been at thy old misdeeds 1090
Of breaking swords and splitting heads?
Thy mad temerity confest,
Hath drawn an old man from his rest.
Curst knave! I have thee at the last!
Seize on him friends, and bind him fast!" 1095
    "Hold, dearest sire, for mercy's sake!
The time is precious; all's at stake.
To day I have a task to do;
To morrow at thy feet I'll bow."
    "Ah, thoughtless, froward, frantic boy! 1100
Thou'st come to combat for a toy;
To fight with one will put thee down,
And for a foe that wears thy crown.
But I'll prevent it. Ne'er shall man
Before my face thy youth trepan. 1105
Sieze on the stripling, I command;
I'll bind him with this aged hand!"
    "Sire, I've already fought and won;
The great decisive deed is done.
This day thy grandson's hand hath slain 1110
Great Eric of the northern main;
Hath gained for thee supreme renown,
And won my father's ancient crown;
And what is more than power or fame,
I've won the flower of all our name!" 1115
    "What? Thou? Young eaglet of the rock!
Brave scion of a noble stoke!
Hast thou our sister realms set free
Of their relentless enemy?
The man who hath for twenty years 1120
Kept us in terror and in tears;
Who all despite to me hath done;
Hath slain my kinsmen one by one;
And my two sons, too rashly brave,
Brought both to an untimely grave! 1125

Ah! knave and vagrant as thou art,
Come let me hold thee to my heart!
   Ye chiefs of Albyn, cease your noise!
List, Colmar, king of Erin's voice!
This is your prince whom I embrace,      1130
The flower of all our royal race;
King Eugene's son of soul refined,
And cousin to your sovereign Hynde.
M,Houston's both, as you know well,
And that old dotard monk can tell.      1135
The truant fled me in disguise,
To seek adventures most unwise;
I followed, and sent men away
To seize him ere the combat day,
Who last night found him in his bed;      1140
He slew my officers and fled!
And, in despite of earth and hell,
Has done this day what you can tell.
   Yet he hath that which man exalts,
For all his foibles and his faults;      1145
O, he is brave! Most nobly brave!
Forgive these tears; I love the knave!
And here to Albyn's fair command
I join the crown of Erin's land.
   Fear not the north's huge power combined; 1150
Ten thousand men come me behind;
Who, with prince Eiden at their head,
Such havock and deray shall breed
'Mong'st that detested brutal host,
Glad shall they be to leave your coast."      1155
   Then the old pagan moved his crown
From off his head, and kneeled him down;
And thus with reverend lifted eye,
Addressed his bright divinity:—
   "Thou glorious SUN, my fathers' god,      1160
Look down from thy sublime abode
On thy old servant's sacred joy,
And bless this brave and blooming boy:
Not with the common light of day
Be thou director of his way,      1165
But on his inward spirit shine
With light empyreal and divine,

For thousands on his reign's success
Depend for mortal happiness.
    And when thou leav'st thy heavenly path,    1170
To sojourn in the realms beneath,
Be charges of him nightly given
Unto thy lovely queen of heaven,
Who with serene and modest face
Watches above the human race,    1175
And sways by visions of dismay
The spirits prone to go astray;
For 'tis not hidden from thy sight,
That dangers of the silent night,
Dangers of woman's witching smile,    1180
Of wassail, waik, and courtier's wile,
Far deadlier are to virtuous sway
Than all the perils of the day.
    And now thou source of light and love,
Great spirit of all things that move,    1185
If thou wilt hearken to my prayer,
I'll such a sacrifice prepare
As neer on beal-day morn did smoke
Beneath thy own vicegerent oak.
    O blessed SUN, I here avow    1190
Thee for my only god, and bow
Before thy bright and holy face,
Sublime protector of my race.
Whilst thy omnipotence shalt burn,
Creation's father'd eyes must turn    1195
To thee for life in donative,
And every comfort life can give.
I ask but life for me and mine,
Whil'st thy transcendant glories shine,
If farther world of bliss there be,    1200
To christian souls I yield it free."
    Columba hearing all revealed,
Before the ancient monarch kneeled,
And cried "O king did I not say
That this thy son should Albyn sway?    1205
That he was destined, he alone
To save his fathers' ancient throne?
Thou did'st oppose the high decree
As far as influence lay with thee;

Now it hath hap'd in way so odd                    1210
That man could not the event forebode,
But who can thwart the arm divine?
Thanks to another god than thine!"
   Colmar looked with averted stare
On the good father kneeling there,                 1215
But deeming him below reply,
He only hem'd and strode him bye;
Then, taking Eiden by the hand,
He led him forth along the strand,
Heaving his ample shield in air,                   1220
And wildly shaking his white hair;
Amid deep sobs and laughter blent,
He wept, and shouted as he went,
"Who buckles brand on brigantine
To follow Houston's son and mine?                  1225
The top of Albyn's royal tree!
Who's for King Eiden and for me?"
   The Scottish nobles, mad with joy
At finding there was no alloy
Yet mingled with the metal good                     1230
Of Fingal's and the Fergus' blood,
With shouts, and songs, and one assent,
To battle rushed incontinent.
The Norse came on—As well they might
Have tried to stay the morning light!              1235
The torrent turned by sword and spear;
Or stop'd the storm in its carreer.
   The Danish men came in the van
On Sutherland's and Ross's clan,
And dreadful was their onset shock,                1240
On the small plain beneath the rock;
Thousands were slain; and wo to tell!
There Colmar king of Erin fell,
And Gaul of Ross, as brave a lord
As ever wielded warrior's sword.                   1245
But clan on clan like billows toiling,
Came panting on for battle boiling,
And swept the Danish host before
Like wreck upon the ocean shore,
Which every wave drives on and on.—               1250
So rolled the strife tow'rds Beregon.

To tell of all the deeds of might
That there were done from noon to night,
Would steep my virgin patroness
To the fair bosom in distress.                              1255
And to relate the deeds of doom
Wrought by the royal young bridegroom,
Would class my song mid fabulous lore,
A folly I indulge no more.
Whene'er a breach was made in flank                         1260
Or rear of Albyn's battle rank,
There was M,Houston to supply
The breach, and quell the enemy.
Alas! he struck a foe too late
When brave old Colmar met his fate;                         1265
But yet the sire upraised his head,
And feebly laughed, and bless'd the deed;
Then bending back his rigid form,
Like shrivell'd pine beneath the storm,
He fixed his latest visive ray                              1270
Upon the glorious god of day;
And some weak piping sounds were heard,
As if a joy with terror jarr'd;
The parting spirit's last recess
From dust and dreary nothingness!                           1275
      The battle spread from cliff to shore,
Along the field where late before
The Danes and Norse the battle won,
That drove the Scots from Beregon.
This day that order was reversed,                           1280
The invader's closest files were pierced,
And foot by foot forced to give way;
Till, at the tofall of the day,
Their speed of foot they 'gan to try
Within the city gates to fly:                               1285
They wanted Eric in their van!
Which brave M,Houston overran.
      Cold, stretched upon his ample shield,
King Eric's corse lay on the field;
Deserted in the flame of fight,                             1290
When Norway's files wheeled to the right.
That and old Colmar's, side by side,
Were borne in barge across the tide

That funeral honours might be paid,
When to Iona's isle conveyed.					1295
    The tidings of the battle won,
And mighty deeds the king had done,
And who he was, on wings of wind,
Flew o'er the ferry to Queen Hynde;
Then of her joy supreme, I wot					1300
A bride may judge, but man can not.
    Meantime, as deep the darkness grew,
Eiden marched over Drimna-huah,
And down upon Bornean moor
Descending at the midnight hour,					1305
He found the enemy's camp at rest,
Without a guard to east or west;
Nought there remained in shape of foe,
But wounded men and menials low;
For all within the city gate					1310
Had fled, on learning the defeat;
And many, less intent on prey,
Unto the fleet had stolen away.
Spoil was there none, save armor good,
And hides, and furs, and beastly food;					1315
And ere the dawn of morning came,
That mighty camp was all on flame;
A sight that cheered each Scottish glen,
But woful one to Norway men!
    On the return of morning light,					1320
Full grieveous was that army's plight!
Without a general of respect,
Or prince, or leader, to direct,
Save one was qualified the least,
Odin's most high and potent priest!					1325
At board, at muster, or in field,
No warrior counsel Eric held;
Thro' life he suffered no cabal;
King, general, he was—all and all.
But this bluff priest, in wonderous way,					1330
Held over him perpetual sway;
While his last hest "the gods t' appease"
Made this old fox's powers increase;
Save he, the host would list to none;
They ran to him, and him alone.					1335

Until that time king Eric's word
Had saved the city from the sword,
From pillage, and the thousand woes
That conquer'd city undergoes;
And he had saved the innocent                        1340
From the last throes of ravishment.
But now this foul and bloated beast,
Issued forthwith the loved behest,
To take the city for a prey,
The loss and charges to defray;                      1345
To ravish women great and small,
Whether in city, field, or hall,
By way of fair and just reprise;
But keep the maids for sacrifice!
And once that great oblation made                    1350
Unto the gods, as Eric bade,
The priest would answer with his head,
For Odin's high and heavenly aid.
    The soldiers lauded with acclaim
The priest of Odin's blessed name;                   1355
And darted on the spoil away,
Like hungry tygers on their prey;
Then was a ravishment begun,
Such as in warfare hath been done,
But suits not ear of virgin young,                   1360
Nor aged minstrel's weary tongue.
    One hundred virgins, richly dress'd,
Were brought before this goodly priest;
And out of these selected he,
His god's own number—three times three;              1365
Those that remain'd by lot were shared
Among'st the soldiers of the guard.
O, grievious chance! Sure death was bliss
To such a heideous doom as this!
Well might they say, on such a lot,                   1370
Is there a god in heaven or not?
Unto the top of Selma's tower,
Beyond the reach of human power,
The nine were borne for sacrifice,
With songs and shouts that rent the skies;           1375
And the poor victims of despair
Were stretched upon an altar there.

By this time many a weeping dame
Had fled that hive of sin and shame,
And fled to Eiden's camp on high,　　　　　1380
Still placed upon Doon-Valon-Righ.
All other comforts he disdained,
Compared with the advantage gained;
And there above his foes he hung,
Like osprey o'er the gannet's young.　　　　1385
But Ah! the rueful news that came,
Distracted every warlike scheme;
There lay the victims in their view,
Surrounded by the heideous crew;
And Selma's seven towers could then　　　　1390
Have guarded been by twenty men
Against a thousand. Such a scene
May christian ne'er behold again!
The hymns of Odin that ascended,
Mid screams of death and horror blended,　　1395
Form'd such a dire discordant yell,
As sinner scarce shall hear from hell;
When through the far domains of night,
He takes his drear reluctant flight,
By power unseen impelled behind,　　　　　1400
That sails him swifter than the wind;
To some unfathom'd gulf below,
Which minstrel fears but does not know,
Of utter darkness and of dread,
The very spring and fountain head!　　　　　1405
　　"O, christian sire! if thee 'tis given
To influence the powers of heaven,
For woman's sake, though shun'd by thee,
For hers who nursed thee on her knee,
Now use it; for no earthly power　　　　　1410
Can save in this distressing hour!
Pray him in whom my soul believes,
Trembles before, but not concieves,
To send relief—O, father, cry!"
King Eiden said, with streaming eye.　　　　1415
　　Columba stood amidst the men,
And sung a hymn from David's pen;
Then kneeled upon the flinty rock,
The Almighty's succour to invoke;

But ere his God he had addressed,                    1420
Or suppliant word to him expressed,
The shouts from Selma's turrets sounding,
And tens of thousands these surrounding;
And smoke ascending to the sun,
Told that th' unholy deed was done.                  1425
    The king, the saint, and warrior bands,
Upon their faces laid their hands,
That on such scene they might not look,
Nor the abhorred remembrance brook;
But good Columba bent his eyes                       1430
On heaven, and with most vehement cries
Implored his Saviour and his God,
To smite with his avenging rod
Those rude and violating beasts,
Those vile polluted idolists,                        1435
Who dared to stain the murderous knife
In christian virgin's sacred life.
And, as 'tis told in ancient rhyme,
Some words like these, in tone sublime,
He muttered to the Eternal's ear,                    1440
Which made the kneelers quake to hear:—
    "Father of angels and of men!
Thou whose omniscient heedful ken,
Takes in the ample bounds of space,
Wherever smiles the human face,                      1445
Or seraphs sing, or angels dwell,
Or demons that in torment yell:
Turn here in mercy from above
One glance of justice, and of love;
Of love to those who look to thee,                   1450
And justice on their enemy,
And view a deed that stamps disgrace
On thy beloved human race.
O God can such a deed beseem
Creatures thou died'st to redeem?                    1455
    If thou Jehovah art alone,
And Odin but a God of stone,
Pour down thy vengeance from the skies
On these polluted obsequies.
View but the deed, and ere 'tis done                 1460
In darkness thou wilt veil the sun;

His flaming orb shall cease to burn;
The moon and stars to blood shall turn,
While the broad sky aside shall fold,
And like a garment up be rolled.          1465
    O if thou com'st, as come thou wilt,
Vengeance to take on human guilt;
Then be thy wrath in terror shown,
By thunders from thy awful throne;
Descend in majesty supreme;          1470
Thy chariot be devouring flame;
That all the elements may die
Beneath the lightening of thine eye.
The vales shall yawn, in terror rending,
The mountains quake at thy descending,          1475
Nay bow their hoary heads, and heave
Like skiff upon the yeilding wave.
    Stretch but thy finger from the spheres
Towards these bloody worshippers,
And lo the sinners and the spot          1480
Shall quickly be as they were not;
As things of terror no more seen,
Nay be as they had never been:
Shall be as Israel's sinful Korah,
Or second Sodom and Gommorrah.          1485
    Our eyes are fixed on thee above,
Our hope in thy redeeming love;
Then O in mercy to our race,
Hear in the heavens thy dwelling place!"
    While yet the christian army kneeled,          1490
Ere brow was raised from rock or shield,
Heaven's golden portals were unbarred,
And the Almighty's voice was heard!
It came not forth like thunders loud,
When lightenings through the liquid cloud          1495
Break up the dense and dismal gloom,
With chafe with chatter and with boom;
It came with such a mighty sound,
As if the heavens, the depths profound,
And tempests at their utmost noise,          1500
Cried altogether in one voice.
    Deep called to deep, and wave to wave;
Stone unto stone, and grave to grave;

The yawning cliffs and caverns groaned;
The mountain's tottered as they moaned;                    1505
All nature roared in one dire steven;
Heaven cried to earth, and earth to heaven,
Till both th' offenders and offended
Knew that the Eternal God descended.
  After the voice a whirlwind blew                 1510
Before it every fragment flew
Of movent nature, all in cumber,
And living creatures without number,
Were borne aloft with whirling motion.
It lifted ships out of the ocean;                          1515
And all, without one falling shiver,
Were borne away and lost for ever;
But there were cries of death and dread
Heard in the darkness overhead!
  After the wind, with rending roll                1520
A crash was heard from pole to pole,
As if the Almighty's hand had rent
The ample yeilding firmament;
Or split with jangle and with knell
The adamantine arch of hell;                               1525
And lo! from out the heavens there came
A sea of rolling smouldering flame,
Which o'er the sinners' heads impended,
And slowly dreadfully descended;
While with their shouts the welkin broke,                  1530
"Great Odin comes! our god, our rock!"
  Just while their horrid sacrifice
Still flamed with incense to the skies;
Just when their hearts were at the proudest,
And their orisons at the loudest,                          1535
The liquid sounding flame inclosed them,
And rolled them in its furnace bosom!
That city, filled with lothsome crime,
With all its piles of ancient time,
After the fiery column broke                               1540
Scarce gave a crackle or a smoke
More than a heap of chaff or tinder,
But melted to a trivial cynder!
  Scarce had the eye of trembling hind
Regain'd its sight, with terror blind,                     1545

His heart begun to beat in time,
Or shuddered at the heineous crime,
Ere the appalling scene was o'er!
One single moment and no more
All glittered with a glowing gleen,               1550
Then pass'd as they had never been.
Walls, towers, and sinners, in one sweep,
Were soldered to a formless heap,
To stand until that final day
When this fair world shall melt away,        1555
As beacons sacred and sublime
Of judgement sent on human crime.

            *     *     *     *     *

     Adieu dear maids of Scotia wide,
Thy minstrel's solace and his pride,
The theme that all his feelings move       1560
Of grief, of pity, and of love;
To thee he bows with lowly bend;
His ancient tale is at an end.
More would he tell, but deems it best
That history's page should say the rest.      1565
     There thou may'st read, and read with gain,
Of Eiden's long and holy reign;
How Haco and his winsome Wene
Were Scandinavia's king and queen;
How much he owed her in his sway,        1570
And loved her to his latest day.
He and his inmates to a man,
Dressed in the garb of highland clan,
(Of Sky-men whom they slew in fight
When Donald Gorm was beat by night)      1575
The maids had rescued from the pile,
And bore them to some western isle.
Thence they returned to Albyn's coast,
In wedded love, when all their host,
Save those within the ships that lay,        1580
Had melted from the world away,
And were recieved with greetings kind
By Eiden and his lovely Hynde.
'Twas there that ancient league was framed,

For wisdom, peace, and justice famed
For many ages—Blest is he
Thus hallowed by posterity!

Finis

# Memento of names places &c

*Beregonium* – A celebrated ancient city; the first capital and emporium of the Scots in Albion. Its Castle, according to Boethius and Harrison's Chronologie, was founded by king Fergus, so early as 327 years before the birth of our Saviour, and 420 years after the building of Rome. Around that castle (the Selma of Ossian) the city had continued to extend for the space of several centuries, until at length the marble chair and seat of government was removed to Dunstaffnage, on the southern side of the bay. The site of Beregonium is in that district of ancient Lorn now called Ardchattan, although Boethius includes it in the bounds of Loch-Quhaber. The castle, situated on the top of a huge insular rock, near to the head of a fine bay, and in the midst of a level plain, must, at that period, have been rendered impregnable, without any great effort in fortification. It is altogether a singular and romantic scene; and, being situated on the new road from Dalmallie to Fort-William, by Connel ferry and Appin, it is well worthy the attention of the curious, and, indeed, of every tourist interested in the phenomena of nature. That this city, with its towers and palaces, was destroyed by fire from heaven, tradition, song, and history all agree; and if ever oral testimony from an age so distant was bore out by positive and undeniable proofs, it is this case, so much out of the course of nature and providence. All that remains of this mighty citadel, with its seven towers, is one solid mass of pumice, burnt and soldered together in an impervious heap, wholly distinct from the rock on which it is situated. The outer wall, as well as the forms of the towers, may still be traced, but all are melted down to trivial and irregular circles of this incrusted lava. And as there can be little doubt respecting the existence of this renowned castle and city, so it is manifest, to me at least, that no human operation could ever have effected so mighty and universal a transmutation as is there to be witnessed.–*See* WILLIAMS' *tour*, Edin[r] Ency[dia] &c &c &c

In the place where the city stood, two streets, well paved, are still easy to be traced by a little digging; the one of these is called in Gaelic, Market-street, and the other, Meal-street. In making the new road, a vaulted gangway was here discovered under ground; and about 25 years ago, a man, in digging fuel, found one of the large wooden pipes that had conveyed the water accross the plain to the citadel. These few remains of the famous Beregonium have been preserved in the bowels of the earth; but nothing remains above ground, either of city or walls, but a few irregular lines of trivial cynder.

*M,Houston* – This hero's name is, it seems, wrong spelled throughout; a natural error of a lowlander. It ought, I am told, to have been M,Uiston; signifying the son of Eugene. He was the son of king Eugenius, the third of that name, long the accomplice, but at last the conqueror, of the far-famed Arthur. This Eiden More, (Aiden the great,) on his father's death, was, with his mother and infant brother, removed into Ireland by St

Columba, and afterwards restored to his throne by the diligence and influence of that holy man. In most things regarding him, the poem accords with history. He succeeded his uncle; married his uncle's daughter; embraced christianity; and reigned over the Scots 37 years in great prosperity. Columba lived to an exceeding old age; and, after his death, king Eiden seemed to have no more spirit or pleasure in this life, but quickly followed his great friend and patron to the grave in A.D.597.

*Eric* – The following short translation from an ancient Runic ode was handed me by a correspondent as probably relating to the death of this northern hero.

"Before Beregholmi did we fight with swords. We held bloody shields, and well stained spears. Thick around the shores lay the scattered dead. There saw I thousands lie dead by the ships. We sailed seven days to the battle in which our army fell.

We fought again; and then the bow uttered a twanging sound, sending forth tempests of glittering steel. It was at the time of the evening the foe was compelled to fly. The king of Erin did not act the part of the eagle–he fell by the bay. He was given for a feast to the raven–A great storm descended.–O ye sons of the fallen warriors who among you shall tell of the issue of that dreadful day.–The gods were angry, and before their vengeance who shall stand! THERE ERIC FELL, than whom there was no greater king: The sword dropped from his hand–the lofty helmet was laid low–The birds of prey bewailed him who prepared their banquets."

*Human Sacrifices* – That this picture of Scandinavian worship may not be viewed as an exaggeration I shall quote the words of the learned M. Mallet "The appointed time for their sacrifices was always determined by another opinion, which made the northern nations regard the number THREE as sacred, and particularly dear to the gods. Thus in every ninth month they renewed the bloody ceremony, which was to last nine days, and every day they offered up nine living victims, whether animals or human creatures. Then they chose among the captives in time of war, and the slaves in time of peace nine persons to be sacrificed. The choice was partly regulated by the choice of the bystanders, and partly by lot. The wretches upon whom the lot fell were treated by such honours by all the assembly; they were so overwhelmed with carresses, and with promises for the future that they sometimes congratulated themselves on their destiny. The priests afterwards opened the bodies to read in the entrails, and especially the hearts the will of the gods, and the good or evil fortune that was impending. The bodies were then burned, or suspended in some sacred grove near the temple. Part of the blood was sprinkled upon the people, part of it upon the grove; with the same they also bedewed the images, the altars, the benches, and walls of the temple both within and without." See Intro. Hist. Den.

< *Haco* prince of Norway king Eric's nephew and heir
*St Columba*– The apostle of Scotland
*Laughlan Dhu*–A monk of I

*St Oran* The hater of women
*Gilchrist* lord of Mar
*Diarmid* lord of Lochow and Argyle
*Gillian* lord of Lorn
*Harold* of Caithness
*Allan Bane* thane of Lochaber
*Donald Gorm* the chief of Skye
*Coulan Brand* A chief of the Country since possessed by Keppoch
*Connal Bawn*  An ancient warrior
*Moravius*–Lord of Buchan and Spey
*Sutherland*–lord of Sutherland
Colmar–King of Ireland and grandfather to M,Houston alias prince Eiden
   More
Priests of Odin; chiefs, and champions of Scandinavia &c. &c. &c

## Women
*Hynde*–Queen of Scotland
*Wene*–A noble maiden
Maidens her associates, attendants &c &c

The mountains, bays, castles &c mentioned in the poem are all contiguous
   to the scene, and retain their ancient significant names. >

*Scotticisms* – There are perhaps numbers of these scattered throughout the
   poem, but as I never guard against their introduction, so I neither can
   reccollect nor point them out: as instances
   *Gallow*–To gallow in old English is *to cow to terrify*. But in Scots it is *to make
      a loud broken or discordant noise* and in this sense it is always used here.
      Gallow and Gallo are synonimous, and peculiar to various districts
   *Gleen* to shine–to glitter v. A bright dazzling gleam s.
   *Torfel* To toss, to overpower. Also to roll over, to struggle with an over-
      powering force
   *Collied*–darkened, overshadowed
   *To-fall of day*–The close of day, eventide
   *Steven*–Uproar

# Note on the Text

The final section (pp. lx–lxv) of the Introduction of the present volume sets out the reasons why the Stirling / South Carolina edition of *Queen Hynde* is based on Hogg's manuscript of the poem (Huntington Library HM 12412).[1] In the Introduction, it is argued that *Queen Hynde* exists in two distinct versions. One of these, the manuscript version, is the poem as Hogg prepared it for publication; the poem as it stood when he offered it to the publishing institutions of the day. The other version is the poem as it stood after being processed for public consumption by these publishing institutions; this version of *Queen Hynde* is to be found in the first edition, and in all subsequent printings of the poem until the present one. The Introduction suggests that an editor might usefully edit either of these versions, or indeed both, separately; but it goes on to argue that the need for an edition of Hogg's original version is particularly urgent. The present volume, therefore, offers an edition of the version of *Queen Hynde* to be found in Hogg's manuscript; and the purpose of this Note on the Text is to discuss the details of the policies that have been followed in preparing the manuscript's version of the poem for publication.

One striking feature of Hogg's manuscript immediately poses a problem for the editor: several long passages have been marked for deletion, usually by having two vertical lines drawn through them. Were these deletions made by Hogg himself, before he passed his manuscript into the hands of the publishing institutions of the day? Or were they made by the publishing institutions, as they prepared the poem for its public appearance? In seeking an answer to these questions, it will be useful to examine Hogg's dealings with the publishers and the printer of *Queen Hynde*.

The Introduction of the present volume suggests that the opening portion of the manuscript of *Queen Hynde* was probably written in or around 1817; and further suggests that the manuscript was probably completed in 1824 (pp. xiv, lxvi). Confirmation of this date for the completion of the poem is provided by a letter of 10 July 1824 from Hogg to Robert Southey. Hogg writes:

> I have no news but that I am just sending the last sheets of an *Epic Poem* to press!![2]

The London firm of Longman had published *The Private Memoirs and Confessions of a Justified Sinner* a few weeks earlier, in June 1824;[3] and the same firm had also published Hogg's novels *The Three Perils of Man* (1822) and *The Three Perils of Woman* (1823). It was therefore natural that Longman should become the publishers of the new epic poem that was being completed in July 1824. On 28 October 1824, however, the Longman firm wrote as follows to the Edinburgh publisher William Blackwood:

> Mr Hogg in one of his letters to us expressed a wish that we would grant you a share in his new Poems & the Confessions, & he stated that you were willing to take any share in them. If he be correct, we will with

pleasure let you have a quarter of each we holding the management & settling the accounts annually in the same way as we used to do with Constables House when we published jointly with them.[4]

In the event, *Queen Hynde* was indeed published jointly by Longman in London and Blackwood in Edinburgh; and the Edinburgh publisher wrote as follows to Hogg on 4 December 1824:

Let me hear from you very soon. Queen Hynde was shipp'd for London yesterday and I will publish here on Tuesday[5]

Longman and Blackwood were two of the leading British publishers of the period; and the printing of *Queen Hynde* was entrusted to another firm of high repute, James Ballantyne and Co. of Edinburgh. Although this was not generally known in the 1810s and early 1820s, Hogg's friend Sir Walter Scott had a major financial stake in the Ballantyne firm; and (behind the scenes) Scott took a close and active interest in a printing business that was to play an important part in his financial affairs. The Ballantyne firm enjoyed a high reputation, not least because of its role in printing Scott's Waverley Novels. In short, this was a printing firm at the upper end of the range: a high-quality printer of high-quality texts. The Ballantyne firm guarded its reputation jealously. Nothing dubious could be allowed to appear in a Ballantyne book; and this provided a strong motive for subjecting the Ettrick Shepherd's epic poem to careful copy-editing, with a view to ensuring that the published version did not stray from the paths of correctness and propriety.

The Ettrick Shepherd already had a good deal of experience of Ballantyne's alertness in such matters. For example, in setting down his reminiscences of Scott after his friend's death, Hogg remarks:

When *the Three Perils of Man* was first put to press he requested to see the proof slips Ballantyne having been telling him something about the work. They were sent to him on the instant and on reading them he sent expressly for me as he wanted to see and speak with me about my forthcoming work.[6]

One of the characters in *The Three Perils of Man* was called 'Sir Walter Scott of Buccleuch' in Hogg's manuscript. Scott himself had recently been made a baronet; and, by Hogg's account, the newly-created Sir Walter Scott suggested that the name of the novel's 'Sir Walter Scott of Buccleuch' should be changed, for fear of causing offence to the Duke of Buccleuch, the chief of the clan Scott. A few years earlier, the Duke had given Hogg the farm of Altrive Lake, rent free, for life. Sir Walter reminded Hogg of this; and Hogg accepted the suggestion that the name of the novel's 'Sir Walter Scott of Buccleuch' should be changed. In the first edition of *The Three Perils of Man* (1822), the character in question is duly called 'Sir Ringan Redhough'. *The Three Perils of Man* can be read as a text that partly celebrates and partly subverts Scott's fictions, particularly *Ivanhoe*; and as a result it is possible to feel regret over the disappearance of 'Sir Walter Scott' from the pages of Hogg's novel.

The Ballantyne firm, then, showed an impressive vigilance with regard to *The Three Perils of Man*; and this kind of attention to detail would be likely to appeal to Hogg's publishers. It would be less likely to appeal to the at times indecorous and subversive Ettrick Shepherd, however. In an important paper given at the 1997 James Hogg Society conference, Peter Garside presented new evidence to suggest that for the *Justified Sinner* (1824) the Longman firm wished to have the novel printed by Ballantyne. Hogg seems to have allowed his publishers to believe that their wishes were being followed in this matter, while ensuring that his novel was in fact printed under his own supervision by another Edinburgh printer, James Clarke, with whom he had close ties. Hogg was thus able to get the *Justified Sinner* printed in exactly the way he wished, circumventing the danger that Ballantyne's eagle-eyed copy-editors would tame and tone down any potentially offensive or otherwise 'incorrect' material in the distinctly unreliable Shepherd's manuscript.[7]

The fact that the *Justified Sinner* was being printed in Edinburgh helped the Shepherd to pull the wool over the eyes of his publishers, who were far away in London and out of touch with events. Once bitten, however, Hogg's London publishers were twice shy; and it appears that the Longman firm (ably assisted by Blackwood, their Edinburgh co-publisher) took care to ensure that *Queen Hynde*, the next book by their loose cannon of an author, was really and truly entrusted to the safe hands of the Ballantyne firm. This time the talented but boorish and eccentric Shepherd would be kept on a tight rein, thus avoiding the risk of a repetition of the offensive excesses of the *Justified Sinner*. And, in line with this cautious approach, the first edition of *Queen Hynde* duly offers a carefully polished (and, it might be argued, a carefully neutered) version of Hogg's poem.

From all this, an outline is emerging of the pattern of relationships between the author, the printer, and the publishers of *Queen Hynde*; and this pattern of relationships provides a context for considering the nature of the deleted passages in Hogg's manuscript. It may be useful to begin this discussion by stressing that it is clear that some of the deletions were made by Hogg himself. For example, at Book Fifth line 1485 the manuscript reads:

> For there no preference was to be
> Confered on lineage or degree.
> Nor was it needful, in that age,
> The low estate of vassalage
> <Rendered the peasant being tame
> In dignity of mind and frame>
> Withheld the peasant from the bound
> Of high exploit, or deed renowned.

The two lines enclosed in angle brackets in the quotation above are scored out in the manuscript; and the sense of the passage indicates that these lines are replaced by the two undeleted lines that follow. This particular deletion, it seems, was made because Hogg wished to adjust a passage dealing with a subject about which he doubtless felt strongly. Interestingly, the replacement lines have not been squeezed in as an afterthought. That is to say, it appears that they have been written on what was still blank paper, immediately below the deleted lines they replace. It seems, then, that this particular deletion was made by Hogg while he was writing out the manuscript.

Nevertheless, the Introduction of the present edition (pp.lxi-lxii) suggests that many of the manuscript's deleted passages would have been felt to be objectionable in the increasingly prim climate of the 1820s; and no doubt these passages were deleteded for that reason. Hogg may have made these deletions himself, of course, from motives of self-censorship, during a final revision before delivering his manuscript into the hands of the publishing institutions of his day; but in all the circumstances it seems much more likely that these deletions result from the activity of Ballantyne's alert copy-editors, as they sought to remove what they would have described as 'indelicate' material from the poem.

The manuscript's deleted passages were not printed in the first edition of *Queen Hynde*. As we have seen, some of the deletions are manifestly Hogg's own work; and the passages deleted by Hogg in the manuscript do not find a place in the present edition. Nevertheless, it seems unlikely that Hogg was responsible for all the deletions; and when a deletion cannot be attributed to Hogg with confidence, it is included in the text of the present edition. Such passages, however, have been enclosed within angle brackets < thus >, to record the fact of their deletion in the manuscript.

In the manuscript, several changes have been made in a hand that is manifestly not Hogg's; and these changes provide further evidence of an active process of copy-editing designed to remove what was felt to be potentially offensive or otherwise 'incorrect' material from *Queen Hynde*. The alterations thus marked are duly followed in the first edition and subsequent reprintings. For example, at Book Second line 67 Hogg wrote:

> While the rath herald of dismay,

This describes the precipitate and 'vehement' messenger of line 74; and in this context *rath* (Hogg's spelling of *rathe*) is a word that is entirely appropriate, although unusual. However, it would appear that the copy-editor could not make sense of the manuscript's *rath*; and this unusual word is changed in a hand that is not Hogg's to the more familiar and run-of-the-mill *rude*. As a result *rude* is the word that made its way into the printed text of *Queen Hynde*. The present edition ignores this change, and all the other changes that have been made to the manuscript in a hand that is not Hogg's.

Another serious difficulty for the editor of the manuscript version of *Queen Hynde* arises because the final portion of Book Fifth (from line 1953 onwards) is missing from the manuscript as it now survives. The immediately obvious course of action here would be to fill this gap by reprinting the missing section of the text from the first edition. There is another possible course of action, however. A proof copy of the first edition of *Queen Hynde* survives, and has been deposited on long-term loan in Stirling University Library by Hogg's descendant Mr R. Gilkison of Opua, New Zealand.[8] This is important for our discussion, because the relevant portion of the proofs would have been set up by a compositor working directly from the manuscript leaves that are now missing.

Which, then, should be followed in filling the gap in the manuscript: the proofs or the first edition? In considering this question, much clearly depends on the exact nature of the relationships between the manuscript, the proofs, and the first edition of *Queen Hynde*; and we shall proceed to consider these relationships.

What, then, can be deduced about the proofs? The surviving proof volume is made up almost entirely of marked proof sheets. Some of these sheets carry the manuscript inscription 'Last Proof', while others do not; many (but not all) of the sheets carry the manuscript initials of the 'correctors of the press' (that is to say, proof readers) by whom they have been checked and marked; and one sheet, as we shall see, contains markings in Hogg's hand as well as markings by the correctors of the press. In short, the surviving proof sheets appear to be something of a mixed bag. It would seem that, around the end of 1824, someone in the employment of the Ballantyne firm gathered together and preserved a set of proof sheets of *Queen Hynde* that would otherwise have been scrapped; and the fruit of this activity is the surviving proof volume. It appears, however, that the person who preserved the proof sheets was unable to lay hands on a copy of sheet 2B (first edition pp. 385–400), because this sheet has been supplied in a manuscript copy in the surviving proof volume. The surviving proofs, then, have been preserved by a lucky chance; and they seem to represent a random collection of sheets culled from various stages of the proofing process.

In spite of their random nature, however, the surviving proofs provide valuable evidence. For example, they demonstrate that, in setting up type from the manuscript, Ballantyne's compositors made some errors that appear to result from misreadings. For example, in the manuscript at Book First line 718, the monks of Iona welcome Hynde

> In two long files—a lane between,
> Where pass the maidens and their queen,
> Up to the sacred altar stone,
> Where good Columba stands alone.

In the surviving proof copy (p. 38), 'files' becomes 'piles' as a result of a misreading by the compositor; and the solemn image is somewhat spoiled. Unfortunately, this error was not spotted at the proof-reading stage by Ballantyne's correctors of the press. As a result, the monks remain assembled in piles in the first edition (p.38). Some misreadings *were* caught at the proof-reading stage, however. At Book First line 476 the manuscript has 'wail', but a misreading converts this to 'wait' in the proof. The misreading has been spotted and marked by an alert corrector of the press in the surviving proof copy, however; and the first edition duly restores 'wail' (p.26). The compositors, that is to say, made some mistakes; and some but not all of these mistakes were spotted and put right by the correctors of the press.

The sheets in the surviving proof volume have been extensively marked by Ballantyne's correctors of the press. Many of these in-house markings focus on typographical matters: damaged letters that need to be replaced, the need for extra space between lines, and so on. However, Ballantyne's correctors of the press also make adjustments to such matters as punctuation and spelling. For example, at Book First line 940, an outraged St Oran exclaims in the manuscript:

"The path of truth!!! O God of heaven!

Here as elsewhere, the compositor tends to make the punctuation more elaborate, and a dash is added. The proof reads:

"The path of truth!!!–O God of heaven!  (p.48)

In pursuit of a bland normality, however, the corrector of the press deletes two of the exclamation marks after 'truth'; and the first edition duly reads:

"The path of truth!–O God of heaven!  (p.49)

From time to time Ballantyne's correctors of the press move beyond matters such as punctuation and spelling, and make alterations to the actual words of the text. For example, at Book Fourth line 279 the manuscript has:

> Who feared if once thy deed got wind,
> The blame would fall on royal Hynde.

In the proof the compositor has elaborated the punctuation in the usual way, and he has also made a couple of mistakes. The lines are typeset as follows in the proof:

> Who fear'd, if once the deed get wind,
> The blame would fall on royal Hynde.  (p.200)

Marking the proof, the corrector of the press makes radical changes to these two lines: perhaps he felt that getting wind suggested indelicate ideas. At all events, the following revised version is offered in a hand that is not Hogg's:

> Who dared not this thy deed proclaim,
> Lest royal Hynde should bear the blame.

This revised version duly appears in the first edition (p.200).

It begins to appear, then, that the first edition departs from the manuscript in various ways: it contains mistakes by the compositors; it contains additional punctuation and other changes supplied by the compositors; and it contains numerous alterations, revisions, and adjustments made by Ballantyne's correctors of the press.

There is a further complication, however. In Hogg's period it was customary for more than one set of proofs to be taken. Once corrections had been marked on the first set of proofs, the necessary alterations would be made to the metal type. A new proof, a 'revise', would then be taken to permit further checking and correction. This process might be repeated several times; and as a result the surviving proofs of *Queen Hynde* do not necessarily provide a complete record of the alterations made to the poem during the reading of the proofs. Indeed, a detailed collation of the surviving proofs and the first edition indicates that many changes have been made at a stage later than the surviving proofs. For example, at Book Fourth line 729 the large inland loch now called Loch Awe is given the name 'Lochow' in both the manuscript and the surviving proof copy (p.222). No change to 'Lochow' is marked in the surviving proof sheet, but the first edition has 'Loch-Ow' at this point (p.222). Clearly, this indicates that a change has been made here at a stage later than the surviving proof. It appears, then, the surviving proofs only record part of the extensive alterations made to Hogg's poem during the preparation of the first edition.

By the time it reached the first edition, then, the text of Hogg's poem had been considerably altered by the Ballantyne firm. The surviving proofs do not represent the final stage in that process. Therefore, in seeking to reconstruct the text in the missing leaves of the manuscript, the present edition uses the proofs rather than the first edition as its main guide.

This is not to suggest that the present edition has followed the proof without alteration, in its attempt to reconstruct what was in the missing part of the manuscript. Throughout *Queen Hynde* both the proof and the first edition leave blank lines between verse paragraphs; but the manuscript does not. The present edition follows the manuscript in this as in other matters; and, as a result, its attempted reconstruction of the missing section of the manuscript silently removes the proof's blank lines between verse paragraphs. Similarly, throughout the poem the compositors regularly change the manuscript's 'M,Houston' (and similar names) to 'M'Houston' (and the like). The present edition's attempted reconstruction therefore silently substitutes 'M,Houston' for the proof's 'M'Houston', and 'M,Righ' for the proof's 'M'Righ'.

Furthermore, it appears from the discussion above that the compositors sometimes made mistakes as a result of misreading the manuscript. The surviving proofs have therefore been treated with due caution in the attempted reconstruction, as will be seen from the List of Emendations which follows the present Note on the Text.

A further complication arises because there is evidence that Hogg read proofs of *Queen Hynde* as it made its slow way through the laborious processes of hand printing that still prevailed for book production in the early 1820s. In a letter to the Longman firm of 13 November 1824, Hogg writes:

> I have this day looked over the last sheets of Queen Hynde and as I leave town will trust to you to correspond with Mr Blackwood regarding the title page as that cannot be thrown off it seems till he hear from you and till you fix the price &c &c.[9]

Clearly, then, Hogg read proofs of *Queen Hynde*; but there is much to be said for proceeding with caution at this point in the argument. The phrase 'looked over' has a somewhat cursory ring to it. Furthermore, when Hogg says that he has 'looked over the last sheets of Queen Hynde', this leaves open the possibility that he may have 'looked over' *only* the last sheets of the poem. It seems, then, that the letter quoted above does not *necessarily* show that Hogg's involvement in reading the proofs of *Queen Hynde* was either extensive or detailed. It is also worth bearing in mind that we know from other evidence that Hogg did not always make a point of reading the proofs of his books with particular care.[10]

As it happens, only a handful of changes in Hogg's hand appear in the surviving proofs of *Queen Hynde*, and all these changes are to be found in gathering Y. This printed sheet (pp. 337–52 in the first edition) covers Book Fifth lines 1905–2233; and this means (oddly enough) that it approximately matches the gap in the surviving manuscript. It would not be safe, however, to jump to the conclusion that Hogg made proof markings *only* in gathering Y. As we have seen, the surviving proofs do not provide a complete record of the changes marked on all the various revises; and, for sheets other than gathering Y, Hogg might have marked his corrections on a revise later or earlier than the surviving proof sheet. It is thus perfectly possible that Hogg made proof markings in various gatherings; but that, as chance has had it, only the ones he made in gathering Y have survived.

If Hogg did make proof changes other than the ones in his hand that have survived in the extant proof copy of gathering Y, then these changes may well still be traceable among the variants in wording between the manuscript and the first edition. An examination of these variants suggests that most of them can readily be interpreted either as misreadings, or as examples of the work of Ballantyne's correctors of the press. For example, at Book Third line 518 'old Diarmid of Argyle' rises, in the manuscript, with 'brow serene and placid smile'; but in the first edition (p.136) this becomes 'brow severe and placid smile'. The original 'serene' fits the context much better than 'severe'; and the two words look alike. It would therefore seem reasonable to interpret this particular variant as the result of a misreading by the compositor.

Another example is provided by Book Sixth line 303, which forms part of Columba's curse on Eric for his barbaric and pagan mistreatment of Wene and her maidens. The manuscript renders this line thus:

> Be hence thy valour siderated,

According to the *Oxford English Dictionary*, 'siderate' is an obsolete verb, chiefly used in the passive, meaning 'to be blasted, struck with lightning'. This makes it an entirely apt word for Columba's curse, as it looks forward to the fate of the Vikings at the end of the poem. However, this unusual word seems to have puzzled the correctors of the press. In the surviving proof (p.375) it is underlined and marked with a cross in the margin; and in the first edition it is changed to 'pall'd in dread'. It seems that the publishing institutions of the day were unable, in this instance, to cope with the self-educated shepherd's extensive vocabulary.

Still another example emerges at Book Fifth line 2260, in a verse paragraph in which the Shepherd writes scathingly of the affectations of some modern middle-class female readers:

> He next debars all those who dare,
> Whether with proud and pompous air,
> With simpering frown, or nose elate,
> To name the word INDELICATE!
> For such may harp be never strung,
> Nor warbling strain of Scotia sung;
> But worst of guerdons be her meed,
> The garret, poll, and apes to lead:
> Such word or term should never be
> In maiden's mind of modesty.

In the manuscript, the verse paragraph ends here; and this verse paragraph remains unaltered in the suviving proof. However, in the first edition (p.354) two additional lines are inserted at the end:

> But little is the bard afraid
> Of thee, to whom this tale is said.

Someone has decided that it would be prudent to soften the sting of what Hogg had written; and this seems typical of the process of toning down imposed on *Queen Hynde* by the publishing institutions of the day.

Examples might be multiplied: but the point is that most of the variants in wording between the manuscript and the first edition can reasonably be attributed to the compositors or the correctors of the press. Nevertheless, it is possible to identify a handful of variants that cannot readily be interpreted in this way; and it seems reasonable to guess that these variants may well reflect changes marked by the author on proof sheets now lost.

The variants in question are to be found in the List of Emendations which follows this Note on the Text; and, as will be seen from that list, all of them are to be found in or after the concluding portion of Book Fifth. That is to say, they all appear in the 'last sheets' of *Queen Hynde*; and this tends to confirm the suspicion that Hogg may indeed have 'looked over' *only* the 'last sheets' of his epic at the proof stage. Why, then, should this have been the case? A possible answer to this puzzle emerges from an examination of the physical characteristics of the manuscript of *Queen Hynde*.

The separate leaves of Huntington Library HM 12412 have been mounted on stubs, and have been bound up into a single volume. The opening section of the manuscript consists of leaves measuring 23 x 18.5 cms, with one page of Hogg's manuscript on each side of each leaf. Originally, this section of Hogg's manuscript would have consisted of larger sheets of paper, folded to provide four pages per sheet. The folded sheets would then have been brought together to form a booklet. However, the binder of the volume which is now Huntington Library HM 12412 has divided the sheets along the centre fold of the booklet, before mounting the resulting leaves on stubs.

The opening section of the manuscript of *Queen Hynde* contains the text of the first two Books of the poem, together with the first 1071 lines of Book Third; that is to say, it ends at the point at which Hogg set the poem aside in

1817. The manuscript resumes on paper of a slightly different size (22.3 x 18.5 cms); and this second section carries the text of the poem to line 986 of Book Fifth. A third section of the manuscript consists of much larger leaves (38.2 x 23.7 cms). It seems clear that, in contrast to the other sections of the manuscript, the sheets of this section have never been folded to form a booklet. Again in contrast to the other sections of the manuscript, Hogg writes here in double columns. The leaves of this third section carry the text to line 1952 of Book Fifth; but, as we have seen, the remaining lines of Book Fifth are now missing from the manuscript. A fourth and final section of the manuscript contains the whole of Book Sixth, together with Hogg's concluding 'Memento of names places &c'. This final section returns to t he 'divided booklet' pattern, and consists of leaves measuring 22.3 x 18.5 cms.

Peter Garside has demonstrated that, during his period as a mature professional writer, Hogg normally composed poems in draft, and then prepared a fair copy for the printer.[11] The first two sections of the manuscript of *Queen Hynde* have been prepared with some care, and would appear to be fair copies of this kind. These sections are reasonably fully punctuated, apparently in Hogg's hand; and Hogg has made various revisions to the words of the text. Some of these revisions are squeezed in above deleted words or lines; and it is possible that such revisions may have been made during a final re-reading before the manuscript was sent off to begin the process of preparation for publication.

The third section of the manuscript (Book Fifth lines 987-1952) has likewise been prepared for the printer with some care; it is, for example, fairly fully punctuated. However, the fact that Hogg has here written in double columns on larger pages suggests that this section may be a draft that has been spruced up for the printer, rather than a fair copy made from a draft. Time was no doubt short as the process of composition neared its end, and publication approached; and it may be that Hogg's draft (on large paper) of the latter part of Book Fifth was pressed into service to save time by avoiding the need for making a fair copy.

The final section of the manuscript, containing Book Sixth, is on paper of the size and quality Hogg used for fair copies; but nevertheless there may never have been an earlier draft of this part of the poem. On the fifth page of this section of the manuscript there is the following note in Hogg's hand:

> The printers will take care of these leaves there being as usual no other copy existing

Peter Garside has shown that Hogg, seeking to avoid loss of his manuscripts, liked to encourage care by giving the impression that the documents he sent to publishers and printers did not exist in other copies: hence the 'as usual' here.[12] However, in the manuscript of *Queen Hynde*, Hogg makes his plea for care only at this point, and does not do so in the earlier sections of the document. It may be felt that this suggests that the manuscript for Book Sixth *was* in fact the only copy; and that Hogg, in this section of his epic, made his first draft serve as his fair copy. This suggests that, in completing the manuscript of *Queen Hynde*, Hogg was writing with a certain fluency. Interestingly, he writes as follows in *Memoir of the Author's Life* about his completion of the poem in 1824:

> Several years subsequent to this, at the earnest intreaties of some literary friends, I once more set to work and finished this poem, which I entitled "Queen Hynde," in a time shorter than any person would believe.[13]

It appears, then, that Hogg, in the final portion of *Queen Hynde*, departed from his usual practice in preparing his poems for the publication process. In this instance, he seems to have missed out the stage of preparing a fair copy; and his draft therefore went directly to the printer. In these circumstances, it would not be astonishing if Hogg took the trouble to look over the last sheets of *Queen Hynde* before leaving town, as his letter to Longman of 13 November 1824 indicates: this would provide an opportunity for the kind of final revision that he would normally undertake while making a fair copy for the printer.

In his surviving proof markings to gathering Y, Hogg provides his own fine-tuning of the text; but he does not engage with the alterations that had been made by the compositor and by Ballantyne's correctors of the press. This may have been because Hogg did not have his manuscript to hand while looking over the proofs; but it may also reflect a realistic assessment of the extent to which the publishing machinery of the gentlemanly elite would allow a self-educated shepherd to undo its corrections of his perceived errors, whether in grammar or in taste. Be that as it may, the present edition sets out to take on board Hogg's own final fine-tuning of his poem at the proof stage, noting that he appears to have made proof changes only in the 'final sheets'.[14] Further details are given in the List of Emendations which follows this Note on the Text.

Consideration has been given to the problems posed by the deleted passages in the manuscript; to the problems posed by the alterations in the manuscript in a hand other than Hogg's; to the problems posed by the missing section of the manuscript; and to the problems posed by Hogg's proof corrections. There remains the question of how the manuscript version of *Queen Hynde* can best be presented to the reader. One possible way forward would have been to present the text of the poem by means of a photographic facsimile of Huntington Library HM 12412. Such a procedure would, of course, generate a faithful and accurate rendering of the version of *Queen Hynde* to be found in the manuscript; but the resulting volume would not provide an opportunity to read the poem in a free-flowing and unimpeded way. Bearing this in mind, the present volume offers the manuscript's version of the poem in the form of a typeset transcription. As we shall see, however, various difficulties arise in the process of converting the text contained in the manuscript into print. In attempting to cope with these difficulties, the present editors have sought to keep two needs firmly in mind: the need to provide an uncluttered text that lends itself to fluent reading; and the need to provide a text that is faithful to the content, flavour, and spirit of Hogg's manuscript.

An examination of Huntington Library HM 12412 makes it clear that, in spite of the care Hogg has taken in preparing his manuscript for the printer, he nevertheless here and there forgets to insert a full stop at the end of a sentence. This is particularly liable to happen when the sentence in question concludes a verse paragraph, or concludes a page of the manuscript. Equally, Hogg sometimes forgets to open or to close inverted commas in direct speech. These missing full stops and inverted commas have been silently supplied in the present edition. This policy seeks to assist fluent reading of *Queen Hynde* by completing Hogg's own system of punctuation.

Similarly, there are a very few occasions in the manuscript (for example at Book Third line 1309) where Hogg inadvertently begins a line of verse with a lower-case rather than an upper-case letter; and in these instances an upper-case letter has been silently supplied, in accordance with Hogg's normal practice in this manuscript. Likewise, a standard pattern can be perceived in the headings Hogg gives to the various Books of the poem in the manuscript. He sometimes departs from his standard pattern in minor ways; but when this happens the present edition silently implements the standard pattern. The standard pattern may be set out as follows:

Queen Hynde
Book First

However, in Book Fourth, for example, Hogg has 'fourth' rather than the expected 'Fourth'; and the expected capital letter is silently supplied in the present edition.

Nevertheless, there is no attempt in the present edition to undertake a full-scale tidying-up of the manuscript. Like several other writers of his period, Hogg exhibits some eccentricity in spelling and similar matters: thus *heideous* apears for *hideous*, *ideot* for *idiot*, *invain* for *in vain*, and so on. In such matters, the idiosyncracies of the manuscript have been retained. It might be felt that this policy of faithfulness to the manuscript gives the text of the present edition a somewhat rough and unpolished feel; but the flavour of Hogg's manuscript is preserved, and the idiosyncrasies involved are not of a kind likely to cause serious disturbance to the flow of reading.

In any literary manuscript, it would be unsurprising to find evidence of authorial second thoughts and revisions; and, in the manuscript of *Queen Hynde*, Hogg sometimes scores out what he had originally written, and substitutes a revised version. With the need to facilitate fluent reading in mind, the text offered by the present edition makes no attempt to incorporate a record of what Hogg has rejected while making revisions. Rather, this edition seeks to offer an uncluttered presentation of the text as Hogg revised it in the manuscript.

When Hogg scores out what he had originally written and substitutes a revised version, he sometimes leaves the revised version unpunctuated, even although his original version had been punctuated. For example, at Book Fourth line 1137, Hogg originally wrote:

> But all was one distorted shoal,
> A vision of the troubled soul,

He later deleted this from 'shoal' onwards, substituting the following:

> scene
> The vision of a soul in pain

Read in context, the commas of Hogg's original version of these lines perform a useful function. Furthermore, Hogg's revision of the words does not alter the structure of his sentence, so the need for the commas remains. What seems to be going on here is a tinkering with words, in a process that does not appear to address itself to the punctuation of the sentence. On this view of the matter, the best way for an editor to be faithful to the text in the manuscript would seem to be to follow the revised form of words, while retaining the original punctuation. This is the procedure adopted in the present edition in such cases; and as a result the lines under discussion appear as follows:

> But all was one distorted scene,
> The vision of a soul in pain,

At some places in the manuscript of *Queen Hynde*, words or phrases have been marked in pencil; and in some such cases a revision has been made in ink in Hogg's hand, apparently in response to the pencil marking. For example, at Book Third line 604 of *Queen Hynde*, Hogg originally wrote:

> Still God's dread work was but begun,
> At man's behest he staid the sun
> Still in the midst of heaven's high cone,
> And the moon paused o'er Ajalon;

A pencil cross has been added in the margin at this point, and 'cone' has been underlined in pencil. Someone has spotted that the sky, strictly speaking, does not form a cone; and Hogg responds by providing the following new version of the third of the lines quoted above:

> Arrested, fixed in heaven he shone

It may be that someone (Hogg's wife, perhaps, or a friend) read the manuscript of *Queen Hynde* for him before it went off to the printer, marking in pencil places that might need attention. At all events, Hogg made some revisions in response to these pencil markings. The present edition follows these revisions; but where Hogg did not respond to the pencil markings, the pencil markings are ignored.

The policy discussed above may be summed up briefly: the present edition follows Hogg's manuscript where the manuscript survives; at the point where there is a gap in the manuscript, the present edition follows the surviving proof copy; and the present edition seeks to incorporate the revisions Hogg made to the text of the poem at the proof stage, insofar as these revisions can be recovered.

## Notes

1 It seems clear that Huntington Library HM 12412 is the manuscript from which the Edinburgh printers James Ballantyne and Co. set up the type for the first edition of *Queen Hynde*. Printers in the 1820s often marked the manuscripts from which they were setting type, in order to indicate the points at which various pages or gatherings begin in the printed version. Such marks are present in Huntington Library HM 12412; and these marks correspond with the pages and gatherings of the first edition of *Queen Hynde*.

2 National Library of Scotland (hereafter NLS) MS 2528, fol. 40.

3 See Hogg, *The Private Memoirs and Confessions of a Justified Sinner*, ed. by John Carey (London: Oxford University Press, 1969), p. xxv.

4 Longman Archives part 1, Item 101, Letter-book 1820-25, no. 469C: typed transcript.

5 NLS MS 2245 fols 84–85. In the 1820s, when a book was published at the end of a year, it was not unusual for some copies to bear the date of the following year on the titlepage. In accordance with this practice, some copies of the first edition of *Queen Hynde* have the date 1824 on the titlepage, while others have the date 1825. Nevertheless it seems clear from Blackwood's letter that Hogg's epic poem was in fact published in December 1824, some six months after the publication of *The Private Memoirs and Confessions of a Justified Sinner*. As is indicated in the Introduction (p. li), reviews of *Queen Hynde* began to appear in December 1824.

6 Hogg, *Memoir of the Author's Life* and *Familiar Anecdotes of Sir Walter Scott*, ed. by Douglas S. Mack (Edinburgh: Scottish Academic Press, 1972), p.100. Oddly enough in view of Hogg's anecdote, the first edition of *The Three Perils of Man* was printed, not by James Ballantyne, but by another Edinburgh printer, John Moir. However, there were close links between some of the Edinburgh printers of the period. For example, Nan Jaboor and B. J. McMullin write: 'Press figures can be used–in certain cases with absolute confidence–to identify work ostensibly by Ballantyne but in reality by other printers [...]. The reverse is also true: work ostensibly by other printers may be (at least in part) the work of Ballantyne.'. See Jaboor and McMullin, *James Ballantyne and Press Figures* (Melbourne: Ancora Press, 1994), p.19.

7 Peter Garside's conference paper will appear in *Studies in Hogg and his World*, 9 (1998); and these matters will also be discussed in his forthcoming edition of *The Private Memoirs and Confessions of a Justified Sinner* in the Stirling / South Carolina Research Edition of James Hogg.

8 The titlepage of this proof copy mentions only the London firm of Longman as publishers of *Queen Hynde*. However, in a letter to Blackwood of 13 November 1824 the Longman firm gives instructions with regard to a revised imprint on the titlepage, in order to take account of Blackwood's involvement: see Longman Archives part 1, Item 101, Letter-book 1820-25, no. 472: typed transcript.

9 NLS MS 9634, fols 11–12.

10 See Douglas S. Mack, 'The Transmission of the Text of Hogg's *Brownie of Bodsbeck*', *The Bibliotheck*, 8 (1976–77), 7–46 (p.11).

11 See Peter Garside, 'Vision and Revision: Hogg's MS Poems in the Turnbull Library', *Studies in Hogg and his World*, 5 (1994), 82–95 (pp.88–91).

12 Garside, 'Vision and Revision', pp.84–87.

13 Hogg, *Memoir* and *Scott*, pp.40–41.

14 The final sheets would include the title-page and other preliminaries: in Hogg's period these were normally printed last. Proofs of these preliminaries, marked by Hogg, have been bound up with the manuscript of *Queen Hynde*, and are discussed in notes on the *title-page* and *dedication* in the present edition's Notes.

# List of Emendations

The Note on the Text, above, outlines the present edition's textual policy; and, among other things, it sets out the situations in which emendations have been silently made. For example, Hogg sometimes forgot to supply full stops at the end of sentences in his manuscript, and he sometimes forgot to open or to close inverted commas in direct speech. In such cases, the missing full stops and inverted commas have been silently supplied. All the present edition's silent emendations are discussed in the Note on the Text at pp. 227 and 231–32, above. Apart from these silent emendations, all the present edition's emendations are listed below.

For the reasons set out in the Note on the Text, the present edition follows Hogg's manuscript where it survives. However, the emendations listed below have been made in order to correct what appear to be slips of the pen on Hogg's part.

| **Book First** | **manuscript** | **emendation** |
|---|---|---|
| l. 80 | gallants | gallant |
| l. 398 | maiden s | maiden's |
| l. 594 | Scotand's | Scotland's |
| l. 690 | brthren | brethren |
| l.1095 | boundess | boundless |

| **Book Second** | | |
|---|---|---|
| l. 350 | Knight | Knight, |
| l. 440 | houshold | household |
| l. 687 | Th' Effect | Th' effect |
| l. 814 | "Then Bring | Then "Bring |
| l. 850 | from of her | from off her |

| **Book Third** | | |
|---|---|---|
| l. 542 | I thank, you | I thank you, |
| l. 648 | bedwork | bedework |
| l. 753 | hat sat | had sat |
| l. 1021 | thou can'st dissolve; | thou can'st not dissolve; |

[The 'not' is needed by the sense, even although it disturbs the rhythm. The first edition (p.159) re-casts the whole line in an attempt to resolve the problem.]

| | | |
|---|---|---|
| l. 1025 | father's | fathers |
| l. 1038 | thou art under | thou art not under |

[The 'not' is needed by sense and rhythm, and has been added in the manuscript in a hand that is not Hogg's.]

| **Book Fourth** | | |
|---|---|---|
| l. 86 | in the ground. | in the ground |
| l. 317 | There bodies | Their bodies |
| l. 481 | measur'st | measures |
| l. 605 | The Victory | The victory |
| l. 1002 | ire to brow | ire to brow? |
| l. 1033 | Shall it it be | Shall it be |

| Book Fifth | manuscript | emendation |
|---|---|---|
| l. 667 | Their darted | There darted |
| l. 673 | in glorious | in the glorious |

[The 'the' is needed by the sense, and has been added in the manuscript in a hand that is not Hogg's.]

| | | |
|---|---|---|
| l. 775 | Is their a | Is there a |
| l. 1057 | momtuous | momentuous |

[Compare 'momentuous' at Book Fourth line 775.]

| | | |
|---|---|---|
| l. 1061 | Presumtuous | Presumptuous |
| l. 1136 | Trusless | Trustless |

[In the manuscript an *l* seems to over-write a *t* in the middle of this word; the hand may well be Hogg's.]

| | | |
|---|---|---|
| l. 1290 | captain's | captains |
| l. 1295 | trumpet s | trumpet's |
| l. 1470 | All man | All men |
| l. 1565 | "Feldborg | Feldborg |
| l. 1622 | made it a wheel, | made it wheel, |

[In the manuscript, Hogg makes a deletion and revision here; the sense suggests his failure to delete 'a' was a slip.]

| | | |
|---|---|---|
| l. 1851 | ponerous | ponderous |
| l. 1910 | wrested | wrestled |

**Book Sixth**

| | | |
|---|---|---|
| l. 158 | Travelled | Travailed |
| l. 527 | steril | sterile |
| l. 605 | thence.–the | thence.–The |
| l. 634 | "Behold, All | "Behold, all |
| l. 1181 | courtir's | courtier's |
| l. 1362 | dress d, | dress'd, |

**Memento**

| | | |
|---|---|---|
| p. 218, l. 7 | goverment | government |
| p. 218, l. 14 | road From | road from |
| p. 219, l. 7 | 579 | 597 |
| p. 220, l. 8 | *Brand.* | *Brand* |
| p. 220, l. 19 | contigous | contiguous |

As explained in the Note on the Text, the present edition follows the surviving proof sheets for that part of the text for which the manuscript is now lost. The emendations listed below seek to correct what appear to be errors of transcription made by the compositors who set up the proofs.

| Book Fifth | proof reading | emendation |
|---|---|---|
| l. 1963 | Beragon | Beregon |
| l. 1982 | circumverted | circumvented |
| l. 1988 | Does'nt | Doesn't |
| l. 2092 | Keilo | Keila |
| l. 2161 | mian, | main, |
| l. 2223 | state | stale |
| l. 2272 | an | on |

One surviving proof sheet (of gathering Y) contains revisions and corrections marked in Hogg's hand; and these revisions and corrections were duly implemented in the first edition, with minor adjustments. The present edition accepts the changes marked by Hogg in the surviving proof of gathering Y; and these changes are listed below.

| Book Fifth | original reading | Hogg's change in proof |
|---|---|---|
| l. 1911 | dreadful | strain and |
| l. 1922 | but | though |
| l. 2027 | cheek | cluck |
| l. 2079 | Eric's | Erin's |
| l. 2123 | the | thy |
| l. 2175 | thirst in thee, | burning thirst |

l. 2176　That longing for a bliss to be, **(original reading)**
　　　　　That hath annoyed thee from the first **(Hogg in proof )**

　　　　[Hogg's alteration of lines 2175–76 is unpunctuated, but does not seem to call for the removal of the end-of-line commas after 'thee' and 'be'.]

| | | |
|---|---|---|
| l. 2183 | [Paragraph break requested here by Hogg in proof.] | |
| l. 2215 | perverseness | frowardness |
| l. 2233 | monkish | maukish |
| l. 2234 | all | roll |

Furthermore, the present edition accepts the following readings from the first edition, which are taken to reflect proof changes made by Hogg in proof sheets that are now lost.

| Book Sixth | original reading | first edition |
|---|---|---|
| l. 79 | bonny breast; | virgin breast; |

l. 278　Where are the hostages were thrust
　　　　Into thy hand in sacred trust? **(original reading)**

　　　　Where be the maidens that were sent
　　　　As hostages unto thy tent? **(first edition)**

| | | |
|---|---|---|
| l. 287 | instant | moment |
| l. 293 | course | fate |

**Memento**

p. 220　[The first edition adds two entries at the end of the list of Scotticisms, as follows:]

　　　　*To-fall of day*–The close of day, eventide.
　　　　*Steven*–Uproar.

# Appendix: Beregonium

At the very end of *Queen Hynde* Hogg announces, 'The mountains, bays, castles &c mentioned in the poem are all contiguous to the scene, and retain their ancient signficant names' (p.220). What may seem like a throwaway line, however, reveals the strong sense of place that underpins the narrative. Typically, Hogg plays unabashedly with chronology, historical accuracy, and character; but he does not tend to manipulate geography. In *Queen Hynde*, the settings are precisely placed and meticulously described to the best of Hogg's knowledge (which, given his travels around Scotland, is considerable). But though Hogg is typically careful about geography, in *Queen Hynde* that tendency is heightened, perhaps because the poem is presented as an *epic*, concerned with the origins of a people.

Beregonium is the legendary capital city of Scottish Dál Riata (conventionally spelled Dalriada); and the *Ordnance Gazetteer of Scotland* of 1882–85 cites Hector Boece's application of the name Beregonium to 'a very large vitrified fort in Ardchattan parish, Argyllshire, on the E side of Ardmucknish Bay, $2\frac{1}{2}$ miles NNW of Connel Ferry, and $5\frac{1}{2}$ NNE by boat of Oban'. The *Gazetteer* is somewhat dismissive of claims that this fort was 'the seat of a monarchy far earlier than the Christian era, the Selma of Ossian, the place of the residence of Fingalian kings'.[1] Nevertheless, such claims were undoubtedly in circulation in the early nineteenth century; and, in a lengthy note to *Queen Hynde*, Hogg gives Boece's account as evidence to support the idea that the Beregonium of Ardmucknish Bay was indeed an ancient home of kings.

Hector Boece (Boethius) was born in the 1460s and died in 1536. He held university posts in Paris and Aberdeen (where he was Principal); and his Latin history of Scotland (from the earliest times to the beginning of the reign of James III in 1460) was published in Paris in 1526. Boece's history was translated into Scots by John Bellenden ( *fl.* 1533–87); this translation was published in 1536. There followed a translation into English by William Harrison (1534–94), which formed part of the chronicle of Scotland produced by Raphael Holinshed (d.1580?). Holinshed's chronicles of Scotland, England, and Ireland were published in 1577;[2] and his *Scottish Chronicle* was readily available to Hogg, for example in a two-volume edition printed in Arbroath in 1805.[3] Boece and Holinshed drew on myth and legend in their account of Scotland's origins, and their colourful narratives can no longer be regarded as authoritative and respectable history; but it is important to recognise that Holinshed's chronicles carried enough weight in their day to be used extensively by Shakespeare as source material. Even as late as Hogg's period it was possible to regard *The Scottish Chronicle* as a standard work; and Hogg's note on p. 218 takes it for granted that 'Boethius and Harrison's Chronologie' are authoritative.

References to Beregonium are scattered matter-of-factly throughout the text of Holinshed's *Scottish Chronicle*. We read (in the Arbroath edition at I. 44) that 'Ferguse' founded the 'kingdome of the Scotishmen [...] in Albion', an event that took place 'in the yeare after the creation of the world 3640, which is (as *Harison* saith in his chronologie) before the incarnation of our Saviour 327, after the building of Rome 420, and after the entring of Brutus into Britaine 790'. We are told (I.48) that Ferguse 'builded also the castell of Beregonium in Loughquhabre on the west side of Albion, over against the western iles, where he appointed a court to be kept for the administration of justice'. Later (at I.63) we read that King Ewin 'builded a castell not farre distant from Beregonium, which he named after his owne name Enonium: but afterwards it was called Dunstafage'. Likewise, at I.65 we are told that Cadall 'gat first all the best fortresses into his hands, as Beregonium, Dunstafage, and other'. Dunstaffnage, like Beregonium, features prominently in *Queen Hynde*.

Giving detailed directions to potential tourists, Hogg places Beregonium 'on the new road from Dalmallie to Fort-William, by Connel ferry and Appin' (p. 218). The site in question is the vitrifed fort of Dun mhic Uisneachan (pronounced 'Doon Vic OOSH-nah-han'), which may have approximated 'M,Houston' to Hogg's ear: see Hogg's note on *M,Houston*, pp. 218–19. This fort overlooks Ardmucknish Bay, which does indeed lie 'on the west side of Albion, over against the western iles'. Drawing on a tradition already in circulation, Hogg calls Beregonium 'the Selma of Ossian' (p. 218); and this traditional belief is reflected in the fact that 'Port Selma' may be found in modern maps in the immediate vicinity of the ancient hill fort. Under its Gaelic name, Dun mhic Uisneachan is connected with the sad story of Deirdre (Macpherson's 'Darthula') and the sons of Uisneach, quite a different tale from that associated with the Scottish kings of Beregonium. The legendary Irish beauty Deirdre, tragically foretold to bring about the downfall of the House of Ulster, was exiled to Glen Etive on the coast of Scotland, where she fell in love with Naoise of the House of Uisneach. When the jealous Irish king, Conchobar, treacherously tried to claim her for himself and plotted Naoise's murder, Deirdre took her own life. Her Gaelic 'Lament for Alba' is still sung. Typically, for *Queen Hynde* Hogg seems to have collapsed the legends into one, though conjoining these two in particular is suggested by some accounts.

Either written records of Beregonium have been lost or the city existed only in legend, perpetuated through the oral tradition and then entering written history as records of oral accounts. In his account of Beregonium, however, Hogg apparently relied in part on the entry for Ardchattan in the first *Statistical Account of Scotland*. According to the *Statistical Account*, at this point late in the eighteenth century traditional stories of Beregonium were very much alive:

> the famous city of *Beregonium* [...] was situated between two hills, one called *Dun Macsnichan*, "the hill of Snachan's son," and the other, much superior in height, is named *Dun bhail an righ*, "the hill of the king's town." A street paved with common stones, running from the foot of

the one hill to the other, is still called *Straid-mharagaid,* "the market street;" and another place, at a little distance, goes by the name of *Straid namin*; "the meal street." About 10 or 11 years ago a man, cutting peats in a moss between the two hills, found one of the wooden pipes that conveyed the water from the one hill to the other, at the depth of 5 feet below the surface. On *Dun Macsnichan* is a large heap of rubbish and pumice stones; but no distinct traces of any building or fortification can now be seen on either of the hills, the foundations having been dug up for the purpose of erecting houses in the neighbourhood.[4]

The supposed wooden water pipes of Beregonium turn up in *Queen Hynde* when Hogg makes use of this passage from the *Statistical Account* in his note on *Beregonium* (p. 218); and they cause much hilarity in the discussion of Hogg's epic in the 'Noctes Ambrosianae' of the January 1825 number of *Blackwood's Edinburgh Magazine*. 'ODoherty' assures 'Hogg' that these ancient objects 'turn out to be the gas-pipes' of Beregonium. The Hogg of the 'Noctes' is not too disturbed by this introduction of a very modern technology into the Scotland of more than a thousand years ago: 'Like aneugh. I never saw them mysell. But how can ane tell a gas-pipe frae a water-pipe?' ODoherty replies: 'Smaller in the bore, you know. And, besides, the stink is still quite discernible'.[5]

The *Statistical Account* (p. 180) goes on to suggest the basis for Beregonium's untimely end:

> There is a tradition, among the lower class of people, that Beregonium was destroyed by fire from heaven. In confirmation of this tradition, it may be mentioned, that a high rock, near the summit of *Dun bhail an righ*, projecting and overhanging the road, has a volcanic appearance and a most hideous aspect. Huge fragments have tumbled down from it. Adjoining to this place, is a fine, open, spacious bay, with a sandy bottom, capable of containing the whole navy of Great Britain.

For the purposes of his poem, following a practice common throughout his work, Hogg takes for granted that Beregonium is historical; but in his note he expands on the idea that its fiery end was an act of God (see p. 218).

James Macpherson clearly incorporated traditional accounts of Selma into his *Ossian* poems, a point that Hogg may have found articulated expansively in notes by Alexander Stewart in Sir John Sinclair's 1807 edition of the *Ossian* poems 'in the original Gaelic'. Under the heading 'Topography of Some of the Principal Scenes of Fingal and his Warriors', Stewart writes:

> there is every reason to believe that Selma, so often mentioned in the poems of Ossian, as the principal residence of his father Fingal was situate in that part of Argyleshire called upper Lorn, on a green hill of an oblong form, which rises on the sea shore at equal distances from the mouths of the lakes Eite [Etive] and Creran. It is now called by the inhabitants of the place "DUN-MHIC SNITHEACHAIN," i.e., the fort of the son of Snitho; but by some of our historians Berigonium, and by them

said to have been the capital of the kingdom of the Gaels, or Caledonians.[6]

It is clear, too, from various contemporary accounts of travels in this area that stories of Beregonium were in circulation. Prominent among the tours was that of Thomas Pennant, detailed in *A Tour in Scotland and Voyage to the Hebrides*. Pennant made this tour in 1772, and he describes the scene meticulously:

A mile from *Connel*, near the shore, is *Dun-mac-Sniochain*, the antient *Beregonium*, or *Berogomum*. The foundation of this city, as it is called, is attributed, by *Apocryphal* history, to *Fergus* II, and was called the *Chief* in *Scotland* for many ages [...]. Along the top of the beach is a raised mound, the defence against a sudden landing. This, from the idea of here having been a city, is styled, *Straid-a mhargai*, or, market-street: within this are two rude erect columns, about six feet high, and nine and a half in girth: behind these a peat-moss: on one side a range of low hills, at whose nearest extremity is an entrenchment called *Dunvalirè*. On the Western side of the morass is an oblong insulated hill, on whose summit, the country people say, there had been seven towers: I could only perceive three or four excavations, of no certain form, and a dike round them.[7]

In *Journal of a Tour in the Highlands and Western Islands of Scotland in 1800*, John Leyden details his travels in search of vitrified forts and the authenticity of Macpherson's Ossian poems. There he writes, 'on the opposite side of Loch Etive I saw the supposed site of the ancient Berigonium, marked by rocks which have no resemblance to ruins. The ruins as well as the history of this city have perished, and it hardly lives in tradition'. Leyden adds, 'From the same spot I had a view of the ruins of Dunstaffnage Castle'.[8] Leyden probably gleaned the story from his many investigations into both antiquities and contemporary oral accounts.

Scott toured the area by sea in September 1814, as part of a voyage round Scotland in the 'Lighthouse Yacht' with the Commissioners of the Northern Lights. In the diary he kept during this tour he describes the site of Beregonium as follows:

On the right, Loch Etive, after pouring its waters like a furious cataract over a strait called Connell-ferry, comes between the castle [that is to say, Dunstaffnage] and a round island belonging to its demesne, and nearly insulates the situation. In front is a low rocky eminence on the opposite side of the arm, through which Loch Etive flows into Loch Linnhe. Here was situated *Beregenium*, once, it is said, a British capital city; and, as our informant told us, the largest market-town in Scotland. Of this splendour are no remains but a few trenches and excavations, which the distance did not allow us to examine.[9]

Scott's reference to his 'informant' underscores the suggestion by Leyden that

Beregonium had not passed entirely out of the oral tradition of the area.

Beregonium has attracted more than poetic interest. In *The History of Scot-land*, J. H. Burton locates 'Dun Macsniachain' and says the Gaelic name 'has been set down as the Rerigonium spoken of by the monkish chroniclers as the capital of the Pictish kings'. He notes, 'Among the people of the neigh-bourhood the Latin name thus conferred on it by the learned seems to have, with an alteration in the first letter, superseded its native name, and the inhab-itants speak of it as "Beregonian"'.[10] In *The Pictish Nation: Its People & its Church*, Archibald B. Scott makes a Gaelic connection with the otherwise Roman name of Beregonium. The capital of the 'Western Picts' he calls '*Barr-an-Righ*', 'better located through the name of the adjoining fort *Barr-nan-Gobhan*, George Buchanan's "Beregonium"'. *Barr-an-Righ* he glosses as 'The King's (fortified) height', and *Barr-nan-Gobhan* as 'The (fortified) height of the Armourers'. He situates Barr-nan-Gobhan 'by the northern shore of Lower Loch Etive, on the precipitous height which ends *Beinn Laoire*' and adds that 'Dr. Carmichael, author of *Carmina Gadelica*, describes it in his notes to *Deirdere*'.[11] G. A. Frank Knight documents Columba's presence here: 'At the head of Ardmucknish Bay, at Selma in Benderloch, is Kilcolmkill, or Keil, where a small burial ground and some mouldering stones witness that Columba erected a chapel on the spot'.[12]

R. Angus Smith, a chemist visiting the site in 1867, made a detailed per-sonal examination of the site and reported his findings in three papers given before the Society of Antiquaries of Scotland in the early 1870s. He writes that he had been advised by locals 'to visit the vitrified fort Dun mhic Uisneachan, let us say, Dun MacUisneachan; it is frequently called there, Beregonium'.[13] Smith mentions the 'old St Columba church' in the nearby cemetery and the evidence of pagan worship in the area (p. 82). He learned that the fort had been 'fancied as a palace of Fergus, and by others as the seat of Fingal' (p. 82). Even in 1867, Smith encountered a living tradition regard-ing the site: 'the story [...] everybody tells you of six kings having lived there, and of its having been burnt' (p. 88). The burning, Smith argues, 'is, prob-ably, a fabrication caused by observing the vitrifaction; so may the kings be. We do not hear of six sons of Usnoth or Uisneach' (p. 88). Closely investigat-ing the physical location, Smith reports a distinguishable zig-zag road, known as 'Queen Street, or Sraid a Bhan Righ' (p. 86); and visiting the hill of Ledaig, he remarks that its name is 'Dun Valanree [...] or Dun Bhaile an righ, the fort of the king's town', which suggests a 'time when a chief lived at the fort' (p. 87). Finding an ancient well on 'Dun Bhaile an righ' (where Eiden establishes his camp in *Queen Hynde*), Smith challenges the story of the wooden pipes: the well 'has been imagined to communicate with [...] Dun Mac Uisneachan, but I saw no reason for thinking so. The story of wooden water-pipes leading to the well in the fort has grown uncertain, requiring corroboration' (p. 87).

In another of Smith's presentations to the Society of Antiquaries of Scot-land, he describes the story of Deirdre and the sons of Uisneach ('the oldest heroes of Loch Etive'), a story which 'according to the given accounts [...] ought to have been some three hundred years old in the time of Fingal'.

We are not told how long this family stayed at Loch Etive, but it was long enough according to the story, to give them power in the country, and long enough, as we know to a certainty, to have connected their name with the fort to this very day, notwithstanding the attempts of guidebooks and histories to give it a Latin and foreign designation [i.e., 'Beregonium'].[14]

Some modern travel guides perpetuate the stories of Beregonium. In *The Companion Guide to the West Highlands of Scotland*, W. H. Murray points out a spot on the shore of Ardmucknish Bay:

> At the south end of the beach, near the old railway station, a grassy hillock bears on its top the faint trace of *Dun Mhic Uisneachan*, the Fort of the Sons of Uisneach.
>
> Some historians consider the fort to have been Beregonium, the seat of Pictish kings, and it was so named by George Buchanan (sixteenth century) in his Latin *History of Scotland.* Support is given to the notion by the local tradition that Pictish kings were buried on the island of Lismore, which lies only one and a half miles off the Benderloch coast. Beregonium, like the Scots' fort on Dunadd, was a multiple structure incorporating several forts on the one hill. The upper fort was vitrified.[15]

The community of Benderloch preserves the traditional accounts of the rock outcrop that presides over its bay. In *By Sword & Pen: Benderloch & Balcardine, their Story*, a book published in Oban in 1997, Liam MacClarich describes the setting of Beregonium: the 'magnificent view from the top which gives its name to the area—Selma—*sealla' ma'*—fine view'. MacClarich summarises the various historical and traditional accounts of Dun MacUisneachan, and points to Hogg's use of the setting for *Queen Hynde*.[16] The mingling of traditional and historical would have delighted Hogg, who placed a higher value on the validity of oral sources than many of his contemporaries. A crofter whose cattle graze in the area recently told the editors that the zig-zag remnants of 'Queen Street' (mentioned by Smith) are associated with the regal Hynde herself.

## Notes

1. Francis H. Groome, *Ordnance Gazetteer of Scotland*, 6 vols (Edinburgh: Thomas C. Jack, 1882–85), I, 149.
2. Hector Boethius, *Scotorum historiae a prima gentis origine* ([Paris, 1526]); *Heir beginnis the hystory and croniklis of Scotland*, translatit laitly in our vulgar and commoun langage be maister Johne Bellenden (Edinburgh: Thomas Davidson, [1536]); and Raphael Holinshed, *The firste volume of the chronicles of England, Scotland, and Irelande*, 3 vols (London, 1577).
3. Raphael Holinshed, *The Scottish Chronicle*, 2 vols (Arbroath: printed by J. Findlay, 1805). This edition was 'SOLD BY MESSRS. MAGNAY, *and* PICKERING, R. OGLE, J. ROACH, *London;* W. *and* J. DEAS, *Edinburgh;* A. WILSON, *Glasgow*'; and it describes

itself on its title-page as 'an accurate narration of the beginning, increase, proceedings, wars, acts, and government of the Scottish nation, from the original thereof unto the year 1585'. Subsequent references to *The Scottish Chronicle* are to this edition, and are given in the text.

4. Ludovick Grant, 'United Parishes of Ardchattan and Muckairn', in Sir John Sinclair, *The Statistical Account of Scotland*, 21 vols (Edinburgh: W. Creech, 1791–99), VI, 174–82 (p. 180).

5. 'Noctes Ambrosianae no. XVIII', *Blackwood's Edinburgh Magazine*, 17 (January 1825), 114–30 (p. 128).

6. *The Poems of Ossian, in the Original Gaelic, with a Literal Translation into Latin, [...] together with A Dissertation on the Authenticity of the Poems, by Sir John Sinclair, Bart.*, 3 vols (London: G. and W. Nicol, 1807), III, 498.

7. Thomas Pennant, *A Tour in Scotland and Voyage to the Hebrides; MDCCLXXII* (Chester: John Monk, 1774), p. 356.

8. John Leyden, *Journal of a Tour in the Highlands and Western Islands of Scotland in 1800* (Edinburgh: Blackwood, 1903), p. 31.

9. J. G. Lockhart, *Memoirs of the Life of Sir Walter Scott, Bart.*, 7 vols (Edinburgh: Cadell, 1837–38), III, 258.

10. J. H. Burton, *The History of Scotland*, 8 vols (Edinburgh: Blackwood, 1897), I, 87.

11. Archibald B. Scott, *The Pictish Nation: Its People and its Church* (Edinburgh: Foulis, 1918), p. 220. George Buchanan (1506–82) was a Scottish historian and scholar; his fame in Hogg's period is indicated by the fact that his portrait appeared on the cover of all numbers of *Blackwood's Edinburgh Magazine*.

12. G. A. Frank Knight, *Archaeological Light on the Early Christianizing of Scotland*, 2 vols (London: James Clarke, 1933), II, 20.

13. R. Angus Smith, 'Descriptive List of Antiquities near Loch Etive. Part I', *Proceedings of the Society of Antiquaries of Scotland*, 9 part 1 (1870–71), 81–106 (p. 81). Further references to this article are given in the text.

14. R. Angus Smith, 'Descriptive List of Antiquities near Loch Etive. Part II', *Proceedings of the Society of Antiquaries of Scotland*, 9 part 2 (1872), 396–413 (pp. 407, 403).

15. W. H. Murray, *The Companion Guide to the West Highlands of Scotland* (London: Collins, 1968), p. 150.

16. Liam MacClarich, *By Sword & Pen: Benderloch & Balcardine, their Story* (Oban: Bardic Books, 1997), pp. 43–44.

# Notes

In the Notes below, page references are followed by line numbers in brackets. Thus 46(606) refers to p. 46 and line 606 of Book Second, which appears on that page. For Hogg's prose 'Memento of names places &c' at the end of *Queen Hynde*, page references in the Notes below include a letter enclosed in brackets: (a) indicates that the passage concerned is to be found in the first quarter of the page, while (b) refers to the second quarter, (c) to the third quarter, and (d) to the final quarter. Where it seems useful to discuss the meaning of particular phrases, this is done in the Notes: single words are dealt with in the Glossary. Quotations from the Bible are from the Authorised King James Version, the translation familiar to Hogg and his contemporaries. For references in the Notes to plays by Shakespeare, the edition used has been *The Complete Works: Compact Edition*, ed. by Stanley Wells and Gary Taylor (Oxford: Clarendon Press, 1988). Michael Lynch, *Scotland: A New History* (London: Pimlico, 1992) is referred to below as 'Lynch, *Scotland*'; *The Poems of Ossian and Related Works*, ed. by Howard Gaskill, with an introduction by Fiona Stafford (Edinburgh: Edinburgh University Press, 1996) is referred to as '*Ossian*, ed. Gaskill'; and Raphael Holinshed, *The Scottish Chronicle*, 2 vols (Arbroath: J. Findlay, 1805) is referred to as '*The Scottish Chronicle*'. This narrative of Scotland's story, an important source for *Queen Hynde*, draws on myth and legend in its version of the earliest stages of Scottish history; and this early part of its narrative is similar in nature to the well-known legends of King Arthur and the Round Table. By the time *The Scottish Chronicle*'s narrative has reached the sixth century, however, some historical figures (for example Columba and Aedán) mingle with the people and events of legend. For further details on *The Scottish Chronicle*, see the Appendix: Beregonium, at p. 238. The Notes that follow are much indebted to *The Oxford English Dictionary* (*OED*).

[1] **Title-page** Hogg's manuscript has a title-page in his own hand, transcribed here. Bound in with the manuscript is a printed proof title-page. This proof title-page follows the words of Hogg's manuscript title-page, with the addition at the foot of the page of 'PATERNOSTER-ROW, LONDON' (the address of the Longman firm), and the date '1824'. On the proof title-page, Hogg has written an expanded version of the statement of authorship, as follows: 'By James Hogg (The Ettrick Shepherd) / Author of The Queen's Wake, Poetic Mirror, Pilgrims of / the Sun, &c &c &.'. The proof title-page is printed in roman type, and Hogg adds the following handwritten comment at the top: 'I should like the Black letter of the queen's wake as well as this. Ask Mr Blackwood'. On the title-page of the first edition as published, 'Queen Hynde' and 'in six books' duly appear in Black Letter (Gothic) type, instead of roman; and Hogg's expanded version of the statement of authorship is adopted, with the omission of '(The Ettrick Shepherd)'. Furthermore, 'William

Blackwood, Edinburgh' is added as joint publisher with the Longman firm; and some copies give 1825 rather than 1824 as the date of publication. This kind of variation of date on title-pages is not unusual in the hand-printed books of the period, especially when (like *Queen Hynde*) the book concerned was published at the very end of a year.

[3] **Dedication** the dedication in Hogg's manuscript is transcribed here. In the manuscript, the word 'virgin' has been scored out; and this word has been enclosed in angle brackets in the transcription in order to indicate this fact. It is not clear whether this deletion was the work of Hogg himself, or part of the copy-editing process to which the manuscript has been subjected (see Note on the Text). Hogg's original phrase underscores the motif of the 'Blessed Virgin Mary' so prevalent in the pre-Reformation world of his poem, particularly in his presentation of Hynde as 'virgin sovereign' and his comments on the power of virginity (pp. 13–15). The 'Blessed Virgin' appears elsewhere in Hogg during this period, most notably in 'Kilmeny' (1813) and *Pilgrims of the Sun* (1815). See also Douglas S. Mack, 'Hogg and the Blessed Virgin Mary' in *Studies in Hogg and his World*, 3 (1992), 68–75.

A proof copy of the dedication is bound in with Hogg's manuscript of *Queen Hynde*: this proof omits 'virgin', and also omits the heading 'Dedication'. Otherwise, however, it follows the words of the manuscript's dedication leaf. Hogg writes 'This very neat' at the top of the proof page devoted to the dedication; and he writes 'This line Black letter' against the line of the proof which reads 'The Daughters of Caledonia'. The first edition duly prints this line in Black Letter. Someone has scored out 'throughout' in the proof dedication in an ink different from that used by Hogg on this page; but 'throughout' nevertheless makes its way into the first edition. Indeed, apart from re-setting one line in Black Letter, the first edition makes no change to the proof dedication as typeset.

By addressing in his dedication the daughters of Caledonia 'throughout', Hogg draws attention to the poem's narrative framing device: a Scottish bard telling the epic tale of Scotland's origins to a modern audience. 'Caledonia' was the Roman designation for ancient Scotland, referring primarily to the central Highlands. Subsequently the name was adopted into common usage to mean Scotland generally. James Macpherson glosses 'Caledonians' as follows:

> When South-Britain yielded to the power of the Romans, the unconquered nations to the north of the province were distinguished by the name of *Caledonians*. From their very name, it appears, that they were of those *Celts*, or *Gauls*, who possessed themselves originally of Britain. It is compounded of two *Celtic* words, *Caël* signifying *Celts*, or *Gauls*, and *Dun* or *Don*, a hill; so that *Caël-don*, or Caledonians, is as much as to say, the *Celts of the hill country*. The Highlanders, to this day, call themselves *Caël*, and their language *Caëlic*, or *Galic*. ('A Dissertation', in *Temora: An Ancient Epic Poem* (London: T. Becket and P. A. De Hondt, 1763), p. v.)

In the 1765 edition, Macpherson adds that the Romans 'softened' *Caëloch* into *Caledonia*: see *Ossian*, ed. Gaskill, pp. 207 and 476. Stirling University Library holds a small number of books that once belonged to Hogg. One of these contains three separate books bound into one volume: the 1762 edition of *Fingal*, the 1763 edition of *Temora*, and James Thomson's *The Castle of Indolence* (London, 1748).

## Book First
**5(1) There was a time—but it is gone!** see lines 1–9 of Wordsworth's 'Ode', published in 1807 and retitled in 1815 'Ode. Intimations of Immortality from Recollections of Early Childhood'. Wordsworth begins 'There was a time [...]' and laments, 'It is not now as it has been of yore' (*William Wordsworth*, ed. by Stephen

Gill, The Oxford Authors (Oxford: Oxford University Press, 1984), p. 297).
Coleridge's 'Dejection: An Ode' appropriates both the line and the sentiment
(*Samuel Taylor Coleridge*, ed. by H.J. Jackson, The Oxford Authors (Oxford: Ox-
ford University Press, 1985), p. 115). Amelia Opie also begins her poem 'To a
Maniac' with the phrase (see *The Warrior's Return and Other Poems*, 1807), and it
occurs in Burns's 'On the Destruction of Drumlanrig Wood' as well as in poems
by Charlotte Smith, James Thomson, and William Cowper. Hogg expands this
phrase, used by other Romantics for lyric reflections, to epic proportions.

**5(2) Albyn** the reference is to *Alba*, the Gaelic name for the combined kingdom of the
Picts and the Scots of Dalriada: Alba (or 'Albaine' as it is called in *The Scottish
Chronicle*) evolved into the modern Scotland, and *Alba* remains the name for 'Scot-
land' in modern Gaelic. The historical setting of *Queen Hynde* is Dalriada, the
ancient kingdom of the Celtic Scots, formed when an Irish clan, the Scots of
Dalriada, expanded from Antrim in Ireland into Argyll on the west coast of Scot-
land, during or before the early sixth century. Hogg's epic focuses on 573, the year
in which Saint Columba (acting, it is said, on the instructions of God as conveyed
by an angel) ordained Aedán as overking of Dalriada (see Lynch, *Scotland*, p. 17).
Alba, the combined kingdom of the Picts and the Scots of Dalriada, came into
being much later, between 850 and 1050 (see Lynch, *Scotland*, p. 39); but in the
world of Hogg's epic, this process seems to have taken place before the time of
Aedán and Columba. Writing about 'the significance of the word Alba itself',
Lynch comments (p. 49):

> Before 900 it had been synonymous with the whole of Britain; after 900 it
> became increasingly identified with the land over which the kings of Scots
> ruled and in which their people lived. By 1034, when Malcolm at his death
> was hailed as 'King of Scotia' or 'Scotland', the process was virtually com-
> plete. A compelling image of a trinity of king, people and land had been
> coined. It would last for centuries.

The Celtic word *Alba* is associated with *Albion*, the Roman name for the island of
Great Britain, and in later centuries a poetical name for the home base of the
British Empire.

**5(2-7) Albyn's throne, / Over his kindred Scots alone [...] Pict of Cimbrian
blood, / Or sullen Saxon** during the time of St Columba (521-597), the Scots of
Dalriada contended against rival peoples such as the Picts and the Saxons. *Queen
Hynde*, however, frequently brings the later history of Scotland into play as it
describes Columba's Dalriada; and the opening lines of the poem appear to refer to
the Union of the Crowns of Scotland and England in 1603. This event took place
when James VI (King of Scots, and as such a descendant of the rulers of Dalriada)
inherited the crown of England, and thus began to rule not only Scots, but also
the 'Saxon' English and the 'Cimbrian' Welsh. This particular occupant of 'Albyn's
throne' can thus be seen as a successor to Queen Hynde; but he (like his succes-
sors on the British throne) no longer ruled 'over his kindred Scots alone'. It
appears, then, that Hogg's poem begins with an expression of nostalgic regret for
the days before the Union of the Crowns. In his manuscript, Hogg originally
wrote 'Scotland's throne' here; but he changed this in the manuscript to 'Albyn's
throne'. Given that the connotations of 'Albion' can be British as well as Scottish
(see previous note), this change helps to give *Queen Hynde* a British as well as a
Scottish dimension. This dual dimension is a characteristic Hogg's epic shares
with many Scottish fictions of the time: for example Robert Crawford writes that
Scott's *Waverley* is 'a Scottish and a British book', adding that *Waverley* 'matters
most as a multicultural novel' (*Devolving English Literature* (Oxford: Clarendon
Press, 1992), p. 130). *Waverley* and *Queen Hynde* (in their very different ways) both
assert that there are things of value to be found in the Scottish past. The relation-

ship between these two texts is discussed more fully in section 2 of the Introduction (pp. xvi–xxxviii).

**5(5) Unmixed and unalloyed they stood** this notion seems to derive from *The Scottish Chronicle*, a major source for *Queen Hynde* (see Appendix: Beregonium, pp. 238–44 above, at p. 238). In *The Scottish Chronicle* (I, 3) the old Highland Scots are described as:

> poeple that have lesse to doo with forreine merchants, and therefore are lesse delicate, and not so much corrupted with strange bloud and aliance. Hereby in like sort it commeth to passe, that they are more hard of constitution of bodie, to bear off the cold blasts, to watch better, and absteine long, wherunto also it appeareth that they are bold, nimble, and thereto more skilfull in the warres.

**5(11) Grampian cliff** the Grampians are a Highland mountain range.

**5(15) targe and claymore** a phrase that suggests traditional Highland weapons. The targe is a shield, and the claymore is a large, one-handed, two-edged longsword.

**5(20–21) Even those the world who over-ran / Were from that bourn expelled** referring to the Romans, whose attempts to subdue the 'barbarian' Scots from the first century AD onwards met with little real or lasting success: see Lynch, *Scotland*, pp. 8–11. In the notes to *Fingal*, Macpherson draws attention to a passage in Book VI where Cuchullin praises Fingal for his success in driving away the Romans, 'returning from the wars of the desart; when the kings of the world had fled, and joy returned to the hill of hinds'. Macpherson writes that the Roman emperor 'is distinguished in old compositions by the title of *king of the world*' (*Ossian*, ed. Gaskill, pp. 103, 435).

**6(35–37) His tabernacle, was the height; [...] His cemetry the lonely cairn** for a reader familiar with the Scottish cultural context, these lines evoke popular traditions about the way in which the Covenanters, in the time of their persecution, worshipped God in the mountains; and they also evoke popular traditions about the execution of Covenanters by Royalist soldiers in lonely moorland places, where their graves would sometimes be marked by cairns. Such traditions make themselves felt in the Introductory chapter of R. L. Stevenson's *Weir of Hermiston* (1896), which focuses on a lonely moorland cairn at the place where 'Claverhouse shot with his own hand the Praying Weaver of Balweary'. The relevance of the Covenanters to *Queen Hynde* is discussed in the Introduction at pp. xxxii–xxxiv.

**6(39) queen Hynde** seemingly, there was no historical queen named Hynde; and no such queen is recorded in *The Scottish Chronicle*. She is Hogg's invention, in short. In Scots, 'hind' means both a female deer and a farm worker; and in naming his queen, Hogg likely is playing on both meanings. In Ossian, 'hind' (meaning a deer) appears frequently: see, for example, the note on 5(20–21) above, related to the Romans being driven from Ossian's 'hill of hinds'. Hogg chooses an archaic spelling of the word.

**6(41) vale of Clyde to Orcady** the River Clyde runs from southern central Scotland north-west to its mouth west of Glasgow. 'Orcady' refers to Orkney, a group of islands off the north-east tip of the mainland of present-day Scotland.

**6(43) dreadful monument** Hogg refers to the vitrified remains of a fortress atop Dun mhic Uisneachan on the shore of Ardmucknish Bay. The hill is associated with the ancient, legendary city of Beregonium where Hogg sets *Queen Hynde*: see Hogg's note on p. 218 and the Appendix: Beregonium, pp. 238–44. Here Hogg links the oral tradition of the legendary city with a specific geographical location, citing the latter as evidence. It is a device that he employed frequently. See, for example, in the *Justified Sinner* the hearsay accounts of the suicide's grave; and in *The Three Perils of Man* the footnote to Isaac the curate's narrative regarding secret underground passages leading from Roxburgh castle to the rivers.

**6(62) virgin sovereign** Hynde is portrayed as a 'Blessed Virgin' figure. Also invoked is the virgin queen, Elizabeth of England. See the related note to 13–14(364–65).

**7(113–14) <I'll leave the nation to its fate, / And every ill subordinate.>** these and the preceding lines can be read as a continuation of the references to James VI and the Union of the Crowns of 1603. Mary Queen of Scots was 'won' by Darnley, who was regarded by many as a 'coxcomb'; and it could be argued that in their son, the distinctly unheroic James VI, 'Albyn's ancient royal blood' ran 'to a weak and spurious brood'. According to such a view, James's inheritance of the English throne in 1603 left Scotland open to 'every ill subordinate'. These lines, and others, are enclosed in angle brackets for reasons set out in the Introduction, pp. lxi–lxii.

**10(204–05) The lord of Moray famed in war, / Proud Gaul of Ross, and lordly Mar** these aristocrats, like many of the other persons of Hogg's Scottish epic, are not portraits of actual inhabitants of Columba's Scotland; rather, they conjure up associations with persons (historical or fictional) from many different centuries. Thus the 'lord of Moray' of *Queen Hynde* calls to mind James Stewart (1531–70), Earl of Mar and afterwards Earl of Moray. A natural son of James V (and thus half-brother of Mary Queen of Scots), Moray became a Protestant leader in the mid-1550s and was Regent after Mary's abdication in 1567. However, the 'lord of Moray' of Hogg's poem also calls to mind the well-known traditional ballad 'The Bonny Earl of Moray', about the second Earl of Moray, James Stewart (d. 1592), who assumed the title in right of his wife, daughter of the Regent Moray. 'Proud Gaul of Ross' suggests the 'Gaul' who figures in the Ossianic *Fingal* and *Temora*, as well as 'Goll mac Morna', Fingalian hero of traditional Gaelic narratives (*Ossian*, ed. Gaskill, p. 563). Hogg's list of the major characters of *Queen Hynde* (p. 220) includes '*Gilchrist* lord of Mar'. Mar, one of the ancient Scottish earldoms, was given to a Gilchrist in the 1180s (see A.A.M. Duncan, *Scotland: The Making of the Kingdom* (Edinburgh: Mercat Press, 1996), pp. 187–88). However, the 'lordly Mar' of *Queen Hynde* also calls to mind later figures, for example the Regent Moray (see above), and John Erskine (c.1510–72), who was given the vacant Earldom of Mar in 1565. This Mar helped suppress the 'Chaseabout Raid' of 1565. Led by the Earl of Moray (half-brother of Mary Queen of Scots), this short-lived rebellion of Protestant magnates was provoked by the queen's marriage to Darnley. One is tempted to think that the oft-mentioned rapidity of the Mar of *Queen Hynde* would have been useful in coping with the Chaseabout Raid. The Mar of the Chaseabout Raid had the honour of carrying the infant king at the coronation of James VI at Stirling in July 1567. The Mar of *Queen Hynde* also connects with another John Erskine Earl of Mar. This particular 'lordly Mar' (1675–1732) was heavily involved in the bribing of anti-Union Scottish noblemen that was necessary to purchase the votes in the Scottish parliament that secured the Union of 1707 between Scotland and England, a Union that paved the way for the Hanoverian British state of the eighteenth century. Finding himself out of favour in the Hanoverian Britain of the 1710s, this Mar duly became a Jacobite and led the unsuccessful rising of 1715. His penchant for changing sides earned him the nickname 'Bobbing John'.

**10(210) Donald Gorm** the reference here is to three well-known, warlike, and quarrelsome chieftains associated with the island of Skye, each called Donald Gorme of Sleat: see A. and A. MacDonald, *The Clan Donald*, 3 vols (Inverness: Northern Counties Publishing, 1896), III, 19–57. These three successive generations of Donald Gormes lived in the sixteenth and seventeenth centuries. In Hogg's poem Donald Gorm comes to represent the archetype of an Island chieftain; and as such he represents the Lords of the Isles, who created much trouble for Scottish monarchs over the centuries. *The Scottish Chronicle* describes an aggressive third-century 'Donald of the Isles', 'a nobleman borne', who 'came over with an armie into Rosse and Murreyland, fetching from thence a great spoile and bootie, not without great slaughter of such as inforced themselves to resist him'. He carried out the raid under pretence of revenging the death of Natholocus, an Argyll nobleman (pp. 122–23).

**10(219) Appin** the Beregonium of *Queen Hynde* is situated in Benderloch, a peninsula which lies between Loch Etive (to the south) and Loch Creran (to the north). Appin is the peninsula immediately to the north and east of Benderloch, and it lies between Loch Creran and Loch Linnhe.

**10(223) Lorn** a district on the western coast of Scotland, located south and west of Benderloch, on the opposite side of Loch Etive.

**10–11(234–47) Blithe was her bosom's guileless core, [...] While thus some viewless being sung** see 'Kilmeny' in *The Queen's Wake*, where another 'guileless' maiden ('For Kilmeny was pure as pure could be') lies down in a natural setting and receives a vision concerning the fate of Scotland.

**11(248) The black bull of Norway** Hogg's song alludes to the Scottish folk tale 'The Black Bull of Norroway', a 'lost-husband' narrative common in the oral tradition. As Elaine Petrie observes in her essay '*Queen Hynde* and the Black Bull of Norroway', the tale appeared in Robert Chambers's 1826 *Popular Rhymes of Scotland*: see *Papers Given at the Second James Hogg Society Conference (Edinburgh 1985)*, ed. by Gillian Hughes (Aberdeen: Association for Scottish Literary Studies, 1988), 128–43 (p. 131). In the *Justified Sinner*, the conflict between George Colwan and Robert Wringham involves events in an Edinburgh tavern called the Black Bull, a name expanded in one place to 'The Black Bull of Norway': see *The Private Memoirs and Confessions of a Justified Sinner*, ed. by John Carey (Oxford: Oxford University Press, 1969), p. 50. It may be that *Queen Hynde* draws on the mention of 'The Black Bull of Norroway' in John Leyden's poem 'The Cout of Keeldar', which appeared in Scott's *Minstrelsy of the Scottish Border*, 2 vols (Kelso, 1802), II, 355–72. In commenting on Leyden's poem, Scott mentions (p. 372) 'the wild fanciful popular tale of enchantment [...] *The Black Bull of Norrway*'.

The invisible voice prophesying the siege of the Black Bull of Norway and warning Queen Hynde that 'the flower of the land shall be lost and won, / Ere ever he turn his tail to the sun' recalls the minstrel's song that another queen, Mary, hears in the Introduction to *The Queen's Wake*: 'Watch thy young bosom, and maiden eye, / For the shower must fall, and the flow'ret die': see Hogg, *Selected Poems*, ed. by Douglas S. Mack (Oxford: Oxford University Press, 1970), p. 8.

**11(258) She deemed she lay on fairy ground** according to folk tradition, mortals abducted to fairyland forget why they are there and lose the will to leave. See, for example, the ballad of 'Thomas the Rhymer'.

**11(278–79) As if the lord of nature furled / Up like a scroll the smouldering world** echoes Isaiah 34.4 and Revelation 6.14.

**13(336) The ravisher comes on his car of the wind** Eric, the Great Bull of Norway, who would soon invade Albyn from Scandinavia.

**13(340–43) Trust not the sea-maid with laurel in hand; [...] lion of Lorn** in the second stanza of Book Second, Columba reveals that this utterance refers to 'chiefs defined by heraldry'. It proves to be an accurate prophecy as the poem unfolds: various Scottish noblemen here 'defined by heraldry' prove unable to protect their young queen from the danger that threatens her; instead, the salvation of this royal hind lies (appropriately enough) with a 'roe-buck' (see next note).

**13(344) the roe-buck with antler of gray** this proves to be an apt descripton of the young man Hynde eventually marries.

**13(345) Temora** in his notes to *Temora*, James Macpherson draws on Irish / Gaelic tradition to gloss Temora as 'the name of the royal palace of the supreme kings of Ireland': see *Ossian*, ed. Gaskill, p. 458.

**13–14 (364–65) For she had heard that maiden's eye / Had some commanding majesty** on the power of virginity, see also pp. 14–15 (lines 412–415), where Hogg cites a 'reverend sage' who places the virgin at the top human link of the Great Chain of Being. Hogg distances himself from this position slightly: 'I love it, and in part believe't' (p. 15, line 417). Compare this, too, with 'Kilmeny'. See Douglas Mack's 'Hogg and the Blessed Virgin Mary' for a discussion of the cult of the Blessed Virgin and of Hogg's attitude toward Catholicism as the religion of pre-Reformation Scotland (*Studies in Hogg and his World*, 3 (1992), pp. 68–75). See also the poem 'Ane Rychte Gude and Preytious Ballande', in Hogg, *A Queer Book*, ed. by Peter Garside (Edinburgh: Edinburgh University Press, 1995), pp. 125–35, where there is a long debate on the subject.

**14 (385) maiden's shield by favouring heaven** see also *The Brownie of Bodsbeck*, where Davie Tait's prayer is an effective protection. (Hogg, *The Brownie of Bodsbeck*, ed. by Douglas S. Mack (Edinburgh: Scottish Academic Press, 1976), pp. 127–29.)

**14–15 (402–15) That elfin spear, or serpent's sting, [...] angels joined to human kind** see Psalm 91.4-13, which offers the one who 'dwelleth in the secret place of the most High' protection from forces including 'the arrow *that* flieth by day', the 'pestilence *that* walketh in darkness', 'the young lion and the adder': 'For he shall give his angels charge over thee, to keep thee in all thy ways'.

**16 (454) Maids of Dunedin** Edinburgh is 'Dunedin' (fortress of Edin). For an earlier address to these 'maids', see the 'Introduction' to *The Queen's Wake* (1813), where Hogg writes, 'Fair daughter of Dunedin, say, / Hast thou not heard, at midnight deep, / Soft music on thy slumbers creep?' (Hogg, *Selected Poems*, ed. by Douglas S. Mack (Oxford: Clarendon Press, 1970), p. 3).

**17 (508–09) Come modalist thy toil renew, / Such scene shall never meet thy view!** according to the *OED*, modalism is 'the Sabellian doctrine that the distinction in the Trinity is "modal" only, i.e. that the Father, the Son, and the Holy Spirit are not three distinct personalities but only three different modes of manifestation of the Divine nature'. Hogg has just suggested the Trinity by describing the 'mortal triad' of Hynde standing in a tower between two maidens, implying that the modalist is too rational and earthbound, or 'Enlightened', to be able to give an adequate explanation of woman's nature, which includes wicked Wene as well as the virtuous Queen Hynde.

**17 (528) Cruachan** a mountain rising between Loch Etive and Loch Awe, east of Oban. It is the chief mountain in the lands of the Duke of Argyll; 'Cruachan' was the war-cry of clan Campbell.

**18 (566) Columba of the holy isle** Colum Cille, better known as St Columba (521–597), the Irish abbot and missionary who came to Scotland in 563, and founded a monastery on the inner-Hebridean island of Iona. Legendary for his diplomatic skills and the influence he exerted over both the rulers of the Scots of Dalriada and the Picts, he supported and presided over the crowning in 573 of the king of the Dalriadan Scots, Aedán mac Gabráin (often written as Aidan, Aedan, or Eiden): see Lynch, *Scotland*, pp. 17, 31. In Scottish tradition, Columba is often credited with bringing Christianity to Scotland, though the historical reality is more complicated than this.

**18 (573) Uan bay** the reference may be to 'Port an Duine', on the shore of Ardmucknish Bay, near the site of Hogg's Beregon.

**19 (576) The gilded barge, with silken sail** in Canto I of Scott's *The Lord of the Isles* (Edinburgh: Constable, 1815), the fleet of Ronald, Lord of the Isles, is 'Streamer'd with silk, and trick'd with gold' (p. 21).

**19 (589) Ila Glas the minstrel gray, / Well noted as they sped away** another reference to *The Lord of the Isles*. The name of Hogg's minstrel resembles the Gaelic 'Ile Ghlas', meaning 'green Islay', Islay being a large and fertile island of the Inner

Hebrides. The minstrel's role in sending off the ships also figures in Canto I of Scott's *The Lord of the Isles*, and in that canto of Scott's poem 'green Ilay' (that is, Islay) is mentioned as a centre of the power of the Lord of the Isles (p. 13 and note p. ix).

**19(610–14) She met the ocean's mighty swell; / Yet bounded on in all her pride** an echo of *The Lord of the Isles* (see two previous notes). At this point in Hogg's poem the bark's progress through the water is joyful, as in Canto IV of *The Lord of the Isles*: 'Merrily, merrily, bounds the bark, / She bounds before the gale' (p. 135).

**20(620) Forth's blue waters playful glide** the river that dominates the eastern half of the central belt of Scotland, widening into the Firth of Forth before flowing into the North Sea near Edinburgh. Hogg suggests that, because of its proximity to Edinburgh, the Maids of Dunedin often would sail on it for recreation.

**20(631) Mull** island in the Inner Hebrides, off the western coast of mainland Scotland, west of Oban. In his account of his summer 1804 tour of the Highlands and Western Islands, serialised in 1808 and 1809 in the *Scots Magazine*, Hogg recounts a rough crossing to 'Loch Don' (now 'Lochdon'), a bay on the eastern coast of Mull, and then describes the island:

> There is some green grass surrounding this bay but most of it is upon land which hath been tilled, and is thereby converted from a moss soil into a rich black loam. The mountains are high, the coast, except in the bays, bold and rocky; some brush-wood interlines the declivities; a good way to the eastward appeared the isle of Kerrara, and beyond that the mountains of Lorn; the ruins of Castle-Duart stood on the point beyond us. (*Scots Magazine*, 70 (1808), p. 737).

**20(636) Iona bay** Iona, the site of Columba's early monastery, is a Hebridean island off the western tip of Mull.

**20(638–39) though no woman might come nigh / That consecrated land of I** this is in line with some traditional accounts: see Shirley Toulson's *Celtic Journeys* (London: Fount, 1995), p. 59. In historical accounts, Iona sometimes appears as 'I', 'Hy', 'Iou', or even 'Hugh'.

**20(642–43) Her sire that isle had gifted free, / And reared that sacred monastry** Hogg gives credit for the monastery to Albyn (Scotland) rather than Erin (Ireland). Some early sources establish the idea that a Dalriadan ruler had given Iona to Columba. Tigernach writes, 'Conall, Comgall's son, king of Dalriata [...] gave as offering the island of Iona of Columcille'; and in the *Annals of Clonmacnoise* appears the sentence, 'Conall, son of Comgall that gave the island of Iona [*Hugh*] to Columcille': see Alan Orr Anderson, *Early Sources of Scottish History*, 2 vols (Edinburgh: Oliver and Boyd, 1922), I, 75.

**20(654) Saint Oran** 'The most ancient building on Iona today—as, indeed, in Johnson's time, although much restored since then—is the twelfth-century "St Oran's Chapel." There was an historical Odhran, the saint whose feast is entered in the calendars under October 27th and whose obituary is entered in the *Annals of the Four Masters* at 548, a full fifteen years before Columba left Ireland. There are place-name dedications which, if they are of sufficiently genuine antiquity, indicate his having been in the southern Hebrides, but the tradition linking him with Iona, like the chapel which bears his name, can be traced no further back than the twelfth century.' (John Marsden, *Sea-Road of the Saints: Celtic Holy Men in the Hebrides* (Edinburgh: Floris Books, 1995), pp. 131–32.) In his hostility towards women, the St Oran of *Queen Hynde* seems to provide an echo of the famous confrontations between the religious reformer John Knox and Mary Queen of Scots.

**22(723) wicked Wene** Hogg uses the word *wene* in 'Kilmeny', the most famous part of his most famous poem, *The Queen's Wake* (1813):

> In yon green-wood there is a waik,
> And in that waik there is a wene,
> And in that wene there is a maike,
> That neither has flesh, blood, nor bane;
> And down in yon green-wood he walks his lane.

It appears that *wene* in 'Kilmeny' suggests a dwelling or bower in the greenwood, a place of danger, beauty, and fairy enchantment: see Hogg, *Selected Poems*, ed. by Douglas S. Mack (Oxford: Clarendon Press, 1970), pp. 34, 162–63. For wicked Wene in the role of Fairy Queen, see the note on 129(265), below.

**26(902–03) the christian cause / Rested on Scotland's throne and laws** the suggestion is that the support of the throne and the state is essential if Christianity is to establish itself *within* Scotland. There is also a suggestion of the Covenanters' belief that Scotland was a nation (like ancient Israel) especially chosen by God: see Introduction p. xxxiii, above.

**27(916–17) He seemed as if with heaven he strove, / And more in anger than in love** compare the Rev. Robert Wringhim struggling with God in the *Justified Sinner*, and receiving assurance that Robert Wringhim the younger is one of the elect. The Rev. Robert Wringhim tells young Robert of this; and young Robert meets Gil-Martin for the first time immediately afterwards. This passage in the *Justified Sinner* seems linked with Genesis 32.24-32, in which the patriarch Jacob (ancestor of the nation of Israel) wrestles with God.

**28(968) Lauchlan Du** 'Lauchlan' is a common Highland name, and 'Du' from the Gaelic 'Dubh' means 'black'. Hogg may be drawing on Scott's character Evan Dubh in *Waverley*.

**29(1024) Old Ila Glas his harp-strings rung** perhaps a reference to the 'wild minstrelsy' that comes from the galleys in the Sound of Mull in Canto I of Scott's *The Lord of the Isles*: see note on 19(589).

**29(1028–29) A lay full tiresome, stale and bare / As most of northern ditties are** in poking fun at the Ossian-style bard Ila Glas, Hogg comments on the melancholy heaviness and fatefulness of Ossian's poems. He argues that he *could* write like Ossian, but he will do something different. The reference to learning the song from a 'Bard in Mull' may refer to a personal experience on Mull or to Macpherson's collecting practice and the discussion of his sources in the Highland Society's *Report* of 1805.

**29(1034)< No more of high important things** an allusion to the first line of Book IX of Milton's *Paradise Lost*: 'No more of talk where God or Angel Guest'.

**31(1080–86) Wing the thin air or starry sheen, [...] Or raise up spirits of the hill** in this *apologia* for his writing, Hogg presents a litany of his major themes and alludes to some of his works. Winging 'the thin air or starry sheen', for example, may refer to *Pilgrims of the Sun*, and the 'fairy's visionary home' recalls 'Kilmeny'. An allusion to Ossian's *Fingal* may be found in Hogg's plea that he be allowed to 'raise up spirits of the hill'. In Book V, Ossian describes the bard Carril's voice as 'pleasant as the gale of spring that sighs on the hunter's ear; when he wakens from dreams of joy, and has heard the music of the spirits of the hill': see *Ossian*, ed. Gaskill, p. 96.

**Book Second**

**32(5–6) He solved the eagle, and the oak, / The hawk, and maiden of the sea** see the riddle of Queen Hynde's dream, p. 13 (lines 334–45). Columba's biographer Adomnán records numerous stories of Columba's prophetic powers, many of which have entered popular consciousness. For his prophecy regarding Aedán as king, see the section headed 'Of the angel of the Lord who was sent to St Columba to bid him ordain Áedán as king, and who appeared to him in a vision while he was living in the island of *Hinba*' (*Life of Columba*, trans. by Richard Sharp (London: Penguin, 1995), pp. 208–09).

33(33) **Morven** Hogg is referring to *Morvern*, a diamond-shaped peninsula on the western coast of the mainland. It is bounded by Loch Sunart to the north and Loch Linnhe to the southeast, and separated from the island of Mull by the narrow Sound of Mull. The site of Hogg's Beregon is on the opposite side of Loch Linnhe from Morvern. 'Morven' is the Ossianic name for Fingal's kingdom ('King of Morven'); in a note to Book III of *Fingal*, Macpherson comments, 'All the North-west coast of Scotland probably went of old under the name of Morven, which signifies a ridge of very high hills' (*Ossian*, ed. Gaskill, p. 428).

33(39) **robes of green** in folk tales and ballads, the colour green is associated with fairies.

33(49) **Barcaldine lea** an area on the south shore of Loch Creran on the peninsula of Benderloch. 'Barcaldine lea' lies a little to the north of 'Beregon', discussed below.

33(62) **Beregon** or 'Beregonium', the legendary Scottish capital in Argyll on the western coast of Scotland. See Hogg's note, p. 218, and the Appendix, pp. 238–44.

34(95–98) **beacon which from Uock shone, [...] Ben-More** the image here is of a chain of warning beacons being lit on high ground to rally the nation's forces to resist an imminent invasion. Beacons of this kind feature in Scott's *The Antiquary* (1816); and they were familiar in Britain during Hogg's lifetime, when invasion by Napoleon's forces was widely expected. Hogg began to write *Queen Hynde* around the time of Napoleon's final defeat at Waterloo.

35(112) **Ardnamurchan** a peninsula on the opposite side of Loch Sunart from Morvern. Ardnamurchan lies to the north of the island of Mull, separated from it by a sound. In the account of his 1804 tour, Hogg describes a frightening attempt to cross from Tobermory at the northern tip of Mull to Ardnamurchan:

> When we reached the point of Ardnamurchan, or the Rhu, as it is com-
> monly called, we were obliged to tack twice in order to weather it, and had
> already got to the windward side of it, when the sea growing prodigiously
> heavy, and the wind continuing to increase, the sailors were affrighted, and
> though ten or twelve miles advanced, turned and run again for Tobermory.

In the November instalment, Hogg continues the harrowing tale:

> We had got within the rocky point which bounds the north side of the
> harbour, and just when endeavouring to put the vessel about for the last
> time on that side, a tremendous gale commenced, which threw her so much
> over, that the main-sail dashed into the sea, and rendered fruitless every
> effort, not only to bring about the ship, but even to get down the mainsheet,
> in order to let her scud out to sea, clear of the rocks. She was, during the
> time of this short struggle, driving with great force straight upon the rocks;
> and the men, not being able to effect any thing in the consternation they
> were in, a moment of awful pause ensued. Every man quitted his hold, save
> old Hugh at the helm, and if my chops had not been so much slackened at
> the inner end, I would have raised the tinker's whistle; when, by a singular
> interposition of Providence, the ship gave a great roll backwards, and the
> main-sail dropped down of itself, the ropes having been previously loos-
> ened, and the vessel whirled round clear of the rocks, tho' within six, or at
> most, seven yards of them. Old Hugh thanked his Maker aloud for this
> signal deliverance, and indeed every heart seemed sensibly affected by it.
> We now stood out to the open sound, intending to weather out the storm
> without risking the vessel among rocks, to gain a harbour a second time.

Because continuing in the direction of the open sea toward Ardnamurchan Point was too dangerous, the group turned east, opting to 'run for Loch-Sunart' (*Scots Magazine*, 70 (October 1808), 738; (November 1808), 809). The exploits of 'Old

Hugh' may have helped to suggest those of M,Houston in Book Third of *Queen
Hynde* (pp. 88–89).

**35(118) Canay** the island of Canna, one of the small islands north and east of
Ardnamurchan. Scott has a note on 'the little island of Canna, or Cannay' in *The
Lord of the Isles* (Edinburgh: Constable, 1815), notes p. xciii.

**36(163) Loch-Sunart** a sea loch running east and west and separating Ardnamurchan
and Sunart (to the north) and Morvern (to the south). Hogg describes it as
follows:

> This Loch-Sunart, and its environs, is a very wild scene, and though not
> destitute of beauty, it is rather of the savage kind, being a group of precipi-
> tate rocks, green hallows, and wild woods; with the sea winding amongst
> them in every direction; and the back ground shaded by a range of black-
> topped mountains, embosomed in which the mean hamlets lie hid from all
> the rest of the world. (*Scots Magazine*, 70 (November 1808), 811.)

**37(210) I swam the Coran** at the Corran Narrows, Loch Linnhe (an arm of the sea)
is only a quarter of a mile wide. To cross here saves a long detour round the head
of the loch; and in modern times a car ferry operates at Corran.

**37(227–28) "I've braved the Briton on the field, / I've met the Roman, shield to
shield** the Britons and Romans were historical enemies of the Scots. For
Macpherson's notes to *Fingal* regarding the Romans, see the note to 5(20–21),
above.

**38(233–52) If there are nations north away, [...] a countless host / Of such now lies
on Scotland's coast** Hogg's epic is based on the premise that the Norse invaded
this part of Scotland in the sixth century, though recorded history indicates no
invasion before the ninth. Some historians hint at the possibility of earlier incur-
sions, however. Rightly or wrongly, the Ossianic *Fingal* is based on this premise
that Norse invasions of Scotland commenced, and were destructive far earlier
than is generally thought; and in *Queen Hynde* Hogg follows the lead of Ossianic
tradition. See also Hogg's *The Three Perils of Man* of 1822 (ed. by Douglas Gifford,
Edinburgh: Canongate, 1996), in which the Poet's tale (pp. 348–49) describes a
Norse threat facing the 'royal maids of Caledon', a situation reminiscent of *Queen
Hynde*. A key source for Hogg's understanding of Norse culture is Paul Henri
Mallet, *Northern Antiquities*, translated [by Thomas Percy] from Mallet's *Introduction a
l' Histoire de Dannemarc*, 2 vols (London: T. Carnan, 1770). Hogg quotes Mallet in
one of his notes on *Queen Hynde* (p. 219).

**38(261) Barra** an island in the Outer Hebrides, south-west of Skye.

**38(264) Creran bay** the peninsula on which Beregon is situated lies to the south of
Loch Creran. Appin lies to the north of Loch Creran.

**39(274) Moidart's clan** Moidart lies between Loch Shiel and the sea, and was the
territory of the MacDonalds of Clanranald, some of whom provided hospitality to
Hogg during his 1804 tour:

> Mr M'Donald caused his sons to row us round the island [Island-Teona, in
> Loch-Moidart], and land us on the mainland in the country of Moidart. On
> our way we passed by a natural canal, so narrow, that there was scarcely
> room to work the oars, and saw the mighty ruins of Castle Tuirim, which
> they said was formerly the residence of Clanranald. (*Scots Magazine*, 70
> (December 1808), 891.)

Visiting the site where 'the unfortunate Prince Charles Stewart first landed on
the mainland of Scotland in the year 1745', Hogg learned from the locals that this
landing had been the occasion on which 'that song, called the "*Eight men of Moidart*,"
was composed' (*Scots Magazine*, 70 (December 1808), 891.)

**40(315–20) High on a rock the palace stood [...] well may trace** Hector Boece
describes Beregon as having seven towers. For a discussion of Boece and Beregon,

see the Appendix, pp. 238–44, and Hogg's note on p. 218. See also *The Three Perils of Man*, where the castle of Roxburgh is described as having 'seven distinct squares or castles, every one of which was a fortress of itself' (p. 452).

**40(322) Selma** Ossian's name for the site known as Beregon or Beregonium: Macpherson's Ossian poem *Fingal* is set there. Modern maps locate a site called Port Selma near the supposed ruins, exactly where Hogg places Beregon in his note, p. 218. See also Hogg's footnote on p. 59.

**40(341) Benderiloch** Benderloch, a low peninsula projecting into the Lynne of Lorn between Loch Etive and Loch Creran. Benderloch is marked by nine bays, including Ardmucknish Bay, the site of Beregon.

**40(342) Etive bay** Loch Etive begins deep in the Highlands of the Blackmound Forest and winds 18 miles before opening into the Lynn of Lorn. The narrow opening at Connel Ferry allows crossing from the south into Benderloch.

**40(342) Cona glen** a glen formed by a river that empties into upper Loch Linnhe. Loch Etive and Cona glen define the southern and northern boundaries of Benderloch and Appin.

**40(343) Connal of Lismore** Lismore is an island off the coast of Benderloch at the point where Loch Linnhe, the Firth of Lorn, and the Sound of Mull meet.

**40(346) Connel's boisterous wave** tides flow very strongly at Connel, through the narrow mouth of Loch Etive, thus producing Ossian's 'Falls of Lora'.

**41(372) dead-lights glimmering in the dale** a luminous appearance supposed to be seen over a dead body; a 'corpse-light' or 'corpse-candle'. An almost identical phrase, 'dead-lights glimmering through the night', occurs in the 'Introduction' to *The Queen's Wake*: see Hogg, *Selected Poems*, ed. by Douglas S. Mack (Oxford: Clarendon Press, 1970), p. 12, l. 344). Dead-lights as a means of tracing a body appear in Hogg's story 'Rob Dodds' (Hogg, *The Shepherd's Calendar*, ed. by Douglas S. Mack (Edinburgh: Edinburgh University Press, 1995), pp. 33–34); and they also appear in 'The Cameronian Preacher's Tale' (Hogg, *Selected Stories and Sketches*, ed. by Douglas S. Mack (Edinburgh: Scottish Academic Press, 1982), pp. 117–18).

**41(391) Loch-Linhe** this extremely long loch (spelled 'Linnhe' on modern maps) cuts off Ardgour, Morvern, and Ardnamurchan from the rest of the mainland.

**41(394–96) When Orion with his golden chain [...] To keystone of the milky way** time is here measured by the movement in the sky of the group of stars known as Orion's Belt. In Hogg's story 'Mary Burnet', 'the set time' of Mary's assignation with Jock Allanson is 'when the King's Elwand (now foolishly termed the Belt of Orion) set his first golden knob above the hill' (Hogg, *The Shepherd's Calendar*, ed. by Douglas S. Mack (Edinburgh: Edinburgh University Press, 1995), p. 201).

**41(395) moors of Tay** the source of the river Tay lies in Highland moorland to the east of Loch Linnhe. The Tay flows into the North Sea.

**42(402) Ossian's airy harp** this phrase combines images from *Ossian*—Hogg keeps *Fingal* very much in view—and the Romantic preoccupation with the Eolian harp as seen especially in Coleridge, Wordsworth, and Shelley.

**42(403–07) rapt spirit [...] The first watch of the morning** in New Testament times, the night was not divided into hours, but into four watches; and the fourth and final watch was called the morning watch. We read in Matthew 14 that Jesus 'went up into a mountain apart to pray' by night, while his disciples remained on a ship:

> But the ship was now in the midst of the sea, tossed with waves: for the wind was contrary. And in the fourth watch of the night Jesus went unto them, walking on the sea. And when the disciples saw him walking on the sea, they were troubled, saying, It is a spirit; and they cried out for fear. But straightway Jesus spake unto them, saying, Be of good cheer; it is I; be not afraid. (Matthew 14. 24–27.)

**42(434) the thousand glens of Lorn** this area is remarkable for its jaggedness; it is carved by glens, rivers, lochs, and high mountains.

**42(435) Spey** a major Highland river, which enters the sea to the east of Inverness.

**42(436) Lomond** Loch Lomond, which is dominated by the mountain Ben Lomond, discharges into the Clyde estuary by the River Leven.

**42(437) Cantire** Kintyre is a long peninsula on the west coast, south of Knapdale and west of the island of Arran; the tip of Kintyre is separated by the North Channel from Ireland. Kintyre is part of the territory of Clan Campbell, and Campbeltown is its most prominent town.

**43(463) Lofodden's thirsty cave** the Lofoten Islands lie off the coast of north-west Norway.

**43(475–76) As if the forest of Lismore / Came struggling on to Appin's shore. / So far that moving wood was spread** an echo of Act V of *Macbeth*, in which Malcolm's army, carrying boughs, makes good the prediction that Macbeth has nothing to fear 'till Birnam Wood / Do come to Dunsinane' (v.5.42–43).

**44(491) old Conal** the Ossianic character Connal appears, for example, in Book II of *Fingal* (*Ossian*, ed. Gaskill, p. 65).

**44(492) "On, warriors, on!"** an echo of the words of the dying Marmion in stanza XXXII, Canto Sixth, in Scott's *Marmion* (1808): 'Charge, Chester, charge! On, Stanley, on! / Were the last words of Marmion'.

**46(606) Keila bay** that is, Ardmucknish Bay, which is overlooked by the site of Beregon. Large-scale modern maps show the remains of a Columban chapel ('Cill Choluim-chille') immediately to the south of the site of Beregon; and this chapel is discussed (as 'Kilcolmkill, or Keil') in the Appendix: Beregonium, p. 242. 'Keil Crofts' lie nearby, a little to the north. Hogg also may be invoking I Samuel 23, where David goes to fight the Philistines attacking the city of Keilah. David had been anointed by Samuel as the chosen future king, in accordance with God's instructions (I Samuel 16.1–13). This parallels the historical accounts of Columba's visionary king-making in promoting Aedán's ascension to the throne of Dalriada and Hogg's account of Columba being told to retrieve Aedán from Ireland. In this case, the Philistines would be equated with the Norsemen.

**48(673) Lennox** the earls of Lennox, prominent in medieval Scotland, were descended from one of the ancient native aristocratic families of the pre-medieval period: see Lynch, *Scotland*, p. 59. Lennox is one of the Scottish thanes in Shakespeare's *Macbeth*.

**48(675) every tongue to me is known** Columba was regarded as the apostle to the Scots; and this passage in *Queen Hynde* may allude to the ability of the original apostles to speak in other tongues, as described in Acts 2. 'And they were all all filled with the Holy Ghost, and began to speak with other tongues, as the Spirit gave them utterance. [...] Now when this was noised abroad, the multitude came together, and were confounded, because that every man heard them speak in his own language.' (Acts 2.4, 6)

**48(679) a bough of holly green** a traditional symbol of peace. It is also a specifically Christian symbol, associated with heaven in traditional songs and ballads, as in the carol 'The Holly and the Ivy'.

**48(689) Haco** a character so named appears in Macpherson's early poem *The Highlander* (1758), which resembles *Queen Hynde* in several ways. The poem opens with the death of an aged Scottish chieftain and impending war between Scotland and Denmark, with the Danes ruled by the 'royal Sueno' about to attack: 'fierce Scandinavia's hostile pow'r, / It's squadrons spread along the murm'ring shore; / Prepar'd, at once, the city to invade, / And conquer CALEDONIA in her head' (*The Highlander: A Poem in Six Cantos* (Edinburgh, 1758), p.4). Macpherson's Haco is the young Danish prince, who 'by more than Sueno's blood, was great; / The promis'd monarch of the triple state'. An Eric appears in the poem, and the description of the maid Culena sounds very like Hogg's account of Queen Hynde:

> The imperial maid moves with superior grace,
> Awe mix'd with mildness sat upon her face;
> High inbred virtue all her bosom warms,
> In beauty rises, and improves her charms.
> Silent and slow she moves along the main,
> Behind, her maids attend, a modest train.
> Observe her as she moves with native state,
> And gather all their motions from her gait. (p. 44)

Thomas Percy's translation, *Five Pieces of Runic Poetry* (London: Dodsley, 1763) includes 'The Funeral Song of Hacon', who was 'a great hero of the Norwegians, and the last of their Pagan kings', slain about 960 in battle with the Danes (p. 59). Another ruler, Hakon IV of Norway, may figure here as well. In 1263, he was defeated by the Scottish army of Alexander III, and as a result the Hebrides (previously under Norse control) were finally incorporated into Scotland: see Lynch, *Scotland*, p. 90.

**49(707) Scania** Scandinavia.

**49(709) Odin** the Norse god of war and father of all the gods.

**49(731) Eric of Norway** the character may be based on the historical Eric the Red, who was killed in a tenth-century Viking raid in Britain. For Hogg's knowledge of Norse culture, see the note to 38(233–52).

**52(834-35) Allan Bane, / Lochaber's fair and goodly thane** James VI traced his ancestry back to Banquo, Thane of Lochaber; and Shakespeare's *Macbeth*, written after James VI had inherited the English crown, praises Banquo's royal nature: see Henry N. Paul, *The Royal Play of Macbeth* (New York: Octagon Books, 1971), p. 173. *The Scottish Chronicle* (I.335) likewise writes of '*Banquho* the *Thane of Lochquhaber*, of whom the house of the *Stewards* is descended, the which by order of linage hath now for a long time injoied the crowne of *Scotland*'. Here as elsewhere, *Queen Hynde*'s portrait of Scotland shows an awareness of *Macbeth*; and the 'fair and goodly' Allan Bane seems to connect with Banquo. Lochaber includes Fort William and Glencoe, and it extends east of the upper portion of Loch Linnhe, to the north-east of Ardmucknish Bay.

**52(837) Argyle** here, as elsewhere, a character in *Queen Hynde* calls to mind figures from later periods of the history of Scotland. The earls (later the Dukes) of Argyle (or Argyll) were chiefs of the powerful Clan Campbell. The name of the geographical area comes from the Gaelic Earra-Ghaidheal (pronounced Er-a-gyl), meaning 'Coastland of the Gael'. Archibald Campbell (1598–1661), 8th Earl and first Marquis, was a champion of the Protestant cause, and figures prominently in Hogg's 'Edinburgh Baillie' (*Tales of the Wars of Montrose*, ed. by Gillian Hughes (Edinburgh: Edinburgh University Press, 1996), p. 272). John, second Duke of Argyll (1678–1743) figures prominently in Scott's *Heart of Mid-Lothian* (1818).

**52(840) Scotish chief** this spelling of 'Scottish' was common in the eighteenth century.

**54(923-27) When here degraded foemen lay [...] Hated and scorned by all but you** French prisoners of war were held in the vicinity of Edinburgh during the Napoleonic struggles: see Karl Miller, *Cockburn's Millennium* (London: Duckworth, 1975), pp. 154–55.

**55(947) Ettrick** a river in the Scottish Borders, giving its name to the valley where Hogg was born.

**55(960-73) For can I deem that beauty's glow, [...] primal sin / To veil unsanctitude within?** in its concern with the 'primal sin' of the Fall, this passage links with that other Christian epic, *Paradise Lost*.

56(985) **Calvin's sweeping creed** the doctrine promoted by John Calvin. Hogg refers particularly to predestination, whereby he can justify (ironically) women's 'crimes of deepest hue' by saying 'They were predestined thee to do'. This passage may best be understood in the light of Hogg's complex treatment of Calvinism in the *Justified Sinner*.

56(1006–07) **I've sung of Wake and roundelay / In beauteous Mary's early day** a reference to *The Queen's Wake* (1813), in which bards meet in a competition staged on the return of Mary Queen of Scots to Scotland.

56(1009) **maiden borne to fairyland** a direct reference to 'Kilmeny', the thirteenth bard's song in *The Queen's Wake* (1813).

56(1010–11) **Of worlds of love, and virgins bright; / Of pilgrims to the land of light** a reference to Hogg's *Pilgrims of the Sun* (1815).

56(1012–13) **I have sung to those who know, / Of Maiden's guilt and failings too** a reference to Hogg's *Mador of the Moor* (1816), in which the heroine has a child out of wedlock.

56(1016–18) **Now I've called forth a patriot queen, [...] And I've upraised a wayward elf** Valentina Bold has identified Hogg's 'balancing of dignified and impish women' as 'typical' of his work. In addition to Queen Hynde and wicked Wene in *Queen Hynde* (1824), Bold cites Gatty and Cherry in *The Three Perils of Woman* (1823) and Oriel and Lady Foambell in *The Royal Jubilee* (1822): see '*The Royal Jubilee*: James Hogg and the House of Hanover', *Studies in Hogg and his World*, 5 (1994), 1–19 (p. 5).

## Book Third

58(12) **the old site of Beregon** Hogg describes the setting of this legendary ancient seat of the Scottish kings in very accurate and concrete terms (indeed, he apparently had seen the site in his travels), and here he acts as tour guide, pointing out specific features of the prospect. It is a poetic version of his note regarding 'Beregonium', p. 218. See also the Appendix, pp. 238–44.

58(30) **songs of Selma's time** a conflation pun on Macpherson's celebrated 'The Songs of Selma' and 'songs of other times', as well as the persistent Ossianic idea of being brightened by songs of old.

59(39) **remnants of the forest pine** remains of the old native Caledonian pine forest, only a few fragments of which now remain, for example on the islands of Loch Maree.

59(43) **Jura's fair bosom** the two main mountains on the island of Jura are thought to resemble a woman's breasts and are known as 'the Paps of Jura'.

59(46) **Proud Nevis on Lochaber's brink** Ben Nevis, Scotland's highest mountain, is located in Lochaber, south-east of Fort William.

59(52) **one so well deserves the name** the name of Selma, that is. Hogg's footnote explains, '*Selma* signifies The beautiful view *Beregon*, or *Perecon*, as pronounced. The serpent of the strait'. In a note to the Ossianic 'Darthula', Macpherson glosses 'Seláma': ' The word in the original signifies either *beautiful to behold*, or a place *with a pleasant or wide prospect* [...] The famous Selma of Fingal is derived from the same root' ('Darthula', in *Fingal* (London, 1762), p.158). *Beregon* is described as '*Perecon*, as pronounced' because there was a well-established literary convention in Scottish texts for rendering the English speech of native Gaelic speakers, according to which [b] is de-voiced to [p], and so on. This convention is discussed by Mairi Robinson in 'Modern Literary Scots: Fergusson and After', in *Lowland Scots: Papers Presented to an Edinburgh Conference*, ed. by A. J. Aitken (Edinburgh: ASLS, 1973), pp. 38–55 (p. 39).

59(57) **Bornëan height** Hogg may have meant *Borean*, which means 'pertaining to the north', or 'northern'.

**59(59) Barvulen ridge** Baravullin Ridge is approximately one mile directly north of the site of Beregonium.

**62(167) We wish with him to be alone** in her role as Queen Hynde, Wene adopts the royal 'we'.

**63(228–41) O titled rank, [...] scoundrel scrutiny** Hogg's ambiguously satirical address to the aristocracy, in which he is doubtless commenting on the Royal Visit of George IV to Edinburgh in 1822. See Valentina Bold, '*The Royal Jubilee*: James Hogg and the House of Hanover', *Studies in Hogg and his World*, 5 (1994), 1–19.

**65(287–88) to your Albyn's present bound / Unite our islands all around** refers to Viking possession of islands around Scotland, incuding Shetland, Orkney, and the Western Isles.

**67–68(372–411) Loth would Dunedin's daughter be [...] In what a school thy mind was bred!** in these three sections, Hogg chastises his readers for unduly censoring work by such writers as Lord Byron, John Galt, and Thomas Moore, and by extension himself, all of whom were criticised for 'indelicacy' in some sense.

**68(439–41) motely tribes of Spey, [...] Mordun Moravius** according to *The Scottish Chronicle*, 'Britains, Scots, Picts, and Moravians' combined to fight against the Romans (I, 86), but were defeated. However, 'the Moravians which escaped from the discomfiture, had that portion of Scotland assigned foorth unto them to inhabit in, that lieth betwixt the rivers of Torne and Speie, called even unto this day Murrey land' (I, 87).

**68(442) from the Dee's wild branching flood** the river Dee flows into the North Sea near Aberdeen.

**68(451) From far Cantyre to dark Lochow** defines the limits of the territory of the Argyll family, chiefs of Clan Campbell.

**69(456–57) pagan standards broad unfurled, / The remnants of a heathen world** in Book IV of *Fingal*, the hero rallies his forces:

> Raise my standards on high,—spread them on Lena's wind, like the flames of an hundred hills. Let them sound on the winds of Erin, and remind us of the fight. Ye sons of the roaring streams, that pour from a thousand hills, be near the king of Morven: attend to the words of his power. Gaul strongest arm of death! O Oscar, of the future fights; Connal, son of the blue steel of Sora; Dermid of the dark-brown hair, and Ossian king of many songs, be near your father's arm.
>
> We reared the sun-beam of battle; the standard of the king. Each hero's soul exulted with joy, as, waving, it flew on the wind. It was studded with gold above, as the blue wide shell of the nightly sky. Each hero had his standard too; and each his gloomy men. (*Ossian*, ed. Gaskill, pp. 86-87).

Macpherson notes, 'Fingal's standard was distinguished by the name of *sun-beam*; probably on account of its bright colour, and its being studded with gold. To begin a battle is expressed, in old composition, by *lifting of the sun-beam*' (*Ossian*, ed. Gaskill, p. 431). This passage from *Fingal* is one that can be traced to a genuine Gaelic source: see *Ossian Revisited*, ed. by Howard Gaskill (Edinburgh: Edinburgh University Press, 1991), p. 43.

In *Queen Hynde*, Donald Gorm of Skye carries the standards that the Fingalian heroes might have borne; the description of the flags as 'pagan' sets up Donald Gorm as representative of an outmoded force for Scotland's development, as opposed to the Christianity of Columba.

**69(461) Harold with his Caithness men** Caithness forms the extreme north-east corner of the mainland of Scotland. It was for long under Scandinavian control and influence; and 'the earldom of Caithness was formerly possessed by a family of the name of Harold' (Sir John Sinclair, *The Statistical Account of Scotland*, 21 vols (Edinburgh: W. Creech, 1791–99) XX, 534). 'Harold' is an appropriately Norse name: in Ossian's 'Fragment of a Northern Tale', Harold is a ruler of 'Lochlin', glossed by Macpherson as the Gaelic name for Scandinavia (see *Ossian*, ed. Gaskill, pp. 410–11). Hogg may also refer to Scott's poem *Harold the Dauntless*, which Edgar Johnson describes as 'an experiment in the manner of the Norse Skalds' (*Sir Walter Scott: The Great Unknown*, 2 vols (London: Hamish Hamilton, 1970), I, 562–63). According to the opening lines of Scott's poem, Harold the Dauntless was 'Count Witikind's son'; and Count Witikind 'roved with his Norsemen the land and the main'. *Harold the Dauntless* was published anonymously in January 1817, around the time Hogg was writing the first section of *Queen Hynde*.

**69(475) deep and monkish art** the speculation about Columba's activities may be viewed in the light of Gothic fiction popular at the time, in which monks were often associated with sorcery, reflecting a strong anti-Catholic sentiment. See, for example, M.G. Lewis's Ambrosio in *The Monk* (1796) and Ann Radcliffe's character Schedoni in *The Italian* (1797). The Friar in Hogg's *The Three Perils of Man* (1822) provides an interesting contrast: a religious figure who, though acquainted like Michael Scott with the study of occult mysticism, effects his 'miracles' through science.

**71(555–57) Albyn's fierce invading foes, [...] To him had pesterous neighbours been** the Vikings made themselves particularly troublesome on the islands (such as Skye), which were vulnerable to invasion by sea.

**72(590–609) There stands one record, never lost, [...] What arm of angel had begun** the biblical source of this story is Joshua 10.1–14, and Joshua is the one Hogg refers to as 'Captain of the Lord's own host'.

> Therefore the five kings of the Amorites, the king of Jerusalem, the king of Hebron, the king of Jarmuth, the king of Lachish, the king of Eglon, gathered themselves together, and went up, they and all their hosts, and encamped before Gibeon, and made war against it. And the men of Gibeon sent unto Joshua to the camp to Gilgal, saying, Slack not thy hand from thy servants; come up to us quickly, and save us, and help us: for all the kings of the Amorites that dwell in the mountains are gathered together against us. So Joshua ascended from Gilgal, he, and all the people of war with him, and all the mighty men of valour. And the LORD said unto Joshua, Fear them not: for I have delivered them into thine hand; there shall not a man of them stand before thee. Joshua therefore came unto them suddenly, *and* went up from Gilgal all night. And the LORD discomfited them before Israel, and slew them with a great slaughter at Gibeon, and chased them along the way that goeth up to Beth-horon, and smoke them to Azekah, and unto Makkedah. And it came to pass, as they fled from before Israel, *and* were in the going down to Beth-horon, that the LORD cast down great stones from heaven upon them unto Azekah, and they died: *they were* more which died with hailstones then *they* whom the children of Israel slew with the sword. Then spake Joshua to the LORD in the day when the LORD delivered up the Amorites before the children of Israel, and he said in the sight of Israel, Sun, stand thou still upon Gibeon; and thou, Moon, in the valley of Ajalon. And the sun stood still, and the moon stayed, until the people had avenged themselves upon their enemies. (Joshua 10.5–13)

In *Queen Hynde*, Argyle is arguing that Columba's disappearance is not abandonment of Beregon, but in accordance with a mission on the city's behalf; i.e., God listens to prophets and therefore will hear Columba's request and act on it. Like the famous eighth Earl of Argyll who lived almost a thousand years later, the Argyle of *Queen Hynde* is a wily and influential politician, as well as being a man motivated by strong religious feeling: see the note on 52(837).

**72–73 (614–27) At holy Samuel's sacrifice, [...] all their country overthrown** an allusion to I Samuel 7.9–11, where God takes the prophet's offering and answers his prayer:

> And Samuel took a sucking lamb, and offered *it for* a burnt offering wholly unto the LORD: and Samuel cried unto the LORD for Israel; and the LORD heard him. And as Samuel was offering up the burnt offering, the Philistines drew near to battle against Israel: but the LORD thundered with a great thunder on that day upon the Philistines, and discomfited them; and they were smitten before Israel. And the men of Israel went out of Mizpeh, and pursued the Philistines, and smote them, until *they came* under Bethcar.

**73(631) The prayer of a righteous man** 'The effectual fervent prayer of a righteous man availeth much' ( James 5.16).

**74(696–703) The first of Albyn's race supreme [...] Else it is lost to Albyn's line** Aedán (or Aidan) the Great, king of the Dalriadan Scots, who is discussed in a note on 18(566). In this passage, Hogg alludes perhaps to the account of the dream in which, as the legend has it, Columba was told to support Aedán's claim to the throne rather than that of his brother. According to Saint Adamnan's account of the historical Columba's vision,

> Once when the praiseworthy man was living in the island of *Hinba*, he saw one night in a mental trance an angel of the Lord sent to him. He had in his hand a glass book of the ordination of kings, which St Columba received from him, and which at the angel's bidding he began to read. In the book the command was given him that he should ordain Áedán as king, which St Columba refused to do because he held Áedán's brother Éoganán in higher regard. Whereupon the angel reached out and struck the saint with a whip, the scar from which remained with him for the rest of his life. Then the angel addressed him sternly:
>
> 'Know then as a certain truth, I am sent to you by God with the glass book in order that you should ordain Áedán to the kingship according to the words you have read in it. But if you refuse to obey this command, I shall strike you again.'
>
> In this way the angel of the Lord appeared to St Columba on three successive nights, each time having the same glass book, and each time making the same demand that he should ordain Áedán as king. The holy man obeyed the word of the Lord and sailed from *Hinba* to Iona, where Áedán had arrived at this time, and he ordained him king in accordance with the Lord's command. As he was performing the ordination, St Columba also prophesied the future of Áedán's sons and grandsons and great-grandsons, then he laid his hand on Áedán's head in ordination and blessed him.
>
> (*Life of St Columba*, trans. by Richard Sharpe (London: Penguin, 1995), pp. 208–09)

In Hogg's poem, the visitor warns Columba that Eiden must take the throne or it will be lost to Scotland ('Albyn's line'). Here as elsewhere *Queen Hynde* makes connections with Shakespeare's *Macbeth*. James VI was King of Scots about a thousand years after Aedán; and *Macbeth*, written in honour of James VI after he became James I of England in 1603, may echo the ancient story of Columba's dream in its 'show of eight kings, the last with a glass in his hand' (IV.1.127). James VI would have regarded these kings as his own ancestors, the inheritors (like himself) of Aedán's throne.

**75(712–43) And art thou come, [...] In shadows of Eternity** Columba's questioning of the ghost recalls Hamlet's father's ghost being forbidden to tell the secrets of his after-death experience in *Hamlet* I.5.13–22.

**75(736) When once the bourn of death is passed, / A veil o'er all beyond is cast** this passage resembles *Hamlet* III.1.80–84.

**76(752) christian Conran** according to the account of *The Scottish Chronicle* (I, 197), Conrane (or Conranus), King of Scots, was murdered in his bedchamber, and succeeded by his nephew Eugenius, who was supposed by many to have been involved in planning the murder.

**76(756) He died. His brother seized his Crown** there are echoes here not only of the actions of Eugenius in *The Scottish Chronicle* (see previous note), but also of the actions of Claudius in *Hamlet*.

**76(757) Eugene** Queen Hynde's father in Hogg's poem. The character is based on Eugene (or Eugenius) who, according to *The Scottish Chronicle*, had fought with Arthur against the Saxons, and who had begun his reign as King of Scots following the suspicious death of his uncle Conran: see *The Scottish Chronicle* (I, 197), and the note on 76(752), above. Hogg recasts *The Scottish Chronicle*'s Conran as Eugene's brother rather than his uncle; and in doing so he in effect conflates Conran with Eugene's brother Convall, who (according to *The Scottish Chronicle*) became King of Scots after Eugene's death (I, 203). In the poem, it will be remembered, Queen Hynde comes to the throne after her father Eugene's death: but Queen Hynde is Hogg's invention. At all events, Convall is described in *The Scottish Chronicle* as a particularly pious Christian (compare 'Christian Conran', l. 752), whose fame 'mooved that holie man *St. Colme* or *Colombe*, to come over forth of *Ireland* (where he had the the governance of sundrie houses of monks) with twelve other vertuous persons into *Albion*' (I, 203).

**76(760–61) When Conran died, Columba then / Bore his young son across the main** according to *The Scottish Chronicle*, the young 'Aidan' was taken to Ireland for his safety:

> The talke [of Eugene's involvement in the murder of Conrane] was so common in all mens mouths, namelie amongst the common people, that the queene *Dowager* late wife to king *Conrane*, doubting not onlie the suertie of her owne life, but also of her two sons (which she had by the said *Conrane*, the one named *Reginan*, and the other *Aidan*) fled with them over into *Ireland*, where within few yeares after, she died with the one of her sons, that is to say, *Reginan*: the other *Aidan* was honorablie brought up by the king of that countrie, according to his birth and degree. (*The Scottish Chronicle*, I, 197.)

Hogg gives Columba, rather than the mother, the role of taking the young Eiden to Ireland.

**76(765) Colmar, King of Erin's land** Erin is a name for Ireland. The character of Colmar in *Queen Hynde* is based on the king of Ireland who, according to *The Scottish Chronicle* (I, 197), raised Aidan after his escape from Scotland. Hogg seems to have derived the name (though not the character) from the Ossianic poem 'Calthon and Colmar', in which Colmar is son of Rathmor of Clutha, brother of Calthon, who is imprisoned and then killed by Dunthalmo as Ossian's army approaches: see *Ossian*, ed. Gaskill, pp. 171–73, 465, 557.

**77(806) Temora bay** see note on 13(345).

**77(813) truant monks** according to traditional stories, Columba came to Scotland because he was driven into exile from Ireland 'as penance for causing a battle to be fought in defence of his making an illicit copy of a psalter': see John Marsden, *Sea-Road of the Saints: Celtic Holy Men in the Hebrides* (Edinburgh: Floris Books, 1995), p. 49.

**79(880) There was a day, but it is past** see the opening line of Book First.

**80(931–32) some great power beneficent, / That rules around, above, below** Hogg establishes Colmar and Eiden as pagans of a different order from the worshippers of Odin. Rather, Colmar and Eiden perceive a 'great power beneficent', a 'great spirit', in nature; but they have not yet associated this power with the Christian God. *Queen Hynde* posits an Irish royalty that is heathen, which was not so at the time of Columba. In *Queen Hynde*, however, this approach allows Eiden / M,Houston to be converted to Christianity by Columba, thus underscoring Columba's crucial role in establishing Scotland as the Christian country that would become the second Israel (through the Covenants of the seventeenth century). The Covenanters saw the Covenant of Wednesday 28 February 1638 as 'the glorious marriage day of the Kingdom [Scotland] with God' (David Stevenson, *The Covenanters: The National Covenant and Scotland* (Edinburgh: Saltire Society, 1988), p. 1); and Columba prepares the kingdom for this in converting Eiden / M,Houston.

**80(945) Prince Eiden** see Hogg's endnote on M,Houston, pp. 218–19; and *The Scottish Chronicle*, I, 197–211. The character is based on the historical Aedán: see the note to 74(696–703).

**80(948) Cuithone** perhaps an echo of the female Ossianic character 'Cuthona': see *Ossian*, ed. Gaskill, p. 560.

**82(1025–29) "I worship, as my fathers did, [...] I kneel beneath the green oak tree** Hogg's Irish king follows the tenets of Druidism, a form of sun-worship among the Celtic peoples. Canon MacCulloch calls Celtic religion, 'in the main, a cult of the powers of growth and fertility, perhaps because the poetic temperament of the people kept them close to the heart of nature. [...] The cult of nature-spirits preceded and outlived that of the anthropomorphic gods' (quoted in F. Marian McNeill, *The Silver Bough*, (Edinburgh: Canongate, 1989), p. 26). Interestingly, in *Pilgrims of the Sun*, Hogg locates Heaven in the sun. The oak is a magic tree in Scottish folk tradition; F. Marian McNeill describes an old rhyme listing 'nine sacred types of wood [...] used to kindle Druidical fires at Beltane and Hallowe'en: "Choose the oak of the sun"' (p. 84). For druids and oaks, and Columba and oaks, see M.A. Fitzgerald, *The World of Colmcille* (Dublin: O'Brien, 1997), pp. 26–27. The oak, besides being a symbol of Druids, is a symbol of the Stuart line.

**82(1031–32) the weak tenets of thy school, / All founded on a woman's words** in the Christian story of the Annunciation, Mary made the Incarnation possible by acceptance of her role: 'be it unto me according to thy word' (Luke 1.38).

**83 Continuation of Book 3d** this is the point at which the break comes between the early (c. 1817) section and the late (1824) section.

**84(1081) Cunninghame** part of Ayrshire in Scotland, it lies to the east of the northern part of Ireland.

**84(1082–93) When this strange guest, [...] In sooth a fearful wight was he** Hogg's description of M,Houston resembles some descriptions of Hogg himself as a rustic.

**87(1238) Isla** the Hebridean island of Islay, off the coast of the peninsula of Kintyre, is more or less on the direct route to Beregon; but M,Houston heads more directly before the storm, for the nearer shelter offered by Kintyre.

**88(1258) The bark flew on before the wind** see Scott's *The Lord of the Isles*, Canto IV, referred to in the note to 19(610–14). This passage is reminiscent too of Coleridge's 'Rime of the Ancient Mariner', which was first published in the 1798 *Lyrical Ballads*, but reappeared in its revised form in Coleridge's *Sibylline Leaves* (1817).

**88(1269) feind-like crew** 'We were a ghastly crew' (Coleridge, 'The Rime of the Ancient Mariner', *Samuel Taylor Coleridge*, The Oxford Authors (London: Oxford University Press, 1985), p. 57, l. 340).

**89(1287) (Gods how the monks and rowers held!)** with the plural 'Gods', Hogg plays here with M,Houston's religion and his audience, fusing M,Houston's voice with that of the bard.

**89(1313) he hollo'd out** see Coleridge's 'The Rime of the Ancient Mariner', in which the albatross comes to 'the mariners' hollo' (l. 74). The imagery of sea birds predominates in this section of Hogg's poem.

**89(1318–21) At this dire moment, [...] they knew not how** Columba's emergence here echoes the Gospel story of Christ's stilling of the storm:

> And there arose a great storm of wind, and the waves beat into the ship, so that it was now full. And he was in the hinder part of the ship, asleep on a pillow: and they awake him, and say unto him, Master, carest thou not that we perish? And he arose, and rebuked the wind, and said unto the sea, Peace, be still. And the wind ceased, and there was a great calm. And he said unto them, Why are ye so fearful? how is it that ye have no faith? And they feared exceedingly, and said one to another, What manner of man is this, that even the wind and the sea obey him? (Mark 4.37–41)

Columba, 'washed from his hold', provides a somewhat unheroic echo of Christ; but the Apostle operates on a different level from the Son of God. In *Queen Hynde*, Columba's personal heroic stature is not what matters; what matters is the cause he serves. In the manuscript, Hogg originally wrote l. 1321 as 'Washed from his hold, the lord knew how,'; thus hinting at the possibility that the Lord knew exactly what He was doing in washing His Apostle on to the deck at this particular juncture. Perhaps afraid that his more stuffy readers would object to an apparently flippant tone in dealing with serious matters, Hogg then changed the ending of the line to 'they knew not how,'.

**90(1335–37) at the point of low Kintyre, [...] Still fright the coasting mariner** the Mull (point) of Kintyre is the part of Scotland nearest to Ireland, where the Firth of Clyde opens into the sea. The meeting of the waters produces rough water.

**90(1352) "Who *art* thou?" said Columba then** in 'The Rime of the Ancient Mariner', the Hermit who encounters the Mariner after his mysterious voyage asks, 'What manner of man art thou?' (l. 77). There is also an echo of Mark 4.41, which is quoted in the note on 90(1318–21): 'What manner of man is this, that even the wind and the sea obey him?'.

**91(1386–91) 'Twas he who reared the roe-deer's brood, [...] And all for poor M,Houston's use** M,Houston credits the sun with an act of creation that seems to echo the act of creation attributed to God in Genesis 1 and 2: see especially Genesis 2.19–20.

**91(1410–11) strength of mind, / In such low rank of human kind** echoes a favourite theme of Burns's, expressed for example in the song 'Is there for honest poverty': 'The rank is but the guinea stamp, / The man's the goud for a' that'.

**92(1414) he resolved to win the youth / Unto the holy Christian truth** M,Houston will prove to be Scotland's kingly saviour from the pagan Vikings; and it is thus richly significant that he is converted to Christianity by Columba (the Apostle to the Scots) at the moment at which he arrives in Scotland. There is perhaps a hint here of Jacobite notions about the king from over the water who will return to save the land.

**92(1416) Dalrudhain's lonely bay** referring to a bay on the coast of Kintyre, which the writer of the *Statistical Account* for the parish of Campbeltown describes as the original site of the Dalriadan kingdom. The Rev. Dr John Smith writes, 'the oldest name of Campbelton, by which a part of it is still known, is *Dalruadhain*, from its having been the capital of the ancient Scottish or Dalreudinian kingdom' (Sir John Sinclair, *The Statistical Account of Scotland*, 21 vols (Edinburgh: W. Creech, 1791–99), x, 517).

**92(1431) Loch-Fyne** an arm of the sea in Argyll, south of and running parallel to the freshwater Loch Awe.

**92(1450) Orchay's vale** the Orchy, known as a fast and dangerous river, begins in the Black Mount range and rushes twelve miles down Glen Orchy to flow into the northern end of Loch Awe.

93(1461-62) "I've journeyed many a day, / From hill of Zion to the shore Columba's journey seems metaphorical rather than literal; the legends about his life do not include a trip to the Holy Land.

93(1480) The storm hath all unequaled been Hogg's fascination with 'unequaled' storms emerges frequently in his work. See especially 'Storms' in *The Shepherd's Calendar*, ed. by Douglas S. Mack (Edinburgh: Edinburgh University Press, 1995), pp. 1–21.

94(1509) Loch-Ow the modern Loch Awe, spelled 'Lochow' elsewhere in *Queen Hynde*.

### Book Fourth

95(1) the harp of that land the harp refers to Ossian, and the 'land' is the Highlands. Hogg would take up Ossian's harp to sing this epic of Scotland's origins.

95(15) Scythia an ancient region extending over a large part of European and Asiatic Russia (see *OED*). In *The Scottish Chronicle* (I, 42), 'Scythia' is identified as Denmark. The word 'Scythian' in literary contexts of the day is often linked with 'barbarian'.

96(42) Dwina's dark flood there are two rivers named Dvina in Russia, one coming out in the White Sea at Archangel ('Northern Dvina') and the other in the Gulf of Riga ('Western Dvina'). Hogg also refers to the 'Dwina' in his poem 'The Last Stork': see *A Queer Book*, ed. by P. D. Garside (Edinburgh: Edinburgh University Press, 1995), p. 184.

96(48) stound in English, a sharp pain or pang; in Scots, a thrill as of delight. Hogg's use of the word seems to draw on both meanings as he describes the effect Hynde has on King Eric. See Burns's 'Blue-eyed Lassie', where 'aye the stound, the deadly wound, / Cam frae her een sae bonnie blue'.

97(114) Valon-Righ Hogg's spelling approximates the sound of this dun's name, which is 'Dun bhail an righ', the hill overlooking Dun mhic Uisneachan (Beregonium).

98(146) First of these fiends was Donald Gorm Hogg's portrayal of this character as hot-tempered agrees with accounts of at least one historical Donald Gorm, who in 1601 reportedly killed MacLeod of Dunvegan 'in a quarrel which had arisen between them'. According to the story collected by John Gregorson Campbell, when confronted by the dead man's son with the question 'Was it not you who killed my father?' Donald Gorm replied, 'It has been laid to my charge that I killed three contemptible Highland lairds [...] and I do not care though I put the allegation on its fourth foot to-night'. Drawing his dirk, he continued, 'There is the dirk that killed your father; it has a point, a haft, and is sharp edged, and is held in the second best hand at thrusting it in the west'. When MacLeod asked the identity of the other, Donald Gorm 'shifted the dagger to his left hand, raised it, and said, "There it is"' ( J. G. Campbell, *Clan Traditions and Popular Tales of the Western Highlands and Islands*, ed. by Jessie Wallace and Duncan MacIsaac (London: David Nutt, 1895), pp. 59–61).

103(334) sacrifice of human blood see the note on p. 219 regarding 'Human Sacrifices'.

103(336) Thor the Scandinavian god of thunder.

104(407) Donald of the Isle Donald Gorm of Skye.

105(444) M,Ola's royal race from MacColla, Clan Donald.

106(489) Rimmon, bard of Turim's hall MacRimmons were hereditary bards in Skye. For 'Turim's hall' see note on 39(274).

106(492) The winged isle on a map, Skye looks as though it has wings.

106(496) Duich's heights of moor and fell Loch Duich is connected to Loch Alsh, on the mainland just east of Skye.

107(502) Milesian rhyme an Irish rhyme, unidentified and perhaps fabricated for

Hogg's purposes. Macpherson glosses the 'Milesians' as the legendary colonists of
Ireland: see *Ossian*, ed. Gaskill (Edinburgh: Edinburgh University Press, 1996), pp.
217, 219, 224, 487.

107(506) **gods of wood and stone** a frequent Biblical phrase to describe false gods: see
Deuteronomy 4.28, 28.36 and 64, 29.17; II Kings 19.18; Isaiah 37.19; Ezekiel
20.32.

108(542) **Loke** Loki is an evil god in Norse mythology. He is discussed by Mallet in
*Northern Antiquities*, II, 85–89, 154–58. For *Northern Antiquities*, see note on 38(233–
52).

108(578) **Turim's ancient bard** see note on 106(489).

109(616) **the roundelay** this 'Hymn to Odin', apparently one of Hogg's fabrications,
drew some of the most hostile criticism from contemporary reviewers.

110(652) **The master spirit of the age** 'The choice and master spirits of this age'
(*Julius Caesar* III.1.164).

110(657) **That morning rose in ruddy hue** a bad omen ('Red sky at morning, sailors
take warning').

111(684–86) **the shadows closed around, / Until the noontide of the day / Looked
like a twilight in dismay** this passage contains biblical resonances; see Deuter-
onomy 28.29 and Job 5.14, as well as the darkness that comes over the land at the
Crucifixion, Matthew 27.45.

112(722) **men of Dee** the Dee is a river in north-east Scotland.

112(723) **Athol** a Highland district in northern Perthshire.

112(729) **Rannoch** a vast, triangular moor east of the mountainous Lochaber.

112(730) **Pulled the blue bonnet o'er the brow** the blue bonnet is a traditional item
of male Scottish dress.

119(1033) **Lochy's side** a loch north-east of Fort William in Lochaber.

120(1059–60) **as a charm, / Bound golden bracelet round his arm** gold arm-bands
were given as a reward for bravery in battle: for the Viking background, see Else
Roesdahl, *The Vikings*, trans. by Susan M. Margeson and Kirsten Williams, (Lon-
don: Penguin, 1998).

**Book Fifth**

123(5) **Lovely mythologist** a mythologist is 'one who is versed in myths or mytholo-
gies', according to the *OED*. The maid, then, is an expert in stories; and Hogg
would rather pay attention to her expertise than that of the 'official' critics.

125(100) **This city of our fathers' names** a name associated with the fort at the
supposed site of Beregonium is *Dun mhic Uisneachan*, the Fort of the Sons of Uisneach.
See Hogg's note regarding M,Houston, pp. 218–19, where he explains his associa-
tion (however erroneous) of this name with the lineage of Eugenius.

128(215) **"Ohon an Banrigh!"** in Gaelic, 'Alas, oh Queen!' Hogg uses similar Gaelic
expressions in *The Three Perils of Woman*, among them 'Ohon an bochd daoine!'
meaning 'Alas, the poor man!' (ed. by David Groves, Antony Hasler, and Douglas
S. Mack (Edinburgh: Edinburgh University Press, 1995), p. 273).

129(265) **Twelve pages, glancing all in green** a hint of the Fairy Queen's procession
in ballads, with Wene in the role of the glamorous and deceptive Fairy Queen. The
name *Wene* carries suggestions of fairy enchantment: see note on 22(723).

129(271–72) **All were sincere, you may believe't. / How oft poor minstrels are
deceived** an example of a rhyme that works in Scots, in which the -ed ending is
pronounced 'it'.

132(366) **Frotho, the old chamberlain** in the Norse, 'Frothi' means 'the wise one'.
Many 'Frothis' and 'Frodas' appear in Old Norse and Old English literature.

135(519) **without the line** outside the circle (of the festivities).

137(581) **Dunstaffnage** reputed to be the site of the capital of the later Dalriadan kings until the reign of Kenneth I in the ninth century. Dunstaffnage is situated on the southern side of the mouth of Loch Etive, about 2 miles by sea across Ardmucknish Bay from the site of Beregonium. Dunstaffnage castle, the ruins of which survive, was built before 1275, and was captured by Robert the Bruce in 1309: it features in Scott's poem *The Lord of the Isles*.

**137(600–01) ray of heaven and flash of hell / Together upon mortals fell** lightning from both heaven and hell also features in Hogg's story 'Mr Adamson of Laverhope', which, like *Queen Hynde*, was first published in 1824. See Hogg, *The Shepherd's Calendar*, ed. by Douglas S. Mack (Edinburgh: Edinburgh University Press, 1995), pp. 38–56.

**138(615) Freya** Norse goddess of love, marriage, and the dead; wife to Odin.

**138(615) nine times nine** nine is a mystic number in Norse mythology.

**138(629) Valhala** the palace of bliss for the slain heroes of Scandinavian mythology. It has daily battles, and nightly feasts enhanced by maidens and bards.

**139(684) Job** the Biblical book of Job meditates on the question 'Why does God allow the good to suffer?'. Job, a righteous man, suffers severely; and God's decree to this effect is imagined as bringing joy to Satan, who had once been an angel. See Job 1.6–12, on which this passage (lines 669–686) is based. The Priest of Odin is associated with Satan.

**140(712) red rose of Damascus** according to the *OED*, the 'damask rose' is 'a species or variety of rose, supposed to have been brought from Damascus'. The word 'damask' is used to describe the 'blush' colour of this rose and, poetically, the blush of a woman's cheek: in *Twelfth Night* (II.4.110), Shakespeare writes, 'She never told her love, / But let concealment, like a worm i'th' bud, / Feed on her damask cheek'. In Christian tradition, red is the colour of the martyrs; the Blessed Virgin Mary is symbolised by the rose; and St Paul was converted to Christianity on the road to Damascus.

**141(771) sceptical philosophy** see Hogg's comments on scepticism in his *Lay Sermons*, ed. by Gillian Hughes with Douglas S. Mack (Edinburgh: Edinburgh University Press, 1997), pp. 110–20.

**141(777) "What is man?"** echoes Job 7.17, 15.14, and Psalm 8.4.

**141(778–79) What *he hath been*, the world can see. / Thou only know'st *what he shall be*!** echoes ideas expressed in 1 Corinthians 13.9–12.

**147(1001) Possessed by the great Gordon now** Alexander Gordon, fourth Duke of Gordon (1743–1827). An earlier Gordon chief (George Gordon, 1st Marquis of Huntly) features prominently in Hogg's 'Edinburgh Baillie', from *Tales of the Wars of Montrose*.

**147(1021) hector of the northern main** a reference to Homer's Trojan hero.

**150(1125) Donald Bane** Allan Bane, like the Banquo of *Macbeth*, is Thane of Lochaber: see note on 52(834–35). In *Queen Hynde* Donald Bane is Allan Bane's brother; and in *Macbeth* Donalbain is one of King Duncan's sons.

**150(1134) Lochourn leans o'er his tarnished oak** Loch Hourn, Loch Duich, and the Sound of Sleat form boundaries of the headland of Glenelg, a mountainous area on the mainland east of the island of Skye. The 'oak of Loch-Orn' features in the prophecy at p. 13, lines 334–45.

**150–51(1158–1160) Lwin [...] Glen-Roy** the place-names suggest that Brande's extensive territories lie to the north and east of Beregon.

**153(1254) Illium's classic plain** an allusion to Troy that invites comparison with Homer and Virgil. Here the Ettrick Shepherd is underscoring his audacious assertion that *Queen Hynde* is an epic.

**153(1271) Navern dale** Loch Naver is in Sutherland.

**153(1273–74) Gaul, the lord of Tain, / And Ross's wild and wide domain** Tain is an ancient royal burgh in Ross and Cromarty on the shores of the Dornoch Firth, in the far north-east of Scotland.

**154(1303–1307) The royal city now was lost, [...] That for a thousand years had stood** Hogg imaginatively reconstructs the fall of Beregon, which eventually takes on biblical proportions. In enemy hands, and with the horrible transgression of human sacrifice, Beregon goes the way of a Sodom or Gomorrah. *The Scottish Chronicle* puts the building of Beregon at 327 BC (see Appendix: Beregonium, p. 239); and Columba lived towards the end of the sixth century AD; so on this basis 'a thousand years' does not require very much rounding up.

**154(1320–21) Her court, her treasures, and her throne / Safe in Dunstaffnage they did place** implicit in these lines is the idea that Beregon preceded Dunstaffnage as home of the Stone of Destiny: see the note on 'the marble chair' at 218(a).

**157(1415) hill of Kiel** the remains of 'Keil', the Columban chapel mentioned in the note on 46(606), lie immediately below Dun bhail an righ (see Appendix: Beregonium, pp. 238–44).

**158(1458) In honour of this hero slain / Contend in every manly game** the funeral games for Coulan Brande echo the funeral games in Homer's *Iliad* (Book 23).

**158(1485–88) For there no preference was to be [...] The low estate of vassalage** Hogg comments forthrightly on peasantry, social hierarchy, and himself. At this point in *Queen Hynde* there appears to be a questioning of the assumptions that lie behind the famous shooting contest of the popinjay in the opening chapters of Scott's *Old Mortality* (1816). In this contest the 'peasant' Cuddie Headrigg competes and does well; but (not unexpectedly in a novel by Scott) he fails to do well enough to defeat his gentlemanly rivals Henry Morton and Lord Evandale, between whom the contest is finally settled.

**158(1492) The creature of a chief supreme** Hogg comments elsewhere on the subservience of Highlanders to their chief: see for example 'Julia M,Kenzie', in *Tales of the Wars of Montrose*, ed. by Gillian Hughes (Edinburgh: Edinburgh University Press, 1996), at p. 144.

**160(1544–59) Feldborg the Dane [...] Eon of Elry** the contest between Feldborg and Eon is mentioned in the hostile review of *Queen Hynde* in the *Westminster Review*, 3 (April 1825), 531–37. The writer remarks:

> Many gentlemen claim the Queen's hand, and our readers will be not a little surprised to find among them no less a personage than *Professor Wilson*, equally qualified to fill the chair of Moral Philosophy at noon, and of Ambrose's ale-house at night. Our readers will scarcely believe us, when we state, that this person figures by his name, very little disguised, in a poem professing to be the record of things that took place 1,300 years ago [...]. The passage is far too long and dull for entire quotation; but it details a running match, which actually took place between professor Wilson and a teacher of languages at Edinburgh, called Feldborg, who is named at full length.

'Eon of Elry' is John Wilson ('Christopher North'): poet, novelist, influential critic, and a moving force of *Blackwood's Edinburgh Magazine*, including its 'Noctes Ambrosianae'. He was also an athlete in his youth. Eon M,Eon (l.1575) is 'John, son of John' in Gaelic, and Wilson's home in the Lake District was called 'Elleray'.

**169(1950) the son of David's sway** see Matthew 1.1, where Jesus's descent from King David is traced.

**172(2045–46) for one punishment condign, / Thy hate to Odin's heavenly line** see Mallet's *Northern Antiquities*, II, 154–58. For *Northern Antiquities*, see note on 38(233–52).

**172(2078–80) poor M,Houston was his name, / Though some there were, on Erin's shore, / Call'd him M,Righ, and Eiden More** the character of M,Houston is based on *The Scottish Chronicle*'s account of the historical King Aedán: see the notes on 18(566), 74(696–703), and 76(760–61). *Mac Righ* (here 'M,Righ') is Gaelic for

'Son of the King'; and *Eiden More* renders the Gaelic for 'Aedán the Great'.

**174–75(2145–92) Fair maid of Albyn's latter day, [...] What has thy bard to hope for now?** this passage (and in particular lines 2167–92) seems to refer to and echo 'On the Death of a Favourite Cat, Drowned in a Tub of Goldfishes', by Thomas Gray (1716–71):

> From hence, ye Beauties, undeceived,
> Know one false step is ne'er retrieved,
>   And be with caution bold:
> Not all that tempts your wandering eyes
> And heedless hearts, is lawful prize,
>   Nor all that glisters, gold.

Hogg echoes Gray in having a female figure (woman / cat) leaning over a tempting but dangerous brink (in Gray, the cat tempted by goldfish in a bowl). Other echoes include the mock-formality of religious or classical terms ('seraph' in Hogg, 'Nymph' in Gray); the phrase 'angel form' (in Gray, describing fish); and the fact that both passages are cautionary: a woman who falls cannot be reinstated to virtue.

**176(2217) great foe on primal day** a reference to the Fall in Genesis, in which Eve is ensnared by Satan's subtlety.

**176(2223) some stale review** Hogg's opinions on these, and especially on the *Edinburgh Review,* appear in his sermon on 'Reviewers' in *Lay Sermons,* ed. by Gillian Hughes with Douglas S. Mack (Edinburgh: Edinburgh University Press, 1997) pp. 99–107.

**177(2257–58) foreign monstrous thing above / Their native measures** see Hogg's 'Preface' to *The Forest Minstrel* (Edinburgh: Constable,1810), pp. ix–x.

**177(2267) The garret, poll, and apes to lead** an allusion to Shakespeare's *Taming of the Shrew,* which refers (at II.2.34) to the traditional belief that old maids lead apes in hell. This line of *Queen Hynde* also contains an allusion to the conventional picture of an old maid leading a lonely life in a garret, with only a parrot (poll) for company.

**177(2287) Warm friends profest, yet covert foes** the concluding lines of Book Fifth can be read as an extended comment on Hogg's uneasy relationship with the group of writers associated with *Blackwood's Edinburgh Magazine.* One example is provided by the ferociously hostile review of Hogg's novel *The Three Perils of Woman* published in *Blackwood's,* 14 (October 1823), 427–37. This review was by Hogg's 'warm friend profest', John Wilson.

## Book Sixth

**179–82(1–121)** Hogg opens Book Sixth with his poem 'The Queen of the Fairies', just published separately in the first volume of the annual *The Literary Souvenir.* Writing to the annual's editor Alaric A. Watts on 2 February 1825, Hogg remarks:

> The Queen of the Fairies was so decidedly in my best stile that I could not help popping her into the last book of Queen Hynde, and I regretted that my work appeared so soon after yours; however it has rather had a good than bad effect, for the reviewers of The Souvenir quote it on the one hand, and the reviewers of Hynde on the other, and even the same reviewers quote it without at all seeming aware that it is in both works. (National Library of Scotland MS 1002, fol. 102)

**179(8–9) an air of heaven, in passing by, / Breathed on the mellow chords** Hogg's version of the Eolian harp, that Romantic symbol of poetic inspiration. See also the final stanza of *The Queen's Wake*: Hogg's 'loved harp' has 'taught the wandering winds to sing'.

**179(25) Thou lovely queen of beauty** the Queen of the Fairies.

**179(34) Thou queen of the land 'twixt heaven and hell** according to tradition, fairies occupy an otherworld distinct from the Christian heaven or hell. See especially the ballad of 'Thomas the Rhymer', in which the Queen of Elfland shows the captive True Thomas 'ferlies three':

> O see ye not yon narrow road,
>     So thick beset with thorns and briers?
> That is the path of rightousness,
>     Though after it but few enquires.

> And see ye not that braid, braid road,
>     That lies across that lily leven?
> That is the path of wickedness,
>     Though some call it the road to Heaven.

> And see ye not that bonny road
>     That winds about the fernie brae?
> That is the road to fair Elfland,
>     Where thou and I this night maun gae.

'Thomas the Rhymer' draws from a passage in the Sermon on the Mount to which Hogg refers frequently in his fictions: see, for example, *The Three Perils of Woman*, ed. by David Groves, Antony Hasler, and Douglas S. Mack (Edinburgh: Edinburgh University Press, 1995), p. 26. In the Sermon on the Mount (Matthew 7.13–14), Christ preaches:

> Enter ye in at the strait gate: for wide *is* the gate, and broad *is* the way, that leadeth to destruction, and many there be which go in thereat: Because strait *is* the gate, and narrow *is* the way, which leadeth unto life, and few there be that find it.

**180(39–40) thy halls of the emerald bright, / Thy bowers of the green** green is the colour of the fairies.

**180(44) my loved muse, my Fairy Queen** Hogg proclaimed himself 'king o' the mountain and fairy school' of poetry, by way of contrast with Scott's 'chivalry school': see the Introduction, p. xv.

**180(50) the bells of her palfrey's flowing mane** a common element in descriptions of fairies and fairy processions. See the ballad of 'Thomas the Rhymer', in which True Thomas spies the Queen of Elfland riding near the river, and 'From ilka tett of her horse's mane / Hung fifty siller bells and nine'. Hogg aligns himself with that great Scottish poet and prophet, Thomas of Ercildoune, who according to legend was abducted and given the gift of prophecy by the Queen of Elfland herself. See also 'Tam Lin', in which Janet hears 'the bridles ring' as the fairy procession approaches. These traditional fairy ballads make their presence felt in Hogg's poem 'Old David', which forms part of *The Queen's Wake*.

**180(54) old Edmunds lay** a reference to Edmund Spenser's *The Faerie Queene*.

**180(56–57) waked the bard of Avon's theme / To the visions of his Midnight Dream** a reference to Shakespeare and *A Midsummer Night's Dream*.

**180(58–59) the harp that rang abroad / Through all the paradise of God** Hogg's romantic reading of John Milton's *Paradise Lost*, which ('Kilmeny' fashion), intertwines the Heavenly and the Fairy.

**180(60) sons of the morning** there is a well-known hymn beginning 'Brightest and best of the sons of the morning', by Reginald Heber (1783–1826).

**181(83) purple and [...] green** purple suggests royalty, and green is the colour of the fairies: so these are appropriate colours for the Fairy Queen.

**181(92) blackamoor pioneer** the mole. There is an allusion to *Hamlet* 1.5.164–65: 'Well said, old mole. Canst work i'th' earth so fast? / A worthy pioneer'.

**181(105) Where the sun never shone, and the rain never fell** this line and its context echo Hogg's 'Kilmeny', which describes a heavenly and fairy world 'Where the rain never fell, and the wind never blew': see Hogg, *Selected Poems*, ed. by Douglas S. Mack (Oxford: Clarendon Press, 1970), p. 33.

**181(118) now I have found thee, I'll hold thee fast** see the ballad of 'Tam Lin', wherein Tam instructs Janet to 'hold me fast, and fear me not'. In many folk narratives, holding fast to a supernatural being (or one under supernatural influence)—no matter what happens—is rewarded by achievement of a goal or receipt of a gift.

**182(150) To force the Connel and the Croy** to get to Dunstaffnage from Beregon, Eric has to get over the narrow mouth of Loch Etive at Connel. The editors have been unable to identify 'the Croy'.

**184(235–39) Beard Eric of the northern world, [...] And beat the blue and bloody Hun?** reflects the extensive conquests of the Vikings.

**188(374) The evening came, and still no knight / Had proffered life for Scotia's right** this passage offers a parallel to the Arthurian story in *Sir Gawain and the Green Knight*, where the knights are reluctant to step forward to accept the Green Knight's challenge on behalf of Arthur.

**192(547) damask rose** see note on 140(712).

**193(581) The shadow falls not to the east** see the end of Hogg's 'Mary Burnet', where Mary's family await her arrival by watching the shadow of the Holy Cross until 'it fell due east' (*The Shepherd's Calendar*, ed. by Douglas S. Mack (Edinburgh: Edinburgh University Press, 1995), p. 221). The east is a source of blessing in Christian tradition.

**193(617) The will of God be done!** 'The will of the Lord be done' (Acts 21.14).

**194(647–51) threw away his belted plaid; [...] ruby's burning gem** this emergence of a royal figure from a disguise of poor clothing connects with traditional stories of James V's habit of travelling in disguise among his people. These traditional stories about James V underpin Scott's *Lady of the Lake* (1810) and Hogg's *Mador of the Moor* (1816).

**195(672) Harold of Elle, a Danish knight** for associations of the name *Harold*, see note on 69(461).

**195(688–91) both wings, as with assent, [...] 'Twixt Eric and his foeman new** the others pause while the two main heroes fight as in the contest between Burley and Bothwell at Loudon-hill in Scott's *Old Mortality* (1816).

**196(706–07) two wild bulls of bison brood, / The milk-white sovereigns of the wood** echoes the charge of the white bull early in Scott's *The Bride of Lammermoor* (1819).

**196(720–21) Such wars have been since Eden's day, / When thou first erred, and peace gave way** a reference to the Biblical story of Eve succumbing to temptation in the Garden of Eden (Genesis 3). Here 'thou' is the Maid, standing in for woman in general.

**198(802–07) The conqueror's plume began to bow, [...] He reach'd the rail and leaned thereon** in Scott's *Ivanhoe* (1820), too, the hero falls after victory in a tournament.

**199(860) He tried to leap the circling piles** this echoes *The Scottish Chronicle* (II, 44), in which it is said that a feud between '*Clankaies*' and '*Clanquhattans*' was fought out at Perth in 1369, before the king (Robert III), each clan being represented by thirty warriors. The fight was carried on 'with such desperate fury, that all those of *Clankaies* part were slain, only one excepted, who to save his life, and after he saw all his fellows slain, lept into the water of *Tay*, and swam over, and so escaped'. This clan battle features prominently in Scott's *The Fair Maid of Perth* (1828).

**200(888) leeches plied with license brief** commonly used in eighteenth-century medicine to draw blood, leeches are still used today as a remedy for certain medical conditions.

201(928) **Eiden More** at this point M,Houston is revealed to be Eiden More (Aedán the Great).

206(1132–33) **King Eugene's son of soul refined, / And cousin to your sovereign Hynde** see notes on 218(d).

206(1148–49) **here to Albyn's fair command / I join the crown of Erin's land** this is similar to *Fingal*, in which the Irish Cuchullin and the Scottish Fingal join forces to repel the invading Scandinavians.

206–207(1160–69) **"Thou glorious SUN, [...] for mortal happiness** see Ossian's address to the sun in 'Carthon' (*Ossian*, ed. Gaskill, pp. 133–34). Such addresses are common in Gaelic tradition.

208(1228–31) **The Scottish nobles, mad with joy [...] Fingal's and the Fergus' blood** see also Book First, lines 5–7. The Ossianic hero Fingal was king of Morven (*Ossian*, ed. Gaskill, p. 562); and according to *The Scottish Chronicle* 'Ferguse' founded the 'kingdome of the Scotishmen' (I, 44) and 'builded also the castel of Beregonium' (I, 48).

210(1294–95) **funeral honours [...] Iona's isle** Iona served as a royal burial place for centuries.

211(1365) **His god's own number–three times three** Hogg discusses this in his note on Human Sacrifices, p. 219.

212(1381) **Doon-Valon-Righ** Dun bhail an righ. Hogg's spelling approximates the pronunciation in Gaelic.

212(1417) **a hymn from David's pen** a psalm.

213(1456–57) **If thou Jehovah art alone, / And Odin but a God of stone** see note on 107(506). This scene concludes *Queen Hynde*'s great contest between Columba (priest of Jehovah) and the priests of Odin; and it echoes I Kings 18, in which Elijah defeats the prophets of Baal by calling down fire from heaven.

213(1461) **In darkness thou wilt veil the sun** in scientific terms Hogg describes an eclipse, but this seems to be a reference to the Gospel accounts of the Crucifixion, in which darkness falls during daylight hours. See Matthew 27.45 and Luke 23.44–45 ('The sun was darkened').

214(1464) **the broad sky aside shall fold, / And like a garment up be rolled** echoes Isaiah 34.4 and Revelation 6.14. The passage from Isaiah is traditionally interpreted as a prophecy concerning God's judgments against the enemies of the church; while the passage from Revelation describes the great day of God's wrath.

214(1484–85) **Israel's sinful Korah, / Or second Sodom and Gommorrah** Sodom and Gomorrah are the sinful cities destroyed by God, in the account of Genesis 19.24–25:

> Then the LORD rained upon Sodom and Gomorrah brimstone and fire from the LORD out of heaven; And he overthrew those cities, and all the plain, and all the inhabitants of the cities, and that which grew upon the ground.

For the spectacular fate of the sinful Korah, see Numbers 16:

> And the earth opened her mouth, and swallowed them up, and their houses, and all the men that *appertained* unto Korah, and all *their* goods. They, and all that *appertained* to them, went down alive into the pit, and the earth closed upon them: and they perished from among the congregation.

214(1502) **Deep called to deep, and wave to wave** from Psalm 42.7: 'Deep calleth unto deep at the noise of thy waterspouts: all thy waves and thy billows are gone over me'.

215(1510) **a whirlwind blew** echoes Job 38.1: 'Then the LORD answered Job out of the whirlwind'.

**215(1532–43) Just while their horrid sacrifice [...] melted to a trivial cynder** according to popular tradition, Beregonium was consumed by fire from heaven: see Hogg's note on p. 218, and the Appendix to this volume (pp. 238–44).

**218(a) Beregonium** for discussion of Hogg's note, see the Appendix: Beregonium, pp. 238–44.

**218(a) Boethius and Harrison's Chronologie [...] Fergus** see the Appendix (p. 238) for a discussion of Boethius and *The Scottish Chronicle*. According to *The Scottish Chronicle*, 'Ferguse' founded the 'kingdome of the Scotishmen [...] in the yeare after the creation of the world 3640, which is (as *Harison* saith in his chronologie) before the incarnation of our Saviour 327' (I, 44). *The Scottish Chronicle* adds that 'Ferguse' 'builded also the castel of Beregonium' (I, 48).

**218(a) the Selma of Ossian** see the notes on 40(322) and 59(52).

**218(a) the marble chair** a reference to the Stone of Destiny, the stone on which the coronation of the Scottish kings traditionally took place. Taken to London in the 1290s as part of the spoils of war of Edward I of England, it was subsequently used there in the coronations of English (and later British) monarchs. The Stone made a brief return to Scotland in the 1950s, when a group of young Scottish nationalists removed it by night from Westminster Abbey; and it was returned to Scotland once again in the 1990s, as the Conservative government of Britain sought to gain the approval of Scottish opinion as the general election of 1997 approached. The Stone taken to London by Edward I in the 1290s is a flat piece of sandstone. However, some of the early references to the Scottish coronation stone describe it as a marble chair; and it is for this reason that *The Scottish Chronicle* (I, 197) declares that Eugenius began his reign as King of Scots when he was placed 'upon the chaire of marble'. As the flat sandstone block taken to London in the 1290s is manifestly not a marble chair, it is sometimes argued that Edward I did not in fact get hold of the genuine Scottish coronation stone, which was successfully concealed by the Scots to prevent it from falling into Edward's hands. There is a tradition that asserts that the Scottish coronation stone was kept in Dunstaffnage before being removed to Scone in the ninth century: for Dunstaffnage, see the note on 137(581) and the Appendix: Beregonium, pp. 238–44.

**218(b) Ardchattan** the parish in which Beregonium lies.

**218(b) Loch-Quhaber** according to *The Scottish Chronicle* (I, 48), Beregonium is 'in Loughquhabre'; but the district of Lochaber in fact lies a little to the north of Ardchattan.

**218(b) the new road From Dalmallie to Fort-William, by Connel ferry and Appin** the road Hogg describes is now called the A828. The site that Hogg describes is discernible on large-scale maps as ruins of ancient forts on the water's edge at Port Selma on Ardmucknish Bay, adjacent to Benderloch.

**218(c) one solid mass of pumice, burnt and soldered together in an impervious heap** the hill indeed appears volcanic, and the ruins of the fort show signs of vitrifaction. See the Appendix on Beregonium, pp. 238–44.

**218(c) WILLIAMS' *tour*** John Williams, *An Account of Some Remarkable Ancient Ruins, Lately Discovered in the Highlands, and Northern Parts of Scotland; in a Series of Letters to G. C. M. Esq.* (Edinburgh: William Creech, 1777). This pamphlet is an account of vitrified forts in the Highlands, and it associates these forts with Ossian's Fingal. However, Williams places the ruins of Selma at Knockfarril near Dingwall, rather than Ardchattan (pp. 5, 20). In the first edition of *Queen Hynde*, the reference to 'WILLIAMS' *tour*' is replaced by a reference to a relevant book recently published by the publishers of Hogg's poem: John MacCulloch's *The Highlands and Western Isles of Scotland, Containing Descriptions of Their Scenery and Antiquities, with an Account of the Political History and Ancient Manners [...]*, 4 vols (London: Longman, 1824).

MacCulloch, unlike Williams, is distinctly sceptical in his comments on Beregon. The first edition thus subverts Hogg's attempt to provide scholarly support for Beregon; this was perhaps done simply to advertise the publisher's new book.

**218(c) Edin^r Ency^dia** David Brewster's *Edinburgh Encyclopedia* appeared in 18 vols, 1810–1830. The early volumes, as first published, contained an entry on *Beregonium*; but by the time these volumes were being reprinted in 1830 this entry had been dropped, perhaps because the comments of John MacCulloch (see previous note) and others had turned the tide of opinion against Beregon. Nevertheless, in the 1830 printing the entry for *Argyleshire* still contains a cross-reference to the old entry on *Beregonium*.

**218(c) two streets, well paved [...] large wooden pipes** see the quotation from the 1791 *Statistical Account* for Ardchattan in the Appendix, pp. 239–40.

**218(d) son of king Eugenius** however, according to Book Third at lines 751–765, M,Houston is the son of Conran, while Hynde is the daughter of Eugenius: see notes on 76(752), 76(756), 76(757), and 76(760–61). This confusion about the fathers of Hynde and M,Houston can be regarded as a result of Hogg's carelessness; or it can be seen as a part of the teasing game that the Ettrick Shepherd (as narrator of *Queen Hynde*) is constantly playing with his readers as he proceeds with his idiosyncratic new performance of *The Scottish Chronicle*'s narrative of Scottish national origins. On the latter view, the confusion about fathers can be interpreted as a deliberate muddying of the waters, a playful testing of the reader's alertness, as the Ettrick Shepherd (for his own poetic purposes) re-draws the shape of the old story of the Scottish royal family at the time of St Columba, by inventing a queen called Hynde, and by conflating Conran and Convall (see the various notes to p. 76). Interestingly in this context, Hogg makes a carefully worded claim, at the top of p. 219, to the effect that 'in most things [...] the poem accords with history' with regard to Aedán. The Shepherd, deadpan, then goes on to assert that the historical Aedán 'married his uncle's daughter', while omitting to mention the far from trivial detail that there had never previously been a suggestion (in *The Scottish Chronicle* or elsewhere) that Aedán's 'uncle's daughter' was a queen called Hynde.

**218(d) Eugenius [...] long the accomplice, but at last the conqueror, of the far-famed Arthur** this statement tallies with the account of the reign of Eugenius in *The Scottish Chronicle* (1, 197–203).

**218(d) Eiden More (Aidan the great)** Hogg's character is based on the historical Aedán, who is discussed in the notes on 18(566), 74(696–703), and 76(760–61).

**219(a) short translation from an ancient Runic ode** this seems in fact to be based on a version of 'The Dying Ode of Regner Lodbrog', which appeared in several translations in the late eighteenth century, among them Paul Henri Mallet's in *Introduction a l'histoire de Dannemarc* (1755), which was translated by Thomas Percy and published as *Northern Antiquities*, 2 vols (1770), II, 228–33; Percy's own translation appears in *Five Pieces of Runic Poetry* (London: Dodsley, 1763). Regner Lodbrog was a Danish hero, not of the sixth but of the ninth century. In the introduction to *Five Pieces of Runic Poetry*, Percy quotes Mallet regarding him:

> King Regner Lodbrog was a celebrated Poet, Warrior, and (what was the same thing in those ages) Pirate; who reigned in Denmark, about the beginning of the ninth century. After many warlike expeditions by sea and land, he at length met with bad fortune. He was taken in battle by his adversary Ella king of Northumberland. War in those rude ages was carried on with the same inhumanity as it is now among the savages of North-America: their prisoners were only reserved to be put to death with torture. Regner was accordingly thrown into a dungeon to be stung to death by serpents. While he was dying he composed this song, wherein he records all the valiant atchievements of his life, and threatens Ella with vengeance; which

history informs us was afterwards executed by the sons of Regner.

It is, after all conjectured that Regner himself only composed a few stanzas of this poem, and that the rest were added by his *Scald* or poet-laureat, whose business it was to add to the solemnities of his funeral by singing some poem in his praise. (pp. 23–24)

This hero had acquired his name, according to Percy because he 'cloathed himself all over in rough or hairy skins' before he killed a large serpent to win the hand of a Gothic princess; 'Lod-brog' signifies 'ROUGH or HAIRY-BREECHES' (p. 25). Percy's poetic translation of the ode comes close to the passage that Hogg claims to have received from a correspondent:

We fought with swords, before Boring-holmi. We held bloody shields: we stained our spears. Showers of arrows brake the shield in pieces. The bow sent forth the glittering steel. Volnir fell in the conflict, than whom there was not a greater king. Wide on the shores lay the scattered dead: the wolves rejoiced over their prey. (pp. 31–32)

**219(c) M. Mallet** Paul Henri Mallet (the M. is for *Monsieur*), whose writings provided the major source of Hogg's knowledge of Norse culture: see previous note and the note on 38(233–52).

**220(b) Scotticisms** Hogg's remark may have been seen by his contemporary readers in sharp contrast to the attitude of Enlightenment writers who attempted to purge their writing of Scotticisms.

# Glossary

The reader of *Queen Hynde* encounters a wide-ranging and eclectic vocabulary. Partly in accordance with the ancient subject matter, Hogg calls into service many archaic or obsolete words and uses them in ways that may be unfamiliar. Additionally, the poem is peppered with 'Scotticisms', whose presence Hogg (in his note on p. 220) acknowledges but declines to explain. The aim of this Glossary is to provide a guide to many of the unfamiliar words and orthographical variants. Explanations of phrases, expressions, and idioms of more than one word may be found in the Notes. For further study of Hogg's use of Scots, see *The Concise Scots Dictionary*, ed. by Mairi Robinson (Aberdeen: Aberdeen University Press, 1985), and *The Scottish National Dictionary*, ed. by William Grant and David Murison, 10 vols (Edinburgh: Scottish National Dictionary Association, 1931–76). The present Glossary is much indebted to *The Scottish National Dictionary* and *The Oxford English Dictionary*.

*acquest:* the act of acquiring, an acquisition

*ahight:* on high (echoes *The Tragedy of King Lear*, IV.5.58)

*aloof:* away at some distance, apart

*altern:* in turns, one after the other, alternately

*amain:* at once

*amate:* to equal or match

*amind:* in mind, disposed (to do something)

*anchoret:* a recluse, a hermit

*anodyne:* a medicine or drug which alleviates pain; anything that soothes wounded or excited feelings, or that lessens the sense of misfortune

*apothegm:* an apophthegm; a terse, pointed saying, embodying an important truth in few words; a pithy or sententious maxim

*appeach:* to impeach (a person); to cast imputation on; to asperse (honour, character, etc.)

*aright:* rightly, properly; straight, straightway; directly

*armipotent:* mighty in arms

*aslant:* across in a slanting direction, athwart

*aspin:* an aspen

*avale:* to yield, to submit; to degrade, to lower, to humble

*aye:* ever, always

*baited:* harassed, tormented, attacked

*balach:* a peasant; a young man; a sturdy fellow (*Gaelic*)

*ban:* a formal, ecclesiastic denunciation; a curse

*band:* a cord; a fetter; a bond

*bandelet:* a small retaining band, a ribbon, a string

*ban-dog:* a dog tied up as a watch-dog or because of its ferocity

*bane:* ruin, fatal mischief; woeful or hapless fate

*bark:* a small ship

*basilisk:* a fabulous serpent hatched from a cock's egg whose look and breath were fatal

*basket:* a protection for the hand on a sword, in the form of a small basket

*bavaroy:* a kind of cloak

*bay:* to pursue like a pack of hounds, to bring to bay

*beal-day morn:* 'beal an latha' (*Gaelic*), literally 'mouth of the day', i.e. dawn *bealfire:* a beacon fire

*beam:* the side of a ship

*beck:* to beckon; (in Scotland) to make a sign of recognition, respect, or obeisance; to nod, make a slight bow; to curtsey

*bedes-man:* a beadsman, a man of prayer who prays for the soul or spiritual welfare of another; (in Scotland) a public almsman or licensed beggar

*bedight:* equipped, furnished, arrayed

*behest:* a vow, a promise

*behoof:* use, benefit, advantage

*belay:* to besiege, to beleaguer, to waylay

*benison:* a blessing

*bent:* reedy or rush-like grass

*beseem:* to become, to befit, to be in accordance with the appearance or character of

*bestead:* situated, circumstanced (*hard bestead:* hard pressed)

*betimes:* at an early time, early in the morning

*bewray:* to divulge, to disclose, to declare, to make known, to show

*bier:* the stand on which a corpse is placed before burial; that on which it is carried to the grave

*bill:* a military weapon (obsolete) used chiefly by infantry, varying in form from a simple concave blade with a long, wooden handle to a concave axe with a spike at the back and its shaft terminating in a spearhead

*bluff:* big, surly, blustering

*bode:* to foretell, to presage, to predict

*boon:* (adjective) gracious, bounteous, benign; (noun) a favour, a gift; a benefit, a blessing or advantage to be thankful for

*bore (the gree):* won (the prize)

*boreal:* pertaining to the north; northern

*bornean:* borean; pertaining to the north wind, northern

*bothy:* a dwelling for farm servants

*bound:* territory situated on or near a boundary; border-land; also land within certain limits

*bourn, bourne:* a boundary; a limit; the terminus of a race, journey, or course

*brae:* a hill; a bank

*brake:* a clump of bushes, brushwood, or briers; a thicket

*brand:* a sword

*brangle:* to brawl, to wrangle

*brigandine, brigantine:* body armour composed of iron rings or small thin iron plates, sewed upon canvas, linen, or leather, and covered over with similar material

*brog:* a coarse, stout sort of shoe

*broil:* a tumult

*brook:* to put up with, to endure, to tolerate

*brow:* to form a brow to, to be on the brow of; (Scots) to face, to browbeat

*browst:* brewing; brewage; brew

*buckler:* a small shield used in parrying

*buckram:* stiff, starched; that has the false appearance of strength

*bulwark:* defensive rampart or fortification

*burgonet:* a light sixteenth-century helmet

*buskin:* a covering for the foot and leg, reaching to the calf or to the knee; a half-boot; to cover as with a buskin

*cabal:* a small body of persons engaged in secret or private machination or intrigue; a secret or private intrigue of a sinister character engaged in by several persons

*cairn:* a heap of stones, often one raised over a grave

*caitiff:* a captive; a prisoner; a wretched, miserable person

*capperkailzie:* a wood-grouse

*car:* a chariot or carriage, with poetic associations of dignity, solemnity, or splendour

*carl:* a man; a man of the common people, particularly a country-man (sometimes used disparag-ingly); (Scots) a fellow, especially one possessing the qualities of sturdiness or strength

*casement:* a frame forming a window or part of a window, opening on hinges

*casque:* a helmet

*casualty:* chance, accident

*chancel:* the eastern part of a church, used by those who officiate in services

*chaperoon:* a hood or cap formerly worn by nobles

*churl:* a countryman, a peasant, a rustic, a boor (often used as term of disparagement or contempt)

*Cimbrian:* Welsh (from 'Cymreig', *Welsh*)

*clave:* past tense of 'cleave'

*claymore:* a large, one-handed, two-edged longsword

*cleave:* to adhere; to split

*clour:* to bash, to knock

*coil:* a noisy disturbance; tumult, turmoil, confusion

*collied:* blackened, overshadowed

*compeer:* one of equal rank or standing; an equal, a peer

*cormorant:* a web-footed sea bird known to have a voracious appetite

*coronach:* a funeral song or lamenta-tion in the Highlands of Scotland and in Ireland

*correi:* a hollow between hills

*corslet:* a piece of defensive armour covering the body

*cotquean:* a man who meddles in matters generally associated with

a housewife (used disparagingly)

*countervail:* to act against, to counter-balance

*covert:* covering, that which serves for concealment, protection, or shelter; a hiding place, a shelter

*cowled:* furnished with or wearing a cowl

*craunch:* to crunch

*craven:* a confessed or acknowledged coward

*crimosin:* crimson

*crosier:* the pastoral staff or crook of a bishop or abbot

*cuirass:* a defensive breastplate

*cumber:* overthrow, destruction, rout; the condition of being cumbered

*cumberous:* obstructing and impeding progress, troublesome

*cygnet:* a young swan

*damask:* a species or variety of rose supposedly brought from Damascus; the colour of the damask rose

*darkling:* in the dark; in darkness; characterised by darkness

*dastard:* coward

*debel:* to put down in fight, to subdue, to vanquish; to expel by force of arms

*denizen:* a citizen, one who dwells within a country

*deport:* behaviour, bearing, deport-ment

*depose:* to deposit, to lay down, to put down

*deray:* disorder, disturbance, tumult, confusion

*dern:* dark, sombre, solitary, wild, drear

*despight:* outrage, injury, malice

*diadem:* crown; (figuratively) sover-eignty

*die:* (figuratively) chance, hazard, luck

*dight:* to equip, to fit out, to furnish

*discreet:* courteous, civil, polite

*dole:* grief, sorrow, mental distress

*donative:* a donation, a gift, a present

*doon:* a dun, a pre-historic fort

*dotard:* an imbecile; a silly or stupid person; often, one whose intellect is impaired by age and second childhood

*dragonet:* a small dragon; a small kite

*dun:* of a dull or dingy brown colour; dark, dusky; murky, gloomy

*eke:* also

*elate:* lifted, raised; lofty, proud

*emporium:* a principal centre of commerce

*empyreal:* pertaining to the highest heaven or to the sky; celestial, sublime, elevated, superior, rare; fiery

*empyrean:* of or pertaining to the sphere of the highest heaven; in ancient cosmology, the sphere of the pure element of fire; in Christian use, the abode of God and the angels

*ensign:* a banner, a flag

*enthrall:* to enslave

*equivocal:* of uncertain nature

*erst:* before the present time, formerly, earlier

*even tide:* evening

*ewe-flower:* the common daisy

*fabulous:* belonging to fable, mythical, legendary

*fain:* glad, rejoiced, well-pleased

*falchion:* a broad sword

*fane:* a temple

*fare:* to go, to journey, to travel, to make one's way

*fascine:* a brushwood faggot used, for example, to fill ditches or to protect a shore

*fence:* defence

*festal:* pertaining to a feast or festivity

*fillet:* a head-band; a ribbon or band of material worn around the head

*firth:* an arm of the sea; an estuary of a river

*flagrant:* ardent, burning, intensely eager or earnest

*fleer:* a mocking facial expression or speech; a sneer, a gibe

*fleet:* to move swiftly; to flit, to fly

*flew:* the large chaps of a deep-mouthed hound (e.g., the bloodhound)

*flexile:* easily bending, pliant, supple, flexible

*flout:* a mocking speech or action; to jeer, to scoff

*flurr:* to scatter, to throw about

*fond:* foolish, silly; foolishly tender or affectionate, infatuated; mad, idiotic; trifling, trivial

*for aye:* forever

*forebode:* to predict, to foretell

*forefend:* to avert, to keep away or off, to prevent

*fosse:* a ditch, moat, trench, or canal

*freak:* a sudden causeless change or turn of the mind; a capricious humour, notion, whim, or vagary

*frippery:* empty display, especially in speech or literary composition; showy talk; ostentation

*frith:* an arm of the sea, especially a river-mouth

*froward:* disposed to go counter to what is demanded or what is reasonable; perverse, difficult to deal with, hard to please; adverse, unfavourable

*fulgency:* brightness, splendour

*fund:* a source of supply

*furbelow:* a plaited border or flounce; a superfluous ornament

*gage:* a pledge, usually a glove thrown on the ground, of a person's appearance to do battle; a challenge

*galliard:* lively, brisk, gay, full of high

spirits; valiant, hardy, sturdy

*galliardise:* gaiety, mirth, revelry

*gallow:* to cluck; to scream

*garret:* an apartment formed within the roof of a house, an attic

*gasconade:* extravagant boasting; vainglorious fiction

*gastful:* aghast

*gauntlet:* a glove worn as part of medieval armour, usually made of leather, covered with plates of steel

*gelid:* extremely cold, icy, frosty

*giglet:* a giddy, laughing girl (originally a wanton woman)

*glaive, glave:* a sword, especially a broadsword

*gleen:* a gleam of light; a warm blaze of sunlight; to shine

*glewed:* gelid, icy

*goggle:* to turn the eyes to one side or other, to look obliquely, to squint; to look with widely opened, unsteady eyes, to roll the eyes about; to sway or roll about; to move loosely and unsteadily

*gorget:* a piece of armour for the throat

*gree:* pre-eminence; superiority; mastery; victory in battle; hence, the prize for a victory

*green:* a piece of public or common grassy land near a town or village; grassy ground

*guerdon:* reward, requital, recompense

*haberdine:* dried salt cod

*hacqueton:* a stuffed jacket or jerkin worn under the mail; a jacket of leather plated with mail

*hawser:* a rope or cable used to moor a ship

*hector:* a warrior like Hector, the Trojan hero of the *Iliad*

*heideous:* hideous

*helm:* a helmet; the handle, tiller, or wheel of a ship

*henchman:* the personal attendant of a Highland chief; hence, a trusty follower or attendant who supports his chief or leader

*hest:* bidding, command, injunction, behest

*hight:* called, named

*hind:* a female red deer; a farm-hand, a rustic

*hoar:* grey or greyish white as with age; venerable, ancient

*hoe:* a false singular, found in Scots, of 'hose', a stocking

*host:* consecrated bread

*immane:* monstrous in size or strength; huge, vast, enormous, tremendous

*immolate:* to offer as sacrifice; to kill as a victim

*jobbernole:* jobbernowl; a stupid person, a blockhead

*just:* to joust

*justle:* to jostle

*keep:* the central tower of a medieval castle

*ken:* mental perception or recognition; to perceive or recognise

*kern, kerne:* an Irish foot-soldier; sometimes used (as in this case) to mean a Scottish Highlander; a rustic peasant, a boor

*khan:* a prince or chief in North Asia; a governor in Persia

*kithe:* to make known by action or appearance; to manifest

*knell:* a sound made by a bell when struck or rung, especially slowly and solemnly, as after a death or a funeral; a doleful cry or dirge

*knurl'd:* covered with hard excrescences in the flesh

*lambent:* playing lightly upon or gliding over a surface without burning it; shining with a soft clear light and without fierce heat

*larum:* alarm

*lattice:* a window, gate, or screen constructed of cross-pieces of wood or metal

*lave:* to wash against, to flow along or past; the action of laving

*leveret:* a young hare, in its first year

*levin:* lightning

*lightsome:* cheerful, merry

*links:* the undulating sandy, grassy ground near the sea

*list:* to please, to choose, to like, to care, to desire; a place or scene of combat or contest

*lorn:* lost, perished, ruined, doomed to destruction; bereft, desolate, wretched, forlorn

*louring:* gloomy, dark, threatening

*mace:* a heavy staff or club, either entirely of metal or having a metal head, often spiked, used as a weapon of war

*main:* the high sea, the open ocean

*malison:* a curse, a malediction

*matin:* a morning song (especially of a bird)

*maugre:* in spite of, notwithstanding

*meed:* recompense, reward

*meet:* suitable, fit, proper

*mein:* mien; the air, bearing, or manner of a person, as expressive of character or mood

*mere:* a boundary, or landmark indicating a boundary

*mew:* a gull

*misprised:* scorned, despised, contemned

*misprision:* contempt, scorn; failure to recognise a thing as valuable

*modalist:* one who professes the Sabellian doctrine that the distinction in the Trinity is 'modal' only, i.e., that the Father, the Son, and the Holy Spirit are merely three different modes or manifestations of the Divine nature

*momentuous:* momentous

*monition:* instruction, direction, admonition

*mote:* a moat

*movent:* moving

*muir:* a moor

*mull:* a promontory

*nervous:* sinewy, muscular; vigorous, strong

*noiance:* annoyance, nuisance

*noul:* head

*oblation:* the action of offering a sacrifice

*obsequies:* funeral rites or ceremonies

*obstreporous:* obstreperous; clamorous, noisy; vociferous, turbulent or unruly in behaviour

*o'erhie:* to overtake by hastening after

*ogle:* an amorous, languishing, or coquettish glance; to cast such a glance

*opine:* to hold an opinion; to think, to suppose

*or:* before

*orisons:* a prayer; a speech or oration

*ostent:* display, especially vainglorious display; ostentation

*outgo:* to go out, to pass

*painim creed:* non-Christian, especially Muslim, belief

*palanquin:* a covered litter or conveyance consisting of a box with shutters, carried by poles projecting before and behind

*palisades:* a fence made of poles or stakes fixed in the ground, forming an enclosure or defence

*palm:* emblematic for victory, triumph; supreme honour or excellence, prize

*panoply:* complete suit of armour worn by a soldier of ancient or medieval times

*passenger:* a passer by or through; a traveller (usually on foot), a wayfarer

*pate:* a head, a skull

*pelloch:* a porpoise

*pesterous:* having the quality of pestering; troublesome

*phalanx:* an array of battle

*philabeg:* kilt worn by Highland men

*pilaster:* a square or rectangular column or pillar

*pile:* pointed head of a dart, lance, or arrow

*pinnace:* a small, light sailing vessel, generally two-masted and schooner-rigged

*poignantly:* sharply, piercingly, acutely, keenly

*poll:* a parrot

*post:* to convey hurriedly, as by courier

*poy:* a pole used to propel a barge or boat; a float used to buoy up the head of a sheep when swimming in the washing-pool

*pruriginious:* mangy, itching

*pule:* to cry querulously, to whine

*rabid:* furious, raging; madly violent in nature or behaviour

*rath:* rathe; quick in action; eager, earnest, vehement; coming early

*ravelin:* in fortification, an outwork consisting of two faces which form a salient angle, constructed beyond the main ditch and in front of the curtain

*reave:* to commit robbery; to plunder, to pillage

*reaver:* a robber or plunderer

*reef:* to reduce the extent of a sail by taking in or rolling up a part and securing it

*reif:* the act or practice of robbery; reavery

*reign:* a kingdom, a realm

*remede:* remedy, redress

*reprise:* a return or compensation received or paid

*resistless:* irresistible, unresisting

*restiff:* resisting control of any kind

*rhynde:* the bark of a tree

*rokelay:* a short cloak worn by women in the eighteenth century

*romage:* rummage

*rood:* the cross (as a symbol of Christianity)

*rout:* a fashionable gathering or assembly, a large evening party or reception much in vogue in the eighteenth and early nineteenth centuries

*rueful:* pitiable, lamentable; doleful; disordered

*runkled:* wrinkled, rumpled

*russet:* a coarse homespun woolen cloth of a reddish-brown, grey, or neutral colour; rustic, homely, simple

*ruth:* sorrow, grief, distress, lamentation

*saraband:* a slow Spanish dance

*scald:* a skald, an ancient Scandinavian poet; more generally, a poet

*scan:* to perceive, to discern; to climb

*scath, scathe:* hurt, harm, damage

*sciolist:* a superficial pretender to knowledge

*scion:* an heir, a descendent

*scowered:* scoured

*sea-mew:* a seagull

*seared:* dried up, withered

*shallop:* a small boat, propelled by oars or by a sail; a dinghy

*shaw:* a small wood

*sheen:* brightness, shining

*shelvy:* overhanging

*siderate:* to blast, to strike by lightning

*sleight:* craft or cunning; artifice, strategy, trickery; cleverness, skill, dexterity *slieve:* a sleeve, a covering for the arm

*snood:* a fillet, band, or ribbon for confining the hair, generally worn by women

*solan:* a gannet, a large white sea-bird with black-tipped wings

*sooth:* truth, verity

*sough:* a rushing or murmuring sound; to make such a sound

*soughing:* rushing, rustling, murmuring

*sparry:* having qualities of the crystalline mineral spar

*sped:* succeeded, prospered, accomplished (something)

*speed:* success, profit, advancement, furtherance

*spheral:* spherical

*spheres:* the concentric, transparent hollow globes imagined by ancient astronomers as revolving round the earth and respectively carrying with them the several heavenly bodies

*stager:* one qualified by long experience

*staid:* stayed, halted

*steven:* outcry, noise, tumult, din

*stound:* (Scots) a thrill as of delight; (English) a sharp pain or pang

*strait:* a narrow strip of land with water on each side

*strick:* strict

*suffragan:* assistant

*sun-fawn:* perhaps a yellow patch of sunlight, moving through clouds

*sward:* the grassy surface of land; green turf

*swart, swarth:* dark in colour; swarthy

*swath:* to envelop, to wrap up

*sway:* dominion; position of power or authority

*swither:* to rush, to swirl

*tabour:* a small, drum-like tambourine without jingles, usually played with one stick, along with a pipe

*targe:* a traditional Highland shield

*tarn:* a small mountain lake

*teen:* affliction, trouble, suffering, grief, woe; damage

*terrene:* earthly, terrestrial

*thane:* the chief of a clan; a Scottish lord

*thrall:* bondage, servitude; captivity

*thrift:* prosperity, success, good luck

*tide:* time, season

*tofall:* the close (of the day or night)

*toil:* a trap or snare

*top-mast:* a smaller mast fixed on the top of a lower mast

*torfel:* to toss or tumble about; see Hogg's definition, p. 220

*tourney:* a tournament

*trepan:* to catch in a trap; to entrap, to ensnare, to beguile

*triad:* a group or set of three, collectively or in connexion, especially applied to the Trinity

*troth:* one's plighted word; a promise, a covenant; truth

*trow:* to believe, to think, to suppose, to imagine

*trucculence:* truculence; fierceness, savageness

*unguent:* an ointment, a salve

*unmeet:* unfitting, unsuitable, unbecoming, improper

*untoward:* difficult to control or manipulate; awkward, clumsy; unruly, perverse

*van:* the foremost division of a military force

*vantage-ground:* a position which offers an advantage for defence or attack

*varlet:* a knave; a barbarian

*vassal:* in the feudal system, a tenant in fee; a subordinate, a subject

*verge:* a rod or wand carried as an

emblem of authority or symbol of office

*vespers:* evening prayers or devotions; evensong

*vicegerent:* a ruler acting as representative of the Deity; applied to priests as representatives of God or Christ

*viewless:* invisible

*visier:* vizier; a high state official or minister; chief minister; vicegerent

*visive:* of or pertaining to the eye; sent out from the eye

*vouchsafe:* to show a gracious readiness or willingness, to grant readily, to condescend or deign (to do something)

*waik:* a festival

*wain:* the group of seven bright stars in the constellation called the Great Bear

*wale:* a piece of timber extending horizontally round the top of the sides of a boat

*ward:* in a fortress, the (inner or outer) circuit of the walls of a castle; an appointed station or post

*ware:* prudent, cautious

*wassail:* spiced wine; riotous festivity, revelling

*weal:* well; well-being

*ween:* to know, to think, to fancy, to believe, to expect

*weetless:* unknowing

*weir:* war

*welkin:* the sky, the firmament

*wem:* a blemish, a defect; a scar

*wight:* a human being, a person

*wildered:* bewildering, confused, disordered; pathless, wild

*wis:* to know

*wist:* past tense of 'wit', to know

*wit:* to know

*withe:* a band, tie, or shackle consisting of a tough flexible twig or branch, or of several twisted together

*withouten:* without

*won:* past tense of 'win', to gain; to reach

*wont:* accustomed, used; in the habit of (doing something)

*wore:* past tense of 'wear', to move in a slow, cautious manner

*wot:* to know or to discern

*wreak:* to punish, to avenge

*yare:* ready, prepared; nimble, active, brisk, quick